The Dirty Dust: Cré na Cille

MÁIRTÍN Ó CADHAIN

TRANSLATED FROM THE IRISH BY ALAN TITLEY

YALE UNIVERSITY PRESS ■ NEW HAVEN & LONDON

A MARGELLOS
WORLD REPUBLIC OF LETTERS BOOK

English translation copyright © 2015 by Yale University and Clo Iar-Chonnacht.
Originally published in Irish as *Cré na Cille*. Copyright © 1949 by Sáirseál agus Dill.

Yale University Press books may be purchased in quantity for educational, business, or
promotional use. For information, please e-mail sales.press@yale.edu (U.S. office) or
sales@yaleup.co.uk (U.K. office).

Set in Electra and Nobel types by Tseng Information Systems.
Printed in the United States of America.

The Library of Congress has cataloged the hardcover edition as follows:
Ó Cadhain, Máirtín.
[Cré na cille. English]
The dirty dust : cré na cille / Máirtín Ó Cadhain ; Translated from Irish by Alan Titley.
    pages   cm. — (The Margellos World Republic of Letters)
"Originally published in Irish as Cré na Cille. Copyright © 1949 by Sáirseál agus Dill."
ISBN 978-0-300-19849-2 (cloth : alk. paper) 1. Ireland—Fiction. 2. Cemeteries—
Fiction. I. Titley, Alan, translator. II. Title.
PB1399.O28C7413 2015
891.6'2343—dc23
2014034533

ISBN 978-0-300-21982-1 (pbk.)

A catalogue record for this book is available from the British Library.

10 9 8 7 6 5 4 3 2 1

More praise for *Cré na Cille* and praise for *Dirty Dust*:

"*Cré na Cille* is in essence a savage, uproarious, scabrous, obnoxious, and hilarious protest . . . a smirking linguistic vampire, an apparently moribund language that declares: go ahead and kill me if you want; I'll still come back and bite you on the neck."—Fintan O'Toole, *New York Review of Books*

"Among the best books to come out of Ireland in the 20th century . . . it bristles with black comedy."—Max Liu, *The Independent*

"Titley's effort to translate the untranslatable, with full knowledge of its inevitable imperfections, is courageous and timely. . . . By exhuming Ó'Cadhain's zany chorus of cadavers, Titley has opened this masterpiece to the wider audience it so richly deserves."—Niamh Ni Mhaoileoin, *The Millions*

"Like many Modernist texts and art works *The Dirty Dust*, mixing energy and exhaustion, makes up its own rules, and it depends on the reader, and indeed the translator, to decipher them as we go along. Titley deserves our gratitude for making this novel available in English for the first time."—Colm Toibin, *Irish Times*

"Titley renders the tirades and flytings with the exact ear for dialogue which has characterized his own novels. . . . Here at last is a version done by a scholar who is also an artist."—Declan Kiberd, *Times Literary Supplement*

"A classic Irish novel, the translation of *The Dirty Dust* was long overdue. Alan Titley's vigorous translation fits the dialogue-intense work well. . . . *The Dirty Dust* does a great deal within the limits of its inspired premise."—M. A. Orthofer, *Complete Review*

"*The Dirty Dust* is to be savored on its own terms, as an extraordinary one-off. After the voices fade out at the end . . . the characters become embedded in one's mind—so much so that the reader is impelled to turn at once back to the first page and listen to them all over again."—Roy Foster, *New Statesman*

"The high energy of the Irish masterpiece is translated to another kind of energy. . . . Titley is one of the few—in the world—who possesses the necessary combination of linguistic and literary skills required for the task, and he has made a difficult work readable and accessible in more ways than one."—Éilís Ní Dhuibhne, *Financial Times*

"A ceaseless and often hilarious torrent of chatter and bickering. . . . By allowing his characters to speak only after they have died, Ó Cadhain removes his characters' need to dissimulate, laying bare aspects of humanity we might wish to forget."—Eric Jett, *Full Stop*

"Ó'Cadhain's greatest accomplishment, it seems to me, was to achieve a perfect synthesis of style and subject. It's a lesson still being absorbed that small Irish towns are utterly unsuited to the conventions of literary realism, and in opting instead for this anarchic symphony—the book is a kind of wind machine blowing out gales of yammer and yap—he evolved a narrative structure capable of snagging the native genius of such places."—Kevin Barry, *The Guardian*

"[A] rollicking romp. . . . Shocking, uproarious, and heartrendingly tender by turns."—Cindy Hoedel, *Kansas City Star*

"[T]his long-overdue translation of Ó Cadhain's classic revels delightfully in the gossip of village life as a cemetery's inhabitants engage in lively conversation."—Angel Gurria Quintana, *Financial Times*

"For a novel that takes place six feet under ground, Ó Cadhain's *The Dirty Dust* is quite the lively affair. . . . Alan Titley's translation resuscitates it wonderfully for an entirely new population of modern day readers to ponder over and enjoy."—Aaron Westerman, *Typographical Era*

CONTENTS

In *The Dirty Dust* everyone is dead. This may seem an unlikely way to write a novel, but Máirtín Ó Cadhain* was not your usual author. He was both traditional and experimental as he willed, and the device he chose for this novel suited his own genius and the community he was depicting.

The characters in the novel may be dead, and lying down in their graves, but they do not shut up. It is the fact that the dead do not shut up that gives life to the novel. The novel is composed entirely of heard and of unheard conversation, apart from the introductions to some of the chapters (which are called interludes) that are spoken by the Trumpet of the Graveyard and act as a kind of a linguistic and philosophical contrast to what is going on below. What is going on below is a continuation of what was going on above before all the residents of the cemetery died. It is a novel that is a listening-in to gossip and to backbiting and rumours and bitching and carping and moaning and obsessing about the most important, but more often the most trivial, matters of life, which are often the same thing. It is as if, in an afterlife beneath the sods, the same old life would go on, only nothing could be done about it, apart from talk.

And talk is the principal character in this novel. Although the introductory pages of the novel say that the time is eternity, which is

---

* Máirtín Ó Cadhain may seem difficult to pronounce to anybody without knowledge of the Irish language. His name has never been Anglicised and we are not going to do it here. But for the sake of pronunciation it might be rendered as something like Marteen O'Kine.

understandable, in fact, the locus of the novel is a graveyard some-where in Connemara in the west of Ireland in the early 1940s. In that Connemara of the thirties and the forties there was no radio, except in the priest's and the teacher's houses; there was no cinema and few shops, and television had never been heard of.

The only culture was talk.

There were songs and music and some dancing, but talk was the centerpiece of creativity. This novel attempts to capture the talk and the never-ending gabble and gossip of which the community was made. It might be said that all human communities before the onset of common literacy were simply made of talk. While anthropologists tell us that there are "loquacious" communities and "reticent" ones, there is no doubt whatsoever into which of those boxes Ireland fell. In that sense of never-ending chatter this novel is a better reflection of the concerns of ordinary humanity over thousands of years than those which deal with the great and the good. These concerns are not always that pleasant, of course, no more than are those of the great and the good, but at least they don't do as much harm.

All these dead voices in the unquiet grave are concerned only with the immediate quotidian—the stolen seaweed, who is marry-ing whom, a donkey's trespass, what somebody's will contains, how the publican robbed them—although there are distant echoes of na-tional politics and even of the Second World War. But all human life is here; and if you were to transfer yourself to any part of the world even today and to listen to the clatter of local voices, it would be not that much different from what you will encounter in *The Dirty Dust*.

This book is generally seen as one of the greatest achievements of the Irish* novel. Although the Irish language can boast the longest

---

* Just in case of ambiguity, "Irish" here refers to the Irish language, and "Irish lit-erature" refers to writing in the Irish language, just as "English literature" generally refers to that which is written in English, or "Spanish literature" to that which is written in Spanish. The term is linguistic and not geographical. "Irish" is sometimes erroneously referred to as "Gaelic." The Irish language should never be referred to as "Gaelic" because doing so is historically, socially, formally, and linguistically wrong. "Gaelic" is now correctly applied to the principal historical language of Scotland,

unbroken vernacular literature in all of Europe with the exception of Greek, and indeed, one of the greatest of all European literatures until the modern period, its development was ruptured during the English conquest. Thus the novel came late in Irish, as it did in most noncosmopolitan pre-urban societies. While Irish did have a lively prose tradition up until the middle of the seventeenth century, for political and social reasons it went into rapid decline during the following two hundred years. As literacy in the language was minimal, there was little chance of developing the novel. This changed with the resurgence of interest in the language in the late nineteenth century and in particular after the independence of the new Irish Free State, when a fresh generation of Irish readers appeared.

A common theme in the early Irish novels was a depiction of life in Irish-speaking communities, often referred to as the *Gaeltacht*. While Gaeltacht originally meant Irish speakers, it came to mean those areas in which Irish was the dominant language. Most of these were in the west of Ireland, one of the largest being in Connemara, where Ó Cadhain was born. These novels often painted the Gaeltacht and its people in a glowing idyllic light, or if they didn't, they were perceived to do so. One writer, Séamus Ó Grianna, remarked that he would never knowingly write a word of which his mother would be ashamed. *The Dirty Dust* burst in upon this world with its robust talk, its mean-spirited characters, its petty pursuits, and its great mirth.

Its publication met with immediate acclaim, but not universal. One critic damned it as "a dirty book," when dirty books were banned in the hundreds. Another claimed he would never have supported the Irish language if he had thought it would lead to such abuses as this. Yet another, that such conversation shouldn't be put into the mouth of a dog. On the other hand, it was widely read out loud in Ó Cadhain's own Gaeltacht, rapidly became a best-seller, and gained

---

although it also was referred to (in English) as "Irish" for most of its history. The distinction is not subtle: "Irish" refers to the native language of Ireland, and "Gaelic" refers to the major native language of Scotland, although the term came into common usage only in the past two hundred years, or less.

classic status among Irish-speakers. One writer remembers that his mates in secondary school would wait eagerly for the next instalment when it was first being serialised in a newspaper. The author recalls walking through a crowd at a football match and hearing a spectator mutter, "There goes *The Dirty Dust*." It was referenced in the *Dáil*, the Irish parliament. There has been a bigger critical literature around it than around any other single Irish novel, and like all major works of art there is no single consensus as to what it "means."

Máirtín Ó Cadhain believed that speech was the best way to depict what was going on inside people's heads, which explains a good deal about the narrative structure of the novel. It was said that it was based on a short story by Dostoyevsky on the one hand, and Edgar Lee Masters's *Spoon River Anthology* on the other. In reply to this wild speculation about its origins, he recounted an incident that happened in his own area some years previous to his writing it. A woman was being buried on a particularly miserable rainy day in Connemara and the gravediggers had inadvertently opened the wrong grave. The day was so bad they couldn't dig another, so they chucked her into the one they had already opened. Then someone realised that they were putting her coffin down on top of an old adversary. One of the onlookers muttered: "Oh holy cow, there's going to be one almighty gabble!"

Máirtín Ó Cadhain was born in 1906 in a completely Irish-speaking area. He said that he never heard English spoken until he was six years of age. He trained as a primary schoolteacher in Dublin and taught in various schools throughout Connemara and east Galway. He became involved in illegal republican politics and in community activism and was dismissed from his position as a teacher after a row with the parish priest in 1936. He had already begun to write stories and translated a really bad novel by Charles Kickham for *An Gúm*, which is best described as a government publishing house. He moved to Dublin in search of employment but continued his republican activities.

Shortly after the outbreak of the Second World War he was imprisoned without trial in an internment camp which the then government had put aside especially for dissenters. Although he had one book of stories published in 1939, it is claimed that his years of imprisonment were his real education as a writer. His letters show that he read voraciously and wrote furiously. It is no surprise, then, that his first great burst of creativity took place immediately after the war, the period in which this novel was written.

He was a prodigious writer, with five collections of short stories published during his lifetime and another after his death. His collected works include novels, stories, lectures, letters, polemics, political tracts, history, translations, satires, and other writings which are entirely unclassifiable. Having worked at various slave labour jobs, he was appointed to a lectureship in Irish in Trinity College Dublin because of his deep and abiding knowledge of literature garnered from tireless reading and his almost unsurpassed knowledge of contemporary Irish speech. He eventually was appointed to the Chair of Irish in the same university the year before his death.

The Dirty Dust should best be read as a symphony of voices, although a cacophony of voices might be more appropriate. It is at turns a series of monologues, which can become duologues, rise up to vindictive diatribes and fade out at judicious and injudicious moments. There is a narrative, but you have to listen for the threads. There is more than one story, but they are all interrelated. We have to suss out what each person is saying according to each's own obsession—a phrase can tell us who is talking—or each's one singular moan, or each's big bugbear like a signature tune. It is like switching channels on an old radio, now you hear this, and then you hear this other. Once you get the knack, the story rattles on with pace. It was natural for it to be made into a hugely successful radio play; it has also been staged several times, and even more surprisingly, it has been made into a darkly comic film.

The novel is also replete with references to Irish storytelling traditions, to mythology, to sagas, and to songs, which were all part of the common discourse. Indeed, there are verses of songs thrown in which were often meant to be extempore. One person would cast out a few lines as a challenge, and another person had to answer them.

This was all normal in the community, whereas nowadays people's points of reference may well be TV shows or the doings of some flash celebrity. The mental furniture of another time and a different place is never easily transferred, but we must at least recognise it for what it is.

The main character, if it can be said that such exists, is Caitriona Paudeen. She is not a woman you would have liked to meet in real life, although meeting her in the next would be just as scary. If she has a love of her life it is well hidden, but the hatred of her life is her sister, Nell. Their bitterness sweetens the story throughout. Everyone in the community is dragged into this hatred, old sores are opened, old scores are maintained, and permanent grudges are given new life. We are given a full picture of a closed community largely indifferent to the outside world, a picture with warts and more warts, but we are also energised by their wonderful and beautiful and terrible and gruesome and magic humanity.

It should not be thought that this was Ó Cadhain's only view of life in his community. His choice to write in this fashion was an artistic one, while many of his other stories dealing with the traditional life from which he came can be tender, tragic, and sensitive. While many of the women in *The Dirty Dust* are savage amazons, much of his writing is concerned with the personal and societal entrapment of women, either in economic slavery, or in barrenness, or having lost children. He knew well the price of poverty and the crushing of the human spirit that it often brought.

Translating this novel into English was a linguistic challenge. Translating the simplest story is a huge challenge, as languages are not algebraic equations. There has not been much modern Irish prose translated into English or into other languages, and some of what has been translated has been rendered into Anglo-Irish Synge-like gobbledegook. While this may have its own charm for some, it makes its Irish speakers sound like peasants and idiots and simpletons and clodhoppers. The Irish speakers of Irish Ireland were just as normal and as intelligent and as thick as the people of any other community, ever. I felt that the tradition of making good Irish people speak like bog trotters, hayseeds, and hillbillies should be avoided. There is also the added difficulty that what we used to call Hiberno-English is now as dead as the diplodocus. Whatever the parlous state of the Irish language, which has been under unrelenting pressure for hundreds of years, it has far more life in it than the fag ends of the peculiar way English used to be spoken in Ireland. Apart from a phrase here and there, English in Ireland is as undistinguishable as English in the U.S. or the U.K., and even the erstwhile pronunciation of many Irish people is being rapidly smoothed out by contact with our betters.

On the other hand, to use some version of sub–Jane Austen–like polite urbanities and words of pleasantly standardised appropriateness would be a total denial of the energy and manic creativity of Ó Cadhain's prose. Is not the word "appropriate" the most disgusting word in the entire English language? It means no more than that snobby people do not like unsnobby things. The challenge was to get some of the tone and vivacity of the original across without seeming too bizarre. English is a much standardised language with a wonderful and buzzing demotic lurking beneath. I tried to match the original Irish common speech with the familiar versions of demotic English that we know, mixing and mashing as necessary, and even inventing when required. But slang is always a trap. The more hip you are, the sooner you die. Language changes unsubtly from one half-generation to the under-ten-year-olds just coming after. There is no imaginable way to keep up with the whirl of changing language. Irish is no different, and much of the Irish of *The Dirty Dust* in the original would be incomprehensible and even weird to many native Irish speakers now. That Irish, after all, was the Irish of a generation born in the nineteenth century, when knowledge of English was minimal, and is a language much changed today, when nearly all of its speakers are bilingual.

There are some constants within this change, however. The characters in *The Dirty Dust* call to one another by their names, as this is far more common in Irish than in English. A familiar halloo is commonly greeted by using someone's name. I have tried to follow this, but have on occasions left it out, as it would appear tiresome and unnatural. Likewise there is much that might be seen as "bad language."

As someone who fervently believes that there is no such thing as bad language except that which is tired and dull and clichéd going forward outside the box, the language of *The Dirty Dust* pulsates with energy and brio and gutsiness. It is full of creative curses and inventive imprecations. If one objects to some of the crudity from a linguistically puritanical point of view, it should be remembered that the most common curses in Irish derived from the "Devil" himself, and to those who believed in him and his works and pomps, this was far worse than any "fuck" or "shit"' or their attendant pards. "Damning" someone to the horrors of Hell for all eternity was probably the worst that you could do. Modern "bad language" is a mild and ghostly shadow of the serious stuff of the past.

Ultimately, as we know, there is no easy equivalence between languages. It is not the meaning itself which is the problem but the tone, and feel, and echo. I have no idea whether this works or not in this translation. It may do so for some, and not for others. There is no such thing as a literal translation, as the simplest small word beyond "cat" and "dog" expands into a foliage of ambiguity. Even a fairly direct word like *baile* in Irish throws up difficulties. It appears all over the country, most usually as "Bally" in place-names, and usually refers to a town or a village. This, however, is a more recent growth, as the original Irish most probably refers to a cluster of houses, not quite "settlement," not quite "town land," more like "just around here where I live."

The title itself raised some problems, but also some mirth. The most literal translation of *Cré na Cille* might be "The earth of the graveyard," but this doesn't have any sense of the ring of the original. I must presume that Ó Cadhain put in the alliteration for his own purposes as he had done with other titles. On the other hand, *Cré* can also mean "creed," or "belief" — perhaps a pun for the discerning reader, to whom "The Common Creed" might come to mind. "Cemetery Clay" certainly also gives the necessary consonants, but I just don't like it. If I was determined to stick with those lovely Cs, there was always "Cemetery Chatter," "Crypt Comments," or "Coffin Cant." I toyed with a title such as "Six Feet Under," which would be a normal colloquialism for being buried, and it does retain a certain aptness. Once I was on this road, however, many suggestions rose up from the deep: "Graveyard Gabble," "Talking Deads," "The Last Words," "The Way of All Trash," "Undercurrents," "Tomb Talk," "All the Dead Voices," "Beneath the Sods," "Deadly Breathing," "Biddies in the Boneyard," and much more, culminating in "A Hundred Years of Verbitude." Ó Cadhain's first book of stories is entitled *Idir Shúgradh is Dáiríre* (Between joking and seriousness), and he once observed that if there ever was a single particular Irish trait it was the ability, even the necessity, to mix fun with solemnity. He might have preferred some of the above to *The Dirty Dust*, which I finally settled on in order to maintain some sense of the rhythm of the original, along with the biblical echoes that dust we are and "unto dust we shall return," while not forgetting that what goes on below amongst the skulls and cross words is certainly dirty.

I have taken some liberties with this translation, but not many. Certainly not as many as those which Máirtín Ó Cadhain took in his very first work of translation. His first manuscript version of that bad Charles J. Kickham novel *Sally Kavanagh* was returned to the publisher with nearly twice as many words as the original! There was always a tradition in translation in Ireland of taking some freedoms, and it would have been untraditional of me not to do likewise.

The main reason that Máirtín Ó Cadhain was so profligate with words was that he couldn't help it. His supreme gift was his torrent of words which gushed and laughed and overflowed in a flush of excess. Not only was this the way he wrote, it was also the way he spoke. But every writer's supreme gift is also his weakness, as he cannot be everything. The writer Liam O'Flaherty once advised him to take a scissors to his prose, although he probably meant a bill-hook. If he had, he would not have been Máirtín Ó Cadhain, but only an anaemic version of him.

His inability to be unable not to let fly meant that although he tried his hand at drama, he was singularly unsuccessful. Drama demands some sense of structure and control of time, traits which he lacked. While *The Dirty Dust* does have a definite structure, it is big and baggy enough for him to dump everything into. Readers therefore might find it odd that in this graveyard there are elections, and Rotary clubs, and writers, and even a French pilot who was washed up on the shore and interred with the others. If you are wondering what they are doing there, it is quite simply that Ó Cadhain as a public polemicist could not resist the temptation of taking subtle and not-so-subtle swipes at colleagues and at issues which intrigued or pissed him off. Much of the novel is satire, not only on the easy pieties of country life but on the snobbery, pretence, and charlatanry which were as much a part of his country then as they are now.

This satire goes deep in Irish literature and links it with texts at least as far back as the eighth-century *Fled Bricrenn* (The feast of Bricriu) and the twelfth-century *Aislinge meic Conglinne* (The vision of Mac Conglinne), but you don't have to know anything about this to enjoy Caitriona Paudeen's poison tongue, the Old Master's abiding jealousy, Nora Johnny's whoring after "culture," and the entire interlocking spite that gives them life while they are dead. There have only been about three hundred novels written in Irish since the start of the twentieth century, and if there were a typical mould, this certainly wouldn't be it. Like all great novels it is unique and is to be enjoyed as a feast of language, the kind of language you might hear outside a door when everybody inside is tearing themselves apart; or in a country graveyard in the dark light of day.

I would like to thank both Garry Bannister and the late David Sowby for their interest in this translation, and for their many helpful and often invaluable suggestions, which were a great assistance to me.

CHARACTERS AND DIALOGUE CONVENTIONS

Primary Characters

CAITRIONA PAUDEEN Newly buried

PATRICK CAITRIONA Her only son

NORA JOHNNY'S DAUGHTER Wife of Patrick Caitriona. Living in
   Caitriona's house

MAUREEN Patrick Caitriona and Nora Johnny's Daughter's
   young girl

NORA JOHNNY Toejam Nora. Patrick Caitriona's mother-in-law

BABA PAUDEEN A sister of Caitriona and of Nell. Living in
   America. Her will expected soon.

NELL PAUDEEN A sister of Caitriona and of Baba

JACK THE LAD Nell's husband

PETER NELL Nell and Jack's son

BLOTCHY BRIAN'S MAGGIE Peter Nell's wife

BLOTCHY BRIAN JUNIOR Peter Nell and Blotchy Brian Maggie's
   son. Going for the priesthood.

BLOTCHY BRIAN Maggie's father

FIRESIDE TOM Relation of Caitriona and Nell. The two of them
   vying for his land.

MAGGIE FRANCES Neighbour and bosom friend of Caitriona

Other Neighbours and Acquaintances

BIDDY SARAH Keening woman, but fond of the drink

COLEY Traditional storyteller. Can't read.

KITTY Neighbour of Caitriona's who claimed to have lent her a pound but never got it back.

DOTIE A sentimental woman

MARGARET A friend of Kitty's

CHALKY STEVEN He didn't go to Caitriona's funeral because he "hadn't heard" about it

PETER THE PUBLICAN Pub owner. Still alive.

HUCKSTER JOAN Shopkeeper

MICHAEL KITTY Lying on top of Huckster Joan

TIM TOP OF THE ROAD Lives in a hovel at the end of the town land. Accused of stealing by neighbours.

MANNIX Lawyer who dealt with Caitriona and her family

JOHN WILLY He had a dicey heart

BREED TERRY Wants only peace and quiet in the grave

GUZZEYE MARTIN, GUT BUCKET, BLACK BANDY BARTLEY, PADDY LAWRENCE, THE FOXY COP, THE OLD MASTER, REDSER TOM and others.

Guide to Dialogue Conventions

—	Beginning of Talk
—...	Middle of Talk
...	Conversation, or Missing Talk

THE DIRTY DUST

Time

For Ever

Place

The Graveyard

Range

Interlude 1: The Black Earth
Interlude 2: The Scattered Earth
Interlude 3: The Sucking Earth
Interlude 4: The Grinding Earth
Interlude 5: The Muck Manuring Earth
Interlude 6: The Mangling Earth
Interlude 7: The Moulding Earth
Interlude 8: The Heating Earth
Interlude 9: The Wasting Earth
Interlude 10: The Good Earth

Interlude 1
THE BLACK EARTH

1.

Don't know if I am in the Pound grave, or the Fifteen Shilling grave? Fuck them anyway if they plonked me in the Ten Shilling plot after all the warnings I gave them. The morning I died I calls Patrick in from the kitchen, "I'm begging you Patrick, I'm begging you, put me in the Pound grave, the Pound grave! I know some of us are buried in the Ten Shilling grave, but all the same . . ."

I tell them to get me the best coffin down in Tim's shop. It's a good oak coffin anyway. I am wearing the scapulars. And the winding sheet . . . I had them ready myself. There's a spot on this sheet! Like a smudge of soot. No, not that. A daub of finger. Who else but my daughter-in-law! 'Tis like her dribble. Oh, my God, did Nell see it? I suppose she was there. Not if I had anything to do with it . . .

Look at the mess Kitty made of my covering clothes. I always said that that one and the other one, Biddy Sarah, should never be given a drop to drink until the corpse was gone from the road outside the house. I warned Patrick not to let them near my winding sheet if they had a drop taken. All they ever wanted was a corpse here, there, or around the place. The fields could be bursting with crops, and they'd stay there, if she could cadge a few pence at a funeral . . .

I have the crucifix on my breast anyway, the one I bought myself at the mission . . . But where's the black one that Tom's wife, Tom the crawthumper, brought me from Knock, that last time they had to lock him up? I told them to put that one on me too. It's far nicer than this one. Since Patrick's kids dropped it the Saviour looks a bit crooked. He's beautiful on this one, though. What's this? My head must be like a sieve. Here it is, just under my neck. 'Tis a pity they didn't put it on my breast.

They could have wrapped the rosary beads better on my fingers. Nell, obviously, did that. She'd love it if it fell to the ground just as they were putting me in the coffin. O Lord God, she better stay miles away from me . . .

I hope to God they lit the eight candles on my coffin in the church. I left them in the corner of the press under the rent book. You know, that's something that was never ever on any coffin in the church, eight candles! Curran had only four. Tommy the Tailor's lad, Billy, had only six, and he has a daughter a nun in America.

I tells them to get three half-barrels of porter, and Ned the Nobber said if there was drink to be got anywhere at all, he'd get it, no bother. It had to be that way, given the price of the altar. Fourteen or fifteen pounds at least. I spent a shilling or two, I'm telling you, or sent somebody to all kinds of places where there was going to be a funeral, especially for the last five or six years when I felt myself failing. I suppose the Hillbillies came. A pity they wouldn't. We went to theirs. That's how a pound works in the first place. And the shower from Derry Lough, they'd follow their in-laws. Another pound well spent. And Glen Booley owed me a funeral too . . . I'd be surprised if Chalky Steven didn't come. We were at every single one of his funerals. But he'd say he never heard about it, 'til I was buried.

And then the bullshit: "I'm telling you Patrick Lydon, if I could help it at all, I would have been at her funeral. It wouldn't have been right if I wasn't at Caitriona Paudeen's funeral, even if I had to crawl on my naked knees. But I heard nothing, not a bit, until the night she was buried. Some young scut . . ." Steven is full of crap! . . .

I don't even know if they keened me properly. Yes, I know Biddy Sarah has a nice strong voice she can go at it with if she is not too pissed drunk. I'm sure Nell was sipping and supping away there also. Nell whining and keening and not a tear to be seen, the bitch! They wouldn't have dared come near the house when I was alive . . .

Oh, she's happy out now. I thought I'd live for another couple of years, and I'd bury her before me, the cunt. She's gone down a bit since her son got injured. She was going to the doctor for a good bit before that, of course. But there's nothing wrong with her. Rheumatism. Sure, that wouldn't kill her for years yet. She's very precious about herself. I was never that way. And it's now I know it. I killed myself working and slaving away . . . I should have watched that pain before it got stuck in me. But when it hits you in the kidneys, actually, you're fucked . . .

I was two years older than Nell anyway . . . Baba. Then me, and Nell. Last year's St. Michael's Day, I got the pension. But I got it before I should have. Baba's nearly ninety-three, for God's sake. She'll soon die, despite her best efforts. None of us live that long. When she hears that I'm dead, she'll know she's done for too, and then maybe she'll make her will . . . She'll leave every bit to Nell. The bitch will have one up on me after all. She has Baba primed. But if I had lived another bit until Baba had made her will, she'd have given me half the money despite Nell. Baba is quick enough. She wrote to me mostly for the last three years since she abandoned Blotchy Brian's place and took off to Boston. It's a great start that she has shagged off from that poisonous rats' nest anyway.

But she never forgave Patrick that he married that cow from Gort Ribbuck, and that he left Blotchy Brian's Maggie in the lurch. She would never have gone next or near Nell's house that time she was home from America if it wasn't for the fact that her daughter married Blotchy Brian. And why would she? . . . A real kip of a house. A real crap kip of a house it was too. Certainly not a house for a Yank. I haven't a clue how she put up with it having been in our house and in fancy homes all over America. She didn't stay there long though, she soon shagged off home . . .

She'll never come back to Ireland again. She's finished with us. But you'd never know what kind of a fit would hit her when this war is over, if it suited her. She'd steal the honey from a bee's hive, she is so smarmy and sweet. She's gutsy and spirited enough to do it. Fuck her anyway, the old hag! After she buggered off from Blotchy Brian's place in Norwood, well, she still had a lot of time for Maggie. Patrick was the real eejit that he didn't listen to her, and didn't marry the ugly bitch's daughter. "I wouldn't marry Meg if she had all of Ireland . . ." Baba hurried off up to Nell's place as if you had clocked her on the ear. She never came near our place again, but just about stood on the floor the day she was returning to the States.

—. . . Hitler's my darling. He's the boy for them . . .

—If England is beaten, the country will be in a bad way. The economy has already gone to the dogs . . .

—. . . You left me here fifty years before my time, you One Eared Tailor git! You lot were always twisted. Couldn't trust you. Knives, stones, bottles, it didn't matter. You wouldn't fight like a man, but just stab me . . .

—. . . Let me talk, let me talk.

—Christ's cross protect me!—Am I alive or dead? Are the people here alive or dead? They are all rabbiting on exactly the same way as they were above the ground! I thought that when I died that I could rest in peace, that I wouldn't have to work, or worry about the house, or the weather, that I would be able to relax . . . But why all this racket in the dirty dust?

2.

—. . . Who are you? How long are you here? Do you hear me? Don't be afraid. Say the same things here as you said at home. I'm Maggie Frances.

—O may God bless you. Maggie Frances from next door. This is Caitriona. Caitriona Paudeen. Do you remember me, or do you forget everything down here? I haven't forgotten anything yet, anyway.

—And you won't. This is much the same as the "ould country" except that we only see the grave we are in, and we can't leave our coffin. Or you won't hear any live person either, and you won't have a clue what they're up to, except when the newly buried crowd tell you. But, hey, look Caitríona, we are neighbours again. How long are you here? I never noticed you coming.

—I don't know, Maggie, if it was St. Patrick's Day, or the day after that I died. I was too weak. I don't know how long I'm here either. Not that long, anyway . . . You've been buried a long time now, Maggie . . . Too true. Four years this Easter. I was spreading a bit of manure for Patrick down in Garry Dyne when one of Tommy's young ones came up to me. "Maggie Frances is dying," she said. And what do you know, Kitty, the young one, was just going in the door when I reached the end of the haggard. You were gone. I closed your eyes. Myself and Kitty laid you out. And thanks to us, well, everyone said that you looked gorgeous on the bed. Nobody had any need to complain. Everyone who saw you, Maggie, everyone said that you were a lovely corpse. Not a bit of you, not a hair out of place. You were as clean and smooth as if they had ironed you out on the bed . . .

. . . No I didn't hang on that long, Maggie. The kidneys had packed up a long time ago. Constipation. I got a sharp pain five or six weeks ago. And then, on top of that I got a cold. The pain went into my stomach and then on my chest. I only lasted about a week . . . I wasn't that old either, Maggie, just seventy-one. But I had a hard life. I really had a hard life, and I looked every bit of it. When it hit me, it really hit me, left its mark on me. I had no fight left . . .

You might say that Maggie, alright. That hag from Gort Ribbuck didn't help me a bit. Whatever possessed my Patrick to marry the likes of her in the first place? . . . God bless you, Maggie, you have a heart of gold, but you don't know the half of it, and a word about it never passed my lips. A full three months now and she hasn't done a stroke . . . The young one. She just about made it this time. The next one will really put her to the pin of her collar, though . . . Her brood of kids out of their minds except for Maureen, the eldest one, and she was in school every day. There I was slaving away washing them and keeping them from falling into the fire, and throwing them a bit of grub whenever I could . . . Too true, too true. Patrick's house will be a mess now that I am gone. Of course that hag couldn't keep a decent house any way, any woman who spends every second day in bed . . . O, now you're talking, tell me more . . . Patrick and the kids, that's the real tragedy . . .

It was so. I had everything ready, Maggie, the clothes, the scapulars, the lot . . . 'Tis true, they lit eight candles for me in the church, not a word of a lie. I had the best coffin from Tim's place. It cost at least fifteen pounds . . . and, wait for it, not two plates on it, but three, believe me . . . And every one of them the spitting image of the fancy mirror in the priest's house . . .

Patrick promised he'd put a cross of Connemara marble on my grave: just like the one on Peter the Publican, and written in Irish: "Caitriona, wife of John Lydon . . ." He said it himself, not a word of a lie. You don't think I'd ask him do you, I wouldn't dream of it . . . And he said he'd put a rail around it just like the one on Huckster Joan's, and that he'd decorate it with flowers—I can't remember what he called them, now—the kind that the School Mistress wore on her black dress after the School Master died . . . "That's the least we could do for you," Patrick said, "after all you did for us throughout your life." . . .

But listen to me, what kind of place is this at all, at all? . . . Too true, too true, the Fifteen Shilling plot . . . Now, come on Maggie, you know in your heart of hearts that I wouldn't want to be stuck up in the Pound plot. Of course, if they had put me in there, I could have done nothing about it, but to think that I might want that . . .

Nell, was it . . . I nearly buried her. If I had lived just a tiny little bit more . . . That accident to her boy, that really shook her . . . A lorry hit him over near the Strand about a year or a year and a half ago, and it made bits of his hip. The hospital didn't know whether he would live or die for about a week . . .

O, you heard about it already, did you? . . . He spent another six months on the flat of his back . . . He hasn't done a thing since he got home, just hobbling around on two crutches. Everyone thought he was a goner . . .

He can't do anything for the kids, Maggie, except for the eldest fucker and he's a bollocks . . . that might be the case alright . . . Like his grandfather, same name Big Blotchy Brian, a total asshole. Who cares, but then, his grandma, Nell . . . Nell and her crowd never harvested anything for the last two years . . . That injury has really shagged the two of them, Nell and that Brian Maggie one. I got great satisfaction from that bitch. We had three times as many spuds as her this year.

Ah, for God's sake, Maggie Frances, wasn't the road wide enough for him just as it was for everybody else to avoid the lorry? . . . Nell's boy was thrown, Maggie. "I wouldn't give you the steam of my piss," the judge said . . . He let the lorry driver come to court in the meantime, but he didn't allow Nell's youngfella to open his mouth. He's bringing it to the High Court in Dublin soon, but that won't do him any good either . . . Mannix the lawyer told me that Nell's crowd wouldn't get a brass farthing. "And why would he," he said, "wrong side of the road." . . . No truer word, Maggie. Nell won't get a hairy cent from the law. It's what she deserves. I'm telling you, she won't be going past our house so easily from now on singing "Ellenore Morune" . . .

Ara, poor Jack isn't that well either, Maggie. Sure, Nell never minded him one bit, nor did Blotchy Brian's daughter since she went into their house . . . Isn't Nell my own sister, Maggie, and why on earth would I not know? She never paid a blind bit of attention to Jack, and not a bit of it. She was wrapped up in herself. She didn't give a flying fuck about anyone, apart from herself . . . I'm telling you, that's the God's honest truth, Jack suffered endlessly because of her, the slut . . . Fireside Tom, Maggie. Just as he always was . . . In his hole of a hovel all the time. But it will fall down on him someday soon . . . Ah, for God's sake didn't my Patrick go and offer to put some thatch on it . . . "Look, Pat," I said to him, "you have absolutely no business sticking thatch on Tom's wreck of a house. Nell can do it if she wants. And if she does so, then so will we" . . .

"But Nell has nobody at all now since Peter's leg was smashed," said Pat.

"Everybody has enough to do for himself," I said, "everyone has to thatch their own place, even a kip like that prick Fireside Tom."

"But the house will collapse on him," he says.

"It can if it wants to," I says, "Nell has enough on her plate without filling up Tom's mouth with shite. That's it, Pat, my boy, keep at it. Fireside Tom is like rats being drowned in a bath. He comes crawling to us to keep out of the rain" . . .

Nora Johnny, is it? . . . It's a queer thing to find out more about her here . . . I know far too much about her, and every single one of her breed and seed, Maggie . . . Listening to the Master every single day, is that it . . . The Old Master himself, the wretch . . . the Old Master reading to Nora Johnny! . . . Nora Johnny! . . . ah, for Christ's sake . . . he doesn't think much of himself, does he, the master . . . Reading stuff to Nora Johnny . . . Of course, that one has nothing between her ears. Where would she get it from? A woman that never darkened the door of a school, unless it was to vote . . . I'm telling you it's a queer world if a schoolmaster spends his time talking to the likes of her . . . What's that, Maggie? . . . that he fancies her . . . I don't know who she is . . . If her daughter lived in the same house as him for the last sixteen years, as she has here, he sure as hell would know who she was then. But I'll tell him yet . . . I'll tell him about the sailor, and the rest of it . . .

— "Johnny Martin had a daughter

As big as any other man . . ."

— Five-eight's forty; five-nine's forty-five, five ten's . . . sorry sir, I don't remember . . .

— "As I roved out to the market, seeking for a woman to find"

— I had twenty, and I played the ace of hearts. I took the king from your partner. Mrukeen topped me with the jack. But I had a nine, and my partner out of luck . . .

— But I had the queen, and was defending . . .

— Mrukeen was going to play the five of trumps, and he'd beat your nine. Wasn't that what you were going to do, Mrukeen?

— But then the mine blew our house up into the air . . .

— But we'd have won the game anyway . . .

— No way. If it wasn't for the mine . . .

— . . . A lovely white-headed mare. She was gorgeous . . .

— I can't hear a thing, Maggie. O my God almighty and His precious mother . . . a white-headed mare . . . The five of trumps . . . I can't listen to this . . .

—I was fighting for the Republic . . .

—Who asked you anyway . . .

—He stabbed me . . .

—Then he didn't stab you in the tongue anyway. Bugger the lot of you. My head is totally screwed up since I came here. Oh, Maggie, if you could just slink away. In the other world, if you didn't like someone's company you could just leave them there, and shag off somewhere else. But unfortunately, the dead can't budge an inch in the dirty dust . . .

3.

. . . And after all that they shagged me into the Fifteen Shilling Place. After all my warnings . . . Nell had a grin on her as wide as a barn door! She'll surely get buried in the Pound Place now. I wouldn't be a bit surprised if it was she put Patrick up to sticking me in the Fifteen Shilling Place instead of the Pound. She wouldn't have the neck to darken the door of my house, only that I was dead. She didn't put a foot on my floor since the day I married . . . that is, if she didn't sneak in unknown to me while I was dying.

But, Patrick is a bit of a simpleton. He'd give in to her crap. And his wife would agree: "To tell God's truth, but you're right Nell. The Fifteen Shilling Place is good enough for anybody. We're not millionaires . . ."

The Fifteen Shilling Place is good enough for anyone. She would say that. She would say that, wouldn't she? Nora Johnny's One. I'll get her yet! She'll be here for sure at her next delivery. I'll get her yet, I'm telling you. But I'll get her mother first—Nora Johnny herself—in the meantime.

Nora Johnny. Over from Gort Ribbuck. Gort Ribbuck of the Puddles. It was always said they milk the ducks there. Doesn't she just fancy herself. Now she's learning from the Master. It was about time for her to start anyway. No schoolmaster in the world would speak to her, except in the graveyard, and even then he wouldn't if he knew who she was . . .

It is her daughter's fault that I'm here twenty years too soon. I was washed out for the last six months looking after her mangy children. She's sick when she's expecting a child, and sick when she's not. The next one will take her away. Take her away, no doubt about it . . . She was no good for my Patrick anyway, however he would get on without her . . . You couldn't talk to him. "It's the only one thing I'm going to do," he said, "I'll feck off to America and I'll leave the place go to hell, seeing as you don't give a toss about it . . ."

That was when Baba was home from America. She did everything she could to get him to marry Blotchy Brian's Maggie. She really took a fancy to that little ugly hussy of Blotchy Brian's for some reason. "She looked after me well when I was in the States," she said, "especially when I was very sick, and all my own people miles away. Blotchy Brian's Maggie is an able little smarty, and she has a bit put aside herself, as well as what I could give her. I had more time for you, Caitriona," she says, "than for any other of my sisters. I'd prefer to leave my money in your house than to anyone else belonging to me. I'd love to see your own Paddy get on in the world. You have two choices now," she said to him, "I'm in a hurry back to America, but I won't go until I see Blotchy Brian's young girl fixed up here, as she is having no luck at all over there. Marry her, Paddy. Marry Brian's Maggie and I won't see you stuck. I have more than enough to see me out. Nell's son has asked her already. Nell herself was talking to me about her only the other day. She'll marry him, Nell's son, I'm telling you, if she doesn't marry you. Marry her, or marry who you like, but if you marry who you like yourself . . ."

"I'd sooner take to the roads," said Patrick. "I won't marry any other woman who ever sniffed the air other than Johnny Nora's daughter from Gort Ribbuck."

He did.

I had to put the clothes on her back myself. She didn't have as much as a penny towards the wedding, not to mention a dowry. A dowry from the crowd of the Toejam trotters? A dowry in Gort Ribbuck of the Puddles where they milk the ducks? . . . He married her, and she is like death warmed up ever since. She couldn't raise a pig or a calf, or a hen or a goose, or even a duck, and she knew all about them from Gort Ribbuck. Her house is filthy. Her kids are filthy. She's totally clueless whether she's working the land or scavenging stuff on the shore . . .

There was some decent stuff in that house until she came along. I kept it as clean as a whistle. Every single Saturday night without fail I washed the stools and the chairs and the tables out in the stream. I spun and I carded. I had bags of everything. I raised pigs and calves and fowl . . . as long as I had the go in me to do it. And when I hadn't I shamed Johnny Nora's one enough that she didn't sit on her arse completely . . .

But what will happen to the house now without me? . . . Nell will get great satisfaction anyway . . . She can afford to. She has a fine woman to make bread and spin yarn on the floor of her house now: Blotchy Brian's Maggie. She can easily be jeering about my own son who only was a bit of a waster, a messer. She'll be going up past our house every second day now saying: "Bejaysus, we got thirty pounds for the pigs . . . It was a great fair if you had some cattle. We got sixteen pounds for the two calves" . . . Even though the hens aren't laying right now, our Maggie has always a few tricks up her sleeve. She brought eighty eggs to the Fancy City on Saturday. We had four clutches of chicks this year. The hens are laying twice as many eggs. I had another clutch yesterday. "The little speckled oat coloured clutch," Jack called them, when he saw me handling them . . . She'll have ants in her pants when she's going past our house. She'll know I'm not there. Nell! The Bitch! She might be my sister, alright, but I hope and pray that not one other corpse will come to the graveyard before her . . . !

4.

—. . . I was fighting for the Irish Republic, and you had me executed, you traitor. You fought for the English, just the same as fighting for the Free State . . . You had an English gun in your hand, English money in your pocket, and love of England in your heart. You sold your soul and your ancient heritage for a mess of porridge, for a "soft bargain," for a job . . .

—That's a lie! You were a criminal, fighting against the legitimate Government . . .

—. . . I swear by the oak of this coffin, Margaret, I swear I gave her, I gave Caitriona the pound . . .

—. . . I drank forty-two pints . . .

—I remember it well, you scumbag. I bollixed my ankle that day . . .

—. . . You stuck the knife in me, straight between my gut and the top of my ribs. Through the skin of my kidneys. Then you twisted it. The foul stroke always by the Dog Eared crowd . . .

—. . . Let me speak. Free speech . . .

—Are you ready now for an hour's reading, Nora Johnny? We'll start a new novelette today. We finished "Two Men and the Powder Puff" the other day, don't you remember? This one is called "The Berry Kiss." Listen carefully now:

"Nuala was an innocent young girl until she met Charles ap Rice in the nightclub . . ." Yes, I know. There isn't any chance to get away here, or to talk about culture . . . and just as you say, Nora, they are always talking about small stupid insignificant stuff here . . . cards, horses, booze, violence . . . we are totally pissed off about his racing mare every bloody day . . . that's the whole truth, undoubtedly, Nora . . . Nobody has a snowball's chance in hell of developing their intellect here . . . Right on, that's the complete truth . . . this place is as bad-mannered, as thicko, as barbaric as whatever happens over in the dregs of the Half Guinea place . . . we are really back in the dark ages since the *sansculottes* started scrimping money together from the dole to be put in the Fifteen Shilling Place . . . I'll tell you how I would divide this place up, if I had my way: those who went to university in the Pound Place, those who . . . No, no, that's not it Nora! Yes, it's a crying shame that some of my own past pupils are lying next to me here . . . It really depresses me to learn how ignorant they still are, after all I burst my guts for them . . . and sometimes they are pig ignorant rude with me . . . I just don't know what's happening to the young crowd . . . that's it, Nora . . . no chance whatsoever of culture . . .

"Nuala was an innocent young girl until she met Charles ap Rice in the nightclub . . ." A nightclub, Nora? . . . You were never in a nightclub? . . . Well, a nightclub isn't that different from this place . . . Ah, no, Nora, ah no. Nightclubs aren't the same places as sailors hang out. They are "dives" really, but cultured people go to the nightclubs . . . You'd like to go to one of them . . . Not a bad idea really to put the finishing touch, the last notch, to bring a proper *cachet* to your education . . . I was in a nightclub once, just that time when they had raised teachers' salaries, just before they reduced them again, twice. I saw an African prince there . . . He was as black as the sloe and was drinking champagne . . . You'd love to go to a nightclub, Nora! Aren't you the brazen hussy . . . oh, the "naughty girl" . . . Oh Nora, so "naughty . . ."

—You thieving bollocks! Johnny the Robin's daughter out from Gort Ribbuck! Where did she say she wanted to go, Master . . . ? Her tricks will get her yet! Don't take a gnat fart's notice of her, I'm telling you. If you knew her like I do you'd keep your trap firmly shut. I've been dealing with herself and her daughter for the last sixteen years. You shouldn't bother your arse wasting your time with Toejam Nora. She was hardly a day at school, and she wouldn't know the difference between the ABC and a plague of fleas in her armpit . . .

—Who's this? Who are you . . . ? Caitriona Paudeen. I don't believe you're here at last . . . Well, however long it takes, this is where you end up . . . Welcome anyway, Caitriona, you're welcome . . . I'm afraid, Caitriona, that you are . . . How will I put it . . . You are a bit hard on Toejam No— . . . Nora Johnny . . . She has come on a bomb since you used to be . . . What's that the way you put it . . . That's it . . . dealing with her . . . We find it hard to measure time, but if I get you correctly, she's three years here already under the positive influence of culture . . . But listen here Caitriona . . . Do you remember the letter I wrote for you to your sister Baba in America . . . 'Twas the last one I wrote . . . The day after that, my last sickness hit me . . . Is that will still in dispute . . . ?

—I got many letters from Baba since you were writing them for me, Master. But she never said either "yea" or "nay" about the money. Yes, we got an answer from her about that letter, alright. That was the last time she mentioned the will: "I haven't completed my will yet," she said. "I hope I do not pass away suddenly or by happenstance, as you have suggested in your letter. Do not be concerned in this matter. I'll execute my will in due course, when I know what is required of me." I know what I told her when I caught up with her. "I'm sure the schoolmaster wrote that for you. No one of us ever spoke like that."

The Young Master—he succeeded you—he writes the letters for us now. But I'm afraid that the priest writes for Nell. That hag can pull the wool over his eyes with her chickens and knitted socks and her twisted tricks. She is a dab hand it, Master. I thought I'd live another few years yet and see her buried, the maggot . . . !

You did your best for me anyway, Master, about the will. You could handle the pen. I often saw you writing a letter, and do you know what I thought? I thought that you could knit words together just as well as I could put a stitch in a stocking . . . "May God have mercy on the Old Master," I'd say to myself. "He would always do you a good turn. If God allowed him to live, he'd have got the money for me . . ."

I'd say it won't be long now until the Mistress—that is to say, your good wife, Master—it won't be long until she gets her act together. No doubt about it. She's a fine good-looking young thing yet . . . Oh, I'm very sorry Master! Don't take a bit of notice of anything I say. I'm often romancing like that to myself, but sure, no one can help who they are themselves . . . I know, Master, I shouldn't have told you at all. You'll be worried about it. And I thought you'd be absolutely thrilled to hear that the Mistress was getting her act together . . .

Ah, come on, don't blame me, Master . . . I'm not a gossip . . . I can't tell you who the man is . . . Ah, please, Master, don't push me . . . If I thought it would really make you so cranky I wouldn't have said as much as a word . . .

She swore blind that she wouldn't marry another man, did she, Master? Oh, come on! . . . Did you never hear it said that married women are the best . . . You were hardly cold in your grave when she had cocked her eye at another guy. I think, honestly, that she was always a bit flighty . . .

The Young Master . . . Ah, no, not him, never, Master . . . The teacher in Derry Lough. He's a good guy. Doesn't touch a drop. Himself and the priest's sister—that dark fancy slip of a thing with the pants—they are to get married soon. They say he'll get the new school there . . .

Ah, no, certainly not the Foxy Policeman either. He has a lump of a nurse hanging out of him in the Fancy City, or so they say . . . nor the spuds guy . . . Go on, have another guess, Master. I'll give you as many as you want . . . Paddy is gone to England. They took the lorry from him, and sold it. He never went up a road for turf without letting a string of debts behind him. Guess again, Master . . . That's him, dead on, exactly, Billy the Postman. Well done getting it like that, just as a pure guess. Never mind what anyone else says, Master, I think you have a great head on your shoulders . . .

Careful now with Nora Johnny. I could tell you things, Master . . .

Ah, forget about that now, get over it Master, and don't let it bother you . . . Maybe you are dead right . . . It wasn't just letters that had him coming to the house . . . Ah, come off it, Master . . . She was always a bit flighty, your wife . . .

5.

—. . . They were sent as plenipotentiaries to make a peace treaty between Ireland and England . . .

—I'm telling you you're a filthy liar. They were only sent over as messenger boys, they exceeded their authority, and betrayed us, and the country is buggered up ever since . . .

—A white mare. She was a beauty. No bother for her to carry a ton and a half . . .

—. . . By the oak of this coffin, I swear Nora Johnny, I swear I gave Caitriona the pound . . .

—. . . "That daughter of Big Martin John
    Was just as tall as any man

When she stood up on the hill . . ."

—. . . Why don't you go stuff your England and its markets. You're just scared shitless of the few pence you have in the bank. Hitler's the boy! . . .

—. . . Now, Coley, I'm a writer. I read fifty books for every one that you read. I'll sue you if you think I am not a writer. Did you read my last book, "The Dream of the Jelly Fish?" . . . You didn't Coley . . . My apologies Coley. I'm very sorry. I forgot that you couldn't read . . . It's a great story though . . . And I had three and a half novels, two and a half plays, and nine and a half translations with the publishers, The Goom,* and another short story and a half "The Setting Sun." I never got over the fact that "The Setting Sun" wasn't published before I died . . .

—If you're going to be a writer, Coley, remember that it's taboo for The Goom to publish anything that a girl would hide from her father . . . Apologies, Coley. I'm sorry. I thought you intended becoming a writer. But just in case you get that blessed itch . . . There isn't an Irish speaker who doesn't get that itch sometime in his life . . . they say it's the stuff on the coast around here that causes it . . . Now, Coley, don't be rude . . . It's the duty of every Irish speaker to find out if he has the gift of writing, especially the gift of the short story, plays, poetry . . . These last two are far commoner than the gift of the short story, even. Take poetry, for example. All you have to do is to start at the bottom of the page and to work your way up to the top . . . either that, or scribble from right to left, leave a huge margin, but that isn't half as poetic as the other way . . .

Apologies again, Coley. I'm really sorry. I didn't remember that you can't read or write . . . But the short story, Coley . . . I'll put it like this . . . You've drunk a pint, haven't you? . . . Yes, I understand . . .

---

* The Goom (An Gúm) was a state publishing house established in 1927 to publish books in Irish for the general public and for schools. Máirtín Ó Cadhain's early stories were published by An Gúm, but he always had a fractious relationship with them. This is one of the many asides in the novel where he is poking fun at his literary adversaries.

You drank lots of pints of stout, and often . . . Don't mind how much you drank, Coley . . .

—I drank forty-four pints one after the other . . .

—I know that . . . Just hang on a minute . . . Good man. Let me speak . . . Get an ounce of sense, Coley, and let me speak . . . You've seen what's on the top of a pint of stout. The head, isn't it? A head of useless dirty froth. And yet, the more of it that's there on the pint, the more your tongue is hanging out for the pint itself. And if your tongue is hanging out for it you'll drink it all the way down to the dregs, even though it tastes flat. Do you see now, Coley, the beginning, the middle and the end of the short story . . . Be careful now that you don't forget that the end has to leave a sour taste in your mouth, the taste of the holy drink, the wish to steal the fire from the gods, to take another bite of the apple of knowledge . . . Look at the way I'd have finished that other short story— "Another Setting Sun," the one I was working on if I hadn't died suddenly from an attack of writer's cramp:

"Just after the girl had uttered that fateful word, he turned on his heels, departed the claustrophobic atmosphere of the room, and went out into the fresh air. The sky was dark with threatening clouds that were coming in from the sea. A weak faceless sun was entering the earth behind the mountains of the Old Town . . ." That's the *tour de force* Coley: "a weak faceless sun entering the earth"; and there should be no need for me to remind you that the last line after the last word has to be richly splattered with dots, writer's dots as I call them . . . But maybe you'll have the patience to listen to me reading it all to you from start to finish . . .

—Wait now, my good man. I'll tell you a story:

"Once upon a time there were three men . . ."

—Coley! Coley! There's no art in that story: "Once upon a time there were three men . . ." That's a hackneyed start . . . Wait now a minute, Coley, patience one minute. Let me speak. I think that I'm a writer . . .

—Shut your mouth you old windbag. Keep going, Coley . . .

—Once upon a time there were three men, and it was a long time ago. Once upon a time there were three men . . .

—Yes, go on, Coley, go on . . .

—Once upon a time there were three men . . . ah yes, there were three men a long time ago. I don't know what happened to them after that . . .

—". . . I swear by the book, Jack the Lad . . ."

—. . . Five elevens fifty-five; five thirteens . . . five thirteens . . . nobody learns that . . . Now, Master, don't I know them! Five sevens . . . was that what you asked me, Master? Five sevens, was it? . . . five sevens . . . five by seven . . . wait now a second . . . five ones is one . . .

6.

—. . . But I don't get it, Margaret. Honest Injun, I just don't get it. She—that's Caitriona Paudeen, I mean—was badmouthing me to the Master. You wouldn't mind, but I did nothing to her? You know yourself, Margaret, that I wouldn't stick my nose into anybody else's business, I'm too busy with culture. And there's a big flashy cross on my grave too. Smashing, the Old Master says. She insulted me, Margaret . . .

—I think you had better start getting used to Caitriona's tongue, Nora Johnny . . .

—But all the same, Margaret . . .

—. . . "Like an eel on a hook, by crook or by luck
     Caitriona would snare Nora Johnny."

—But she has it in for me all the time, she never stops, I just don't get it, honest . . .

—. . . "Each morning that dawned Nora Johnny came over
     To make bits of Caitriona like she would with a fish . . ."

—. . . "My beautiful daughter, she married your Paddy
     Your hovel is better for all she brought in . . ."

—"Caitriona, you maggot, you were never ashamed
     For disgracing yourself you were the best thing . . ."

—. . . All his lies, Margaret! Honest to God! I wonder what does she say to Dotie . . . Hey, Dotie . . . Dotie . . . What does Caitriona Paudeen say about me . . .

—God save us all. I don't know who you are at all at all. I wish they had brought my sod of clay east of the Fancy City and laid me down on the flat surface of the Smooth Meadow in Temple Brandon with my ancestors . . .

—Dotie! I told you already that that kind of talk is only sentimental tosh. What did Caitriona say . . .

—I heard the filthiest talk you could imagine from her about her own sister Nell. "May not another corpse come to the graveyard before her," she said. You'd never hear that kind of talk on the Smooth Meadow.

—Dotie! But just about me . . .

—About your daughter.

—. . . "Not a coat on her back, and I paid for that too,
    Nor as much as a shirt to get married in . . ."

—She said that you were of the Toejam crowd, and that you were riddled with fleas . . .

—Dotie! De grâce . . .

—That there were sailors . . .

—Parlez-vous français, Madame, Mademoiselle . . .

—Au revoir! Au revoir! . . .

—Mais c'est splendid. Je ne savais pas qu'il y avait une . . .

—Au revoir. Honest, Margaret, only that Dotie knows me well she'd believe all those lies . . . Dotie! That old sentimentality again. You are my fellow mariner on the illimitable sea of culture, Dotie. You should be able to distil every twisted prejudice and every prejudged notion out of your head, just like Clicks did in "Two Men and the Powder Puff" . . .

—. . . The Poet did it, I'd say . . .

—Oh, was it that chancer . . .

—No certainly not. It wasn't him. He wouldn't be that lucky. Big Micil Connolly made it up:

    "Bonking an Old Yank was our Baba Paudeen
    And there was no one just like her in all of Maine . . ."

—Honest, Margaret, I've forgotten all that business about Caitriona Paudeen in the place above. It's the culture, Margaret. It raises the mind up to the noble heights and exposes the magic fairy forts in which the hidden elements of sound and vision dwell, just as Nibs said in "Evening Tresses." You don't have any interest any more in normal inanities nor in the petty pastimes of mortal life. My mind is possessed by a glorious disorder for this last while as a result of the rushing wonders of culture . . .

—. . . "And there was no one just like her in all of Maine

She came back home dressed up to the nine

With money the old hag left to her name . . ."

—Baba Paudeen never married, but she was looking after an old crone since she went to America. What do you know, but the old one left her all of her money—well nearly all—when she was dying. Baba Paudeen could fill all the graves in this cemetery with golden guineas, at least that is what they say about her, Dotie . . .

—. . . It was Coley who made up all that rubbish. What else?

"'Ara, Baba, my darling,' said Caitríona's cat

'Don't yield a farthing,' said Nell's cat back.

'If I only got the money,' said Caitríona's cat

'It's all for me, honey,' said Nell's cat at that."

—Caitriona would prefer, better than another thousand years, to scrub Nell from Baba's will . . .

"'I have a nice deep pocket,' said Caitriona's pussy.

'I have a nice deep pocket,' said Nell's pussy back."

—"'For an old hag's money,' said Caitríona's pussy.

'Baba didn't promise you,' said Nell's pussy at that."

—She had every single teacher in the whole area totally driven out of their minds getting them to write to America for her . . .

—And Mannix the Counsellor . . .

—The Old Master told me he wrote very cultured letters for her. He picked up a lot of Americanese from the films . . .

—That time when he used to bring the young mistress to the Fancy City in his car . . .

—The thing that really pisses Caitriona off is that she died before

Nell. I often heard her going up the lane and muttering to herself: "I'll bury her yet before me in the Cemetery Clay."

—. . . Tell the truth, Coley. Did you write that rubbish?

—Big Micil Connolly did it. He did "The Ballad of Caitríona" too, and "The Ballad . . ."

—. . . But Nell is still alive. She'll get what's in Baba's will now. There's no other brother or sister, only herself . . .

—I'm not sure about that, Margaret. Baba was very fond of Caitriona.

—Do you know what my boss used to say about all of them, the Paudeens: "Weather cocks," he'd say. "If one of them went to market to buy a cow, he'd come home with a donkey. Then he'd say to the next person who made some smart remark about the donkey: 'I'm sorry now I didn't buy a cow instead of that old bag of bones of a donkey. She'd be a lot more useful . . .'"

—. . . "Would you come along home with me, I'll shelter you under my cloak,

     And I swear young Jack the Lad, we'll have songs until we croak . . ."

—. . . It's a strange nickname for a man, alright, Dotie . . . Yes. Jack the Lad. He lives up there at the top of the town land where Caitriona and myself lived. I knew the original Lad himself, Jack's father . . . The Old Lad. He was one of the Feeneys, really . . . No need to laugh, Dotie . . . Dotie! "Lad" is just as handy as "Dotie" any time. Even if you do come from the Smooth Meadow, I'm telling you, we weren't pupped by hens no more than yourself . . .

—De grâce, Marguerita . . .

—. . . " 'I'll marry Jack,' said Caitríona's dog.

     'I'll marry Jack,' said Nell's dog too . . ."

—Caitriona refused many men. One of them was Blotchy Brian. He had a good chunk of land and pots of money. Her father advised her to hook up with him. He was so worthless, according to her, she wouldn't give him the time of day . . .

—. . . Start that song again, and sing it right this time . . .

—"The Lad's son he got up and went . . ."

—. . . You'd nearly think that God gave Jack the Lad a soul so that he could go about singing. If you heard his voice just once it would haunt you for the rest of your life. I don't know at all what exactly to call it . . .

—A musical dream.

—That's it, Nora. Just like a strange and beautiful dream. There you are on the edge of a cliff. A drowning hole down below you. Your heart thumping with fear. Then, suddenly, you hear Jack's voice wafting up from the depths. Your desire immediately banishes your fear. Then you seem to let yourself go . . . You feel yourself sliding down and down . . . and down . . . getting nearer all the time to that voice . . .

—Oh my, Margaret! How thrilling! Honest . . .

—. . . I never met anyone who could remember exactly any song that Jack sang. We would forget everything but the soul he put into his voice. Every young girl in the place would lick the winding path which he trod to his door. I often saw the young ones up on the bog and as soon as they caught a glimpse of Jack the Lad over at his own turf they would crawl through muck and glob just to hear him sing. I saw Caitriona Paudeen doing it. I saw her sister Nell doing it . . .

—Smashing altogether, Margaret. Cultured people call it the eternal triangle . . .

—. . . "Jack the Lad rose up and took the early morning air
    And went off chasing women with the frolics at the fair . . ."

—. . . Too true. It was at the Big Pig Fair that Nell Paudeen and Jack the Lad took off together. Her people were fit to be tied, for all the good it did them. I don't know if it's the way you do things over on the Smooth Meadow, you know, that the eldest daughter has to get married first . . .

—. . . "She carried him off through bog-holes, swamps and mucky glob
    Disturbing all the curlews whose chicks had open gobs . . ."

—Jack was up on the bog and all he had was waste scrub and some drowned moorland . . .

—Ara, Maggie Frances, I never saw a more awkward pathway

up to a house than that of Jack the Lad's. Didn't I twist my ankle that night coming home from the wedding at . . .

—. . . You did, because you made a pig of yourself, as usual . . .

—. . . The night of the wedding in Paudeen's house Caitriona was holed up in a corner in the back room with a face as miserable as a wet week. There was a small gang of us there. Nell was there. She started ribbing Caitriona: "I really think you should marry Blotchy Brian, Caitriona," she said. She knew right well that Caitriona had already refused him . . .

—I was there, Margaret. "I've got Jack now," Nell said. "We'll leave Blotchy Brian for you, Caitriona."

—Caitriona went ape. She stormed out, and she wouldn't go near the room again until the next morning. Nor did she go to the church either the following day . . .

—I was cutting a bunch of heather that day, Margaret, and I saw her winding her way up through the bog by Tulla Bwee even though the wedding was over the other way at the Lad's house . . .

—She didn't put one foot, right or left, across the threshold of Jack the Lad's joint from that day to this. You'd think Nell was riddled with some kind of nasty pox the way she used to give her a wide berth. She never forgave her for Jack . . .

—. . . "Brian is a darling with his land and his cows

But he'll never be right without a woman and a house . . ."

—. . . Despite all his wealth, Blotchy Brian failed utterly to get a woman. It's a small wonder he didn't come crawling to her again . . .

—. . . "'By japers,' says Triona, 'here's a fine pig for scalding,

Turn the kettle to the fire: he might get the warning.'"

—They'd use the handle of the pot over beyond the Fancy City. That time Pat McGrath came knocking . . .

—We refuse them that way too on this side of the city, Dotie. Honest. In my own case, for example . . .

—Did you hear what the Tailor's sister did when an old dribbling dunderhead came over from Derry Lough looking for her? She took a long knife out of the press, and started sharpening it in the middle of the floor. "Keep it for me," she said . . .

—Oh, she'd do that alright. The Dog Eared crowd . . .

—After all that, what do you know, Caitriona married John Thomas Lydon from our own place, and never said either "yea" or "nay" when he came for her . . .

—I swear, Margaret, John Thomas was far too good for her . . .

—He had a fine plot of the best rich soil . . .

—And the willingness to work it . . .

—A fine spacious house . . .

—She drooled for the place, certainly. To be better off and have more money than Nell. And to be close enough so that Nell could see every single day that she was better off and had more money than her to the end of her days . . .

—"'I have a huge haggard,' said Caitríona's cat

'I have the best fat cows, and butter as well . . .'"

—"'I am sleek and useful and friendly and cuddly

Quite just the opposite of that kitty of Nell's . . .'"

—Letting Nell know that she didn't get the worst of the bargain, and that Nell could suck on her disappointment and failure. That much came out of Caitriona's own unforgiving mouth. It was her revenge . . .

—Oh my! But that's very interesting. I don't think I'll bother with the reading session I have with the Old Master today . . . Hey there, Master . . . Let's skip the novelette today . . . I'm doing something else intellectual. *Au revoir* . . .

—Caitriona was particular, thrifty and nifty in John Thomas Lydon's house. I know that well, as I was next door to her. The sun never woke her up in bed. Her card and spinning wheel often chattered and gabbled through the night . . .

—And it looked every bit of it, Margaret. She had stuff and more . . .

—. . . I wandered into Barry's betting shop up in the Fancy City. I had my hand in my pocket just as if I had a pile. All I had was one shilling. I made a racket chucking it on to the counter. "'The Golden Apple,'" I said. "'The three o'clock. A hundred to one . . . It better win,' I muttered putting my hand in my pocket and sauntering out" . . .

—. . . It's a pity I wasn't there, Peter, I wouldn't let him get away with it. You shouldn't let a black heretic like that insult your religion.

"Faith of our fathers, Holy Faith,
We will be true to thee 'til death,
We will be true to thee 'til death . . ."

—You're a bloodless wimp, Peter, letting him talk like that. I wasn't there to . . .

—Put a cork in it! Neither of the two of you have shut up going on about religion for the last five years . . .

—They say, however, Margaret, after all the savaging that Caitriona did of Nell that she would have been glad of her when her husband died. She was in a bad way that time, as Patrick was only a toddler . . .

—That I would have been glad of Nell! That I would have been glad of Nell! That I would take anything from Nell. God Almighty Father and his blessed angels, that I'd take anything from that hog face! I'm going to burst! I'm going to burst! . . .

7.

—. . . "The nettle-ridden patches of Bally Donough," you say.

—The little pimply hillocks in your town land couldn't even grow nettles with all the fleas on them . . .

—. . . Fell from a stack of corn . . .

—By the hokey, as you might say, myself and the guy from Menlow were writing to one another . . .

—". . . Do you think that this war is 'The War of the Two Foreigners'?" I says to Patchy Johnny.

—Wake up, you lout. That war's been over since 1918 . . .

—It was going on when I was dying . . .

—Wake up, I'm telling you. Aren't you nearly thirty years dead. The next war is on now . . .

—I'm twenty-one years here now. I can boast something that nobody else here can: I was the first corpse in this cemetery. Don't you think that the elder in this place would have something to say. Let me speak. Let me speak, I tell you . . .

—Caitriona had stuff and plenty, no doubt about it, Margaret...

—She certainly had, but despite that her place was better than Nell's, Nell didn't let things slide either . . .

—God bless you. Margaret! Neither herself nor Jack ever did a toss except gawk into one another's eyes and sing songs, until Peter, the son, grew up and was able to do some work on that old swamp and clear some of the cursed scrubs . . .

—Nell didn't have a penny to her name until Blotchy Brian's Maggie brought her dowry.

—However much you dress up her place, the truth is that what saved her was being near a river and a lake, with some wild grouse around. Of course, there's no telling what money hunters and fishermen gave her. I myself saw the Earl slipping a pound note into the palm of her hand: a nice crisp clean pound note . . .

—. . . Over on the Smooth Meadow, you call your swamps "fens," don't you, Dotie? I also heard that you call the cat "a rat catcher," and the thongs "the fire friend." . . . No doubt about it, Dotie, that's not the proper and correct "Old Irish" at all . . .

—God save us all! . . .

—. . . "'We'll send pigs to the market,' said Caitríona's cat
'You'd do better with bullocks,' said Nell's cat back."

—. . . It's not one smell of an exaggeration that Caitriona would add bits to her prayers for Nell to shrivel away. She was thrilled to bits if a calf died, or if her potatoes rotted . . .

—I won't tell one word of a lie about her, Margaret. God forgive me if I did! That time when the lorry crocked Peter Nell's leg, Caitriona said straight up my face: "I'm glad it hit him. The road is plenty wide enough. It serves the maggot right . . ."

—"Nell won that round anyway," she admitted, the day her husband, John Thomas Lydon, was buried . . .

—He was buried in the eastern graveyard. I remember it well, and I had good reason to. I twisted my ankle, just where I slipped on the stone . . .

—Where you made a pig of yourself, as you usually did . . .

—. . . To have more potatoes than Nell; more pigs, hens, hay;

have a cleaner smarter house; her children to have better clothes: 'twas all part of her vengeance. It was her vengeance . . .

—. . . "She ca-me back ho-me dressed to th-e nines
As she fi-lched a sta-ck from the old grey hag."

—Baba Paudeen got laid low by some sickness in America, and it took her to death's door. Blotchy Brian's Maggie looked after her. She brought Maggie back home with her . . .

—. . . "Baba was holed up in Caitríona's house . . ."

—She rarely went near Nell. She was too out of the way and the path was too awkward after her sickness. She seemed to like Caitriona a lot better for some reason . . .

—. . . "Nell's house is only a rotting hovel
She needn't bother be spouting lies
The fever was there, no use denying it
If that plague gets you, you'll surely die . . ."

—. . . Caitriona only had one son in the house, Padd . . .

—Two daughters of hers died . . .

—No, three did. Another one in America. Kate . . .

—I remember her well, Margaret. I twisted my ankle the day she left . . .

—Baba promised Caitriona's Paddy that she wouldn't see him short for the rest of his days if he married Blotchy Brian's Maggie. Caitriona really hated Blotchy Brian's guts, and she was the same way with her dog and her daughter. But she had a big dowry, and Caitriona had a notion that Baba would more than fancy leaving money in her house as a result. Just to best Nell . . .

—. . . "Baba was holed up in Cat-rion-a's house
Until Paddy rejected the Blotchy's Maggie.
Nora Johnny has a lovely fair maiden
Without cows or gold I took her fancy . . ."

—High for Gort Ribbuck! . . .

—Nora Johnny's daughter was a fine piece of work, I swear . . .

—. . . That's what turned Caitriona against your daughter in the first place, Nora Johnny. All that old guff about the dowry is only an excuse. From the day your daughter stepped into her house, married to her son, she had it in for her like a pup with his paw on a bone and another pup trying to whip it from him. How often did you have to come over from Gort Ribbuck, Nora . . .

—. . . "Each morning that broke, Nora Johnny came over the way . . ."

—Oh my! We're getting to the exciting part of the story now, Margaret, aren't we? The hero is married to his sweetheart. But there's another woman lurking away in the background. She's been wounded by the conflict, and there will be lots of trouble ahead . . . Anonymous letters, sly gossip about the hero, maybe a murder yet, certainly a divorce . . . Oh! My! . . .

—. . . "'I wouldn't marry Blotchy Brian,' said Caitriona's kitty . . ."
Add a few lines to that yourself . . .

—"'But you thought for to hurt him,' said Nell's kitty back . . ."

—"'But I'd marry his daughter,' said Caitriona's puss to that."

—"Said Nell's kitty then, 'That's a chance you won't get.'"

—It pissed Caitriona off even more that Baba took off and stayed in Nell's house more than Nell's son got the money and the dowry that had been promised to her own Paddy . . .

—I remember well, Margaret, the day that Baba Paudeen went back to America. I was cutting hay above in the Red Meadow when I saw them coming down from Nell's house. I ran over to say goodbye to them. As God is my witness, just as I was jumping across the furrowed dyke, I twisted my . . .

—Don't you think, Margaret, isn't it twenty years since Baba Paudeen went back to America? . . .

—She's gone sixteen years. But Caitriona never took her beady eye off the will. If it wasn't for that she'd be dead a long time ago. It added years to her life to be badmouthing her son's wife . . .

—Yes, Margaret, and the pleasure she got in going to funerals all the time.

—And Fireside Tom's land . . .

—. . . Listen to me now, Curran:

"A great big altar as a kind compensation . . ."

—Don't mind that little scut, Curran. Sure, he couldn't compose a line of poetry . . .

—The story is getting a bit boring now, Margaret. Honest. I thought they'd be a lot more hassle by now . . .

—. . . Listen, Curran. Listen to the second line:

"And to add to my pride, to be in the Pound Place . . ."

—. . . Honest, Margaret. I thought there'd be at least a murder and a divorce. But Dotie can assess every prejudice . . .

—. . . By japers, I have it now Curran. Listen:

"The cross above me will drive Nell to distraction
And in the cemetery clay I'll have won the race . . ."

8.

—Hoora, Margaret! . . . Can you hear me, Margaret? . . . Nora Johnny has no shame talking to a schoolmaster . . . Of course, that's true, Margaret. Of course, everyone knows she's my inlaw. You wouldn't mind but there is no place here you can get a bit of privacy, or get out of the way. Sweet God almighty! A bitch! A bitch! She was always a bitch. That time when she was a skivvy in the Fancy City before she got married they used to say—we don't want to even think about it!—that she used to hang around with a sailor . . .

Sure thing, Margaret . . . I said it to him. "Patrick, my darling," I said, just like this. "That thing from Gort Ribbuck that you are determined to marry, did you hear that her mother was hanging around with a sailor in the Fancy City?"

"So what?" he said.

"Ah, Patrick," I said. "Sailors, you know . . ."

"Hu! Sailors," he said. "Couldn't a sailor be just as good as any other person? I know who this girl's mother was hooking up with in the Fancy City, but that's a long way from America, and I haven't the faintest clue who Blotchy Brian's Maggie was knocking around with over there. With a black, maybe . . ."

Sure thing, Margaret. If it wasn't that she couldn't warm to Nell and didn't want to give her the money, there's some chance that I'd let my son bring a daughter of Blotchy Brian into my house. I swear, I could have been fond of Blotchy Brian's daughter. The night that Nell got married, that's what the cow threw in my face. "I have Jack," she said, "You can have Blotchy Brian now, Caitriona."

Do you know what, Margaret, but those few words hurt me far more than all the other wrongs she did me. What she said was like a plague of stoats buzzing back and forth through my brain spitting out venomous snots. They never left my head up to the day I died. They never did, Margaret. Every time I saw Blotchy Brian I'd think of that night in the room at home, and on the gloating grin on Nell's puss because of Jack the Lad. Every time I'd see Brian's son or daughter, I'd think of that night. Every time somebody even mentioned Blotchy Brian, I'd remember it . . . on the room . . . on the grin . . . on Nell in Jack the Lad's arms! . . . in Jack the Lad's arms . . .

Blotchy Brian asked me twice, Margaret. I never told you that . . . What's that Nora Johnny calls it? . . . The eternal triangle . . . the eternal triangle . . . That was her silly shite, alright . . . But, Margaret, I didn't tell you, did I? . . . You're mistaken. I'm not that kind of a person, Margaret. I'm not a blabbermouth. Anything that's my own business, anything I saw or heard, I took it into the clay with me. But there's no harm talking about it now when we are gone the way of all flesh . . .

He asked me twice, I'm telling you. The first time I was hardly more than twenty. My father was trying to get me to do it. "Blotchy Brian is a good decent man, with a nice little spot, and a decent stash of money," he said.

"I wouldn't marry him," I said, "even if I had to borrow the shawl from Nell and stand out in front of everyone in the middle of the fair."

"Why's that?" said my father.

"Because he's an ugly git," I said. "Look at his ridiculous goatee beard. See his sticky out teeth. His nasal whine. His bandy leg. See the dirty dive of a hovel he lives in. See the coat of filth all around it. He's three times as old as me. He could be my grandfather."

And I was right. He was nearly fifty that time. He is nearly a hundred now, still alive and not a bother on him, apart from the odd bout of rheumatism. He'd be going to collect the pension same time as me when we were up there. The ugly gom! . . .

"Every brat to her own device," my father said, and that was all he ever said about it.

Nell wasn't married long when he came slavering for me again. I was just getting a cup of tea in the evening as the shades of night came down. I remember it well. I had put the teapot down on the hearth trying to blow some life into the embers. This guy comes in totally unexpectedly even before I had a chance to recognise him. "Will you marry me, Caitriona," he said, just like that. "I think I deserve you, coming like this the second time. And as it's not doing me any good, living without a nice woman . . ."

I'm telling you straight, that's exactly what he said.

"I wouldn't marry you, you rotten poop, even if cobwebs grew out of me for want of a man," I said.

I had put the thongs down and I had the boiling kettle in my hand. I didn't blink an eye, Margaret, but went for him in the middle of the floor. But he had vanished out the door by then.

I know I am hard to please when it comes to men. I was good-looking enough and had a decent dowry . . . But marry Blotchy Brian, come on now like, Margaret, after what Nell said . . .

—. . . "It'd better win," I said, sticking my hand in my pocket and hightailing it out the door. "When you lose, you're screwed," I said, taking the ticket from the wench. She smiled at me: that kind of innocent smile from a young innocent heart. "If 'The Golden Apple' wins," I said, "I'll buy you some sweeties and take you to the pictures . . . Or would you prefer a bit of a dance . . . or a few quiet drinks in the snug in the Great Southern Hotel? . . ."

—. . . Qu'est-ce que vous dites? Quelle drôle de langue! N'y a-t-il-pas là quelque professeur ou étudiant qui parle français?

—Au revoir. Au revoir.

—Pardon! Pardon!

—Shut your gob, you shitehawk!

—If I could reach that gander, I'd shut his trap for him. Either that, or he'd talk proper. Every time he mentions Hitler he starts sputtering away in a torrent of talk. Sweet jumping Jesus, but if he really knew I don't think he'd be that happy about Hitler at all . . .

—Didn't you notice that every time that Hitler's name is mentioned, he calls him a "whore" immediately. Who are we to say he hasn't picked up that much Irish . . .

—Oh, if only I could get my hands on him! High for Hitler! High for Hitler! High for Hitler! High for Hitler . . .

—Je ne vous comprends pas, monsieur . . .

—Who is that, Margaret?

—That's the guy who was killed in the airplane. Don't you remember? He went down in the middle of the bay. You were alive that time.

—Sure, didn't I see him laid out, Margaret . . . He had a fantastic funeral. They said he was some kind of a hero . . .

—He jabbers away like that. The Master says that he's French, and that he'd understand him if his tongue wasn't worn away by the time he spent in the sea . . .

—So, the Master doesn't understand him, Margaret?

—Not the slightest clue, Caitriona.

—I always knew, Margaret, that the Old Master wasn't very learned. It doesn't matter if he doesn't understand a Frenchy! I should have known that yonks ago . . .

—Nora Johnny understands him better than anyone else in the graveyard. Did you not hear her answering him just a while back? . . .

—Ara, would you get an ounce of sense, Maggie Frances. Do you Mean Toejam Nora with the smelly feet? . . .

—Ils m'ennuient. On espère toujours trouver la paix dans la mort, mais la tombe ne semble pas encore être la mort. On ne trouve ici en tout cas, que de l'ennui . . .

—Au revoir. Au revoir. De grâce. De grâce.

—. . . Six sixes, forty-six; six sevens fifty-two; six eights, fifty-eight . . . Now, amn't I great, Master! I know my tables up to now. If I had gone to school as a kid, there'd be no stopping me. I'll say all the tables from the beginning now, Master. Two ones are . . . Why don't you want to hear them, Master? You've been kind of neglecting me for the last while, since Caitriona Paudeen told you about your wife . . .

— I swear by the oak of this coffin, Curran, I gave her the pound, I gave the pound to Caitriona Paudeen. But I never got a gnat's glimpse of it since.

— Ababoona! Holy cow! You lied, you old bat . . .

— Honest, Dotie. You wouldn't understand: a stranger this way from the rich lands of the Fair Meadow. This is the truth, the unadulterated truth, Dotie. Honest, it is. I was going to swear "by the Holy finger," but that is unbecoming talk. Instead of that, Dotie, I'll say: "I'll put the blessed crucifix on my heart." Margaret told you about herself and Nell, but she never told you about the dowry I lavished on my daughter when she married into Caitriona's house. You should know that story, Dotie. Everyone else here knows it. Sixty pounds, Dotie. Honest! Sixty pounds in golden guineas . . .

— For the love of God Almighty! Margaret! Hey, Margaret! Do you hear me?

I'm going to burst! I'm going to burst, Margaret! I'm going to burst, Margaret! Nora Johnny's young one! . . . sixty . . . dowry . . . for me and us . . . I'm going to burst! I'm going to burst! O my God, I'm going to burst! . . . Goi . . . bur . . . Go . . . burs . . . G . . . bu . . . Burs . . .

Interlude 2

THE SCATTERED EARTH

1.

You were asking for it. If I hadn't stabbed you, somebody else would have stabbed you, and isn't the fool and his lackey all the same? As you were going to be stabbed anyway, wasn't it better to be stabbed by a neighbour than by a stranger? The stranger would be buried miles away, maybe, over on the flat plains of the Smooth Meadow, or up in Dublin, or the arsehole of the country somewhere, and what would you do then? Look at the satisfaction you get chewing me up here. And if the stranger was lying next to you, you would be at a loss to know what to throw up in his face, as you would know nothing about his seed, breed, and generation. Cop yourself on, you knacker. You wouldn't mind, but I stabbed you cleanly . . .

—The Dog Eared Lot often stabbed cleanly! . . .

—. . . A white-headed mare . . . She was gorgeous . . .

—. . . I swear, Huckster Joan, I swear by the oak of this coffin, that I gave her the pound, Caitriona Paudeen . . .

—. . . That's the way it was. Went up to the Bookie's around three o'clock. "'The Golden Apple,'" I said. "She better win," I said, sticking my hands in my pockets and turning on my heels out the door. I didn't have a brass farthing . . .

Won the three o'clock. The race was over. "The Golden Apple" at a hundred to one. Went to collect my fiver. The wench smiled at me again: a sweet innocent smile from a pure heart. It meant a lot more to me than a fiver: "I'll get you sweets, or I'll bring you to the pictures, or to a dance . . . Or would you prefer . . . ?" I was mortified. I didn't finish what I was saying.

"I'll meet you outside the Plaza at a quarter past seven," I said.

Go home. Shave, shower, shite, shampoo, slap on the slime, get ready. Didn't even drink a drop for good luck. I had far too much time for that innocent smile from a pure heart . . .

To the Plaza for seven. Put a hole in my fiver buying her chocolates. The chocolates would really melt her young pure heart, and the glint of the beauty of the rose would appear in her smile like the first rays of the breaking morning. Wasn't I the eejit who had spent so much . . .

—Hang on now 'til I read you the Proclamation that Eamon de Valera put before the people of Ireland:

"Irish men and Irish women . . ."

—Wait now, until I read the Proclamation that Arthur Griffith put before the people of Ireland:

"Irish men and Irish women . . ."

—. . . I drank forty-two pints that night one after the other. And I walked home after that as straight as a reed . . . as straight as a reed, I'm telling you. I delivered a calf from the brindle cow, which was in labour for two hours already. I drove the old donkey out from Curran's oats . . . and I tied up Tommy. I had just taken off my shoes and about to go on my knees to say a bit of a prayer, when the young one comes in. Her breath was totally shagged. "My Mam says to go over straight away," she said "Dad is doing his thing again."

—"I don't give a toss about him doing his thing if it's not the right time," I said, "just as I was about to say my prayers. What's bugging him now?"

"Downing poteen like water," she said.

Off I went. He was out of his tree and nobody in the house was able to hold him down. You couldn't say they weren't a bunch of wimps . . .

"Here, grab this," I said. "Take a hold of this rope, like, right now, before he goes for the axe. Can't you see he's eyeing it . . ."

—I remember it well. I twisted my ankle . . .

—We won the match.

—Not a bit of it. If the mine hadn't destroyed the house . . .

—... "I washed my face in the dew of the morning,
And combed my hair with the wind of my hand ..."

It's not right yet, Curran. There's a stray bit still there. Hang on a minute now:

"I washed my face in the dew of the morning ..." That bit is just dandy, Curran. I already used it in *The Golden Stars.* Hang on a minute now ... Listen to this, Curran:

"I washed my face in the dew of the morning,
And combed my hair with the wind of my hand ..."

That's just perfect. Curran, I knew I'd get it in the end ... Are you listening now?

"I washed my face in the dew of the morning,
And combed my hair with the wind of my hand ...
My shoelaces were as the sparkle of the rainbow ..."

Hang on now, Curran ... Wait a second ... *Eureka* ... "And the Pleiades were holding up my pants ..." I knew I'd get it, Curran. Listen to the whole verse now ...

—Will you go and get lost, and don't be driving everyone around the twist. My mind is numb for the last two years listening to your nonsense verse. I have worse things on my mind, God forgive me: my eldest boy knocking around with the floozie from Up the Way, and the boss of the house all ready to hand the place over to him. And on top of that, I have no idea is it old Gut Bucket's donkeys, or Tim Top of the Road's beasts who are guzzling my corn ...

—You're dead right about that, Curran. They should have stuffed the piece of shit in the eastern graveyard. Mike O'Donnell is there, the guy who wrote "The Song of the Turnip," and "The War of the Hen with the Grain of Corn" ...

—And Big Mike Connolly who made up the "Ballad of Caitríona" and "Fireside Tom's Song" ...

—And "The Psalm of the Cat." That's a fantastic piece of work, "The Psalm of the Cat." I'd never be able to do that, never ...

—... Eight sixes forty-eight; eight sevens fifty-four ... You're not listening at all, Master. You're not with it at all, these days, ... I'm not making one bit of progress ... Is that what you said, Master? Hardly surprising, Master, and the way you have been neglecting me . . . Answer me this . . . How many tables are there anyway, Master? . . . Is that all? Well, fuck me pink if that's it! I thought that there were at least a hundred . . . or up to a thousand . . . up to a million . . . up to a quadrillion . . . we have so much time to be lying in the grave, that's what they say. He who made time, made tons of it . . .

—God help us! Isn't it a tragedy that they didn't transport my mortal bones beyond the Fancy City and to lay me down in Brandon's Temple on the white bleached plains of the Smooth Meadow amongst my own people! There, the clay is gentle and welcoming; there, the clay is soft and silken; there, the clay is quiet and loving; there, the clay is protective and snug. Decay there is not the decay of the graveyard; corruption there is not the corruption of the flesh. But clay will cling to clay; clay will hug and kiss clay; clay will interbreed with clay . . .

—She's gone all sloppy again . . .

—You'd never see anyone as crazy mad as her, only when this stupidity gets her . . .

—It's the way she is, God help us! Caitriona's far worse when she starts going on about Nell and Nora Johnny . . .

—Caitriona's gone over the top altogether. Blotchy Brian was right when he called her a jennet . . .

—Blotchy Brian wasn't right. Honestly, he wasn't . . .

—What's up with you? Are you against that arsehole too, Nora?

—Honest, he wasn't right. The jennet is a very cultured beast. Honest, it is. The Rooters in Bally Donough used to have a jennet when I was going to school, years ago. And it would eat raisin bread from the palm of my hand . . .

—Going to school years ago! Toejam Nora going to school! Raisin bread in Gort Ribbuck! O holy cow and mother of Jesus! Margaret . . . Margaret, did you hear what Toejam Nora Johnny Robin of the Stinky Soles said? O, O, I'm going to burst . . .

... Nora Johnny ... Nora Johnny ... Toejam Nora Stinky Soles ... You weren't happy to leave your lying ways aboveground, but you had to bring it down here too. The whole graveyard knows the devil himself—keep him far away!—gave you a loan of his tongue when you were just a slip of a thing, and you used it so well that he never asked for it back ...

One hundred and twenty pounds dowry for that trollop of a daughter of yours ... My goodness me ... A woman that didn't have a stitch of clothes to put on her the day she got married, only I bought her an outfit ... Toejam Nora had sixty pounds ... There wasn't sixty pounds ever in all of Gort Ribbuck end to end. Gort Ribbuck of the Puddles. I suppose you're too snobby now to milk the ducks ... A hundred and twenty pounds ... A hundred and twenty fleas! No, six thousand fleas. They were by far the commonest creatures that the Toejam Crowd ever had. I'm telling you, if fleas had to give dowries, then that eejit who married your daughter, Noreen, would have enough to make him a knight in a castle nine times over. The two of them had plenty between them coming into my house ...

That was the disastrous day, Noreen, the first day yourself or your daughter ever darkened the door of my house ... The little hussy that she is. Certainly, Nora, she is a credit to you: one who can't put a patch on her child, or make her husband's bed, or throw out the wasted ashes every week, or to comb her own clump of hair ... It was she had me buried twenty years before my time. She'll bury my son too, and before too long, if she doesn't come here soon to keep you company and keep you in gossip at her next delivery ...

Oh, your little yackity mouth is in great form today, Noreen ... "We'll be ..." How's that you put it? ... "We'll be OK then." ... "OK": that's your catch phrase, Noreen ... "We'll be OK then. You'll have your son, and I'll have my daughter, and we'll be together again down here just as we were aboveground ..." The devil's plaything is in great mocking form altogether in your little yackity mouth today, Noreen ...

That time you were in the Fancy City . . . You're telling me I'm lying. It's you're the filthy liar, Toejam Noreen . . .

—Witch!

—Harridan!

—Hag!

—Toejam Crowd . . . Duck milkers! . . .

—Do you remember the night Nell was sitting in Jack the Lad's lap? "We'll leave Blotchy Brian to you, Caitriona . . ."

—I never sat in a sailor's lap anyway, thanks be to God Almighty . . .

—You never got the chance, Caitriona . . . I don't take a devil's blind bit of notice of you. Your endless bitching and lies doesn't leave a scratch on me. I'm far more respected in this cemetery than you are. There's a fine upright cross on my grave, which is more than can be said for yours, Caitriona. Smashing! Honest! . . .

—. . . Well, even if there is, it didn't cost you anything. You can thank that fool of a brother of yours who stuck it up when he was home from America. You'd be a long time getting the money for a cross from milking the ducks in Gort Ribbuck . . . What's that you're saying, Nora? . . . Spit it out. You haven't the guts to say it to my face . . . I have no culture? . . . I have no culture, Noreen? . . . I have no culture, imagine that! . . . Too true for you Noreen. I often saw maggots and crawlies on the Toejam Crowd . . .

What's that you're saying, Noreen? . . . You don't have the time to be yacking with me . . . You're wasting your time yacking with me. For the love of God! You don't have the time to be yacking with me . . . You have something else to do, yea! . . . Now what's that you're saying? You have to listen to another episode of . . . What's that she called it, Master? . . . Master . . . He doesn't hear me. He's totally lost it since he heard about his wife . . . That's it, got it . . . Novelette . . . This is the time that the Master reads a bit of the . . . novelette to you every day . . . If the Master paid any attention to me . . . Oh, Mary Mother of God! . . . A novelette in Gort Ribbuck . . . The Toejam thickos with a novelette . . . Margaret! Hey, Margaret! Can you hear me? The Toejammy Crowd with a novelette . . . I'm going to burst! I'll burst! . . .

3.

—... I swear, Gut Bucket, by the oak of this coffin, I gave her the pound, I gave Caitriona the pound ...

—... God save us all! ... My death would not be like death to me there: for I would lie in the soft warm clay of the plain; the potent clay which can afford to be kind with its own brute strength; the proud clay whose treasures do not decay, nor rot, nor wither in its fertile womb; the seasonal clay which finds it easy to dispense its gifts generously; the renewing clay which takes all its nourishment of food and drink making it fruitful again without waste, deformity, or metamorphosis ... It would recognise its own ...

The gentle buttercup, the moist mossy sward, the pleasant primrose and the creeping grass would grow upon my grave there ...

The sweet warbling of the birds would sing above me instead of the chatter of the waves or the clatter of the waterfall or the sigh of the sedge or the shriek of the cormorant as she plunges with lust upon the small sprats of the sea. O clay of the plain, wouldn't it be good to settle beneath your mantle ...

—She's gone all soppy again ...

—... Pearse said, O'Donovan Rossa said, Wolfe Tone said, that Eamon de Valera was right ...

—Terence McSwiney said, James Connolly, John O'Leary, John O'Mahony, James Fintan Lawlor, Davitt, Emmet, Lord Edward Fitzgerald, Sarsfield himself, they all said that Arthur Griffith was right ...

—Owen Roe O'Neill said that Eamon de Valera was right ...

—Red Hugh O'Donnell said that Arthur Griffith was right ...

—Art McMorrough Kavanagh said that Eamon de Valera was right ...

—Brian Boru, Malachy, Cormac mac Airt, Niall of the Nine Hostages, the two Patricks, Brigid, Colm Cille, and all the Irish saints wherever they are—on land, sea, or sky, and all the Irish martyrs from Dunkirk to Belgrade, and Finn McCool, Oisin, Conan, Caoilte, Deirdre, Gráinne, the Great Professor of Ireland, and Gael Glas all said that Arthur Griffith was right ...

—That's a lie, they didn't . . .

—I'm telling you, you're a liar. The truth hurts . . .

—You treacherously murdered me when I was fighting for the Republic . . .

—You had it coming. Neither God's law nor that of the Church allows the overthrow of a legitimate Government by force . . .

—I have no interest in politics, but I have some regard for the old IRA . . .

—You coward, you were skulking under the bed when Eamon de Valera was fighting for the Republic . . .

—You old bag, you were under the bed when Arthur Griffith was . . .

—. . . "And he went off to market for courting . . ."

—. . . Wait now, my good man, wait 'til I finish my story:

". . . Now send out to me John James

And I'll be for ever without him.

"The fairy lover captured John James in the magic palace and there was no escape for him. Just then, all the waters of the grey green Isle of Ireland, including those around its islands and about its shores, dried up, all except for two bottles of Portuguese aerated water that was thrown up on the Blaskets, and a cask of holy water from Spain that a fishing trawler swapped for some fifty potatoes from the Island of Hens' Eggs . . .

"The maid of the sweet brown ringlets was in Dublin at exactly that time . . ."

—The version I heard from old people around here, Coley, was that it was a nurse in the Fancy City . . .

—A woman in a bookie's shop, I heard . . .

—Oh, so what? It was up in Dublin, anyway. What else? "'I have an arrow,' she said, 'that will rescue John James if he promises me a hundred and one large barrels, a hundred and one large casks, and a hundred and one of the best hogsheads as a dowry . . .'"

—Now, you old Gut Bucket, where are your forty-two pints now? . . .

—Coley, hang on a moment. This is how I would have ended that matter if I hadn't died . . .

—. . . If Hitler gets as far as England, he'll have them living on dead cats . . .

—I'm telling you things weren't as bad until then. You'd hardly get a penny for a cow or a calf. God help the poor man if the cattle get any cheaper. I have a bit of land up on the top of the town, and there's no telling what it costs to look after the beasts. It'll go to waste, as there's not a tosser to be earned on cattle . . .

—"There's no point in rearing cattle!" Take the crap land in your place. Let two rabbits loose, let them at it, and after five years there would still only be two rabbits, even if that many . . .

—You were a gutless pansy, Peter. If it had been me! I swear to Jaysus, I'd have given him what not. If I had a pub, Peter, if I had a pub and dirty heretics coming in through the doors insulting my religion like that . . .

—. . . We,—The Cadavers of the Half Guinea—we are putting forward a joint candidate in this election also. Just like the others—The Cadavers of the Pound Place and the Cadavers of the Fifteen Shillings—we have absolutely nothing to offer to our fellow cadavers. However, we are taking part in this Interred Election because we have a policy—the Half Guinea Party—we have a policy also. If those aboveground can have an election, those of us underground can have one also. There is no democracy without an election. Us, we, here, in the cemetery clay, we are the democrats.

The Pound Cadavers are the party of the rich, of the Conservatives, of the Big Cheese, of the Reactionaries, of what they call Stability. The Cadavers of the Fifteen Shillings are the party of commerce and of merchants, of the professional class, the bourgeoisie, the middle class, property and capital. But we, and us here, my fellow Cadavers, we are the party of the working class, of the proletariat, the peasants, the wage slaves, the nothing nobodies, the utter dependents, the party of the completely dispossessed: the hewers of wood and the drawers of water. We are absolutely bound to stand up for our rights as did the men of old (knocking of skulls and gnashing of teeth clearly heard from the Half Guinea Place) . . .

—. . .

—. . . Our candidate, our joint applicant—our own candidate if you like, the Fifteen Shillings—she's a woman. Don't let that bother you. Her husband was never a Teachta Dála, a Member of Parliament. She made a name for herself by her own ability and cop on. When she came down into the dirty dust three years ago she knew as little as any of the windbags that are spouting rubbish down in the Half Guinea Place. But despite what the Half Guinea crowd say, there are absolutely equal rights and opportunities in this graveyard (more knocking and clapping of skulls). Our candidate is the living proof of that. She is cultured and wise. Let me introduce her to you . . . Nora Johnny! (Even more knocking and clapping of skulls.)

—Toejam Nora! The whore. Milking the ducks . . . Hey, Margaret! . . . Hey Margaret! . . . Nora Johnny . . . I'm about to burst! . . . I'm going to burst! . . .

4.

. . . Toejam Nora standing for election! Jesus Christ Almighty, they have no respect left for themselves in this cemetery, especially if they can't put up anyone else only Fleabag Nora from Gort Ribbuck . . . She won't get elected . . . But who knows? . . . Kitty, Dotie, and Margaret talk to her, and Peter the Publican, and Huckster Joan sometimes. As for the Old Master, it's a total disgrace the kind of things he tells her every day . . . He says they're all in the book, but I can't imagine myself that propriety would allow those kinds of things to be printed:

> "Your curling tresses fair
> Your eye sparkling like the dew
> Your smooth and pointed breasts
> Set my soul ablaze anew."

. . . That's lovely talk altogether for a schoolmaster. The Mistress and Billy the Postman are being driven mad. If he wasn't a bit nuts himself, of course, he wouldn't be praising Nora Johnny: "Her mind has really improved," he said. "She has acquired some culture now . . ."

Wasn't she very quick to remind me about the cross over her grave. "I have a fine big cross," she said, "something you haven't got, Caitriona." She'd only have a small scutty little cross if it wasn't for what that fool of a brother spent on her, something I told her straight up. She'd be down in the Half Guinea place without a plaque or a headstone, in among those gangsters from Clogher Savvy and Derry Lough, and that's where she should be, if the truth be told. That's what they were going to do anyway, until she died. When did anyone ever have a good word to say about any of her lot? Never, I'm telling you. Never ever. Never happened. A useless shower . . .

Having a cross here is like having a big slate house aboveground, a house with a name over the door—The Fox's View, Heavenly Haven, The Fairy Throne, Lovers' Way, Sun Spot, All Saints Grove, Leprechaun Green—and a cement border around it, trees and flowers to the edge of the garden, an iron gate with a bowered arch overhanging it, security and money in the bank . . . The railings on the grave are just the same as the fancy borders around the Earl's house. I never really peeped into the Earl's place without a flutter in my heart. I always thought I would see something miraculous. The Earl and his Lady having descended on their wings from heaven after their dinner. Either that, or St. Peter accompanying them to a table underneath a shady bower; he was carrying a net, having fished on the Earl's Lake; and in it a big golden salmon; his great keys rattling away; and then, he opening his Big Book and inquiring of the Earl which of the people of his district should be allowed into heaven. I always thought that to be in good standing in the Earl's book was the same as to be in good standing in heaven . . .

That shower aboveground are very innocent. "What good will it do them to have a cross over their graves?" they ask. "Not the smell of an oil rag! Those crosses are only snobbery and one-upmanship and a waste of money." If they only knew! But they never get it until they are buried, and then it is far too late. If they knew up there that a cross here earns respect even for the Toejammers, I don't think they'd be dawdling around as they are . . .

I wonder how long will it take to put my cross up? Patrick would never delay that much? He promised me faithfully:

"You'll have it within a year, or even before that," he said. "It's the least we could do for you . . ."

A cross of Connemara marble, and the inscription in Irish . . . It's all the rage to have Irish on your headstone these days . . . and lovely flowers . . .

I often warned Patrick:

"I raised you with love and care, Patrick," I said. "I kept a good house always. God knows that wasn't always easy. I never told you how I suffered after your father died. I never asked anything of anybody because of that. I often felt like buying a strip of pork to give some taste to the head of cabbage; or a fistful of raisins to chuck into the cake; or to hop into Peter's Pub when I felt my throat parched from dust and cleaning, just to ask him for one of those golden bottles that smiled at me every time I went past his place . . .

"But, Patrick, my precious, I didn't. I saved every brass farthing. I hate to give Nell or Blotchy Brian's Maggie the satisfaction now that I wasn't buried properly. Get me a plot in the Pound Place. Put a cross of Connemara marble over me. Have it up a year after I'm buried, at the latest. I know that it will cost a bit, but God will reward you . . .

"Don't give in to your wife if she's nagging you about money. She might be your wife, but I brought you into the world. I never bothered you for anything, only this. You'll be finished with me then. Whatever you do, don't give Nell the satisfaction . . ."

He didn't bury me in the Pound Place after all that. His wife . . . or his wife and that other piece of shit, Nell. Although, Patrick can be sharp enough himself when he wants to. He promised me the cross . . .

I wonder what kind of a funeral I had? I won't know that until the next corpse comes. Biddy Sarah was fading away. But I'd say there's nothing wrong with her yet. And then there's Guzzeye Martin, Black Bandy Bartley, and Breed Terry, and of course, that old gobshite himself, Blotchy Brian, keep his bag of bones away from us! . . . Fire-

side Tom should be dead already with the rain through his roof . . .
If Patrick did what I told him, his shack would have fallen down by
now . . .

My son's wife will be here, she has to be, at her next birth. Nell is a
bit flattened since Peter got injured, and she has rheumatism, the old
snotbag. That isn't likely to kill her, though. She was dead a few times,
according to herself, but the seven plagues of Egypt wouldn't kill
some people. May nobody else come to the cemetery before her! . . .

I haven't a notion if any letter has come from America since. I'm
really afraid that Nell will have it all her own way about Baba's will. If
I only lived another few years . . .

Baba was very fond of me more than anyone else. When we used
to be messing around as young girls in the Hedge Field . . . Wouldn't
you think she could put up a cross over me just as Nora Johnny's
brother did for Nora . . .

—. . . Does anyone know is this war "The War of the Two Foreigners"? . . .

—It's only when you are expecting some real peace and quiet
that these chattering gossips really get going. Isn't what they say up
above a real joke: "She's at home now. She can rest in peace now,
and can forget all the troubles of life in the cemetery clay" . . . Peace!
Peace! Peace! . . .

—. . . If you elect me I promise you I'll burst my gut as good as
any man—I mean any woman—for culture's sake, and for the sake
of enlightened and progressive public opinion . . .

—Margaret! Margaret! Hey Margaret! . . . Did you hear what
Nora Johnny just said? . . . "If you elect me" . . . I'm going to burst! I
swear I'm going to burst! . . .

5.

—. . . "Fireside Tom was dying to get ma-arried,
    As he always wa-as when pla-astered drunk . . ."

—. . . It's really hilarious, isn't it Dotie? . . . Everyone calls him
Fireside Tom . . . He lives in a hole of a dump of a place up on the

top of the town land. He never married. He has no living relations—not in Ireland anyhow—except for Caitriona and Nell Paudeen. I couldn't really tell you, unless I was to give you a very short answer, what exact relation he is to Nell and Caitriona, and not because I haven't heard it often enough . . .

We were first cousins once removed, Margaret. Young Paudeen, Caitriona's father, and Fireside Tom were cousins . . .

—. . . "I've a small bit of land and a nice little shack . . ."

—Fireside Tom's bit of land is rubbing up beside Nell's, and there's a lot more gab about hers than Caitriona's, because hers is farther away, and she has plenty of it anyway . . .

—. . . "And I know two who can pay my rent . . ."

—Caitriona was always crawling her way up to Fireside Tom's place trying to coax him down to her own, not entirely because of his land, but just to spite Nell . . .

—But hang on, Margaret, wasn't she driving Paddy totally nuts . . .

—If he was up to his balls in work she'd be bugging him to go on and help Fireside Tom, anyway . . .

—Paddy Caitriona is a decent guy . . .

—A great neighbour, to tell the truth . . .

—He never had his eye on Fireside Tom's land . . .

—He never felt much like toddling up to help him, but just for the sake of peace . . .

—. . . "And Nell is gre-eat at digging di-itches . . ."

—I rarely got so much fun out of anything, I'd say . . .

—I'd say you never got as much fun out of anything, true . . .

—But you didn't see the half of it . . .

—I saw enough . . .

—If you were in the same town land . . .

—I was near enough to them. What I didn't see, I heard. Wasn't the whole country talking about them? . . .

—There wasn't a single soul in the whole town land that wasn't weak with the laughter from morning to night. You wouldn't believe half of it, even if I told you . . .

—Of course, I'd believe it. Nearly every Friday when we drew the pension myself and Fireside Tom would toddle into Peter's Pub for a couple of scoops, and he'd go through it all backwards and forwards . . .

—Careful now. Do you know that Caitriona Paudeen's buried here a little while—in the Fifteen Shilling Place. Maybe she'd hear you . . .

—Let her for all I care. And everyone else in the Fifteen Shilling Place also, if they want to. Yea, like, I'm really worried about them. Themselves and their airs and graces. You'd think we were only muck and garbage . . .

—All the same I wouldn't want Caitriona to hear me. I was in the same spot as her all her life, and she was a good neighbour, except that she seriously had it in for her sister Nell. Fireside Tom was the only one who really gained in any way from all the spite . . .

—He often told me that when we were having the few scoops . . .

—You'd see Caitriona heading out in the morning driving the cows to the top of the fields. She'd deliberately take the long way round home in order to go by Thomas's hovel:

"How's the form today, Tom? . . . I see those two turf creels you have there are on their last legs. Do you know what, I think I have two of them sitting at home somewhere, and they're not needed at all as Patrick was out weaving baskets only the other day, and he made himself two new ones . . ."

Tom would get the baskets.

Caitriona would hardly have vanished over the brow of the meadow when Nell would be down quicker than shit through a goose:

"How's the form today, Tom? . . . Do you know, I think that those trousers of yours aren't that good. They could do with a few patches . . . But I don't know if they'd be worth it. They're totally in shreds. As it happens, we have a pair at home and they're as good as new for all the wear they got. They were made for Jack, but the legs were too thin, and he didn't wear them twice . . ."

Tom would get the trousers.

—Didn't he tell me as much? . . .

—Another day then Caitriona would be there again:

"How's the form today, Tom? . . . Didn't I just notice that the fences on the field over there are completely flattened . . . The donkeys in this town land are a terrible curse, Tom. God's honest truth. They're a terrible curse when they're not kept locked up in their own outhouse. Gut Bucket's old donkey, and the one that Top of the Road has are bad enough, but the nastiest of all are the ones over there" — she meant Nell — "and she lets them run wild . . . Of course an elderly man like yourself can't be expected to go around driving out donkeys. You have enough to be thinking about. I'll have to tell Pat that the fences are down . . ."

The fences would be repaired for Fireside Tom . . .

—But of course, didn't he tell me himself . . .

—Nell would pop down:

"How's the form today, Tom . . . There's nothing done in this field, God bless you. Nothing sown, only in a tiny little corner. You only have about a fortnight more. But it's hard to do a decent stroke of work if you're all on your own. It's a bit late for sowing spuds now. Isn't the best of May over and done with already! . . . It's a disgrace that that other crowd" — meaning Caitriona's family — "wouldn't give you a day's help, and they're already finished a fortnight ago . . . I'll have to tell Peter to drop around tomorrow. Nothing better would suit the two of us for the rest of our lives, Tom, but to be on both sides of the fire together . . ."

The field of potatoes would be dug for Fireside Tom . . .

—What makes you think he didn't tell me that often enough? . . .

—Nobody would really have the least clue that was going on after that, apart from those from the same place . . . Caitriona was always trying nonstop to rope him in and to have him all to herself, alone. But listen to me now, by the burnt balls of the morning! I'm telling you that Tom was no slouch, despite the way everyone was trying to take him for a ride . . .

—Do you actually think that I don't know this? . . .

—Nobody would really know anything, apart from the closest

neighbours . . . Tom was as fond of that wreck of a hovel as a king would be of his palace. If he hooked up with one sister, then sure as hell, the other would disown him. And neither of them would have the least time for him if he let go of his grubby patch of land. But he didn't. Fireside Tom was a class of a cute hoor and certainly didn't come down in the last shower.

—Do you think I hadn't a clue about all of this already? . . .

—No, you hadn't a clue, no more than anyone else who were not their neighbours . . . But it was when he got really stocious—on a fair day, or a Friday, or whatever—that's when we heard the real fun. That's when he got horny to get married.

—For the love of God, do you think that I didn't often see him scuttered in Peter's Pub? . . .

—I saw him there once, and to tell you the truth, he was a howl. That's not more than five years ago: the year just before I died:

"I'm up for it to get married," he said. "I have a nice patch of land, a pension of half a guinea, and I'm as fit as a spring chicken. I swear to Jaysus, I'll get married. I'm telling you truthfully, I'll get married yet . . . Give me that bottle of whisky, Peter"—Peter was alive then—"only the best now. I swear to Jaysus I'm off on the hunt."

—I remember that day really well. That's when I twisted my ankle . . .

—Just then Caitriona's in the door and whispering in his ear:

"Come on away home with me now, Tom, and our Patrick will go out looking for a woman for you, but just put your heads together about it . . ."

Then Nell comes in and starts whispering in his other ear. "Come on away home with me, Tom my darling. I have a strip of steak and some whisky. As soon as you've had a bite to eat Peter will be off looking for a woman for you . . ."

Tom hightailed it off to Nora Johnny's joint in Gort Ribbuck. "Despite the fact that she's a widow," he says to Nell and to Caitriona, "I'm telling you truthfully, there're no flies on her. She's young in spirit. Her daughter, the one married to your son Paddy, Caitriona, she's hardly thirty-two or thirty-three. No doubt about it, the daughter is a fine strapping young one as far as I'm concerned . . ." He said that, no lie. Did you know that? . . .

— It's ridiculous that you think I didn't know . . .

— How would you have the least clue, as you're not in the same place as they are? . . . It was just as well for them that Tom only had a kip of a dive or they'd be totally ruined, no other house under God's sky got thatched more often. Paddy Caitriona covered the north side from end to end one year. He was an excellent thatcher. He slapped some straw on it. Not the worst of it either. That lovely roof never would have to be covered for another fourteen or fifteen years. The following year Nell's Peter comes along with his hammer and his mallet. Up he goes on the north side. What do you think he did to the roof that Paddy had put up just a year before? He gutted it all out from the roots and chucked it down on to the road. May I not leave this spot if I am telling you a word of a lie. There wasn't as much as a pick of Pat's thatch from end to end that he didn't yank out from the roots.

"That wouldn't have been long dripping down on you, Tom," he said. I swear by all that's holy that I was listening to him! "The cover that went on last year was totally useless. I'm only surprised that it stopped any drop coming down. Half of it was only that soft heathery stuff. All the signs on it, anyway. Jaysus, he didn't cause himself too much hassle gathering it up, always avoiding anything that might cause a bit of effort. If you want to gather that stuff you have to go out into the deep sodden sedgy slobber and get your feet wet. Look at what I have, from out there in the middle of Aska Roe . . ."

He did the two sides of the house, but even so, 'twas a bit of a botched job. Actually, a really botched job! It didn't even last three years. It was a real pain . . .

— You'd think the way you're talking you didn't know that I knew all this . . .

— Nobody would have a clue about it, except those in the same place, neighbours . . .

Another time I saw the two of them at the house at the same time: Paddy Caitriona and Peter Nell. Paddy was up on the north side with his ladder, his mallet and his strip of straw. Peter on the south of the house, with his ladder, his mallet, and his own strip of straw. You never saw work like it in your whole life: they were really at it. Fireside Tom lounging on his butt on the big boulder at the east end, puffing away at his pipe, and talking to the two of them at the same time. He was in exactly the right spot between the two ends of the house. I came along. I sat down on the boulder beside Tom. You couldn't hear yourself think because of the banging of the two mallets.

"Why don't you," says I, "why doesn't one of you drop the thatching for a while and help the other, as Tom isn't helping either of you. Either that, or why don't you take turns helping and thatching . . ."

"Shut your mouth," Tom said. "Can't you see that they're flying ahead one as good as the other now, God bless them! They're brilliant thatchers. I reckon that neither one of them is a hair's breadth or a nail shaving better than the other . . ."

— Easy to tell that you don't know that I realise all about it . . .

— But you don't know, you haven't the least clue . . .

— . . . "Nell knows all about building fences,
      And Cathy's an expert on thatch and felt . . ."

— . . . "Fireside Tom was smirking broadly
      At Cathy Paudeen who paid the rent . . ."

— No, she wasn't! I wasn't! It's not true, Margaret! Oh, Margaret! I'm going to burst! I'm going to burst! . . .

6.

— . . . The Grave Ghoul! He is as big an eejit as you ever saw . . .

— It's a total disgrace, Caitriona, if he has the map, that he couldn't tell one grave from another . . .

— God help you and your stupid map! His stupid map makes as much sense as Eddie East Boss dividing up the land with a tongs, when they were divvying it up in strips long ago . . .

— For all that, Caitriona, I kept that stretch at the top of the fields despite your best efforts, seeing as there wasn't one of you who didn't want it. You couldn't do better than it to fatten up the cattle . . .

—Ho! Do you hear the cricket chirping again? . . .

—It's a disgrace, Caitriona, if the corpses are being put in the wrong graves that someone wouldn't charge him with treason: let the Government know, or at least tell the priest, or the Foxy Policeman . . .

—Ara, God bless the Government! Some Government, since Griffith's crowd were thrown out . . .

—You lied . . .

—You told a big black . . .

—Isn't that just what Blotchy Brian said: they are being chucked into any old hole in the graveyard now, just as if they were fish guts or leftover limpets . . .

—Oh, the dirty fucker! . . .

—If you don't have a proper cross on your grave now, and it well-marked, who knows what day it wouldn't be opened up . . .

—I'll have a cross on me shortly. A cross of the best Connemara marble just like Peter the Publican and Joan . . .

—A cross of Connemara marble, Caitriona . . .

—Wouldn't they let them put up a wooden cross, Caitriona?

—They'd be dumped out on the road the following day . . .

—Isn't that because of the people who make the other crosses? . . .

—Of course, what else? Everyone feathering his own nest. If you were allowed stick up wooden crosses or cement crosses, nobody would bother with their own. Everyone then could just make their own cross . . .

—I'd much prefer no cross at all than one made of wood or cement . . .

—True for you. I'd die of shame . . .

—It's this Government's fault. They get a tax on all the other crosses . . .

—You're a liar. That was the law before this Government . . .

—It's a terrible thing to dump one of your own down beside a stranger . . .

—The apple never falls far from the tree . . .

—That's the Government for you . . .

—You're a liar . . .

—I heard that they stuffed Tuney Mickle Tuney down on top of Tom the Tailor's son last year . . .

—Oh, didn't I up and kick off the murderer from on top of me! It was the other half of the treacherous Dog Eared mob who stabbed me . . .

—I was at Jude's funeral, Jude from our own place, last year. She was shagged down on top of Donal Weaver from Clogher Savvy. They never knew they were digging the wrong grave until they hit the coffin. The dogs on the street know that it's true, I was there, exactly there . . .

—Entirely true. Don't we know you're telling the truth. They dug four graves for the Poet, and in the end he was left down snug on top of Curran . . .

—The devil screw him! I'm driven demented with his trivial waffle. He can go and fuck himself as he didn't stay alive long enough until they put a cross on me . . .

—The little scut . . .

—It wouldn't matter only I had things on my mind, and I didn't realise it was my big farm of land that your one at home gave to the eldest son . . .

—What do you think of Michael Kitty from Bally Donough being clapped in on top of Huckster Joan? Joan didn't even have a cross that time . . .

—Ah, poor Joan . . .

—Poor Joan, you must have been totally in distress . . .

—I told her straight up to her puss without a word of a lie to leave me in the Half Guinea or the Fifteen Shilling place. The last thing I wanted was for that twit to be buried above me. She'd drive me into the next life with the stink of nettles . . .

—Didn't they try to stuff someone in on top of you also, Kitty? . . .

—Some little wretch from Clogher Savvy that I never knew, nor knew anything about her family. By the oak of this coffin, I swear, I got rid of her with a flea in her ear. "I'm really in a bad way if I'm laid out with the beggars of Clogher Savvy in the cemetery clay," I said . . .

—Honest. They had dug my grave also. Some old woman from

Shanakill. "Ugh," I said, "to put that rough diamond from Shanakill down in the same place as me! I wouldn't mind if she had some culture!..."

—Hoora! Do you hear that slattern from Gort Ribbuck of the puddles throwing insults as Shanakill? Listen to me! I'm going to burst!...

7.

—... Fell from a haystack...

—... God help us all! It's a disaster they didn't bring my bones east of the Fancy City... Sunset would not slink slidingly down there. Morning would not break like a strange gypsy woman wandering the byroads of hill and the cliff paths ashamed to face the first begging of the day. The moon itself would not have to shine on innumerable stocks of stone, and ribs of rock, and cursed coves when she chose to come to kiss me. The broad expanse of meadow would be spread before her in a multicoloured tapestry. Rain would not arrive suddenly like the sudden bullet of a sneaky sniper from a smudgy spot, but rather like unto the glorious and majestic appearance of a queen bringing laws and prosperity to her people...

—Dotie! Sentimentality!

—That girlish stupidity again...

—... Look at me, the murderer gave me a lousy bottle...

—... Went to the Plaza at seven... She comes along... That lovely smile again. Takes the chocolates. A film... There was a film in the Plaza—she had seen all the films in the town already. Go for a walk or go to a dance... She had been on her feet in the betting office all day... Tea... She had only just had one. The Western Hotel... Certainly, a short break would do her no harm...

"Wine," I said to the waiter.

"Whiskey," she said.

"Two double whiskeys," I said...

"Two more double whiskeys," I said...

"I have no more whiskey," the waiter said. "Do you know how

much whiskey you have already drunk since seven o'clock: twelve double whiskeys each! Whiskey is scarce . . ."

"Stout," I said.

"Brandy," she said.

"Two large brandies," I said . . .

"Do you not realise," said the waiter, "that it's well past one o'clock, and even if this is The Western Hotel you still have to be careful. A police raid, maybe . . ."

"I'll walk you home, as far as your door," I said, just as the waiter was closing the door of the hotel after us.

"You walk me home to my door!" she said, "The way you are it looks more likely that I have to walk you home. Straighten up a bit or you'll fall through that window. You can't hold your drink, can you? I have my head together, despite the fact I have guzzled more brandy than you! You wouldn't know I touched a drop . . . Watch that pole for chrissake . . . Walk straight. I'll hold your arm, and I'll take you as far as your door. Maybe we'd get another few scoops in Simon Halloran's place on the way up. It's an all-night joint, and never closes 'til morning . . ."

I managed to cadge a look at her in the dim street light. She had a broad smirk on her face. But when I stuck my hand in my pocket and emptied it out, I discovered I only had one shilling left.

—You airhead . . .

—. . . My God almighty, as you say yourself . . .

—. . . I'm telling you God's honest truth, Peter the Publican. Caitriona Paudeen came in to see me. I remember it well. Sometime around November. That was the year when we really gave Garry Abbey's field a proper going over. Mickle was spreading seaweed the same day. I was expecting the kids home from school any minute and I had just turned over the potatoes in the embers for them. Then I sat down in the corner mending the heel of a sock.

"God bless all her," she said. "Same to you," I said. "You're very welcome Caitriona, sit yourself down."

"I can't really stay," she said. "I have my work cut out getting ready for the priest. He'll be in on top of me in about nine or ten days. There's no point in me beating about the bush, Kitty. You sold the pigs at the last fair. Ours won't be ready until St. Brigid's Day, if God spares them . . . I know it's a big favour to ask, Kitty, but I wonder could you loan me a pound until next St. Brigid's Day fair, I would be really extremely grateful to you if you could give me that pound. I have to do something about the chimney, and I've decided to buy a round table for the priest's breakfast. I have two pounds myself . . ."

"A round table, Caitriona?" I says. "But sure, nobody has a round table around here apart from rich people. Why wouldn't he just eat from an Irish table just the same as every other priest we ever had?"

"The last time he was up with Nell," she says, "she had a silver teapot that Blotchy Brian's Maggie got in America. I'll get a loan of a silver teapot from Huckster Joan, as I want to be every bit as good as her, and better as well. The uppity slut!"

I gave her the pound. She bought the round table. Things were cheap that time. She laid out the priest's breakfast on it, and served tea in the silver teapot she got from Huckster Joan.

— By the oak of this coffin, I swear, Peter the Publican, that I gave Caitriona the pound, and I never saw one glimpse of it until the day I died, whatever Huckster Joan did with her teapot . . .

— You lied, you witch of the piddling potatoes. Don't believe her, my dear Peter. I stuffed every brass farthing of it back into her fist when I sold the pigs at the next St. Brigid's Day fair . . . What would you do with her? Your mother didn't often tell the truth either . . . I died as pure as the crystal, thanks be to God . . . Let it never be said that Caitriona Paudeen went to her grave owing as much as a red cent to anybody. Not like you, stingy Kitty of the pissy piddling potatoes. Your family left a heap of debts stringing after them everywhere. Who are you to talk! You killed yourself and your family with your piddling pissy potatoes . . . Don't believe her, Peter . . . Don't believe her . . . I gave her every brass farthing into the palm of her hand . . .

I didn't, you witch? . . . I didn't, is that it? . . .

Hoora, Margaret! . . . Margaret. . . . Did you hear what Kitty said? I'll burst! I'm going to burst! . . .

Interlude 3
THE SUCKING EARTH

1.

I am the Trumpet of the Graveyard. Hearken unto my voice to my voice. You must hearken to what I have to say . . .

For I am the voice that was, that is, and that ever will be. I was the first voice in the shapelessness of the universe. I am the last voice that will be heard in the scattering of the ultimate destruction. I was the gurgling voice in the first pregnancy in the first womb. When the corn is gathered in the barn, my voice will call the last harvester home from the Field of Time. For I am the son of the ancestor of Time and of Life and the governor of their household. I am the harvester, the stacker and the flail of Time. I am the keeper, the custodian and the key holder of Life. Listen to my voice! You have to listen . . .

There is neither time nor life in the Graveyard. Neither brightness nor darkness. There the sun does not go down, neither do floods roar, nor winds blow nor change bite. The day does not stretch out, nor are the Pleiades being hunted by Orion; neither does the living thing dress itself in the garb of Congratulations and Celebration. The glinting eyes of the child are not found there. Nor the simple blush of youth. Nor the rosy cheeks of the young girl. Nor the kind voice of the educated woman. Nor the innocent smile of the old person. Eyes, and blushes, and cheeks, and grins all get mashed into the one undifferentiated alembic mush of the clay. The flush of life does not have a voice there, nor does the voice have the flush of life, because there is neither flush nor life nor voice in the disinterested chemistry of the grave. There are only bones withering, flesh rotting and body parts that were once alive now putrefying. There is only this earthen cupboard and the tattered suit of life to be gnawed by moths . . .

But above the ground there is the light and lively lissom lap of air. The full tide is begotten with gusto in the pulse of the shore. The grass of the meadow is like unto that which had a vessel of fresh milk poured upon it. Every bush and clump and field is like a royal serving girl gently practising her curtsey before she came into the presence of the King. The bird gives voice to his soft melancholy music in the garden. The eyes of the children are magicked by the toys that fall out of the wondrous garden of innocence. The torch of the revival of hope appears in the cheeks of the courageous young. The foxgloves which could be picked in the meadows of eternity light up in the shy cheeks of the young girls. The singular flower of the bright bush blooms in the gentle face of the mother. The youngsters with their ringing laughter are playing hide and go seek in the barnyards, while their high-pitched joy seeks to reach the summit of Jacob's ladder and return by it from Paradise. And the muttering murmur of lovers seeps out from the corners of the backroads like the waiflike whinnying of the wind through flower beds of cowslips in the land of youth.

But the shake of the old man is taking its toll. The young man's bones are stiffening. The grey wisps are blending with the gold in the hair of the woman. A paleness like of serpent's slime is invading the clarity of the child's eye. Questions and querulousness nibble at joy and the carefree spirit. Weakness is beginning to banish strength. Despair is overwhelming love. The shroud is being woven by the baby blanket, and the grave is being prepared instead of the cradle. Life is paying its dues to death . . .

I am the Trumpet of the Graveyard. Hearken unto my voice! You must hearken to what I have to say . . .

2.

—. . . Hoora! Who is that? Who are you? Are you my son's wife? Didn't I tell you she'd be here at her next birth? . . .

—John Willy, no less—unless they have to christen me again in this dive—that's what they called me in the place I came from. The heart . . .

—John Willy. Oh my God. They're putting you down in the wrong grave, Johnny. This is Caitriona Paudeen's grave . . .

—Isn't that how it is in this graveyard, my dear Caitriona. But, I can't talk to the living. There's something at me. My heart . . .

—What kind of funeral did I have, John Willy?

—Funeral? The heart, Caitriona! The heart! I was going to get the pension. I didn't hear a whisper. I drank a sup of tea. I toddled down to the Common Field to get a basket of potatoes. When I was letting them down when I got home the strap ripped and it came down arseways. It gave me a jolt in my side. I was left completely breathless . . .

—What kind of funeral did I have, is what I'm asking?

—The heart, may God help us! The heart was weak, Caitriona. I had a dodgy heart . . .

—Fuck you and your heart! You have to forget about that shite here . . .

—I know but the heart is a poor thing Caitriona. We were making a new pen for the colt that we bought just after Christmas. We were nearly finished except for the last bit. I myself wasn't able to give that much help to the youngfella, but nonetheless, he'd appreciate it. You wouldn't give a damn, only the weather was great for the last while . . .

—Weather! Last while! They're two things you won't have to worry about here, John Willy. You were always a bit of a lazy layabout. Tell me this much! Why are you not taking a blind bit of notice of me? Did I have a big funeral? . . .

—A fine big funeral!

—A fine big funeral, John Willy, did you say? . . .

—A fine big funeral. The heart . . .

—Listen, get stuffed and forget your heart unless it was going to do you some good. Do you hear me? You have to give up that old guff. Nobody will listen to that kind of crap here. How was my altar?

—A fine big funeral . . .

—I know that, but what about the altar? . . .

—A fine big altar . . .

—What altar, I'm asking. Don't be such a dour puss all the time. What altar?

—Peter the Publican had a big altar, and Huckster Joan, and Maggie Frances, and Kitty . . .

Don't I know it! And that's what I'm asking you. Wasn't I above-ground myself that time? But what altar did I have, me, Caitriona Paudeen? Altar! Seventeen pounds, or sixteen pounds, or fourteen pounds? . . .

—Ten pounds twelve.

—Ten pounds! Ten pounds! Now Johnny, are you certain it was ten pounds, not eleven pounds, or twelve pounds, or . . .

—Ten pounds, Caitriona! Ten pounds! A fine big altar, by God. Not a word of a lie, it was a fine big altar. Everyone said it was. I was talking to your sister Nell: "Caitriona had a fine big altar," she says. "I never thought she'd come as much as two or three pounds close to it, or four either." The heart . . .

—Bugger and blast your heart! Give it over, Johnny, for chris-sake! . . . Were the Hillbillies there? . . .

—I'm telling you, that's what she said: "I never thought she'd come as much as two or three . . ."

—The Hillbillies weren't there?

—The Hillbillies! They heard nothing about it. Paddy was to tell them about it: "Ara," Nell says, "why would you be dragging them making them walk all the way down here, the poor creatures." I swear that's what she said. The heart. A dicey heart . . .

—Isn't it a terrible pity that your heart wasn't a poison lump stuck in Nell's gob! Were the Glen Booley crowd there? . . .

—Not as much as a toe of them.

—The people from Derry Lough?

—Huckster Joan's cousin was being brought to the church the other day . . . You wouldn't mind only we have that weather now for quite a while, and we were working away on the pen . . .

— Chalky Steven wasn't there, then? . . .

— We bought a foal after Christmas . . .

— May God be good to you, Johnny, but don't let the people buried here think you haven't a smidgen of sense more than that! . . . Was Chalky Steven there or not?

— Not a bit of him, but Paddy said he was talking to him on the fair day, and he said to him: "Most certainly, Paddy Lydon," he said, "I would have burst my gut to go to the funeral. I wouldn't let it be said . . ."

— "'That I didn't go to Caitriona Paudeen's funeral, even if I had to crawl there on my two knees. But I never heard a hint of it until the night she was buried. A foal with . . .'"

Chalky Steven, he's a total crap artist! . . . What was my coffin like?

— Ten pounds, Caitriona. A fine big altar.

— Are you gabbling on about the coffin or the altar? Why don't you just listen! . . . What price was my coffin? A coffin of . . .

— The very best coffin from Tim's place, three half-barrels of stout, and poteen flowing. Twice as much booze as was needed. Nell said that to him, but there was no talking to him, he had to have the three half-barrels. We were swimming in the stuff. Even if I was the oldfella there, I drank twelve mugs of it that night, not to mention the amount I had the night you were brought to the church, and the day of the funeral. To tell you the whole truth, Caitriona, despite all the respect and affection I have for you, there's no way I would have drunk all that much if I knew that the heart was a bit dicey . . .

— You didn't hear that Patrick said anything about burying me somewhere else in the cemetery?

— I got a little dart in my side, and it clean took my breath away. It was the heart, God help me . . .

— You can keep that to yourself, Johnny. Listen to me. You didn't hear that Patrick said anything about burying me . . .

— You'd have been buried anyway, Caitriona, it didn't matter how much was drunk. Even if I was the one with the dicey heart . . .

— You are the most useless codger ever since Adam took a bite out of the apple. Did you or did you not hear that Patrick said anything at all about me being buried somewhere else in the cemetery?

—Paddy was going to bury you in the Pound Place, but Nell said that the Fifteen Shilling Place was good enough for anyone, and that it was a real pity for a poor person to go into debt.

—The harridan! She would say that, wouldn't she! She was in the house, then?

—A fine handsome foal we bought after Christmas. Ten pounds . . .

—Did you pay ten pounds for the foal? You already said that ten pounds was paid for my altar . . .

—Your altar got ten pounds certainly, Caitriona. Ten pounds, twelve shillings. That was it exactly. Blotchy Brian turned up just as the funeral was turning at the top of the road, and he was trying to give Paddy a shilling, but he wouldn't take it. That would have been ten pounds thirteen, if he had taken it . . .

—He was trying to stuff it down his craw. Blotchy Brian! If the ugly old duffer was looking for a woman, he wouldn't be so slow . . . But listen to me, John Willy, listen to me . . . Good man! Was Nell at the house?

—She didn't leave it from the time you died until the time you went to the church. She was serving the women in the house the day of the funeral. I went into the back room to fill a few pipes of tobacco for the shower from Gort Ribbuck, they were far too wary to come in from the road. Myself and Nell started to talk:

"Caitriona's a lovely corpse, may God have mercy on her soul," I says myself. "And you laid her out so beautifully . . ."

Nell shoved me into the corner out of the way: "I don't really want to say anything," she said. "After all, she was my sister . . ."

I swear, that's what she said.

—But what did she say? Spit it out . . .

—When I was lowering it down going through the town, I got a little dart in my side. Took my breath away, didn't have a puff left. Not even a puff! The heart . . .

—Sweet Jesus help us! Yourself and Nell were ensconced in the corner and she said something like: "I wouldn't really like to say any-thing, John Willy. After all, she was my sister . . ."

—I swear that's what she said. May I never leave this place if that is not what she said: "Caitriona was some whore of a worker," she said, "but she wasn't really as clean, may God have mercy on her soul, as everybody else. If she was, she would have been laid out beautifully. Just see how dirty this shroud now is, Johnny. Look at the smudges on it. Aren't they a disgrace. Wouldn't you think she could have had her laying out clothes scrubbed and ready, and set aside. If she had been laid up for a long time, I wouldn't mind. Everyone is noticing those splotches on the shroud. Cleanliness is very important, Johnny . . ."

—Glory be to God! Jesus, Mary and Joseph! I left them as clean as crystal in the corner of the coffin. My daughter-in-law or the boys mucked it up. Or the gang who laid me out. Who laid me out any-way, Johnny?

—Nora Johnny's one and Nell. They looked for Little Kitty, but she wouldn't come . . . The heart, God help us all . . .

—Some heart! Wasn't it her back that was bugging her? Do you think, just because your own heart was fucked, that everyone else's heart was fucked too? Why in God's name could Little Kitty not come? . . .

—Paddy sent his eldest daughter to get her. I can't remember what her name is. I should remember, I should. But I went too fast. The heart . . .

—She's called Maureen.

—That's it. Maureen. Maureen certainly . . .

—Patrick sent Maureen to get Little Kitty, is that it? And what did she say? . . .

—"I won't go next nor near that town land ever again," she said. "I'm done with it. The journey is far too long now, considering my heart . . ."

—It wasn't her heart, it was her back I'm telling you. Who keened me?

—The pen was ready apart from the roof. Even if I wasn't able to give much help to the youngfella . . .

—You won't be able to give him that much anyway from now on . . . But listen now Johnny. Good man! Who keened me? . . .

—Everyone said it was a great pity that Biddy Sarah didn't come, because when she got her gut full of porter . . .

—Holy cow! Shag that for a game of soldiers! Why the fuck was Biddy Sarah not there to keen me?

—The heart.

—The heart! Why was it the heart? The kidneys, it was Biddy Sarah's kidneys were bollixed, like my own. Why didn't she come? . . .

—When somebody went looking for her she said: "No way, not across the sludge. I keened my eyes out for them, and what do they think of me? I'll tell you: 'Biddy Sarah is always on the bum. On the bum scrounging for something to drink. I swear you won't hear a bleep or a squeal out of her until she is stuffed up to the oxter. She'll keen sweetly then like the choirs of hell.' They can keen her away now, for all I care. I'll keen who I choose from now on." I swear, that's what she said . . .

—A bitch down to her bum, that's Biddy Sarah. She'll know all about it when she gets here . . . Was Nell cosying up to the priest at the funeral?

—The priest wasn't there at all. He was off at a funeral for some cousin of Huckster Joan, as she was very near him. But he lit eight candles . . .

—There were never that many on any corpse before this, Johnny.

—Only that one of them went out, Caitriona. It was just smouldering . . .

—Smoulder my arse!

—And he said no end of prayers and he threw holy water five times on the coffin, something that was never seen before . . . Nell said that he was actually blessing the two corpses together, but I don't really believe that . . .

—Ara, Johnny, and why would that be? God love him and give him health. That would just suit Nell down to the ground. How is her son, Peter? . . .

—Miserable enough. Miserable enough. The heart . . .

—Ara, get away out of that! Why are you blabbing on about his heart? Wasn't it his hip that was bugging him. Or did it get him in the heart in the meantime? That would be even better . . .

—The hip, Caitriona, certainly. The hip. They say it will be in court in Dublin in the autumn. Everyone says it will be thrown out, and Nell won't be left with as much as a tosser, nor Blotchy Brian's one neither . . .

—So be it! With God's help . . . What did you say about Fireside Tom?

—Just after I went to get the pension, I had a sup of tea, and I moseyed down to the Common Field . . .

—Don't worry about it. You'll never go there again with your spindly legs . . . Listen! Listen to me! Fireside Tom.

—Fireside Tom. Wheezing away. His hovel was about to cave in, no roof. Nell wasn't long getting on to your Paddy:

"It's a holy disgrace to leave that old man get soaked with rain," she said. "If it wasn't for what happened to my Peter . . ."

—But the poxy runt gave in to that cute hoor . . .

—He was busy, but he said he'd throw a few straws over the worst bits until he got a chance to do the whole lot . . . The heart . . .

—True for you. The heart. Patrick has a good heart. Too good . . . Did you hear anything about the cross they were to put over me?

—A fine new clean cross of the best Connemara marble, Caitriona . . .

—Recently?

—Recently, certainly . . .

—And my daughter-in-law? . . .

—My daughter-in-law? . . . My son isn't married at all, Caitriona. I told him that when the colt's pen was ready, that the best thing a fine strapping lad like him could do would be . . .

—To go to the doctor about his heart, Johnny, in case he took the weakness from you. My daughter-in-law? My son, Patrick. Nora Johnny's One. Do you get it now? . . .

—Oh, I do. Nora Johnny's One. A bit sick. The heart . . .

—You're a filthy liar. It's not her heart, just sick . . .

—Just a bit sick, Caitriona . . .

—Go away with yourself! I knew that much already. I thought she'd be throwing shapes to get into this place. She'll be here at her next birth, certainly. Did you hear anything about Baba?

—Your crowd's Baba, in America? She wrote to Paddy sympathising with him about your death. She sent him a fiver. She hasn't made a will yet. He told me that the eldest one he has—what's that her name is? I forget. I should remember it, but I went too quickly . . .

—Patrick's eldest one. Maureen.

—That's it, Maureen. There's a shower of nuns down the country somewhere want to take her away and turn her into a schoolteacher, just as soon as she has enough learning . . .

—Maureen is going to be a schoolteacher! Good luck to her! She was always gawping at the books. That'll be one up on Nell anyway . . .

—. . . The joint candidate we have in this Election . . .

—Jesus, come down from the cross! Don't tell me, Caitriona, that there are elections here also. There was one above just the other day.

—How did our people vote . . .

—I got a little stitch in my side. The heart . . .

—He's away with the fairies again. Shut up! How did our people vote? . . .

—Same as ever. What did you expect? Everyone in the town land voted exactly the same way as always, except for Nell's family. Her whole crowd went over to this new gang . . .

—Bad luck to her, the strap! They would, wouldn't they? She'd always stab you in the back . . .

—They say that this new gang promised her a new road up to the house . . . To hell with it anyway, there's no flies on her anyway. She's getting younger. I never saw her looking better in all my life than the day you were buried, Caitriona . . .

—You can go and fuck off, you old bags. No one of yours ever had a good word to say, ever . . . Shag off, this is not your grave anyway . . . The graveyard must be all over the bleedin' gaff if they put you into the same grave as me. Shag off to the Half Guinea Place. That's where you should be. Did you hear about the altar I had? Did you hear what the priest said about me? Your coffin never went beyond five pounds. You can go and fuck off. Yourself and your old heart. You have a cheek! . . . No one of your lot ever had a good word to say. Fuck off as fast as you can! . . .

3.

. . . So I only had ten miserable pounds worth of an altar, despite the fact that I shitted bricks chasing every old skanger and scum bucket putting money on their altars. It's not anybody's time, dead or alive . . . And the Hillbillies didn't come to my funeral . . . Or the shower from Glen Booley or Derry Lough . . . And Chalky Steven didn't come, the gobshite. They'll get their comeuppance someday. They'll come here too . . .

What chance had any of them to come to my funeral when that old tramp Nell was worming her way into Patrick's confidence, and she insisting that nobody should be told that I died. And there she was, laying me out, and dispensing and doling out drink at my funeral. She heard I wasn't alive, she heard that much. The dead can do nothing at all about it . . .

Who would give a toss, only for Little Kitty and Biddy Sarah. They'll get it rough yet. I wouldn't be in the least surprised if Nell put it in their heads and suggested they didn't go near the house, one way or the other. She'd do it, the old bag! Any woman who'd say that I didn't have my clothes properly laid out to be buried in . . . May not one other corpse come to the grave before her! . . .

But Baba sent a fiver to Patrick. He's certainly worth that much. He'll surely hook up now with that slag, Nora Johnny's daughter. She won't be able to say then that she is not responsible for my cross. But that's not a bad sign either. Baba is writing to us . . . If I had only lived for another few years so that she, the wrinkly whore Nell, was buried before me . . .

That's great news that Maureen is going to be a schoolteacher. That'll really piss Nell off and Blotchy Brian's Maggie: we'll have a schoolteacher in our family, and they'll have no schoolteacher at all in theirs. A schoolmistress makes a lot, I believe. I'll have to ask the Old Master what did his wife get. Who knows, maybe Maureen might get a job as a schoolteacher in our own school, especially if the Old Master's wife fecked off, or if anything happened to her? Then Nell would know all about it. Think about it, Maureen strutting up through the church every Sunday in her hat and gloves and parasol, her prayer book as big as a creel of turf tucked neatly under her oxter, strolling with the priest's sister as far as the gallery, and playing the piano. Nell and Blotchy Brian's Maggie would have been gobsmacked—if they were alive. Anyway, they say it's the priest who fixes up the schoolmistresses. If that's the case, I haven't a clue what my best guess would be, as Nell is very friendly with him . . . And who knows what that's about? Maybe he might be transferred soon, or he might even die . . .

And that wench of a wife of Patrick's is still a bit sick . . . It's a feckin' wonder that she's still alive. But, no doubt about it, she will be here at the next birth . . .

Isn't it an awful pity I didn't ask John Willy about the turf, and the planting, the pigs, the calves, and what's up with the fox these days? It was the only thing that was bugging me, if the truth be told . . . But what chance has anyone saying anything to him while he was yapping away about his old heart? It should be easy to get a chance to talk to him in a while. He was stuffed down here right next to me . . .

—Patience, Coley, patience. Listen to me. I am a writer . . .

—Wait now, my good man, wait 'til I finish my story:

". . . 'Ho-row, the chancer!' Fionn said. 'There was no way that he was going to leave Niamh of the Golden Locks with his poor father, even if he was on his own every night since that fast thing Grania the daughter of Cormac Quinn eloped with Muckey More Dooley from the Wild Woods of the Fianna' . . ."

—. . . The most awkward and cunning person I ever had to deal with about insurance, was the Old Master. I tried every trick in the book. I came at him from behind and from the front and from every angle. I sailed towards him on sunny seas and from the frozen wastes.

From the eye of the storm and on the flat of the plain. I came at him in a pincers movement, encircled him, pummelled him, jabbed him and atom bombed him. I was a fawning dog, and a thief in the night. I filled him with the fleets of human charity and jeered him with the jibes of satire. I flooded him with invitations to the princess of Peter's Pub. I fed him with cigarettes for sweet fanny all, and fobbed him off with rides in the car for nothing. I followed him with the sweetest gossip about the intentions of inspectors, and the latest news about the rows between the Master and the Schoolmistress from Barna Townee. I told him fancy stories about young women . . .

But it was completely useless. He thought if he bought an insurance policy from me it would be the worst thing he could do. Even as the head of a family he wouldn't part with a bean . . .

—But I did . . .

—You did, and me too. Hang on a minute. He was the biggest miser in creation. He was so mean he could steal mice at a crossroads, as they say. He never splashed out except that one time when he went to London, the time the teachers got the raise . . .

—That's when he was in the nightclub.

—That was it. He spent the rest of his life telling me all about it, and warning me never to open my big mouth. "If the priest or the Schoolmistress heard about it," he'd say . . .

He married her: the Schoolmistress.

"Maybe," I said to myself, "I might be able to find his weak spot now. The Schoolmistress would be a great help, if I could soft-soap her. And you can always soft-soap her . . ."

There isn't a woman alive who doesn't fancy herself, but she needs to be told. I didn't spend years messing with insurance without learning that much.

—I know that much, too. It's much easier to flog things to women than to men, only to have enough cop on . . .

—I had to give him a while until the novelty of being married wore off. But I couldn't leave it too long, either, in case her influence began to wane, when her magic was fading away. Insurance people know all about that . . .

—And booksellers too . . .

—I gave him three weeks . . . It was a Sunday. Himself and herself, the pair of them, were outside sitting on the front of the house just after dinner.

—"I'm coming to get you, you muppet," I said, "I swear by my balls I'll get you today! . . . You have your week's work all laid out, and those notes you are always going on about, they're all ready. You're stuffed up to the gills, and if your wife is anyway pleasant at all, it'll be easier to get you than ever . . ."

We chatted a bit about politics. I said I was in a bit of a hurry. "Sunday is the same as any other day to me," I said, "always on the lookout 'to see whom I can gobble up.' Now that you're married, Master, the Mistress should encourage you to take out a life insurance policy. You're better off now than ever. You have a spouse to look after . . . My opinion is," I said to his wife, "that he doesn't really love you at all, that he's only out to get what he wants from you, and if you weren't around he'd be off chasing another straight away."

The two of them laughed. "And," I said, "as an insurance man I have to tell you that if he pops off, there is no provision made for you. Now, if there was 'a gilt-edged guarantee' like you there . . ."

She pulled a bit of a face. "That's it," she said to the Master, half serious and wholly in earnest, "if anything happened to you, we'd all be in a proper mess . . ."

"What could happen to me?" he said, grouchily.

"You know not the day nor the hour," I said, "it's the duty of an insurance man to say that kind of thing all the time."

"Exactly," she said. "Of course, I hope nothing would ever happen. God forbid that it would! If it did, I couldn't live without you. We pray that nothing would ever happen, but if you died, and if I didn't die at the same time . . . How would I be fixed then? You have a duty . . ."

And do you know what, he took out a life insurance policy! Fifteen hundred pounds worth. He had only paid up four or five instalments—big fat ones too. She made him take out another two hundred and fifty when he paid the last bit.

"He won't last long," she said jokingly, and winked at me.

True for her. He snuffed it soon after that . . .

I'll tell you about another *coup* of mine. It wasn't half as good as the one I put over on the Old Master.

You played the Old Master just as sharp as Nell Paudeen played Caitriona about Jack the Lad . . .

—Aboo boona, boona! I'm going to burst! I will burst! I'll burst! Burst . . .

4.

Hey, Margaret! Hey Margaret! . . . Do you hear me?

. . . They were dumping John Willy in on top of me, I swear they were, Margaret . . . May God help your head, Margaret! Why would I let him into the same grave as myself? I never collected periwinkles to hock. Didn't he and his whole family live on periwinkles, and I'd soon tell him that. Even though I was only talking to him for a small bit, he nearly drove me nuts yacking on about his old heart . . . That's true, too, Margaret. If they had the cross up over me, it would be much easier for them to recognise the grave. But it won't be long now, Margaret. John Willy told me that much. A cross of the best Connemara marble just like Peter the Publican's . . . My daughter-in-law, is it? John Willy told me she'd be here at her next birth, no doubt about it . . .

Do you remember, Margaret, do you remember our Patrick's eldest girl? . . . That's her. Maureen . . . That's right. She'd be fourteen years old now . . . You got it there. She was only a little strip of a thing when you died. She's in secondary school now. John Willy told me . . . she's going to be a schoolteacher! What else! You don't think, do you, Margaret, that they'd be sending her to secondary school to learn how to boil potatoes or to cook mackerel, or to make beds, or sweep the floor? That might be all right for that bag job of a mother she has, if any such school existed . . .

Maureen also took a fancy to school. She has a great head for learning, for a girl as young as that. She was far better than the

Mistress—that is, the Old Master's wife—before he himself died. There's not one in the school who can hold a candle to her, John Willy tells me.

"She's way beyond them all at learning," he said. "She'll be qualified a year before anyone else."

I swear he said that, Margaret . . . Ah come on now, Margaret, there's no need to be talking like that. It's no surprise at all. Why do you say that it is a surprise? My family always had brains and intelligence to burn, not because I say so . . .

—. . . But that's not what I asked you, Johnny.

—Ah, Master, it was my heart! My heart, for God's sake! I was going for the pension. I didn't hear a whisper . . . Now, come on, Master, no need to be so pissed off. I couldn't help it. I was humping along with a basket of spuds. When I was letting them down . . . But, Master, I am telling you nothing now, apart from the whole truth. But, sure, I haven't a clue, apart from what people say to me. There were other things on my mind. The basket came down skewways. It happened . . . What were people saying then, Master? But, of course, we couldn't say anything, or even hear anything. We were making a new pen for the colt . . .

So, what were people saying then, Master? You know the way it is—somebody like you who has so much education, God bless you—there are bags of people out there who wouldn't be alive if they couldn't gossip. But then, someone with a dicey heart . . . Amn't I telling you what they were saying, Master, but just back off and don't be so crappy with me. It wouldn't have mattered, but we had great weather when we were building the pen . . . It's just people, the way they are, Master. They have a lot more on their minds apart from prayers. But the guy with the dicey heart, God help us! . . .

You were asking about the Mistress? I never saw her so beautiful, God bless her. She's getting younger, no doubt about it. She must have a very healthy heart . . . Ah, sure, people used to be talking. That's the way they are. I swear, myself and the youngfella were caught up with the pen . . . Ah, come on, don't be so pissed off with me. Don't you know, that everyone said that Billy the Postman wouldn't leave that house of yours, no matter what.

It was a fine big colt, Master . . . What good is it for you to be pissed off with me? I couldn't do anything about the lot of you. There was something bugging me, God help me . . . He's often in the house, is that it? I'm telling you, that's the way it is, Master. But you wouldn't mind, only the school. He moseys into the school every day, gives the letters to the kids, and then, himself and the Mistress toddle off into the hall for a chat. Ara, God help your sense, Master! You haven't a clue. There was something bugging me. I hadn't a breath left. The heart . . .

5.

—. . . But, Coley, Coley . . .

—Let me finish my story, my good man:

"'There's absolutely nobody who could instruct me in this case now,' said Daniel O'Connell, 'except one person only—Biddy Early—and she is seven hundred miles removed from here muttering charms for poteenmakers whose moonshine is being stolen by the fairies in a big town called Horse Bones in County Galway back in Ireland. Get ready and saddle up my best horse in the stable so that I will take her as a pillion rider behind me to London in England . . .'

"We went. 'Miss Debonair,' he said to her . . . 'Why would any son of a bitch insult me like that? . . .'"

—. . . Ah come on now, Huckster Joan! Whoring after votes for Peter the Publican! And why wouldn't you? Your son is married to his daughter aboveground. And even if they weren't, yourself and Peter would be as thick as the greatest two thieves ever . . .

—That's all the thanks I get. You'd have been dead long ago only I cut you some slack. Running in scrounging and begging every day: "For the love of God and Mary his mother, lend me a grain of meal or something until I can sell the pigs . . ."

—I paid dearly and sorely for that grain, Joan, you miserable shite! All I ever heard was: "Huckster Joan is a lovely person, kind and charitable. She trusts you." Trust, yea, sure thing, because you knew, Joan, that you would be paid, and for every one person who didn't pay you back there would be another hundred who would . . .

—That is precisely the same principle that obtains in insurance . . .

—I'd get a bag of grain for a pound, if I paid on the button. But if I waited for the fairday, or if I was a sharp shark, then sixty. If I couldn't pay for another six or nine months, then seventy. You were kind and sweet and pleasant with the bigwig hard chaw. You were mean and stingy and tighter than a cow's arse during fly season with the guy who didn't have the ready penny. Thanks be to God that we don't have to give a crap about you and that you can't throw it up in our faces anymore . . .

—Listen, Joan, you sly bitch—a sly supporter of those who had money anyway—Joan, you sly bitch, you done for me eighty years before my time. Without fags . . . I saw you slipping them to the sergeant, a guy you had no dealings with, except in the Fancy City. I saw you giving them to a man in a lorry, you hadn't a clue where he was from, and you didn't get a penny's profit from him. You had them down under the counter.

"Just one," I says, "I could do with one now, and maybe there'll be more tomorrow, the beginning of the month . . ."

"Where would I get fags?" you said. "You don't think that I'm making them! . . ."

"If I was rich enough to give you four or five shillings for a box," I said . . . "You can stuff them . . ."

I went home.

"You'd better spread out that sweep of seaweed you left behind on the field beyond," my mother said.

"Seaweed," I says, "I'm finished with the stuff, with seaweed, mother."

I spat out a glob. It was as stiff as a hard-on. May I never leave here if I'm not telling the truth. There was a little kitten by the fireplace. He started slobbering up the snot. He started to choke with a cough. May I never leave here if he didn't!

"That's no way to be," I says. I took to the bed. Never got up again. No fags. You killed me, you sly bitch—always arselicking people with money . . .

—And my death too. It was the clogs you sold me that finished me off, you old wretch. I gave you forty-five shillings straight up into your fist. It was in the depths of winter and we were hacking out the road to Bally Donough. I was hauling the barrow in the wet muck down below. Fuck that place anyway, and everything about it! That was the spot where I died. I put the clogs on my feet. They wouldn't keep out a drop after two days . . .

I let down the barrow.

"What's up with you?" says one of the guys.

"Everything," I said. I sat down smack bang in the guts of the barrow, and I pulled my pants up from around my ankles. My ankle was as purple as Gut Bucket's nose. I swear it was.

"What's up with you?" the big boss asks when he comes along.

"Everything," I says.

"Everything is right, I'm afraid," he says.

"Huckster Joan's clogs," I say.

"Fuck them clogs, and everything to do with them!" he says. "If she lasts much longer I swear that I won't have any salesman on the road who won't be buried in the grave."

I went home. Lay down on the bed. The doctor was called that night.

"You've had it," he said. "The feet . . ."

"I've had it for sure," I says, "The feet . . . the clogs . . ."

"Huckster Joan's clogs, certainly," he said. "If she survives, I won't be alive . . ."

The priest was called the next morning.

"You've had it," he said. "The feet . . ."

"Had it for sure," I said. "The feet . . . clogs . . ."

"Huckster Joan's clogs, certainly," he said. "If she survives, I won't be alive. But you're a goner anyway . . ."

And by Jaysus he was right. I was on crutches a week from then. It was your clogs, Joan, you old wretch. You killed me . . .

You killed me too, Joan, you hag! Your coffee. Your piss-like coffee! Your jam, yes, your shitty jam, you hag you. Your coffee instead of tea: your jam instead of butter.

That was the fateful day for me—not that I could do anything about it—the day I left you my ration cards, you old cow:

"There's no tea this week. I don't know why they didn't send me any."

"So, no tea came so, Joan?"

"Not a bit."

"So, nobody has any tea this week, is that it?"

"No, I swear to you. But you'll get enough for a fortnight next week."

"But you always say that, Joan, and we were never compensated for the weeks it never came . . . For the love of God almighty, just one pinch of tea, please, Joan. Just a smell of it . . . Just a nail shaving's worth . . . I'm sick with the coffee . . ."

"Don't you know that I can't make tea. If you don't like it, you can give your ration cards to somebody else . . ."

And Joan, you old wretch, you knew full well that I couldn't. There you were hoarding the tea for those who could pay three times as much: the houses that took in learners of Irish, tourists, the big shots, and so on. I saw you with my own two eyes giving some to the priest's girl, and you gave a quarter of a pound to the sergeant's wife. You were hoping the priest wouldn't denounce you from the altar for your underhand dealings, and were trying to bribe the sergeant from squealing on you in court . . .

I toddled off home with my coffee. The wife brewed some.

"I won't drink a drop of it," I said, "God bless you anyway . . ."

"You'll have to have something soon," she said. "You had nothing since yesterday morning."

"So be it," I said. I glugged up another lump of gunge. It was as tough as leather, if the graveyard permits me to say so. The dog started snuffling around me. Didn't stay long. Fecked off and wasn't seen for two days.

"The lining of my guts is not as it should be," I said. "Wouldn't I be better off dying straightaway? I'll die if I drink that bilge of coffee, and I'll die if I don't drink it . . ."

And I did. I couldn't speak a word now, only I spat it out in a sweat when I was laid out. It was your coffee killed me, Joan, you old wretch. You killed me . . .

—And you killed me!

—And me!

—And me!

—. . . I won't vote for you, Peter. You allowed a dirty heretic to insult the church in your own premises. You were a bloodless watery wimp. If that had been me . . .

—You were a complete crook, Peter the Publican. You charged me four bits of coins for a half one of whiskey, and I was so innocent that I didn't know what I should pay . . .

—Your wife would know all about it. She finished off lots of half ones in my place. But I suppose you never knew anything about that either, until now . . .

—You were a crook, Peter the Publican. You were watering down the whiskey . . .

—I was not.

—I'm telling you, you were. Myself and Fireside Tom went into you one Friday after drawing the pension. This was before the war. Whiskey was flowing like tap water everywhere. As soon as you knew that Tom was pissed, you started on at him about women:

"Isn't it a crying shame that you wouldn't get married, Tom," you said, "a man like you with a nice bit of land . . ."

"You never said a truer word," Tom says. "You may as well hand over the daughter now."

"By cripes, she's there alright, and I'm not keeping her from you . . ." you says . . . There was a time when, Peter. Don't deny it . . .

Your daughter came into the pub as luck would have it. She took a crock of jam down from the shelf. Do you think I don't remember it? . . .

"That's neither here nor there now," you says, "She can make up her own mind . . ."

"Will you marry me?" Tom says, pressing up against her.

"Why wouldn't I, Tom?" she says. "You have a nice bit of land, and a half guinea pension . . ."

We were a little while riding away like that, but Tom was half joking, half in earnest. Your daughter was messing around and fiddling with the tie around his neck . . . I'm telling you Peter, that was the day. Don't deny it . . .

Your daughter went down to the kitchen. Tom went after her, to light his pipe. She kept him down there. But she was back fast enough to get another shot of whiskey for him.

"That old bollocks will be pissed soon, and then we'll have him," she said.

You grabbed the glass from her. You half filled it with water from the jug. Then you put whiskey in on top of that . . . That was the day, Peter . . .

Do you think I didn't see you do it? Oh, yes, I noticed right well the jiggery-pokery that you and your daughter were up to behind the counter. Do you think I didn't hear you muttering. Your daughter kept plying Fireside Tom with a concoction of water and whiskey right through the day. And he paid the same amount for the water as he did for the whiskey, after all that . . . Your daughter spent the day teasing him. She even started calling for whiskey for herself, but it was only water all the time. He'd have been killed by a lorry on the way home, only that Nell Paudeen, Jack the Lad's wife, came in to get him . . . That was the day, I'm telling you, Peter. No point in denying it. You were a robber . . .

You robbed me too, Peter the Publican. Your daughter lured me into the parlour, pretending that she had the hots for me. She plumped herself down on my lap. A shower of smart asses came in from the Fancy City, and they were ushered down to the parlour along with me, and this eejit was standing drinks for them all evening. The following day, she was up the same tricks. But there was no smart ass from the city there that day. Instead of that, she hauled a crowd of spongers in from the corner, and into the parlour, and this eejit had to call for drinks . . .

—Oh, I remember it well. I twisted my ankle . . .

—Until I hadn't enough that would make a tinkle on a tin. That was part of your robbery, Peter: your daughter letting on that she fancied every dog's body that you thought had a few bob, until they were milked dry . . .

—You robbed me too, Peter the Publican. I was home on holidays from England. I had sixty hard-earned pounds down in my pocket. Your daughter lured me into the parlour. She sat on my lap. Something was slipped into my drink. When I woke up from my stupor I had nothing at all in the whole wide world except two shillings and a few miserable half pennies . . .

—You robbed me also, Peter the Publican. I had thirty-six quid which I got for three lorries of turf that evening. I dropped into you to celebrate. At half ten or eleven I was on my own in the place. You held your ground. That was another part of your slyness: pretending that you never noticed anything. Went down to the parlour with your daughter. Plonked herself on my lap. Put her arms around me and gave me a big hug. Something went wrong with my drink. When I came to I only had the change from a pound I had before, and that was in my trouser pocket . . .

—You robbed me as well, Peter the Publican. No wonder your daughter had a big fat dowry when she married Huckster Joan's son. I won't be voting for you, I will in my mebs, Peter . . .

—I had intended conducting this Election properly on behalf of the Pound Party. But since you lot, the Fifteen Shilling Party have brought unsavoury personal issues into the contest—things I thought would never have been imputed except by the Half Guinea Party—I will disclose certain information about your own candidate, Nora Johnny. She was a friend of mine, Nora Johnny. Despite the fact that I am against her politically, that doesn't mean that I don't respect her and we can't have a pleasant relationship. That is why I really hate having to say this. It eats into me. I despise it. It disgusts me. But you lot started stirring the shit, you Fifteen Shilling crowd. Don't blame me if I hoisted you with your own petard. You can lie in the bed you made for yourselves. Yes, I was a publican aboveground. Nobody only a filthy liar could say that it wasn't a respectable pub. You are very proud of your joint candidate. She was better than anybody in charm, generosity, and virtue, if what you say is true. But Nora Johnny was a drunk. Do you lot know that hardly a day passed but she wasn't in the door to me–especially on a Friday, when Fireside Tom would be here—and she'd put away four or five pints of stout in the snug behind the shop?

—It's not true! It's not true!

—You're lying, Peter, you are lying . . .

—You're spouting rubbish! It's not true! . . .

—It is true! Not only was she drinking, she was also on the bum. I often gave her drink on tic. But she rarely paid for it . . .

—She never touched a drop . . .

—It's a brazen lie . . .

—It's not true, Peter the Publican . . .

—It's all true, my Fellow Corpses! Nora Johnny was drinking on the sly! Usually when she had no other business in any other shop in the village, she'd hop along the lane, sneak down past the trees, and in through the back door. And she'd come every day of the week, and after closing time at night, and before opening in the morning.

—It's not true! It's not true! Not true . . .

—Three cheers for Nora Johnny! . . .

—Three cheers for the Fifteen Shilling Party!

—Nora Johnny for ever! For ever! . . .

—Good health to you, Peter the Publican! Give it to her up the arse! O, my God Almighty! And I never knew that the bitch was a secret toper! What else would you expect from her? Hanging around with sailors . . .

6.

—. . . The heart! The heart, God help us all! . . .

—. . . God save us all for ever! . . . My friends and my close relations might come, they might genuflect on my grave, warm hearts might catch fire with the explosion of light, sympathetic mouths might murmur prayers. The dead soil might reply to the live one, the dead heart might be warmed in the love of the live one, and the dead mouth might understand the pressing words of the living tongue . . .

Friendly hands may repair my grave, friendly hands may raise my monument and friendly voices may sing out my requiem hymn. Temple Brandon's clay is the clay of my people! The sacred clay of my Zion . . .

But there isn't a Kelly to be found in Gallagh, nor a Mannion in Menlo, or any one of the McGraths to be found anywhere, otherwise my heap of bones would not be left rotting in the unwelcoming clay of granite, in the unfriendly clay of hill and harbour, in the ungenerous clay of rock and rubble, in the unfertile clay of bindweed and seaweed, in the unconformable clay of my Babylon . . .

— She gets very bad when the madness hits her . . .

— Hang on there now, you, wait 'til I finish my story . . .

— "The speckled hen started croaking along the street as loud as her voice would carry: 'I laid an egg! I laid an egg! Fresh hot on the dung heap . . .' 'Go away out of that, and don't bother us with your scutty little egg,' clucked one tough old hen who was listening. 'I've had nine generations, four clutches, six second clutches, sixty stolen eggs, and a hundred and one shell-less eggs since the first day I started crowing on the dung heap. I was done five hundred and forty six times . . .'"

— It's a real shame that I wasn't there, Peter! You shouldn't let any dirty heretic insult your religion . . .

— I drank forty-two pints one after the other. You know that much, Peter the Publican . . .

— I'm telling you, there were no flies on Fireside Tom . . .

— Are you trying to tell me I don't know that . . .

— You have your glue with your rubbishy romancing. And I hadn't a clue at this time that your one wouldn't gift the fat land to the eldest son and to the daughter of Tim Top of the Road . . .

— . . . "Big Martin John had a daughter . . ."

— . . . The murdering bastard gave me a bad bottle . . .

— O Holy God, as you'd say . . .

—I am the old man of the graveyard. Let me speak . . .

—Qu'est-ce qu'il veut dire: "let me speak? . . ."

—I was just putting my hand in my pocket and emptying it out . . .

—It was your clogs, Joan, you piece of crap . . .

—. . . O, Dotie, my darling, I am really worn out by this election. Quarrelling and quibbling all the time. Votes! Votes! Votes! Do you know, Dotie, that an election isn't a bit as cultured as I thought it would be. Honest, I didn't. The language is awful. And insulting. Honest! And full of lies. Honest! Did you hear what Peter the Publican was saying about me? That I used to drink four or five pints every day aboveground. Honest! Stout! If he had even said whiskey. But not stout! The most uncultured drink you could find. Agh! But you don't really believe that I drank stout, Dotie. Agh! Stout, Dotie! It's a lie! Dirty filthy yucky uncultured stout. It's a lie, Dotie! What else. Honest Injun . . .

And that I got drinks on the never never . . . It's a disgrace, Dotie. A disgrace. And that I was on the bum. Agh! All lies and rubbish, Dotie. Who would ever have thought it of Peter the Publican to say such things? I was well got with him, Dotie. There were cultured people in and out to see him . . . Throwing dirt, that's what cultured people call it. The natural thug that's hidden in the corners of our thuggishness— "the old man," as Saint Paul calls him—he can be forgotten about during elections . . . I feel that my own culture is melting away since I took up with those plebs . . .

Fireside Tom, Dotie? Peter said that also. He said that there'd be no problem going to see him except when Fireside Tom would be there with him. It's easily seen what he was trying to say about me . . . Honest, Dotie, I had no need to go after Fireside Tom. It was he who came after me. Honest. There are people, Dotie, who are destined to be romantic. Did you hear what Kinks said to Bliksin in *The Purple Kiss?* "Cupid made you, you sweety pie . . ."

There was never a time when men didn't plague me and have the hots for me. When I was young in the Fancy City, as a widow in Gort Ribbuck, and now right here, I am involved in an *affaire de coeur*, as he calls it, with the Old Master. But there's no harm in it: it's Platonic, and cultured . . .

Dotie! The sentimentality! Forget the bright fields of the Fair Meadows. You should really get this in a way that you dumped every prejudice and preconceived notion out of your noggin. It is the first step on the road of culture, Dotie . . . I was a young widow, Dotie. I married young also. The romantic bug again, Dotie. Fireside Tom didn't give a fiddler's fuck for me when I was widowed:

"I'll tell you one thing for nothing," he'd say, "but I have a nice warm cottage. Not a truer word, and land to go with it. Cows and sheep. I'm still hale and hearty. But it's hard for me to do everything: cattle, sowing, thatching. The place is going to ruin for want of a good woman . . . You're a widow, Nora Johnny, and your son is settled in the house, what good is it for you to be in Gort Ribbuck now? By all that's holy, marry me . . ."

"De grâce, Fireside Tom," I'd say. But there was no point in saying "de grâce" to him, Dotie. He was following me everywhere like a lap dog. As Pips puts it in *The Hot Kiss:* "The pangs of unrequited love have no borders."

He'd be stalking me and then crawling up to me in the village trying to cajole me in for a drink. *Honest!* "De grâce," I'd say, "a drop of drink never passed my lips . . ."

Honest, never, Dotie . . . and the things he would sing to me about love, Dotie . . .

"I'll marry you my Nora Johnny . . .
You're my star of sunshine, my autumn sun,
My golden treasure 'til kingdom come . . ."

Honest, Dotie, he'd sing that. But I knew full well that it was only the fine summer of our romance that was talking, and I'd say:

"O moon, O small moon of Scotland, you will be heartbroken tonight, and tomorrow night, and for countless nights after that, strolling the lonesome sky beyond Glen Lay, seeking the loving haunt of Naoise and Deirdre, the lovers . . ."

He came over to Gort Ribbuck three weeks before I died with a bottle of whiskey. Honestly, he did. He was like a donkey in heat. I might even have encouraged him, Dotie, if it wasn't for the pangs of unrequited love. It was then I said to him:

"The little moon of Scotland will never discover our loving haunt," I said. "It is not written that Naoise and Deirdre will ever again encounter one another in a loving haunt, or taste the sweet joys of passion on the gentle rocks of Glen Lay of the lovers."

"What the fuck are you talking about?" he said.

"The pangs of unrequited love," I says. "Other people get what they want, but I and my true love are separated for ever. We will never have a lovers' haunt except the lovers' haunt of the graveyard. But we will live out the sweet joys of true passion there, for ever and ever . . ."

It nearly broke my heart to say that to him, Dotie. But it was God's truth. Honest, God's honest truth. Caitriona Paudeen came between me and my true love. Small bitchy things. She never wanted to see anybody else darken Fireside Tom's door. She was looking for his land for herself. She didn't leave one thing the sun shone on for him. Honest . . .

—You're lying, you old hag! I never robbed nor swiped anything from Fireside Tom, or from anybody else. You thundering bitch! Secretly supping and deviously drinking in Peter the Publican's snug. Drinking on the sly! . . . Drinking on the sly. Don't believe her, Dotie! Don't believe her! . . .

Hi Margaret! . . . Do you hear me Margaret! . . . Hey, Margaret! . . . Did you hear what the old shrew had to say about me? . . . I'm going to burst! I'm going to burst! I'm going to burst! . . .

Interlude 4
THE GRINDING EARTH

1.

I am the Trumpet of the Graveyard. Hearken unto me! Hearken to what I have to say . . .

Here in the graveyard the monster of Unfeeling is chewing coffins, hacking cadavers, and kneading the refined flesh into one great oven of cold earth. He cares not for the sunlit cheek, or for blonde beauty, or for the flashy smile which is the pride of a young woman. Nor for the muscled limbs, the fleet of foot, the stout chest which defines the pride of the young hero. Nor the tongue which beguiled thousands with its sweet nothings, its mellifluous harmony. Nor the eyebrow which won the laurel crown for beauty. Nor the mind from whence shone the light of knowledge before every sailor on the wide sea of learning . . . As they are all necessary ingredients in the wedding cake which he is preparing for his children and their pards: the grub, the maggot, and the worm . . .

Aboveground the bog cotton is preening itself on every hillock of the moor. The meadow-sweet is a divine chemist along every wold. The seagull's nestling gently brushes the wrack with soft wings. The young boy's playful laugh is loud beside the cascade of ivy on the gable end of the house, the joyful ebullience of the bush in the hedgerow, the protecting canopy of trees in the copse. And the milkmaid's spirited song from the pasture beside the shore is the sweet dulcet lullaby wafting its magic from the Land of Gold . . .

But the flakes of foam on the fringe of the surge of a stream are slurping in towards the shallows of the river where they slobber on the rough sand. The white ripples of the gurgling gullies are being trapped by the willing wind in the rotting mountain sedge. The murmurous hum of the bee fades to despair as it floats to its hive from the foxglove which has yielded up its treasure. The swallow is kissing the top of the barn with its feathers, but the whine of the wind can be heard in its visiting song across the bleak and desolate wastes. The mountain ash is curling itself up against the raw and ruddy wind . . .

The swagger of the youngster is fading away, the whistling of the cowherd is growing faint, and the reaper is laying aside his scythe in the swath which has yet to be cut . . .

The living must pay its dues to the graveyard . . .

I am the Trumpet of the Graveyard. Hearken to what I have to say! You must hearken unto my voice . . .

2.

What's this then? Another corpse, bejaysus! My daughter-in-law, certainly, this time. You'd easily know it . . . A cheapo coffin too. I'm telling you if this is my daughter-in-law . . .

Breed Terry! But it can't be. You should have been here a long time ago. You had the shakes and the snots and the searing heartburn as far as I can remember . . . You fell into the fire . . . And you hadn't the strength to get up again. That wasn't too bad, as it goes . . .

Come here, I want you, word in your ear? . . . Have you any news at all, Breed? Whatever you're having yourself! . . . Oh, you want a bit of peace! That's what they all want, bejaysus, when they come first . . .

You heard they will be putting up my cross soon, Breed. It's already written? How long would that be, now? A fortnight? A month? . . . You haven't a breeze, Breed? In all fairness, now, you never did have much of a clue about anything, now did you? . . .

Ah, sure, I know well. You said that already, you fell into the fire . . . There was nobody there looking after you. Ah well, that's all that they'd want. For an old hag like you! There's no harm at all in it, Breed. It might be better from now on . . . but you won't fall here. Or if you do, you won't have far to fall . . .

Listen now, Breed, just listen . . . Ah come on, Breed, have a bit of cop on and don't make a moaning Minnie of yourself like that John Willy. He's driven everyone mad in the graveyard yacking on about his rotten old heart . . . My daughter-in-law's not too well all the time, is that what you're saying? . . . She had another young one, did she now! Is that true? . . . And it didn't carry her off! Well that's a wonder of wonders. But she'll never recover from this pregnancy . . . I'll bet you anything, Breed, I'll bet you she'll be here with us the next time around . . . And it's a girl . . . My God almighty, Breed . . . And they called her Nora . . . They called her after Toejam Nora! She heard that I wasn't alive! . . .

My daughter-in-law and Little Kitty bitching about one another . . . Scalping the hair out of one another's heads, is that what you are saying? Jumping Jaysus, now you're talking! That's it now, Breed! Nobody ever believed me that that strap of a thing had it in for me since she was forced into my house against my wishes, in from Gort Ribbuck! You can't imagine the tea she served me! And the bedclothes I slept in, I had to wash them myself! She has to vent her savage spleen on somebody else now, as I'm not there anymore for her. Little Kate was a soft touch for her, I'm telling you . . .

It's going to court, you're saying. There'll be a lot of gossip about that, I'm telling you, and it will cost a packet . . . Little Kate said that? She said that Maureen's clothes were got from Jack Chape in the Fancy City! My daughter-in-law wasn't half right then. How would Little Kate know anything then, except that her tongue is as long as a langer? And even if she did, what was that to her? She had no business sticking her nose into a young girl's future going to college. It would be a long time before anyone related to her would ever be a schoolmistress. The law will take care of it, no doubt about it! I certainly hope that Pat Manning the Counsellor will take the case against her. He's the one who would get it out of her . . .

Peace and quiet, is that what you want, you say? Don't we all want that! Well, then you came to the wrong place looking for peace and quiet, Breed . . . That's all the spuds my Patrick has set this year, the Turnip Field? But sure, there's hardly half an acre in all of that

. . . Nell has the two Meadows under spuds! . . . Well now, Breed, there's a fair bit in those two fields but there's hardly an acre and three-quarters, as you say . . .

What was that last thing you said, Breed? . . . Forget that falling into the fire, but just cop on and stop muttering . . . What did you say about Nell's son? . . . He's fine and dandy again! Ah . . . He's doing odd bits of work, is it? . . . Holy Mackerel and Ababoona! I thought, if I could believe John Willy, that he'd never do another day's work in his life! . . .

He was cured at Kill Eeney Well! Fat chance! Didn't that strap of a mother of his know full well where to take him for a cure! That bitch knows a thing or two about life! But I'd never believe, not in a month of Sundays, that he was cured at Kill Eeney Well. Neither do I believe a bit of it, that there's any cure of any kind at Kill Eeney Well. My own son's wife wore out her kneecaps saying prayers and doing the rounds there. There's hardly a well from our own one here to the Well at the End of the World that she hasn't visited, for all the good it ever did her. Always a bit sick. She'll be put to the pin of her collar at the next pregnancy, no doubt about it.

That's another one of Nell's tricks to take him to Kill Eeney Well, and then say he was cured there. That hag is well got with the priest! . . . God bless you anyway and your Kill Eeney Well, Breed! It was nothing like that. This is it. The priest. What else? He gave a copy of St. John's Gospel to her son. That's how he was cured, Breed. What else, like? The priest.

Somebody else is going to have to die instead of him now, though, as he was cured by John's Gospel. Death will have its own. That's what they always said . . .

God bless you, Breed! As if Nell would be the one to die! It's no wonder you fell into the fire, you're so stupid. Not a chance in hell of Nell copping it! . . . Or Blotchy Brian's daughter, either. Or anyone of her brood. Jack the Lad, he's the one they'll drive over the edge. You can be sure that she told the priest to have Jack die, as payment for saving her son. God help us all! She gave poor Jack a really hard time, the skank. She never looked after him. Remember what I'm telling you now, Breed, the finger is pointed at Jack and he'll be here very soon. Nell or Blotchy Brian's daughter couldn't give a fart in a gale. Won't they get a chunk of money from the insurance as a result! . . .

Is that so? The case is still going on, therefore . . . They'll be going to Dublin in the autumn, is that it? . . . I'll tell you something, going to Dublin isn't in any way cheap, Breed . . . Oh, they say it might be put back next time yet again! That'll bleed Nell dry at last, I hope it does! But, Breed, tell me now, if her son is fine again, then surely he won't be getting any money . . . Oh, he only works on the sly, is that the way? . . . He has the crutches laid down beside him anywhere he goes to work! . . . He has statements from doctors saying that his hip will not really mend! He would. You wouldn't mind but taking them out to the field and the bog with him as well! That's more of Nell's slyness. She was always twisted . . .

There's talk of building a road in as far as her house now! The priest and the Gentry will be able to drive up to her door in their cars. Bad luck to that road, anyway! . . . Forget the road, Breed, there'll never ever be a road there! Who'd shift all those boulders? . . .

Peace again, is that it? You'll make a total eejit of yourself if you keep up that talk . . . Biddy Sarah's pretty well fucked by now, is she? The kidneys as usual! Too bad for her! There's not too many people, apart from Nell and my daughter-in-law, that I'd rather see here first . . . And Little Kitty's back is at her again! I hope it gets worse! Another one . . . Blotchy Brian as sprightly as a spring donkey, you said. I wouldn't doubt him! . . . He can go and collect the pension all the time? Some people have all the luck! He's old enough to be my grandfather. God forbid, the poxy gowl! . . .

Listen, Breed, many people fell into the fire just as well as you. You'd lived your life anyway. What's the problem, it was as well the house didn't burn down too . . . Patrick lost two calves . . . With the black leg? God save us! . . . Isn't it just as well that that's how they had to die! . . . Nell fed her own the right stuff in time? That old cow is haunted lucky. And for all that, the black leg was most often on her land. The priest . . .

Patrick didn't cut that much turf at all this year, you tell me? How could he cut turf while he is looking after that floozie of a wife? He should smother her under a pot like you'd do with a cat, as she won't go and die herself . . . Five hens swiped in just one day. My God, that's a massacre! . . . And he didn't get even one of Nell's. Didn't the foxes always hide out on the rough ground around her place. Oh, she has a woman there—Blotchy Brian's daughter—who can mind hens, not like Nora Johnny's daughter from Gort Ribbuck. I think the fox is scared shitless to come near Nell's hens. The priest . . .

Patrick hasn't any pigs now, has he not? Oh, you mean when I went, Breed, the pigs went too. I'd get two lots of pigs ready every year . . . Nell got thirty-five pounds for her own lot! For fuck's sake! . . . Your few pigs were better than hers, Breed, and you only got thirty-two pounds fifteen for them. Nell would get top dollar, whatever. The priest . . .

Do you think there was any news from Baba in America recently? . . . You didn't hear any? . . . Blotchy Brian says Nell will get all of Baba's money . . . "Who do you think that Baba would give her money to," he says, "but to her only sister, Nell? Sure, like, he could hardly give it to a woman who was buried in a hole in the ground . . ."

That's what he said, Breed? What else would he say, of course, isn't his daughter married to Nell's boy? . . .

You heard that Fireside Tom had his lad hanging out all the time to marry someone? The cunt! He should be saying his prayers . . . You think that Patrick doesn't visit him as often as he did when I was alive? I nearly had to whip him to do anything for Tom. That's the kind of guy Patrick was. He wouldn't have kept any kind of decent house without me. Nell will butter him up . . . What's that you tell me, Nell paid some jobber to cut Tom's turf this year? Sweet jumping Jesus! What's that you said, Breed? Don't be muttering and mumbling, I tell you . . . Fireside Tom said that if he didn't get married he'd leave his bit of land and shack to Nell: "Caitriona didn't have as good a heart as Nell," he said. "No way, she didn't. Caitriona only wanted my patch of land . . ." The cunt! The bollocks! The knacker! The fucker! Oh, yes, that's Fireside Tom alright! . . .

Isn't that a great story you have so, Breed Terry! All of Ireland knows that Nell's land is rubbing up against Fireside Tom's? Nobody would ever think the way you're talking, Breed, that Nell deserved Tom's land more than my Patrick . . . Don't I know just as well as you, Breed, that Nell has only a few rocky scraggy bits? . . . Haven't you some cheek to say that to me up to my face. What the fuck do you care who gets Fireside Tom's land? What's it to you anyway? . . .

Peace again! It's what you deserve, you airhead . . . What's that you said, Breed? . . . Move over in the grave to make way for you! You'd easily know it wasn't your grave. Did you know that I'd paid my fifteen shillings for this a year before I croaked? Wouldn't that be just it to have laid out next to me: a bitter woman. You never thought that you or your crowd up there would ever be buried in the Fifteen Shilling Place. Makes no difference now, easy for you. There are five people in your house drawing the dole . . .

I'll give you peace! Piss off so! But you won't sidle up to my side here. I had the best coffin in Tim's shop, and three half-barrels of stout, and the priest threw the holy water . . .

Now, listen, you slag, if you carry on like that, I'll tell the rest of the cemetery who you are . . . What's that you said? . . .

"It is just as rare to saddle a cat as to have any of the Paudeens buried in the Fifteen Shilling Place! . . ."

Ah, come on, Breed, just look at who's talking: one of the beggars. Didn't I rear your father? Coming on over to me anytime it suited him, cadging a cup of tea when he was getting nothing but potatoes and a dry herring. Talk about speaking snottily and an inflated opinion! There's no way that the dungheaps are getting bigger these days . . . What's that you're saying, you hag you? . . . I don't have a cross over me yet as good as Nora Johnny's . . . Get stuffed yourself, you sluttish slag!

3.

Breed Terry, the hag . . . Biddy Sarah the sponger . . . Kitty the small potatoes . . . Little Kate the gossip . . . Fireside Tom, the cunt . . . Blotchy Brian . . .

It's easy enough for that muppet to have bragging rights again and his son-in-law doing OK. What was that John Willy the periwinkles said that he wouldn't do a stroke of work ever again? He was cured at Kill Eeney Well! He was in my arse! Even if he was, it was because that harridan of a mother got John's Gospel from the priest. Jack the Lad will pay for it. He'll try some black magic now instead of John's Gospel. He'll be here soon. And I'm sure they never gave him either a hint or a warning. Great balls of fire! They don't really give a toss!

The priest and Nell and Blotchy Brian's young one gossiping away to one another in secret:

"The way it is," Nell would say, "if anyone is going to plop his clogs, it's likely to be old Jack. It won't be long before he snuffs it. He hasn't been well for ages. But, say nothing about it. It would only bug him. Nobody, really nobody likes to kick the old bucket . . ."

She'd certainly say it, the cute hoor . . . Another young one, she's got so, my daughter-in-law. It's a wonder it didn't take her. But that cow is tough. Just as tough as the rocks of Gort Ribbuck that the road engineers cursed because dynamite couldn't even blast them apart . . . But she'll be here at the next birth. I'd bet anything on that . . .

And they called the kid Nora! Isn't a pity I wasn't there! My daughter-in-law thought she'd try the same trick when Maureen was born. I had her wrapped up in the blanket myself, before we took her out to be baptised.

"What'll you call the little thing, God love her?" says Maggie Frances, who was waiting there.

"Maura," I says. "What else would I call her. After my mother."

"Her mother stretched on the bed says we should call her Nora," Patrick says.

"Toejam Nora," I says. "To name her after her own mother. What else would she do? But why so, Patrick?"

"You're not exactly short of names," Maggie says. "Caitriona or Nell or . . ."

"Fuck the fucking fruitcake," I says. "I'd prefer to give her no name at all rather than Nell . . . No name would suit her better than that of her great-grandmother: Maura."

"Is the kid yours or mine?" Patrick says, and he was getting stroppy. "She will be called Nora."

"But Patrick, my lovely son," I says myself, "think about the child and her future life and what she will have to put up with. Do you remember what I said? Sailors and so on . . ."

"Shut your face, or I'll be totally bollixed . . ."

They were the very first cross words that ever came out of his mouth, that I heard, I think.

"If it's like that," I says, "then off you go. But somebody rather than me will take her to the baptism font . . . I have more respect for myself, God's honest truth. If you are going to call her Nora, then do it! But I might get a bit pissed off what with one Nora toddling up to my house, and the other Nora hardly ever to be seen. If that's the way it's going to be, I won't be hanging around. I'll take myself off, wherever . . ."

I gave Maggie the baby, and I grabbed my shawl from the closed door.

Patrick took off to the back room to Nora Johnny's daughter. He was back as quick as a flash. "Call her whatever damn name you like," he said, "Call her 'Diddly high di dee diddelly dum' if you like. But don't drag me into it. There's not a day that I wake up but that one of you isn't shitting on me . . ."

"It's your own fault, Patrick," I says. "If you had taken my advice, and Baba's . . ."

He was out the door as swift as snot off a shovel. From that day until the day they laid me out there was no talk about calling any of the kids Nora. But his trollop of a wife fancies it, now that I'm gone . . .

The words are all ready for the cross anyway. Poor Patrick is alright even though he doesn't seem to have anything left because of that frump of a woman who couldn't rear a pig or a calf or do any work in the field or on the bog. I know in my heart of hearts that he can't do everything. But when Maureen is a schoolteacher, she'll be able to provide a few bob . . .

Wasn't Breed Terry fast with the quip when she said: "Your cross isn't as good yet as Nora Johnny's." But it will be, you old bat. A cross of Connemara marble like that of Peter the Publican's, or Huckster Joan's, and wreaths, and an inscription in Irish . . .

If I could be bothered, I'd tell Peter the Publican about the cross. I suppose I should be sooner talking to him—as I am going to vote for him—rather than for Margaret, or Kitty, or Dotie. They are the people who have the crosses, of course. It wouldn't be that important only the way he listened to Toejam Nora! But the cat is out of the bag now. Lord Divine Jesus, didn't they tear strips off one another the other day. If Peter the Publican had taken any notice of me in time, I'd have told him what Toejam Nora Stinky Soles was like. But, it's fierce hard to talk to that Pound crowd. They fancy themselves twice as much as anyone else . . .

I won't bother Peter now. He's far too busy bothering about the elections anyway. I'll tell Huckster Joan, and she'll pass it on to the Pound crowd. I'd better say that they'll put the cross on me between now and . . .

—. . . He stabbed me through the three layers of my liver. The Dog Eared crowd were always treacherous . . .

—. . . Didn't we make a right mess of screwing up the English market, Curran? . . .

—. . . "It's 'the War of the Two Foreigners,' Patch," I said . . .

—. . . Honest, Dotie! Our lot were always sharp and smart. Take me, for instance . . . My son had a young fellow, he's married over at Gort Ribbuck, and he was going to school with the Old Master, and he said there was nobody like him. He was really into literature:

"He had culture in his bones," he said. "I could see it in him."

Honest, Dotie, that's what he said. Do you know that daughter of mine that's married to Caitriona Paudeen's boy. She has a girl now who's going to be a schoolteacher. She got that from my daughter. And if she didn't, there's no way she got it from the Lydons or from the Paudeens.

—You're lying up to your teeth, you old cow! Drinking on the sly in the snug in Peter's pub! Drinking on the sly! Hanging out with sailors! Sailors! . . .

Hey, Margaret! Hey, Margaret! . . . Did you hear that? . . . Did you hear what Toejam Nora said? . . . I'm going to burst! I'm going to burst! . . .

4.

—. . . May God Almighty give you a bit of sense, Nora Johnny, and would you ever just leave me alone. You picked a great time to talk about novelettes! I have to have a few words with my old neighbour, Breed Terry. I had no chance to talk to her at all since she arrived, what with yourself and your culture and elections! . . .

Are you there, Breed Terry? . . . Fell into the fire! The first science lesson I ever taught them in school, Breed, was how necessary it was to keep air from a fire. Air fans the flames, Breed. People should know that . . . Oh, there was nobody left to keep the air out, is that it, Breed! . . . In that case the best thing to do was . . . I'm afraid science could do nothing at all about that situation, Breed . . . You want some peace and quiet, Breed! . . . I'm afraid science can do nothing about that situation either . . . What's that you said, Breed? . . . The whole country were at the wedding, oh Breed.

That's the truth, Master. The whole country was at the wedding. You can be rightly proud of your wife, Master. There was no shortage of nothing: bread, butter, tea, and six different kinds of meat, porter, whiskey, and Sam Payne, Master. Sam Payne, Master. When one of our lot—Seamus, it was—got pissed off with the whiskey and the porter, he took off to the parlour and laid into Sam Payne. Every bit as good as the poteen that Ned Tawny has, he said.

Don't worry one bit, Master. It was a great wedding; just as good as if you had been there. The Mistress is a fine woman, Master. She toddled down to us just two nights before the wedding and invited everyone into the house. I was weak to the world, Master. If I wasn't I swear, Master, I swear it's not a word of a lie, but I would have been there.

"Any chance you'd have a bit of a can of buttermilk to spare there, Breed," she says.

"Of course, and I might have two of them also, Mistress," I says myself. "If it was more than that, I wouldn't begrudge it to you, or to your husband who's laid out in the cemetery clay—the Old Master himself—may God have mercy on him!" I says myself.

"I'm determined to have a great wedding," Breed, she says to me. "Myself and Billy the Postman were talking about it," she says:

"'A great wedding,' said Billy the Postman," she said. "That's how he'd love it himself, God bless him!"

"'I am absolutely certain that if he knew, that if the Old Master knew, Billy, that I was going to marry again,' I says myself, Breed, I says, 'that's exactly what he'd say to me, to have a great wedding. And, he'd be happy for the neighbours. And, of course, he'd be happy for me also.' No, he wouldn't either, Breed . . .

"Feck me anyway, Mistress," I says—I didn't really know what I was saying at all, Master, only the words slipped out—"I swear really, Mistress, but I swear I thought you'd never marry again."

"Ah, sure, Breed dear," she says, "I wouldn't have either if it wasn't for what the Old Master said to me a few days before he died. I was sitting on the edge of his bed. I took his hand:

"'What will I do at all,' I says, 'if anything happens to you?'

"He let out a great guffaw, Breed.

"'What will you do?' he says. 'What would a fine young strap of a woman like you do—but get married again?'

"I started sobbing, Breed: 'You shouldn't say something like that,' I tells him.

"'Something like that,' he said, and he was really serious this time, Breed.

"'Something like that,' he said, 'is nothing but the truth. I won't rest easy in my grave unless you promise me that you'll marry again.'

"That's what he said, I swear he did, Breed," she said.

—The hussy . . .

—God forbid that I'd say she told a lie, Master. That's what she said.

"It's going to cost you a lot, Mistress," I says. "You have enough money, and the postboy isn't too badly off either, may God let you enjoy it," I says, "but there's no doubt that a wedding can cost an arm and a leg these days."

"If it wasn't for what he had stashed away before he died, and the insurance money I got from his death, I wouldn't have a chance to afford it, Breed," she says. "The Old Master was very careful with his money, may God bless him," she says. "He neither drank nor went on the tear. He had a nice little nest egg put away, Breed . . ."

—The hussy! The bitch! She wouldn't put a cross over me half as good . . .

—But, sure, didn't I say as much to her, Master:

"You shouldn't do anything at all, Mistress, until you have erected a cross on the Old Master first."

"It's just as well for the Old Master," she says. "The poor Old Master is gone the way of all flesh, and as he has, and as he will be like that, he's not bothered about crosses. And I'm absolutely certain, Breed, that if he knew how myself and Billy are getting along now, he'd say to hell with the cross, but to enjoy ourselves as much as we could. No doubt the Old Master was a good man," she says, "he had a good heart and a good . . ."

That's exactly what she said, Master . . .

—The tramp! The dirty tramp! . . .

—. . . Fell from a stack of barley . . .

—. . . The heart! The heart, may God help us! . . .

—. . . I'm telling you, for Christ's sake, Galway won the All-Ireland football . . .

—In 1941, is that it? If you're talking about 1941, they didn't . . .

—1941, I'm telling you. And they have Kenny to thank for it. Never saw anything like him as a footballer. He clocked, knocked, houghed and ploughed his way through the Cavan team. He was some lad, some footballer, and beautiful to watch. I was looking at him that day in Croke Park in the All-Ireland semifinal . . .

—They won the semifinal against Cavan, but they never won the final . . .

—O they did, certainly! Kenny won it on his own . . .

—In 1941, you're saying? Well, I'm telling you, they didn't win the All-Ireland. They beat Cavan by eight points, but Kerry beat them by a flukey goal and a point in the final . . .

—Ara, God help you, how could they? Wasn't I in Dublin looking at the semifinal against Cavan! Three of us went there on our bikes. I'm not telling you a word of a lie: on our bikes the whole way. It was midnight when we got there. We slept outside that night. We didn't even manage to get a drink. You could have squeezed the sweat out of our clothes. After the match we were in like a flash to meet the players. I, myself, shook hands with Kenny.

"You great ballocks of a boyo, you!" I said. "You're the greatest footballer I ever saw in my entire life. Can't wait for the final in a month's time. I'll be here again looking at you beating the crap out of Kerry . . ." But unfortunately . . .

—1941, you're saying? If so, then Galway didn't beat Kerry, but Kerry beat them . . .

—Ara, God be good to you! Tell that to some twit. "Kerry beat them." You'd easily know you're trying to make a total eejit of me! . . .

—1941, you're saying? Were you even looking at the match?

—I wasn't. Of course I wasn't. But I was at the semifinal against Cavan, I'm telling you. What kind of an eejit are you that you don't understand what I'm saying? We came back again on the Sunday evening on our bikes. We were parched and starved. Our guts were hanging out with the hunger! But still and nonetheless we shouted "Up Galway" in every town we passed through. It was nice and shiny bright on Monday morning when we reached home. I got off the bike at the top of the road. "If it's our good fortune," I said to the other two, "that we come around after this hunger and thirst in a month's time, by Jaysus, we'll go again. I'd love to see Kenny beating seven kinds of shite out of Kerry . . ." And he did, of course. No bother to him . . .

—1941, you're saying? I'm telling you that Kerry won. Were you not at the final? . . .

—I wasn't. I was not. How could I be? Do you think that if I could've I wouldn't? What kind of an eejit are you at all? That day after coming back from the semifinal, didn't I come down sick! I got a cold from all the sweat and from sleeping outside in the air. It went through me straightaway. Five days after that I was here in the dirty dust. How could I have been at the match? You're a terrible eejit altogether . . .

—So what kind of rubbishy crap are you on about so, that they beat Kerry?

—It was no bother to them, no bother . . .

—1941 you're saying. Maybe you're thinking about another year! . . .

—1941. What else. They whacked Kerry in the final . . .

—But I'm telling you that they didn't. Kerry beat them by a goal and a point. A goal and eight points for Kerry, and seven points for Galway. The referee robbed Galway blind. But it wasn't the first time. But the gutty boys from Kerry won the match . . .

—May God grant you an ounce of sense! How could Kerry win it, when Galway did? . . .

—But you were dead. And I was looking at the match. I lived nine more months after that. The game didn't help me one bit. Every day after that I was fading away! If it wasn't for that I was watching them getting thrashed . . .

—God help you! You are the biggest fucking eejit I ever met! Even if you saw it a hundred times, Kerry didn't beat Galway, no way. Wasn't I there, wasn't I there at the semifinal in Croke Park. If only you had seen them that day crushing the bejaysus out of Cavan. It was Kenny! He was the footballer for you! I never wished for even one more day's life when I saw him taking Kerry apart just a month ago . . . No bother to him, none at all! . . .

—The final of 1941, is that it? . . .

—Yes, of course, what else? . . . Yes, of course, what kind of bollocks, are you anyway?

—But they didn't beat them. They . . .

—Oh, yes they did. They did. Kenny would have beaten the whole lot together . . .

5.

—. . . Hey, Margaret! . . . Do you hear me? . . . Why are ye not talking? What's happened to yous lately? There's not a pip or a squeak out of you since the Election. Breed Terry will get some peace now. I hope it does her no good! The little hag! Cursing is better than quiet, for all that . . .

You're not disappointed that Toejam Nora was whipped in the Election, are you, Margaret? That'll teach her not to be so nosy again. She'd go totally out of her tree if she was elected . . .

I voted for Peter the Publican, Margaret. Who else? You'd hardly think that I'd vote for Nora of the sailors, drinking on the QT. I have more respect for myself than that. Vote for a woman who was a sneaky drinker, is that it? . . .

And the Master is very angry with her these days, Margaret. You could hardly keep him under the ground since Breed Terry told him about his wife getting married. Do you know what he said the other day, Margaret, do you know what he said to prickly Nora the other day when she was pissed off he wouldn't read her a bit of the novelette:

"Leave me alone, you piece of shit," he said. "Leave me alone! You're not fit company for a cunt, a cow, or a corpse . . ."

I swear as the day is holy, that's what he said, Margaret . . . What's the point in you saying anything, Margaret? Didn't I hear him? . . .

But anyway, Margaret, something is bugging you all in that part of the graveyard, you're not talking as much as you used to . . . Rotting away, is that it? . . . The writer's tongue wearing away, is it? I doubt if that would bother Coley. He was driven nuts by him . . . Oh, Coley is rotting away nicely too. Don't you see, Margaret, I don't like it one bit. That was a great homely story he had about the hens. I made a packet from the hens, unlike that wretch I left after me: my daughter-in-law . . . It's God's justice, Margaret, to have a maggot in his windpipe, someone who drank forty-two pints . . .

Oh, he's completely putrefied, is he, Margaret . . . They told you in the Half-Guinea Place that he had disintegrated. I didn't think, Margaret, that you'd be bothered trying to chat to the Half-Guinea crowd. How else would they be, Margaret, how else would they be only totally manky? Nobody could be any other way in that place, a half-guinea hole in the ground. If I was you, Margaret, I wouldn't bother my butt with them . . .

What kind of whooping is that, Margaret? . . . The Half-Guinea crowd . . . Celebrating and gloating that their man got in at the Election. They'll deafen the graveyard. The wankers! The horde of rotten runts! Do you hear the way they are carrying on? Jesus, come down off the cross and let me up! It's a terrible affliction to be stuck in the same graveyard as them at all . . . But, by Jaysus, I'd prefer the Half-Guinea guy to get in any day than Toejam Nora . If there was nobody else, I'd have voted for him out of spite . . .

—. . . There was a day like that, Peter the Publican. Don't deny it . . .

—. . . The murdering bastard who gave me the poisoned bottle . . .

—. . . Whiteheaded mare. I bought her at the fair on St. Bartholomew's Day . . .

—I remember it well. I twisted my ankle . . .

—. . . Hitler! Hitler! Hitler! Hitler! Hitler! Hitler! . . .

—. . . Isn't it a disgrace they won't bring my bag of bones . . .

—. . . True for you. She's the gutsiest one in the graveyard until she starts up with that kind of rubbish . . .

—She always hoped to return to the Pleasant Plain . . .

—She knew that the cat had upped there already. Enough to crinkle the old man's cranium beside the fire.

—Maybe he deserved it. She said herself that he didn't give her a day's peace since she married his son . . .

—. . . Let me talk! . . .

—. . . But that was only a gnat's fart compared to when they were thatching his roof . . .

—. . . He had a big broad grin on his face . . .

—Will the two of you, himself and herself, go and shag yourselves! I hope the devil fucks you! What good was his big broad grin to me? You are just as nasty as the little prick of a poet. Big broad grin! Doesn't that one, the daughter of Tim Top of the Road, doesn't she have the same broad silly grin? The devil can fuck her too, isn't she trying to bewitch my boy, my eldest boy. His eyes are glazed over. Glazed over, I'm telling you! She's in the *Freemasons* or some fuck-arse thing like that. Trying to get her claws on my house and land, my big house and land . . .

—. . . Wait 'til I tell you how I managed to sell the books to the Master . . .

—I went into Peter's Pub. The Old Master hadn't been in there that long. I asked him nicely how he was. He didn't fancy Peter's place much anyway. He only came along once in a blue moon. He was a bit of an awkward bollocks. But he wasn't in any way fired up about the Schoolmistress.

"I know," I said, "I have the bait that is going to trap you, my boyo . . .

"The Greatest Love Stories of the World," I said to him. He was as hungry for them as a ravenous baby for the breast.

"Five guineas for a set," I said.

"They're very expensive," he said.

"What do you mean, expensive?" I said. "A half a guinea now, and the rest in bits just as it suits. They're a good-looking set. You won't be ashamed to show them off on your bookshelves at home. Look at the paper! They are the best and brightest of our love stories. Look at the titles there: *Helen of Troy*; *Tristan and Isolde*; the *Fall of the House of Uisneach*; *Dante and Beatrice* . . . You're not married? . . . You're not . . . You're that age and you have never read any of those stories: about Helen, *'the face that launched a thousand ships and burnt the topless towers of Ilium,'* and 'The Only Jealousy of Emer':

      'Once when the Scottish nobles bold
      And the Clan of Uisneach, often blessed,
      To the Lord's daughter of Dunatrone
      Naoise gave a secret kiss . . .'

"Think of yourself, now . . . There you are down in some hollow beside the flowing tide, a young beauty as bright as the sun in your arms, and you can't even tell her any one of the great love stories of the world! . . ."

He started humming and hawing. I moved in on him. But no good.

"They're far too expensive for the likes of me," he said, "Do you have any secondhand?"

"We are a respectable company," I said. "We wouldn't endanger the life or the health of our salesmen or our clients. Who is to say it wouldn't affect you or your wife? . . .

"Oh, I get it. You're not married. But, with the help of God, you will be. You'll really know then what value this set would be. Those long nights at home with the storm howling outside and yourself and your wife sitting comfortably next to the warm fire . . ."

But it was like talking to the wall . . .

I took off to the barracks. The Foxy Cop was the only one there.

"As for books," he said. "I have a room full of them up there. I'll have to burn the lot if nobody comes around looking for waste paper."

"What kind are they?" I asked.

"Novels," he said. "Crap . . . rubbish . . . but they pass the time anyway in this back arse end of nowhere . . ."

We went upstairs. The place was full of them. Crap, as he said himself. The kind of sloppy romantic slush that young prepubescent girls devour. To tell you the truth, most of them had the name of a nurse whom I knew from the Fancy City scribbled on them. I took the best of them, the neatest, and I tore out the first page of my collection. I travelled the schools in the area, and I came back, in a few days to the Old Master. I was a bit cheesed off with myself that I had slagged off secondhand books a few days before.

"I am heading out into the country today, Master," I said, "and I thought to myself that it would be a good idea to pay you another visit. I have a collection of love stories here. Secondhand. A friend of mine in the Fancy City was selling his library and I bought them deliberately, because I thought you might like them . . . They were disinfected, by the way."

He liked the garish covers, and the romantic titles: *The Berry Kiss, Two Men and a Powder Puff, The Russet Tresses* . . .

"Two pounds fifty for you, Master," I said. "That's all I paid for them myself. I won't make anything on it, as they don't belong to the company. But if you don't buy them, I'll be bankrupt . . ."

The bargaining began. He wanted to Jew me down to nothing. I told him in the end to take them or leave them, but there was no way I would let them go for less than two pounds. I got that much from him, by the skin of my teeth. Of course, they weren't worth diddly squish . . .

You knew what you were doing, I'm telling you. But so did I. I never told you about this *coup:*

There were two sisters living next to me. One of them was Nell Paudeen. The other was Caitriona. She's here now. The two of them hated one another's guts . . . Oh, you heard all this stuff before. Off I went and toddled up to Nell. Her daughter-in-law was there also. I told them about the children's insurance; they'd get so much money when they reached such and such an age and so on. You know the way it is. The two of them were very wary. I showed them some of the forms the neighbours had filled in. For all the good it did me.

"There's no chicanery about this," I said, "but you could get a killing. Ask the priest . . ."

He did. In the next fortnight I got insurance on the two kids. And then I apprised them about insurance for the elderly: the price of a funeral and so on. The old one was happy to pay for her husband, Jack the Lad . . .

Off I went down to the other sister, Caitriona. She was the only one in the house.

"Do you see," I said, "these forms that your woman up there filled out for two children and the oldfella. I told her I was going to drop into you on the way down, but she warned me not to . . ."

"What did she say? What did she say?" said Caitriona.

"Ara, I don't really want to be talking about it," I said. "You're neighbours . . ."

"Neighbours! We're sisters!" she said. "Did you not know that, or what? . . . You're a stranger. Yea, that's it, sisters. But even so, and so on, I hope that's she's the next corpse that goes to the graveyard! But what did she say anyway?"

"Ah, sure, there's no need to be talking about it. If it wasn't for the fact that I have a loose tongue, I'd say nothing at all."

"What did she say?" she shouted. "You won't leave this house alive until you tell me."

"As you wish," I said. "She said I'd only be wasting my time coming in here; that the people in this house didn't have enough to pay any insurance . . ."

"The whore! The harridan! . . ." she said. "It would be a sad day when we couldn't pay it just as much as Nell. But we'll pay it. You'll see that we'll pay it . . ."

Her son and his wife came in. The fun started. She was trying to get insurance for two of the kids and they, the couple, they were dead set against it.

"I'm in a hurry," I muttered. "So, I'll just leave you now. Maybe you'll have a decision for me the day after tomorrow; I'll be calling in to Nell again. She told me to call in and she'd take insurance out on the old man who's living up there all on his ownio . . ."

"Fireside Tom," she said. "Lord Divine Jesus! Fireside flippin' Tom. This is another one of her sneaky tricks to grab his land from us. Any way we could take out insurance on him? . . . I'll pay it out of my half-guinea pension . . ."

It was like the Battle of the Bitches after that. They were waltzing through the house as if they were dancing on grease. The son and his one wanted to smash my back out on the street. And all the time, Caitriona was trying to pin me down and keep me inside until the forms were filled . . .

And they were. I had to give in in the end. It was the diciest situation I was ever in in all my time dealing with insurance.

That's how I got around Caitriona. I couldn't really help it. The tricks of the trade, and all that . . .

—You lied! You're a liar, you didn't get around Caitriona! And if you did, you got around Nell too . . .

—Nell never said as much as one word about you, nor about Fireside Tom. The tricks of the trade, Caitriona my beauty . . .

—Hoora, Margaret! . . . Did you hear that . . . I'm going to burst . . .

6.

Peter the Publican is a right sourpuss too. Even after I went against the grain and voted for him, he didn't even thank me, or nothing. If he had any manners he might have come right out and said to me:

"Caitriona Paudeen, I am very grateful that you voted for me. You are a woman with enough balls to face down all of the Fifteen Shilling Lot together. We really screwed Toejam Nora . . ."

But he didn't. He should have remembered—whether during an election or not—that I still had no cross.

I had to tell Huckster Joan a long time ago that they had to put up a cross. So what now, like? It's been a long time since I was depending on her and her friends. But I may as well do it now, now that the great opportunity of the Election has passed . . .

Hey, Joan! Huckster Joan you . . . Are you there? . . . Joan, are you there? . . . Do you hear me, you shower in the Pound Plot? . . . Or are you all asleep? . . . Huckster Joan, that's who I'm looking for . . . It's me Joan. Caitriona Paudeen, John Thomas Lydon's wife. Joan, they'll be putting up a cross of the best Connemara marble on me . . . very soon. Like the one on Peter the Publican, and railings around it, just like your own, Joan . . .

Don't let me bug you, Joan? Is that what you said? I thought you'd like to hear about it, Joan . . . You don't want to have any hand, act, nor part with the Fifteen Shilling gang. I voted for Peter the Publican, Joan. I brought the whole Fifteen Shilling gang down on my head as a result . . . You'd be better off without my vote! . . . It's not right nor proper that you Pound Plot proper snobs should talk to us plebs in the Fifteen Shilling Place! Do you feel any better now? I can wear my tongue out gabbling and yacking away, but you won't take a blind bit of notice of me . . . You're not happy to talk to my likes of a gossip machine! Gossip machine, Joan! Gossip machine, Joan! You don't want to talk any more to a gossip machine like me! . . .

Go piss off so, you clot! You'll talk again when I get going on you! There's plenty of stuff about you, if you only knew about it! . . . Just because you had a bit of a shop up above and you were ripping us off with your clogs . . .

I know what you're on about, you trollop. I voted for Peter the Publican in the Election. It's a pity I did! Yourself and himself are really pissing yourselves because I'm going to get a cross and rails just as fancy as yours. I'll be as good as the two of you then . . .

That wretch, Joan. That's life, by Jaysus . . .

—. . . "Fireside Tom was there with his trousers . . .

Torn from the top to the bottom and then . . ."

—. . . Nora! Nora Johnny! . . .

—Hi! How are tricks? Have you got over the Election yet? I feel a bit shagged myself.

—You'll excuse me now, Nora . . .

—Ara, Peter, my pet, why wouldn't I? A nod is as good as a wink to the wise. There was a bust up—some of them call it a stink—but between ourselves, who cares? "The flighty mind forgives and forgets. The noble mind needs necessity," as Jinks said in *The Russet Tresses*. Honest . . .

—Holy God Almighty! Peter the Publican talking to Nora Johnny again, even though he swore black and blue during the Election that he wouldn't ever ever say another word to her. Oh, what's the effing point in talking! . . .

What's this he called her? A bitch and a whore and a cunt. Toe-jam Nora. Nora the Sailors' Bit. The piss artist from Gort Ribbuck of the puddles and the piddles! He said that she was drinking on the sly in the snug in his pub; that she often had to be carted home; that she started screaming songs at the top of her head when Michael Tooney's funeral was going past; that she fleeced a beast-buyer inside in his own parlour; that she drank the black porter of the black butler that the Earl had; that she'd feck bottles around when she was pissed; that she brought Johnny Colm's buck goat into the shop when she was totally scuttered and installed him behind the counter, and hoisted him up on the barrel of booze and started stroking his beard and plying him with drink; that she tried to grab Fireside Tom and jizz him up . . .

But what's this he called her? . . . It's terrible, I just can't think of it . . . I've got it, that's it. A *So-and-so.* I'll have to ask the Master, if he ever comes around to his senses again, what's a *So-and-so?*

But he called me a *So-and-so* as well, and he'd have called me worse if he could. But for all that he's talking as gently and as quietly to her now as if they never spoke a cross word. And he would never even think of thanking me for voting for him . . .

As there's no cross on me . . . If that's true. Maybe it was just that Nora wouldn't leave him enough booze money, up above. Peter, or any other Peter the Publican, wouldn't have much of a pub if they were depending on me. He knows right well that he'd have neither a cross nor company here if it wasn't for Nora of the pints, and her likes . . . I was never a drunk . . . But for that, and for all that, sometimes it was hard to pass the door . . .

—. . . That's the way, Peter. All the cultured people voted for me, and the Fifteen Shilling Crowd too, apart from Caitriona Paudeen, and God knows that trollop of an airhead never had the slightest bit of culture or manners.

I'd have preferred not to get Caitriona's vote, but I'd have got it anyway except for one thing. Caitriona only voted for you, Peter, because she was scared shitless about what she had left unpaid in your place. *Honest!* . . .

—You're a dirty liar, you *So-and-so!* When I died I wasn't as much as a penny in debt, no more than the bird on the wing, thanks be to God the Father Almighty. You old bat! "What she had left unpaid . . ."!

Hey there, Margaret! Hey Margaret! Did you hear what Nora the Tippler said? I'm going to burst! I'm about to burst! I'm going to burst!

Interlude 5
THE MUCK MANURING EARTH

1.

I am the Trumpet of the Graveyard. Hearken to what I have to say! You must hearken unto my voice . . .

Here in the grave the spool is for ever spinning; turning the brightness dark, making the beautiful ugly, and imbricating the alluring golden ringlets of hair with a shading of scum, a wisp of mildew, a hint of rot, a sliver of slime, and a grey haunting of mizzle. The vespertine veil of indifference and forgetfulness is being woven from the golden filaments of the setting sun, from the silver web of moonlight, from the resplendent cloak of fame, and from the departing wafture of fugacious remembrance. For this weaver's material is none other than the malleable and kneadful clay. His loom is the rickety rack on which he who attached his chariot to the most effulgent star in the firmament climbed with his dreams, or that other who snatched a bunch of the forbidden fruits from the dark of the dubious deep. This old masterweaver has webbed them all: the purr of passing ambition, the ostentation of transient beauty, the desires of unrequited dreams.

Aboveground everything is bedecked in the garments of everlasting youth. Every shower of rain creates a multitude of mushrooms miraculously in the grass. The opium flowers are like unto the dreams of the goddess of plenty laid upon meadow and field. The ear of corn is imbued with a tinge of yellow from the constant kisses of the sun. The somnolent susurrus of the waterfall sloshes silently through the lithe lips of the salmon. The elder wren is happy as he hops amongst the large leaves observing his young nestlings at their pecking play.

The forager is going to sea with a tune on his lips bearing the effervescence of the elements, the tide, wind, and sun. The young woman is seeking the pearlescent purse of promise so that she may clothe herself with lustrous splendour, and wear the precious stones of serenity that her heart so desires as she floats upon the dew in the morning . . .

But some evil warlock has singed the green canopy of the trees with his accursed wand. The golden tresses of the rainbow have been clipped by the nip of the east wind. A tubercular tinge has crept into the crepuscular sky. Milk is indurating in the udders of the cow while she seeks shelter in the inglenook of the ditch. The voice of the young swain who tends the sheep on the hills is suffused with a sadness which cannot be silenced. The stack-maker is beating his arms as he comes down from his covered rick of corn, because bad boils of threatening terrors are gathering in the northern sky and a cackling cloud of grizzled geese are hurrying away to the south . . .

Since the living must pay its dues to the graveyard . . .

I am the Trumpet of the Graveyard. Hearken to what I have to say! You must hearken unto my voice, listen . . .

2.

. . . Who are you? . . . What kind of an old cadaver are they trying to shove down on top of me at all? . . . My daughter-in-law, certainly, this time. Oh, no you're not. You're a man. You're not one of the Lydons anyway. You're a blondie. None of the Lydons were ever blondies. They were all black. Black as the sloe. Nor none of my own people either, apart from Nell, that old trollop of a tramp! . . .

You're related to Paddy Lawrence. I should know you. Are you Paddy Lawrence's second or third son? . . . The third one . . . Only nineteen years of age . . . Young enough to start on this caper, I'm telling you . . . You were three months failing . . . TB. That's the real bitch. This graveyard is stuffed full of them . . .

You were going to go to England only this shit hit you . . . You said you were all packed up and ready to go . . . All the youth of Bally Donough went last week . . . And the ghouls from Gort Ribbuck! May they never come back! . . . That's true, too true, my boy. You can make bags of money there . . .

You said you heard nothing about them putting a cross on me. Nobody's saying nothing about it now . . . Not a whisper, even, you say . . . He brought it up when he was in visiting you. What did he say? . . . Don't be ashamed to tell me, youngfella. You should know by now that I had no time at all for Blotchy Brian . . . All of Clogher Savvy have upped and awayed to England too. Sure, don't you know, that that crowd were always just navvies and wage slaves . . . If you hadn't got sick, you'd be there too . . . to earn money. It's a bit late now to be going on about earning money . . . But what did Blotchy Brian say? Weren't you always arselicking him anyway? . . . "That old bitch doesn't deserve a cross," he said. "Far from crosses they were reared. A man who couldn't feed his own children—Patrick Caitriona— talking about putting up a cross of the best Connemara marble!" He said that! He still hates my guts . . .

You said that Blotchy Brian was up in Dublin. In Dublin! . . . That prick in Dublin! . . . He saw the guy stuck up on the top of the Pillar! It's a pity he, and all that concrete didn't fall down on top of his knob, the scum bucket! . . . There were great pints there, he said! I hope it chokes up his snotty nose! . . . Lashers of women in Dublin too. It's a pity he didn't go there years ago after I had to refuse him, twice. The Dublin women would really fancy his gammy leg and his hunched back . . . He saw the wild animals! There was no wilder or uglier animal than himself, not to put too fine a point in it! . . . And the judge praised him to the skies! . . . He must have been a really thick judge so! . . . "You are really a wonderful old gentleman to come all this way, considering your age, in order to assist the court," he said. Oh, he must have been a really thick judge if he didn't see that he was only there to help his daughter and her husband, the slob-faced skanger! . . .

You'd really think that a youngfella like you wouldn't believe any of that old shite, and yet you'll end up like John Willy and Breed Terry, if you live long enough. I was hoping for some news about the court, but you said that the crowd from Glen Booley had all taken off to England. Bad luck to them! The Glen Booley shower can go and fuck themselves as far as I am concerned! The bastards wouldn't even come to my funeral . . .

For crying out loud! Nell got eight hundred pounds . . . Even though he was on the wrong side of the road. You're sure of that? Maybe Nell, the cute hoor, added five or six hundred to it . . . It was in the paper! You can read it in the paper yourself. Six weeks ago . . . In *The Galwegian*. Don't take a blind bit of notice of that paper . . . It was in *The True News* also, and in *The Irelander*? . . . And you say there's nothing wrong with him . . . He's thrown away the crutches altogether now . . . He's doing all kinds of work . . . And three doctors swore black and blue that he wasn't himself, and would never be himself again. O sweet Jesus! Truly he was a very thick judge. Did they tell him that he was on the wrong side of the road? The priest told him. What else so! . . .

She gave the priest fifty quid for a mass. She would too, the witch. Her son is fine and she has a pot of money . . . She gave him ten pounds to say a mass for me also! . . . She gave it straight to him and into his fist while Patrick was looking, is that it . . . The mass money that that cow would give would do me no good, I'm telling you . . .

The gang from Derry Lough went to England also five weeks ago. There! Tough shit for England that they had to put up with those gougers from Derry Lough . . . They wouldn't come to a funeral to someone half as good as themselves . . . Hang on! Don't vanish until you tell me some more! . . . Jack the Lad isn't that well. You'd easily know it. St. John's Gospel. He'll be here now any day soon. Nell and Blotchy Brian's daughter made up that potion for him. They'll get insurance money from it . . .

They're blasting a road in as far as Nell's place! God help us all! I never thought they'd be able to hack a road into that ugly goddam awful place . . . This new crowd she voted for, they've got it in for her, is that what you're saying. The little piss puss really knew who to vote for! . . . They're chopping off a corner from our land! For Chrissake! That's the field. The Laccard. We don't have any other field next to the path up to Nell's kip of a house . . . My own Patrick gave away a chunk of the Laccard! Aaagh! I knew as soon as I croaked that Patrick would be putty in the hands of that bitch . . . The priest came along to see what was going on . . . That's all part of Nell's sly shy shift shit . . . The priest himself, he laid out the boundaries . . . That was the same day that Nell gave him the money to say masses for me. My God Almighty, what was she thinking about, no flies on that one! That was her sneaky trick to get the road done. There was no other way to do it apart from taking chunks from our land, especially the Laccard . . . You'd think that Patrick was paid for the field? You have your glue! He shouldn't have let her get away with it. Isn't it a pity he didn't live a few more years! . . . That's what Blotchy Brian said: "Ah, come on, like, you don't expect that Nell would pay for a pate bald baldy bollocks of a heap of stones that couldn't ride one another? If Caitriona's Paddy had the least ounce of sense he'd have built some kind of a crappy kip for her heap of bones over there . . . Up over on Laccard . . . And there'd be tons of stuff for headstones there too, no need at all for Connemara marble . . . John Willy and Breed Terry . . . to keep them away from the hedgehog . . ." Oh, the bitch! The nasty bitch! . . .

This is it again: "If I was only in England! Oh to be in England!" Did I stop you? . . . The whole shower from Kin Teer took off six weeks ago! I couldn't give a tinker's curse or an itinerant's malediction where the sun goes down on anybody from Kin Teer. There's a couple of babbling blabbers here for sure, and they add to the place . . .

Are you saying that you heard nothing about my sister Nell's will? . . . Not a word . . . How could you with your itchy langer out trying to go to England? . . . That's all you heard about Fireside Tom? . . . He's still in his old shack . . . He drops in to us every time he's heading down for the pension. A good man! That's great news . . . He sometimes gives my daughter-in-law the pension book to get it for him! Good for him! . . . He's not as sprightly as he was . . . Oh, you mean he also gets Nell and Blotchy Brian's Maggie to get it too! Shag that! . . .

Little Kitty's back is bad again, you say. I hope there's no one else laid up who won't be laid down before her in the cemetery clay! . . . Biddy Sarah is also very crocked. Another one of them. She wouldn't come to keen me, the bloodsucking ghoul! . . .

You never gave a toss about anything except going to England . . . You'd go to England just because the gang from Shan Kyle went there two months ago! Anyone who copied the knackers from Shan Kyle never came to any good. My son's wife, she's still a bit sickly, all the time . . .

God be good to us! . . . She was fighting with Blotchy Brian's daughter! . . . Fighting with her! . . . She went up to Nell's house, straight in the door, and grabbed Blotchy Brian's daughter by the scruff of the neck! You're having me on! . . . Oh, so it wasn't Little Kitty who said that Maureen's college outfit was bought in Jack Chape's. What was Breed Terry on about so, the whore? . . . Oh, it was Blotchy Brian's daughter who said it first to Little Kitty! She always had the bad word. The bitch's daughter! And my daughter-in-law scrawled her hair out, right in her own house . . . She flattened her on the ground! I never thought she had the guts, Toejam Nora's daughter! . . .

She chucked Nell into the fire! Threw Nell into the fire! I love her! She's brilliant! A good one! A good one! You're sure she fucked Nell into the fire? . . . Nell then tried to defend Blotchy Brian's daughter, and my son's one threw her into the fire also! May God give her good health and happiness! She's a good one! My life on you, ya good thing! That's the first bit of good news that has raised my spirits in the cold rag hole of this earth.

They were beating the shit out of one another until Patrick went up and hauled his wife back home! God's curse on him that he didn't leave them at it! . . .

Ara, who knows but the gang from Tawney Lawr mightn't be better off at home. A mob of mangy maggots! They won't leave a crumb after them in England. But hey, my daughter-in-law and Blotchy Brian's Maggie, they'll be in court after this . . .

What, they won't? What do you mean? If she went into the Bright City and persuaded Mannix the Counsellor that her good name had been ruined, she wouldn't be long in putting a big hole in Nell's money. Maybe 'twould cost her five or six hundred pounds . . .

Nell called in the priest to fix it up! She would, wouldn't she . . .

That's what Patrick said about them: "Don't take a blind bit of notice of women clawing and clattering one another," he said. Nell got him to say that. She misses me, the withered old gummy crone! . . .

What's that you said? That my daughter-in-law is very busy these days . . . She's bursting her guts working since the fight . . . She's never sick or slacking now! That's a big change! And I was certain she'd be here any day now . . . Up at the crack of dawn, you say . . . Out in the fields and in the bogs . . . She's raising piglets again! Good for her! They had three or four calves at the last fair! Good for them! Sound man, now you're talking, I'm telling you . . . And you said you heard your mother say that the whole road was swarming with chickens! How many clutches do you think she had this year? . . . It's not your fault, of course, that you know nothing about that . . .

Patrick is away on a hack now, you say. He'll soon best Nell with her eight hundred pounds so. That judge hadn't a clue from Adam. But if my daughter-in-law goes on the way she's flying now, and when Maureen becomes a schoolteacher . . .

You're right about that, youngfella! Patrick was robbed . . . What did he say? What's that Blotchy Brian said? That Patrick would be better off, as he couldn't pay his rent, he'd be better off giving a mortgage to someone else on a handful of land, on his handful of a wife, and take off to England to get some work . . . To call a fine holding like that a handful of land, the scum bucket! . . . "But it's just as well that that old bat of a mother of his isn't around to give him bad advice," he said. The scum bag! The scum bag! The scum . . .

Where have you gone, youngfella? Where are you? . . . They've taken you away from me . . .

3.

You don't know, my good man, why the land in Connemara is so rough and barren . . .

—Patience, Coley! Patience. The time of the Ice Age . . .

—Ara, put a sock in it! The time of the Ice Age, for God's sake! Nothing to do with it, it was the Curse of Cromwell. That time

God banished the Devil down to hell, he nearly didn't succeed. He tumbled from heaven down here. Himself and Michael the Archangel spent a whole summer wrestling it out. They tore the guts out of the land from the bottom up . . .

—You're right there Coley. Caitriona showed me the mark of his hoof up there on Nell's land . . .

—Shut your trap, you nasty grabber! . . .

—You're insulting the faith. You're a heretic . . .

—I've no idea how things would have ended up after their brawl, only the Devil's shoes started to give way. Cromwell had made them. He was a cobbler over in London. His shoes fell off along the shoreline. One shoe broke into two pieces. They're the three Aran islands out there since. But as the Fallen Angel was up the creek without his shoes, he forced Michael to retreat all the way to Skellig Michael. That's an island there facing Carna. He roared and screamed at Cromwell to come and mend his shoes. I've no idea how things would have ended up after the struggle if his shoes had been mended . . .

Cromwell hightailed it to Connacht. The Irish hightailed it after him—not surprisingly—as they were always fighting against the Devil . . .

Michael confronted them, still running away from the Devil, five miles from Oughterard in a place they call Lawbawn's Hole . . . "Stand, you knave," he said, "and we'll give it to you straight in the balls." That's the spot where he was banished to hell, at Sulpher Lake. That's where the Sulpher River rises to flow through Oughterard. Sulpher is the correct name for the Devil in Old Irish, and Sulphera is his wife's name . . .

With all the messing, didn't Cromwell escape their clutches and took off to Aran, and he's been there ever since. It was a holy place until then . . .

—But Coley, Coley, let me speak. I'm a writer . . .

—. . . Go and get stuffed, yourself and your *Yellow Stars*! . . .

—The way it is, as you say yourself, the very best sods were stolen from us . . .

—Who are you to talk about stealing, Tim Top of the Road, when you'd rob the egg from the stork, and the stork after that? I was cursed that my bog was right next to yours and I didn't have a patch of land to dry my turf on except that bit right next to yours. You'd cosy your own cart or donkey up against your own rick, but you'd fill your own load from mine. Do you remember the morning I caught you at it. It was just at daybreak. I told you the night before that I was going to the market with some pigs. You said you were going to the market also . . .

And the day I caught your wife. I saw her heading off to the bog in the cold light of day. I knew there'd be nobody up there. They'd all be down at the shore at full tide. I was going to go there too, but I knew by the look of your one that she was up to no good, off for a bit of stealing . . .

I crawled up on my belly down around the back of Drum, then I shot up and saw her tightening the rope over the top of the load . . .

"However much the fox escapes, he'll be caught in the end," I said . . .

"I'll get the law after you," she said. "You have no business sneaking up on a woman on her own in a lonely place like this. I'll swear it black and blue. You'll be deported . . ."

—And you talking about stealing, Tim Top of the Road, you'd steal the honey from the hive. Selling every clump of your own turf. Not a bit of yours taken in since Hallowe'en, and yet a blazing fire in the kitchen, in the parlour, upstairs . . .

I was in visiting you one night. I recognised the turf I had cut in the bog myself the day before that.

"The way it is, as you say, there's neither heart nor heat in any of that turf," you said. "It should be a lot better . . . The very best sods were stolen from us . . ."

—And you talking about stealing, and you'd whip the sheet from a corpse. You stole the wrack that I had slaved for over from the Island.

"If we can't pile this stuff on the bank either on our backs or with the horse," I said to the wife, "I'd better put some string around the end of it, so we'll know it's ours. It'd be no bother for that shower at the top of the road to swipe it from the shore in the morning."

"You're not saying that they'd go as far as to rob the wrack," the wife said.

"God grant you sense, woman," I said. "If it was spread out there on your own ground, they'd swipe it, not to mention anything else."

. . . The following morning I was coming down from the houses, and I bumped into your daughter at Glen Dyne, with a load of seaweed astride the donkey.

— Oh, that fast one my eldest is hanging around with.

— I recognised some of my own wrack immediately, even though some of the string had been removed from the end.

"You got that in Cala Colum," I said.

"In Cala Lawr," she said.

"No way," I said, "you got it in Cala Colum. Seaweed never comes in to Cala Lawr from the Island with a south wind and a full tide. That's my wrack. If you have any decency at all you'll unload it and leave it to me . . ."

"I'll get the law after you," she said, "assaulting me on my own in a lonely place like this. I'll swear it black and blue. You'll be deported . . ."

— You stole my hammer. I spotted it when you were working on the back of the house . . .

— You stole my sickle . . .

— You stole the rope I left outside . . .

— You stole the thatching stick that I left stuck out in the barn after two rough days in Kill Unurba. I recognised my own two notches on every stick . . .

— If the truth be told, a fistful of my periwinkles were stolen too. I left them in a bag up at the top of the road.

"Come here 'til I tell you," I said to the youngfella, "if we collect as much as this every week from now 'til next November, we'll nearly have enough for a colt."

There were seven big lumps of bags there. The next morning I went down to the periwinkle man. He looked at them. "This bag here is a couple of stone short," he said.

He was right. It had been opened the night before and a couple of stone had been stolen from it.

The truth is always the best. I had some suspicion about Caitriona Paudeen . . .

—Holy moley! Abuboona! . . .

—I had, I'm telling you. She was nuts about periwinkles. I heard someone say that they were just the stuff for the heart. But I hadn't a clue then that I had a dicey heart, God help us! But I got a catch in my . . .

—You old dolt head! Don't believe him . . .

—Usen't I see my old man, John Willy. The old gom, he drank tea morning, noon, and night. I never saw a brass farthing of his pension in the house, and I have no idea where he stashed it away. But there were buckets of tea that time, and he'd buy a pound and a half, or even two pounds, every Friday. Huckster Joan told me he'd often buy two and half pounds. "As long as it's there, it'll do," he'd always say, the poor gom.

Caitriona always just happened to be hovering around when he was on his way home every Friday, and she'd haul him in. He was always gullible that way, the poor gom.

"You'll have a sup of tea," she'd say.

"By hokey, I will," he'd say. "There's two pounds of it there, and as long as it lasts, it'll do."

He'd tell me that up and down the town land. He was a bit simple like that, the poor gom.

The tea would be made. Made, and maybe twice. But he never brought more than half an ounce home to me. May God forbid that I would wrong him, Johnnie! . . .

"I've bought two pounds," he'd always say. "I must have lost it. Would you see if there's a hole in any of them pockets. Maybe I left some of it after me in Caitriona Paudeen's place. I'll get it the next day. And, sure, if I don't what matter? As long as it lasts, it'll do. When you're with Caitriona a lot of tea gets drunk, fair play to her! . . ."

He was a bit simple like that, the poor gom . . .

—That's another lie, you tool you! I never wasted myself feeding him with tea! He was over to me whenever the clock would chime, he was worn out with your spotty potatoes and your salty water, Breed Terry, the beggar. Don't believe her . . .

—I want some peace! Give me some peace! Stop badmouthing me, Caitriona. I don't deserve your bitchy effing and blinding! Peace! Peace! . . .

—I'll tell you the truth, Breed Terry. We had set the Garry Abbey field the same year, and it was bursting with the best of potatoes. It was out towards the arse end of May. Myself and Micil were out on the bog every day keeping an eye on things for the previous fortnight. We were, and we would have been that day too, only Micil was bringing in some dried seaweed until dinnertime. He went into the barn after dinner to get a fist of hay to stuff into the donkey's halter as he was going to be out in the bog the balance of the day.

"You'd never think, Kitty," he said, "that so many of the old potatoes out in the barn would be gone. I would have said something only that the pigs had been sold two weeks ago."

"I swear to God, Micil," says I, "I haven't been next nor near the barn for the last three weeks. There was no panic for me to be there. The kids brought in the spuds for the meal."

"We should have put a lock on it," he said, "since we started working on the bog. Anyone could sneak in there during the day when we're not around and the kids are in school."

"They could, of course, Micil, or even in the dead of night," I said.

"It's closing the stable door after the horse has bolted," Micil said.

Out I go to the barn, Breed, by the new time. I examined the potatoes.

"By the holies, Micil," I said when I came in. "It's closing the stable door after the horse has bolted. There was a corner full of potatoes there a fortnight ago, but there's a big hole in it now. I'm not sure if there's even enough there to get us to the new potatoes. Would you have any hunch at all, Micil, who is knobbling them?"

"I'll head out to the bog," Micil said. "You slip up to the meadow at Ard Monare letting on you're going to the bog just like every other day, then sneak down by the stony slop, and hide near the willow."

I did that, Breed. I slid down behind the willow mending the heel of a sock and kept my eyes glued on the barn beyond. I was a long time there, and I think I was about to doze off when I heard the noise at the barn door. I jumped through the gap in a jiffy. She was there, Breed, and talk about humping potatoes on the hump of her back!...

"You may as well take them away and sell them to Huckster Joan just as you have sold your own all year," I said. "You haven't had a potato of your own to stuff in your mouth since May. That might be alright for one year, but this is what you're up to every year."

"I had to give them to Fireside Tom," she said. "His own rotted."

"Rotted! He never bothered his barney about them," I said. "He didn't mould them, or clean up the ground, or spit a splash of spray on them . . ."

"I'm begging you, and I'm even grovelling, Kitty, please, please don't say a word about it," she said, "and I'll make it worth it. I don't give a toss who'll hear about it, once that piss puss Nell gets no wind of it."

"OK, so, Caitriona," I said, "I won't breathe a word."

And I swear by the oak of this coffin, Breed, I never said nothing to nobody . . .

—Listen to Kitty of the shitty puny potatoes, I always had tons of spuds of my own, thanks be to the Lord God Almighty . . .

—. . . Dotie! Dotie! She didn't leave Fireside Tom with a tosser. I often met him down in the village.

"For fuck's sake Nora, I haven't a farthing that she hasn't filched from me," he'd say. Honest, that's what he'd say.

I'd lend him the price of a couple of glasses of whiskey, Dotie. Honest. You'd really pity him, all on his ownio, and his tongue hanging out like shrivelled flowers in a pot . . .

What's that they're saying about me, Dotie? My own daughter was up to the same tricks? I learned about it here . . . She pulled a fast one on my son in Gort Ribbuck very shortly after I died. Himself and his wife were going to the fair in the Fancy City. My daughter offered to look after the house until they came back. She gathered up anything worthwhile and chucked it into the big press. She had the horse and trap all ready outside. She asked a couple of young bucks who were hanging around to load the press onto the trap. They hadn't a bull's notion about it. She gave them the price of a couple of pints.

"It's my mother's press," she said. "She left it to me." Honest, that's what she said. She took it home. Honest, Dotie.

It was a really well-made press in the traditional way. As strong as iron. But beautiful also. Perfection and practicality all together, Dotie . . .

Who'd give a damn, except for what was in it was worth! Spoons and silver knives. A whole silver toilette that I had when I was in the Fancy City. Valuable books bound in calfskin leather. Sheets, blankets, sacking, blankets, winding wrappers . . . If Caitriona Paudeen had been able to look after them she wouldn't have been laid out in dirty dank dishcloths . . .

Dead on, Dotie! Caitriona never shuts up prattling on about that press . . .

—Knives and silver spoons in Gort Ribbuck of the ducks! Oh, Holy Mary Mother of God! Don't believe her! Don't believe her! The so-and-so. The old sow! Hey, Margaret! Hi, Margaret! Did you hear what hairy Noreen said? . . . and John Willy . . . and Breed Terry . . . and Kitty . . . I'm about to burst! I'm going to burst . . .

4·

—. . . A white-headed mare. She was a beauty . . .

—You had a young mare. We had a colt . . .

—A white-headed mare for sure. I bought her at St. Bartholomew's Fair . . .

—We bought our colt just after Christmas . . .

—A white-headed mare. A ton and a half was no bother to her . . .

—Our young colt is a big strong one, God bless him. We were making a new pen for him . . .

—... "The Golden Apple" won, I'm telling you, a hundred to one.

—Galway won. They beat the lard out of Kerry.

—You're totally off the wall just like that wanker who goes on and on about Kerry winning. Galway whipped them, I'm telling you ...

—But there was no "Galway" running in the big race at three o'clock.

—There was no "Golden Apple" on the team that won the All-Ireland in 1941. Maybe you meant Cannon ...

—... "Fi-ire-side Tom was there with his ..."

—... There were seventeen houses in our town land and every single one of them voted for Eamon de Valera ...

—Seventeen houses! And after all that, not one shot was fired at the Black and Tans in your place! Not as much as a bullet. Not a piss, nor a pellet, nor even one mangy bullet ...

—Ah, come on, like, there was an ambush. The end of a dark night. They crocked Curran's donkey from going into Curran's field up his road.

—I remember it well. I twisted my ankle ...

—... You're one of Paddy Larry's? ... The third youngfella. You used to come to my school. You were a fine strapping youngfella. A head of blond hair. Brown eyes. Beautiful rosy cheeks. You were brilliant at handball ... The Derry Lough gang gone to England ...

The Schoolmistress is fine, brilliant, just great, that's what you said. But Billy the Postman is down and out ... very sick ...

—That's exactly what I said, Master. They say it's rheumatism. They told him he'd have to give the letters to whoever or whoever would be best, and then he had to start distributing them to the houses himself ...

—That's the way he was, the chancer ...

—He was caught out badly on the marsh. He was drowned to the skin. When he came home he took to the bed ...

—Who gives a fuck! The chancer! The robber! The ...

—He was always going on about taking off to England, Master, that's before he was clobbered ...

—Taking off to England! Taking off to England! . . . Spit it out. Don't be afraid . . .

—Some people are saying, Master, that his health wasn't that good since he got married . . .

—Oh, the robber! The swine-swiver! . . .

—She didn't feel a bit like letting him go. When I was ready to pop off, she was talking to my father about it, and she said that if Billy went she'd drop down and die . . .

—The bog pig . . .

—She brought three doctors up from Dublin to look at him, Master . . .

—With my money! She never brought a doctor to see me, the whore . . . the twat twerp . . .

—De grâce, Master!

—. . . "Fireside Tom there, and he whoring to marry . . ."

—I had no intention of getting married. I'd have gone to England except that I took bad. The whole parishes of Derry Lough and Gort Ribbuck have gone . . .

—And Glen Booley and Derry Lough. I know just as well as you who have gone. But are any of the younger gang getting married? . . .

—There's lots of talk about Fireside Tom getting married.

—They'll still be talking about him, the nitwit. But who else? . . .

—The foxy cop with a nurse from the Fancy City. The Young Master also . . .

—Schoolteachers are really up for getting hooked. There must be another raise of pay in the offing.

—They don't have it easy at times. You just heard the Old Master. But who's the young one? . . .

—A lovely girl from the Fancy City. A fine thing, actually! That day when I was drawing pictures in the hope of going to England, I saw the two of them together. They went in to the Western Hotel.

—What kind of cut or shape of a woman was she?

—A long tall sally. Blondy hair dripping down along her back . . .

—Earrings?

—Of course . . .

—Dark eyes?

—I haven't a clue what kind of eyes she had. I wasn't thinking about them . . .

—A broad bright grin?

—She was gawping away at the Master all right. But she wasn't gawping at me . . .

—Did you hear where she hangs out?

—No I didn't. But she's working in Barry's Bookies, if there's such a joint. The Derry Lough master and the priest's sister are getting married next month. They say he'll get the new school.

—The one with the pants?

—The very one.

—Isn't that weird that she'd marry him?

—Why so? Isn't he a fine-looking specimen, and he doesn't touch a drop.

—But all the same. It's not every man would want to marry a woman who wears the trousers. They'd be a bit more pernickety than other women . . .

—Ah, cop on and get an ounce of sense! My own son is married to a French one in England and you wouldn't have the least clue on God's earth what she was gabbling on about no more than the gob-shite buried over there. Shouldn't she be even more pernickity than any one that wears a pair of pants . . .

—God help you and your Frenchie one! My son is married to an Italian in England. Is that good enough for you?

—Forget about yourself and your Italian. My son is married in England to a black. Can you do better than that?

—A black! My son is married in England to a Jew. Can you credit that? To a slylock Jew. A Jew wouldn't be happy to marry any old kind of man . . .

—And not every man would marry her either. Some of them wouldn't fancy her . . .

—There's many more than that who wouldn't fancy the thing your son married. A black. For fuck's sake! . . .

—The big boss is to marry some woman from Glen Booley. That

youngfella of John Willy's, he's made the kip of a shack and all, and they say he's sniffing around looking for a woman. The daughter of your man Tim Top of the Road sent him packing.

— Tim Top of the Road who spent all his time robbing my turf . . .

— And mine . . .

— And my hammer . . .

— Oh, I hope she chokes! Trying to sneak into my land . . .

— It was she who threatened me with the law to ruin me about the wrack. You're telling me that John Willy's boy wouldn't marry her? . . .

— She'd be good enough for him. What was John Willy ever any good for? Periwinkles. And what is he any good for now? Perifucking-winkles . . .

— There was nothing much wrong with the periwinkles ever, there wasn't really. Myself and the youngfella got most of what we needed to buy a colt. And now we have something that you don't have: a fine big colt and a pen that only needed some covering. I told him that when the pen was finished he should get some bit of a thing of a woman for himself . . .

— The youngfella was sent packing as well from the house up above; and Rootey's daughter in Bally Donough refused him, and the carpenter's daughter in Gort Ribbuck . . .

— That youngfella is a totally useless git. Did he say that we nearly got the price of a colt from the periwinkles; that we had made a clean new pen; that we bought a fine new colt after Christmas? He'd never have managed it himself, I'm afraid. If I hadn't gone so quickly myself . . .

— Hey, John Willy, that Rootey in Bally Donough is my cousin. He didn't do half enough rejecting your son. I rejected you about my daughter. Do you remember the time you came looking for her?

— I had neither colt nor pen that time.

— Aren't you so uppity to talk about Rootey from Bally Donough, no more than anyone else. You'd think he was some kind of a snooty snotty Earl or something, and my father rejecting his woman. "Do you think, Rootey tootey," my father says, "that I'd condemn my daughter to live in Bally Donough to live on nettles and the chirping of crickets?"

—Your father refusing the Rootey! My mother also refused him a woman! "There's forty pounds and a cow going with my daughter," she says, "and there's no way she'll be living on the flea-ridden fastnesses of your place with her forty pounds."

—Your mother refused him a woman! Your mother! My father tried to pawn her off on me, but I wouldn't touch her. She was half blind. She had a mole under her ear. She only had a dowry of fifteen quid. I wouldn't touch her . . .

—I wouldn't marry Blotchy Brian. He asked me . . .

—I wouldn't marry Blotchy Brian either. He asked me twice.

—Nor me neither. He asked me three times. I swear by the oak of this coffin. He nearly completely failed to get any woman at all. Caitriona Paudeen would have married him alright the time that Jack the Lad dumped her, but he never bothered coming looking for her . . .

—Holy cow! Abooboona! Kitty you dirty liar! Kitty the small potatoes! . . .

—. . . Honest, Dotie. No way was the place good enough. There was really no way that I would allow my daughter to go there with her sixty pounds dowry, unless I really had no choice in the matter. I was always possessed of a romantic streak and I couldn't let inferior worldly affairs be an insurmountable obstacle to their unfulfilled love. Honest. If it wasn't for that Dotie, do you think I would have allowed my daughter and her sixty pounds to go and live in Caitriona Paudeen's pokey little hovel? . . .

—You little blabbering scum shit! You riffraff so-and-so! Don't believe her! Don't believe a word! Margaret! Margaret! Do you hear what Toejam Nora is saying? And Kitty the dirty liar? . . . I'm going to burst!

5.

—. . . Do you think that this is "The War of the Two Foreigners"?

—. . . The murdering bastard gave me a bad bottle . . .

—... There was every single tiny drop of the forty-two pints lining my stomach when I was tying up Tomasheen ...

—I remember it well. I twisted my ankle ...

—"The doh-og is drinking." *Qu'est-ce que c'est qu'* "the doh-og?" ... *Qu'est-ce que c'est qu'* "the doh-og"? Doh-og. Doh-og.

—Bow wow! Bow wow!

—*Un chien, n'est-ce pas?* Doh-og. Bow wow. Doh-og.

—Dog! Dog! Dog! You headbanger!

—"The dog is drinking." *Le chien boit, n'est-ce pas?* "The dog is drinking." *Mais non!* "The doh-og is crying."

—Like dogs cry all the time, you headbanger! Maybe he was whining, or barking, or even drinking. But he wasn't crying. Crying! I never ever saw a dog crying.

—"The doh-og is crying."

—"The dog is whining. The dog is whining."

—"The doh-og is crying." "Crying: c—r—y—i—i—n—g"! "Crying." *Ces sont les mots qui se trouvent dans mon livre.* "The doh-og is crying." *Pas* "drinking."

—Well, if he was crying let him cry away. We can't do nothing about it, nor about the twit who put it in a book. Maybe the dog went on the drink and then he started to cry about the hangover he got and his empty pockets ...

—*Je ne comprends pas. Aprés quelques leçons peut-être* ... "The white cat is on the mat." "Cat": *qu'est-ce qu'il veut dire?* "Cat"? "Cat"?

—Mi-aw! Mi-aw!

—Mee-ou! Mee-ou! Chat! N'est-ce pas? Chatte.

—Shat. Yes, of course. Shat. What else?

—"The wo-od is go-od. The ha-at is a-pt. The ha-at is tall on Paul. T— ..."

—You're a dirty liar! I never wore a tall hat. It was too low for me anyway. Do you think that I was a bishop? ...

—*Je ne comprends pas.* "Young Paul is not ..."

—You're a liar. I was still only a youngster. I'd have been only twenty-eight by the next Peter and Paul's day.

—*Je ne comprends pas.* Paul is not drinking . . .

—He's not drinking now because he is not thinking, but he drank what he had before this, and that wasn't much.

—*Je ne comprends pas.*

—*Au revoir! Au revoir! De grâce! De grâce!* . . .

—He'll never have a word of Irish as long as he lives.

—Nevertheless, he shouldn't be that long getting the hang of it. There was a guy learning Irish around here the year I died. He hadn't the least clue from Adam, but he was picking up bits and pieces from those small learning books, the same as your man. He'd be there in the kitchen every morning a full hour before I got up and he'd have made a rat's nest of the whole place:

"This is a cat. This is a sack. The cat is on the sack. This is a dog. This is a stool. The dog is on the stool."

He went on like that all day long. He had my mother driven completely round the twist.

"For Jaysus' sake, Paul, take him away over and into the field," she'd say to me.

I was cutting hay in the meadow down by the shore at that time exactly. I hauled him along with me. We were barely there when it was time to come back again for dinner as he read the lesson to everyone we met on the way.

Up and away again after dinner. I tried to teach him some small words: "scythe," "grass," "ditch," "rick," and little bits like that. It was a very hot day. It was a blistering hot day and he couldn't get his tongue around the words. He spat out a few knotty snots. He asked me how would you say "pint" in Irish.

I said "*Pionta.*"

He said "*Pionta*" and nodded to me . . .

We moseyed off along the shore to Peter's Pub. He bought two pints.

Then back to the field.

I gave him another word.

"*Pionta,*" he said.

"*Pionta,*" I said.

Off we went again. Two more pints. Back again to the field. I gave him another word again.

Off again. Back again.

Over and back like that all day long. It was a pint for a word, and a word for a pint . . .

—. . . Fell from a rick of hay, bejaysus . . .

—Do you think that I was raised in a cabbage patch and never saw a film? . . .

—An oldfella like you?

—An oldfella like me? But, I wasn't always old, you know.

—They're absolutely beautiful. I saw magnificent things like them. Big houses just like the Earl's . . .

—And I saw they had fine big crosses, and I'd say they were made of Connemara marble . . .

—I saw lots of women wearing pants . . .

—And black women . . .

—And cultured people, and nightclubs, and down by the quays, and sailing boats and sailors with multicoloured skins. Honest . . .

—And the occasional nasty bitch . . .

—And women with sly slippery smiles just like Huckster Joan when she refused you a fag or two . . .

—And women giving you the "come-here-I-wantcha," just like Peter the Publican's young one standing in the door trying to lure some new sucker into her parlour . . .

—You'd see some fine frisky colts there, I'm telling you! . . .

—And games of football. Up the yard, boy! Cannon would make shite and onions of any footballer's arse . . .

—You'd never see any wrack that came in there . . .

—Or two thatchers on either side of the house . . .

—Or nettles like there was in Bally Donough.

—Or flea-ridden kips like in your town land . . .

—I'd prefer Mae West to the whole lot of them. I'd give anything to see her again. She'd be a great one for the young bucks, I'd say. Myself and the youngfella were in the Fancy City the night before the fair. We downed a few pints.

"That's enough now," I said. "If we went the whole hog we'd soon make a hole in the price of the colt."

"It's too early to go to bed now," he said. "Come on, let's go to the pictures."

"I was never there," I said.

"So what?" he said. "Mae West is on tonight."

"In that case, so," I said, "it's alright with me."

We went.

A woman came out. A fine strap of a thing, and she started leering at me.

I leered back at her.

"Is that her?" I said.

"Who, so?" the youngfella said.

Another babe came out just after that. She kind of ran her hand along his hip. Then she threw a face and started grinning at us. They all started grinning too.

"That's her now," the youngfella said.

"Off you go," I said. "She'd be a great one for the young bucks, I'd say. As soon as the pen is ready, I'm telling you now, but you couldn't do much worse than to get hitched up with a little slip of a thing. But for God's sake, don't get caught up with the likes of her. She'd be a great one for the young bucks alright, but nonetheless . . ."

"But, but, nonetheless what?" the youngfella asked.

Just then another busty broad came out, just like the floozie that is always up for it in Jack the Lad's house, and he was talking to the two of them. He started waxing the air with his hands. Some lick-spittle comes out. The cut of your man who goes fishing in Nell Paudeen's place—Lord Cockton. Mae West said something to him. I swear to God that the youngfella told me what it was, but there's no way I can remember it now . . .

The little fart pulled a face as if his cheeks were swollen up. He dropped the hand down along his sides. He was a filthy fucker, and he knew what he wanted. I'd say he had a dicey ticker too, the poor hoor! . . .

—. . . Just the once Kitty. That's the only time I was ever ever at the pictures. More than anything I'd give anything to see them again. That was the time my daughter was about to deliver, the one who is married in the Fancy City. I spent a week looking after her. She was coming around after the birth that time. Her husband came in after work. He gobbled down his dinner and done himself up.

"Breed Terry," he says, "were you ever at the pictures?"

"What are they?" I says.

"All those pictures that they're showing up in that place?"

"In the church?" I says.

"Ah no," he says, "just pictures."

"Pictures of Jesus and the Blessed Virgin and St. Patrick and Joseph, is that it?" I said.

"Ah, not at all," he said, "but pictures of foreign places and wild beasts and whacky weirdos."

"Foreign places and wild beasts and whacky weirdos," I says to myself. "I don't think I'd like to go there at all. Who knows, God save us from all harm! . . ."

"You have a crude culchie mind," he said, pissing himself laughing. "They're only pictures. They won't do you any harm."

"Wild beasts and whacky weirdos," I says. "What's that all about? . . ."

"It's a picture about America tonight," he said.

"America," I exclaimed. "Is there a chance that I'd see my lovely Breed and Noreen—God love them!—and Anna Liam? . . ."

"You'll see people like them," he said. "You'll see America."

And of course I did. You never saw anything like it! It's more the pity I couldn't do anything about them? That bloody fire that destroyed my mind completely! . . . But I'm telling you Kitty, everything was as clear as if I was there myself. There was an old woman with a rag wiping the door with a face on her just like Caitriona Paudeen when she'd see Nell and Jack the Lad going on past her coming from the fair . . .

—Holy shite! Abooboona! . . .

—And there was a big spacious room with a round table, just like that one Kitty, that you gave the pound to Caitriona to buy, that time she never gave it back to you . . .

—You're a filthy liar! . . .

—And a silver teapot, like the one in Nell's house, laid out on it.

And then this guy, all dressed in black, except for his golden buttons opened the door. I thought it was the Foxy Cop, but then I remembered that it was in America. Then another man came in with a cap on his head like a messenger boy and himself and the first guy started ballocking one another. Himself and the guy with the golden buttons grabbed the man and shagged him down the stairs. I thought he was going to be completely mangled as they chucked him down three or four flights. Then they kicked him headfirst out the door and nearly bowled the old woman over. I swear Kitty, I really felt sorry for her. My head was all fuzzy.

And then the man looked back and shook his fist at the guy who chucked him out. I thought he was the Old Master—the little button nose and the bitty beady eyes—and Billy the Postman threw him out, but then I remembered it was all in America. And I realised whatever about the Old Master being in America there's no way that Billy could be there as he had to deliver the post every day . . .

—The crook! The sneaky lowlife slime sucker! The . . .

—This guy, the spitting image of Billy, went back upstairs, and there was a woman there all in black sporting some flowers.

"That's the Schoolmistress, if she's alive," I said to myself. But then I remembered this was all happening in America, and the mistress was teaching in the school a few days before this . . .

—The dirty cow! . . .

—De grâce, Master! . . . Now, Dotie . . .

—The guy with the golden buttons opened the door again. Another woman with a small cute nose came in wearing a fur coat, just like the one Baba Paudeen wore when she was home from America but that she had to get rid of because of the snots of soot that slopped down on it in Caitriona's house . . .

—You're a filthy liar, you useless crock of crap! . . .

—. . . Oh, it was a wonderful film, smashing, Dotie! Honest! I was both excited and scared shitless. If you had only seen that bit where Eustasia says to Mrs. Crookshank:

"My dear," she said. "There's no point in getting upset about it. Harry and I are married. We were joined together in matrimony in a registry office on Sixth Avenue this morning. Of course, my dear, Bob is there all the time . . ."

Then she rolled her shoulders kind of triumphantly. Oh, it's really a tragedy that you didn't see the face that Mrs. Crookshank pulled, and she struck dumb! I couldn't help thinking—God forgive me!—of what Nell Paudeen said to Caitriona:

"Sure, you can have Blotchy Brian, Kay."

—You whoring whack! . . . You so-and-so . . . Margaret! Margaret! Did you hear that? Did you hear the trollop of the Toejam trotters, and Breed Terry? I'm going to burst! I'm going to burst! . . .

6.

And so Nell wasted the lorry man! Even though her son was on the wrong side of the road. That judge hadn't a clue. So much for Breed Terry that the law wouldn't leave her with a brass farthing? And she got eight hundred pounds after that! It was the priest, wasn't it? And the holy joke had the cheek to say masses for me . . .

They're making a road into her house. They couldn't have made that road only that my Patrick is so simple. She's taking him for a ride now, just like she did with Jack the Lad about John's Gospel. If I were alive . . .

There hasn't been as much as a peep about the cross anymore. And after what that ugly turkey said: "It would be a shame to put a cross up over that dried-up juice box." Easily known he's not a bit afraid of God or of His holy mother. And he's nearly hitting the hundred! I hope his journey to Dublin kills him! . . .

They've forgotten all about me up above. So it goes, God help us. I didn't think Patrick would go back on his word. That's if that little scut got the story right? Probably not. He was far too set on going to England . . .

If only my own Patrick really knew what things were like stuck here in the dirty dust of the cemetery clay! I'm like a hare trapped by a gang of bloodhounds. Totally harassed and heckled by John Willy, and Kitty, and Breed Terry, the whole shower of them. Trying to keep up with them all on my ownio. And neither soul nor sinner round about to say a word for me. But I won't stand it. I'm about to burst . . .

That whore's melt, Toejam Nora, she's egging them on all the time . . .

And the huge change that came over her daughter and all. I was certain she'd be here ages ago. She's a tough woman, alright. I'm delighted now that she married Patrick. You have to tell the truth. That's how it is. I'd forgive herself and her mother every single thing they ever did on me just because she shoved Nell into the fire on the back of her head, and she didn't leave a wisp of hair, or a tatter of rags, or as much as a strip of clothes on Blotchy Brian to cover him up. And she smashed the dishes. She chucked the tub that Blotchy Brian's young one and Nell were churning in upside down. She stamped on a whole clutch of young chicks on the floor. She clattered Nell's silver teapot against the wall, the one she used to show off on top of the dresser. And she flung the clock that Baba gave to that old scrotumface straight out the window. That's what the youngfella said . . .

She's some woman. I'm sorry now I was so hard on her. To shove Nell arse over head into the fire! Something I never had the good luck to do . . .

And she's got over her sickness now. She's raising hens and pigs and calves. If she lives, she'll do a great job yet . . .

But to shove Nell arse over head into the fire! The back of her white hair was burned. I forgot to ask that youngfella was her white hair sizzled. I'd give all that I ever wanted just to see her dumping Nell in the fire. Isn't it a tragedy that I wasn't alive!

I'd shake her by the hand, I'd give her a big kiss, I'd slap her on the back, I'd order one of those golden bottles that Peter the Publican has in the window, we'd drink to our health, I'd say a prayer for her mother's eternal soul and I'd get her to call her next baby Nora on top of that. What am I talking about? Isn't there a Nora already! . . .

But anyway, I'll call Nora Johnny, I'll tell her all about the great deed her daughter did, and how she is so busy now, and I'll tell her that I'm so thrilled that she is married to my son . . .

And what will Maggie, and Kitty, and Breed Terry, and the whole lot of them say? That I used to be bitching about her; calling her a strap and a slut, and Toejam Nora; that I wouldn't vote for her in the Election . . .

They'll say that. And they'll say also—and 'tis too true—that she told lies about me: she said I had robbed Fireside Tom, that her daughter got a hundred and twenty pounds of a dowry . . .

But let them! I'd forgive her everything just because she shoved Nell arse over head into the fire . . .

Hey Nora! . . . Hello, Nora! . . . Nora, my darling! . . . This is Caitriona Paudeen . . . Nora! . . . Nora my lovely! . . . Did you hear that news from above? . . . about your daughter . . .

What's that Nora? What's that you said? . . . Ababoona! That you have no time to be listening to silly stories about life aboveground! . . . Oh, yea, you had no problem getting involved in the silliness of the Election, and it's left you more stuck in the mud! By cripes! . . . You couldn't be bothered listening to my story . . . It's only something silly, ha! . . . You're going to spend all the rest of your time on . . . on . . . on . . . What's that you called it . . . On culture . . . You don't have the time to be bothered listening to my story as it has nothing to do with . . . with culture . . . Sweet Jesus almighty! . . . Toejam Noreen . . . Toej— Noreen from Gort Ribbuck talking about . . . about culture! . . .

Give me that chunk of English again. As pigs can fly, imagine English in Gort Ribbuck. Give it to me again . . .

—"Art is long and Time is fleeting."

—Fleet! Fleet! That's what you're mainly interested in. Fleets and sailors. Holy Mother of God, I must have had no respect for myself to think that I might get through to you, you So-and-so! . . .

Interlude 6

THE MANGLING EARTH

1.

I am the Trumpet of the Graveyard. Hearken to what I have to say! Hearken unto my voice . . .

Here in the graveyard the autocratic overseer is darkness. His cudgel is the melancholy which does not melt on the smart smirk of the young woman. His lock is the lock of unknowing, and will neither be opened by the lustre of lucre nor by the winsome words of wonder. His eye is the penumbra which peeps from the pox at the edge of the wood. His sentence is the sentence of death from which no cavalier can escape with his sword of valour before he expires.

There aboveground the brightness is resplendent in its radiance. The sun sports a rose-mottled mantle hemmed with the music of the sea and stitched with a seam of birdsong while tassels of butterfly wings belt the stars from the Milky Way. His shield is of the serenity of the bride. His sword of light swirls like a child's. His optimum is the corn which is opening on the stalk, the morning panoply of cloud which is penetrated by a shaft of brightness, the young girl whose vision is still lit by the fresh dreams of love . . .

But the sap is sagging in the trees. The aureate voice of the thrush is coppering. The rose is slouching. The dark rust which ruins, ravages, and runkles is corroding the cavalier's blade.

The darkness is besting the brightness. The graveyard must get its due . . . I am the Trumpet of the Graveyard. Hearken to what I have to say! You must hearken unto my voice . . .

2.

—Who's this now, like? . . . Poxy Martin, be the holies! About time for you, too. I'm here long enough, and we're the same age . . . Yes, that's me, the same woman, Caitriona Paudeen . . .

You had bedsores, you say . . .

Ah, Caitriona, my dear, the bed was very hard. Really hard on my poor arse. My back was really in bits. There wasn't a sliver of flesh on my thighs, and there was a very sensitive spot on my groin. You wouldn't mind, Caitriona, but I was laid up for nine whole months. I couldn't turn or twist. My son used to come in, Caitriona, and turn me on my other side. "I can't really budge my old body at all," I'd say. "I'm a long time laid up," I'd say. "Being laid up a long time never told a lie," he'd say. Ah, Caitriona, my dear, the bed was very hard on my poor arse . . .

—Your arse never felt much, Martin. Did it good . . . Well, if you had bedsores, it's all for the better, they'll help you get used to the planks here . . . Biddy Sarah, you're asking about. She's still alive. We're better off without her. She was an ugly trollop aboveground, not to speak badly about her, but I don't think this place would improve her one tiny bit . . . Yourself and Biddy were always in competition to see which of you would live longer, is that it. That's it, alright. That's it. That's how it is, Poxy . . . But she buried you first all the same! We can do sweet fanny all about that, my poor Martin. Bad shit to her anyway, isn't she the long living thing! She should have died ages ago, only she has no shame . . . Too true for you Martin, it's a wonder she wasn't covered with bedsores she was so fond of the bed. She was sick every single day, except when there was a funeral. Every other day she was choking with a cold. But there wasn't much wrong with her voice on those days. "If I wasn't hoarse," she'd say to you after the funeral, "I would really have keened him." The lying latchico! She's still drawing the pension and hauling in half-crowns and shovelling them into her daughter-in-law's apron. As long as she keeps ladling the money into the apron, her daughter-in-law won't let her get any bedsores, I'm telling you. They'll rub butter on those thighs and hips

. . . She doesn't keen anyone now, she says. What a spouter! . . . Red-ser Tom is laid up too. Another one . . . The shack didn't fall down on Fireside Tom yet, you say . . . Ababoona! Nell bought him a table . . . and a dresser . . . and a bed. A fecking bed! There's no way she'd give a bed to anyone if she didn't want some sneaky money back. Oh, that judge didn't have the least clue! . . . She was scared shitless she'd have sores on the old bed. Listen, Poxy Martin, she was scared shitless she wouldn't get his bit of land . . .

Blotchy Brian, what about him? He'll never pop off until they smear him with oil and put a match to him . . . That's God's honest truth, Poxy Martin. That ugly old wagon will never have bedsores . . . They'll pop off together. That's true, pop off together. I hope their old bones rot together! . . .

What's that? . . . They're all throwing-their-guts-up sick again in Letter Ektur! They were always like that, I'm not blaming them! They'll be a great help to this place, anyway. They'll add to it, and addle it . . .

Our own Baba is down sick in America! By the hokey! . . . Ah, come on like! You think she has bedsores too, Poxy! She has an arse twice as big as yours ever was. And she could keep a nice soft bed under it, unlike you, Poxy Martin . . . Have a bit of sense, you stupid prick . . . You think just because your own bed was hard that every other bed is hard too . . . God help you, there are plenty of soft beds in America, especially if you have money! . . . You never heard whether or not she wrote home, did you? You didn't hear anything about Nell trotting up to the priest recently? . . . No doubt about it, Poxy. She'll guzzle up the will, that's the way she's made . . . The priest is doing the writing for her? What next? . . .

That schoolmaster is no good writing for the likes of us . . . He hasn't a clue about anything, Martin! You're right about that. Every-thing is all right as long as he doesn't go squawking to the priest . . . The priest and the master are often seen out strolling together, you say . . . The new road to Nell's house is nearly finished. Why did that eejit of a son of mine have the misfortune to give her Lack Ard! . . .

Nell is talking about building a house with a slate roof! With a slate roof! I hope she never lives to see her house with a slate roof, the piece of poop! Maybe she's got some of the will already? That crowd in Derry Lough got a slice of it, before their brother died at all ... And of course, she had the money from the court case. They'll certainly bury her in the Pound Plot now ...

Jack is still ailing. The poor man! Nell and Blotchy Brian's young one, that long string of misery, they fixed him up with St. John's Gospel! ... You never heard about St. John's Gospel! ... You heard something, you must have! Do you think they'd tell you anything about it! ...

Patrick's wife is up at the crack of dawn every morning! God bless her! ... There are lots of calves on Patrick's land, is that it? ... Wife has taken over all the business from Patrick! ... She does the buying and selling now! Would you believe it! And there I was thinking she'd be here any day soon! ... But, of course, you never know with a young one, do you? ... There was something crippling you. Bedsores ... You'd easily know, Poxy Martin, that you're very new in this place when you're talking like that. Don't you know that you must die from something, and bedsores are as good as anything else ...

Ababoona! You heard that they've given up on the cross! You heard that! ... Now, come on, Poxy Martin, maybe that wasn't what you heard at all, but that you got the wrong end of the stick completely because of all those bedsores you had ... You heard they're not going ahead with it ... That Nell was talking to Patrick about the cross ... You don't know, you don't want to tell a lie, you don't know what she said. Come off it, Poxy Martin, forget about that "don't want to tell a lie" stuff.

"Don't want to tell a lie"! Nell wouldn't be afraid to tell plenty of lies about you, if it suited her ... And you wishing her luck like fuck! You're finished with the bed now, anyway. Spit out your story ... You didn't know how bad it would be! You had bedsores! Listen now, just for a moment even. Maybe Nell said something like this to my Patrick: "Come here to me now, Paddy my dear, you have enough on your plate now not to be thinking of a cross ..." Oh, it was Nora Johnny's one said that! Patrick's wife said that! ... "We'll certainly be on top of things when we can afford to buy a cross . . . There are plenty just as good as her with no cross at all . . . She's damned lucky to be buried in a graveyard at all, and the way things are." She'd say that, alright. The sly slit of the Toejam tipple! But it was Nell taught her. I hope not another corpse comes to the graveyard before her! . . . Patrick won't take a blind bit of notice of them . . .

Patrick's daughter is back at home . . . Maureen is back home! Are you sure she's not just taking a break from school? . . . She failed her exams. She failed! . . . She's not going to be a schoolteacher after all . . . Shag her anyway! Shag her! . . .

Nora Johnny's grandson from Gort Ribbuck has gone . . . On a boat from the Fancy City . . . He got a job on the ship . . . Just like his grandmother, he really likes his sailors . . .

Say that again . . . Say that again . . . Nell's grandson is going for the priesthood. Blotchy Brian's daughter's youngfella is going to be a priest! A priest! That little feckless fart face going to be a priest! . . . He's already gone to the seminary . . . He was wearing the priest's garb at home . . . And the collar . . . And lugging a huge big prayer book around under his oxter . . . Reading his office up and down the new road at Lack Ard! You'd think that he'd never make a priest overnight, just like that . . . Oh, he's not a priest yet, he's just going to the college. Aha, Poxy Martin, they'll never make a priest out of him ever . . .

What then, what did Blotchy Brian say? . . . Don't be chewing and chomping, just spit it out . . . You're afraid to, is that it? You're afraid to! . . . Because Blotchy Brian is related to me by marriage. It's to that wench of a sister he's related. Spit it out . . . "My daughter has money to burn to make a priest." Money to burn on a priest. The wrinkly old wretch! . . . Spit it out, or go to hell! Hurry up or they'll have whipped you off too. You don't think that I'd let you down into this grave and you riddled with bedsores for months . . . "Caitriona Paudeeen's boy couldn't even do that much . . ." Spit out the rest of it, you old gimp . . . "He didn't have enough to put as much as a stitch of a college petticoat on his daughter." Blotchy bastard Brian! The bumming bastard! . . .

Screw you! You're muttering again . . . Nell is singing "Eleanor

'Aroon" up and down the road every day! Get stuffed, you mangy rash-arsed mong. You never had a good word to say, nor anybody belonging to you . . .

3.

—. . . Do you think this is "The War of the Two Foreigners"? . . .

—. . . There I was giving a word for every pint to the Great Scholar, and he was giving me a pint for every word . . .

Over and back again the next day. The third day he had the car under his arse. The journey over and back was flaying us out.

"Paul, darling," my mother says to me that evening, "there should be a good bit of drying on the grass from now on."

"What do mean, drying, Ma?" I says. "You could never dry that crappy grass . . ."

She was on about it for a fortnight before I succeeded in making a few haycocks. Then I took it down again, and turned it up and turned it over and turned it around.

It was like that until one day when it pissed rain and the two of us were inside in Peter's Pub. I had to up and lay it all out again to give it some more sun.

Then I gutted the gullies, flattened the fences, built them up again, then I cut the grass on the side of the road, brushed away the bracken, bundled the briars out of the way. I carved out culverts. We spent nearly a month in the front field, except that we'd be over and back in the car to Peter's Pub all the time . . .

I never met anyone as nice as him. And he wasn't stupid either. He collected about twenty to thirty words of Irish every day. He had bags of money. A big fat Government job . . .

But the day he headed off without me Peter the Publican's daughter took him into the parlour and started to jizz him up . . .

I was really very fond of him. The week just after he left, I got flattened and that was the end of me . . . But hey, Postmistress . . . Hoora, Postmistress! . . . How do you know that he never paid for his lodging? You opened the letter my mother sent about it to the Government . . .

—And how do you know, Postmistress, how do you know that The Goom didn't accept my collection of poetry, *The Yellow Stars?* . . .

—Ah, for feck's sake, it's too bad about you. They'd have published you yonks ago if you did as I said and wrote from the bottom to the top of the page. But, hey, how about me, *The Irelander* rejected my short story "The Setting of the Sun," and the Postmistress knew that too . . .

—And the Postmistress knew well the advice I gave to Cannon how to crock the Kerry team in the letter I sent him two days after the semifinal . . .

—And how was it, Postmistress, that you knew about what I had said to the Judge about the Dog Eared crowd when we were taking them to court? . . .

—And how was it, Postmistress, that your own daughter, who just happens to be a postmistress now, how come she knew that I wouldn't be allowed into England because I had TB, how come she knew it before me? . . .

—You opened a letter that Caitriona Paudeen sent to Mannix the Counsellor about Fireside Tom. The world and its mother knew what was in it:

"We will take him to the Fancy City in a car. We will get him drunk. If you had a couple of hot broads in the office getting him turned on, maybe he'd sign over the land to us. He's a whore for the young ones when he's pissed . . ."

—Abuboona! . . .

—You slitted open letters from the woman in the bookies in the Fancy City that she sent to the Young Master. You used to have tips about the horses before he had a clue about them himself . . .

—Holy God, Mary, Joseph, and all the saints! Ababoona! . . .

—You opened a letter that Caitriona Paudeen sent to Blotchy Brian saying she'd marry him no problem . . .

—Abuboona, boona boona! That I would marry foul fuckmouth Blotchy bastard Brian . . .

—Just so, Postmistress, I had nothing to thank you for. You always had the kettle simmering away in the back room. You opened a letter my son sent to me saying he married a Yid. The whole country knew about it, and we said neither a jot nor a tittle about it to nobody. What was that about? . . .

—You opened a letter that my son had sent me from England telling me he had married a black. The whole world knew about it, although we weren't mentioning a word about it to anyone.

—I wrote to de Valera advising him what he should say to the people of Ireland. You kept it buried in the Post Office. You shouldn't have done that . . .

—Every single love letter that Caitriona's Paddy wrote to my daughter, you opened it first. I never opened one of them that I didn't know that you had peeped at it already. Honestly. I remembered the letters I got long before that. I warned the postman he had to give them to me directly into my paw. Their lovely exotic smell. Exotic paper. Exotic writing. Exotic stamps. Exotic postmarks that were poetry to my ears: Marseilles, Port Said, Singapore, Honolulu, Batavia, San Francisco . . . The sun, oranges, blue seas. Sun beauty skin. Peninsulas of Paradise. Gold-rimmed garments. Ebony-toothed glittering grins. Lusty lapping lips . . . I'd suck them to my heart. I'd kiss them with my mouth. I'd cuddle them to my heart . . . I'd open them up . . . I'd take out the *billet doux*. And it's only after that, Miss Postmistress, that I would see your slimy slinky paw on any of them. Ogh! . . .

—You opened the letter I sent home to my wife, when I was working on the turf in Kildare. I had nine pounds in it. You kept the lot . . .

—And why not? Why didn't you register it? . . .

—And don't you think that The Old Man of the Graveyard might have something to say also? Let me speak. Let me speak . . .

—Most certainly, Postmistress, there's no way I'd be grateful to you or to your daughter, or to Billy who gave you a hand in the back room. Every single letter that came to me from London, after I came home, you had opened it. There was an *affaire de coeur,* as

Nora Johnny might say, involved. You told the whole world about it. The priest heard about it, and the Schoolmistress—my wife—heard about it . . .

—That's slander, Master. If you were aboveground I'd sue you . . .

—That time when Baba wrote to me from America about the will, Nell, the blabbermouth, was able to tell Patrick what she said:

"I haven't made my will yet. I hope I won't come to a sudden end, as you hoped in your letter . . ."

You opened it, you pisshead pustule . . . You got that nasty streak from Nell.

—Not at all, Caitriona Paudeen, I didn't open the letter about the will at all, but a letter from O'Brien Solicitors in the Fancy City threatening you with the law within seven days if you didn't pay Holland and Company for the round table you had purchased five or six years previously . . .

—Abuboona! Don't believe her, the mangy maggot! Margaret! Margaret! . . . Did you hear what the Postmistress said? I'm going to burst! I'll burst! . . .

4.

—. . . I'll tell you a story now, my good man:

"Colm Cille was in Aran when St. Paul visited him there. Paul wanted to have the whole island for himself.

"'I'm going to open a pawnshop,' Paul says.

"'You will in your balls,' says Colm Cille, 'but I'm telling you straight up in plain Irish to get the fuck out of here.'

"Then he spoke to him in Legalese. Then he spoke to him in Latin. And then in Greek. In childish gibberish. In Esperanto. Colm Cille knew the seven languages of the Holy Ghost. He was the only one to whom the apostles gave the gift of tongues, when they were dying . . .

"'OK, so,' says Colm Cille, 'seeing as you won't fuck off, by virtue of the powers that have been invested in me, we'll fix it like this. You'll go off to the arse end of Aran and I'll go to the west of the island as far as Bun Gowla. Both of us will say Mass at the crack of dawn tomorrow. Then we will walk towards one another, and howsomuchever of the island we will have walked when we meet, we will own that much.'

"'That's a deal, then,' Paul said, in Yiddish. Colm Cille said the Mass and off he walked towards the arse end of Aran, and that's where we get the saying, 'being caught arse-ways' . . ."

—But, hey, Coley, John Kitty in Bally Donough used to say that Colm Cille never said a Mass in his life . . .

—John Kitty said that! John Kitty is a heretic . . .

—So what if John Kitty says what he likes? Didn't God himself—all praise to him—reveal himself there? The sun was up just as Colm Cille was saying his Mass. Then it went down, and God kept it down until Colm Cille had walked to the arse end of Aran. And it was only then that St. Paul saw it rising for the first time! . . .

"'You may as well toddle off now, Shnozzle,' says Colm Cille. 'I'll leave you weeping when you return to the Wailing Wall: the exact same horsewhipping you got when Christ drove you out of the Temple. You should be ashamed of yourself! Who would give a damn only that you are so greasy and sneaky as you slither away . . .'"

"That's exactly why no Jew boy settled in Aran ever since . . ."

—This's the way that I heard that story from oldfellas in my own place, Coley: when the two Patricks—Old Patrick *alias* Cothraighe, *alias* Calprainnovich, and Young Patrick—when they were hawking around Ireland trying to change the country . . .

—Two Patricks! That's a heresy . . .

—. . . There was a day like that, Peter the Publican. Don't deny it . . .

—Master, my darling, the bed was very hard. Really very hard underneath my poor arse, Master . . .

—I was only in it about a month, Poxy Martin, and I found it very hard . . .

—My back was totally flattened, Master. There wasn't even a screed of a shred of skin left on my backside . . .

—Not as much as a screed, Martin, you poor hoor . . .

—Not as much as a screed, my dear Master, and there was a very tender spot in my groin. The bed was . . .

—Let us forget about the bed until some other time. Tell me this much, Poxy, how is . . . ?

—The Mistress, Master. O, she's flying, not a bother. She earns her money every day at school, Master, and then she looks after Billy from then until the morning. She flashes over from the school twice a day to look after him, and they say that the poor thing hardly sleeps a wink, but is only sitting on the edge of the bed giving him his medicine . . .

—The cuntish gash . . . the brasser . . .

—Did you hear, Master, that she brought him three doctors from Dublin? Our own doctor visits him three times every day, but I'd say, Master, that it's kind of wasted on Billy. He's been laid up so long now that he couldn't not be riddled with bedsores . . .

—I hope he lies and never rises! I hope he gets the thirty-seven diseases of the Ark! I hope all his tubes get glutted and his bunghole stuffed! That he gets a clubfoot and a twisted gut! The Ulster flies! The yellow bellies! The plague of Lazarus! Job's jitters! Swine snots! Lock arse! Drippy disease, flatulent farts, wobbly warbles, wriggly wireworm, slanty eyes, and the shitty scutters! May he get the death rattle of Slimwaist Big Bum! The decrepit diseases of the Hag of Beare! May he be blinded without a glimmer and be gouged like Oisín after that! The Itch of the Women of the Prophet! His knees explode! His rump redden with rubenescence! Be lanced by lice! . . .

—Bedsores are the worst of them all, dear Master . . .

—May he get bedsores too so, Poxy Martin.

—She makes the Stations of the Cross twice a day, Master, and the trip to Killeana's Well every week. She did the Mountain Pilgrimage this year, and Croagh Patrick, and Colm Cille's Well, Mary's Well, Augustine's Well, Enda's Well, Bernine's Well, Cauleen's Well, Shinny's Well, Boadakeen's Well, Conderg's Bed, Bridget's Pool, Lough Nave, and Lough Derg . . .

—Isn't a great pity I'm not alive! I'd drain Brickeen's Well on the thief, on the . . .

—She told me too, Master, that if it wasn't for the way things are so dicey at the moment she'd go to Lourdes.

"Lough Derg is the worst of them, Poxy Martin," she said. "My feet were pumping blood for three whole days. But it didn't matter to me how I suffered as long as it did poor Billy some good. I'd crawl from here to . . ."

—The thundering bitch . . .

—"I was heartbroken after the Old Master," she said . . .

—Oh, the whore of a thundering bitch! . . . If you only knew, Poxy! Ah, but you wouldn't understand. There'd be no point in telling you . . .

—Well, anyway, Master, the truth is the bed was too hard . . .

—Will you hump off to hell hollering on about that bed, and just listen to her! . . . Oh, the things that that bitch of a one said to me, Martin! . . .

—I know that's all true, Master . . .

—The pair of us sitting down in Crompaun. The gentle susurration of the suds caressing the rocks at our feet. A young seagull calling to his father and mother to thrill about his first flight, not unlike unto a shy bride approaching the altar. The shades of evening sliding across the shafts of sunlight on the crest of the waves, like the young kestrel slowly shaping to snatch the unready. The oars of the currach returning from its fishing grounds plashing in the water. She's in my arms, Martin. A wisp of her gorgeous hair gently touching my cheek. Her hands are around my neck. I am quoting poetry:

> "Glen Mason:
> Rock high, sun facing.
> We slept all evening
> On its sward and apron
>
> "'If you come, my love, come like one creeping,
> Come to the door that admits no creaking
> If my father asks who it is I'm seeking
> I will say it's the wind outside that's keening.'"

Either that or reciting love stories, Martin . . .

—I get that alright, Master . . .

—The Sons of Uisneach, Diarmaid, and Gráinne, Tristan and Isolde, Strong Tom Costello and Fair Una McDermott, Carol O'Daly and Eleanor Aroon, *The Hot Kiss, The Powder Puff* . . .

—I get that too, Master . . .

—I bought a car straight up, Martin, just to take her out and about. I could hardly afford it, but I thought she was worth it anyway. We'd go into the pictures in the Fancy City, to dances in Derry Dav, to teachers' meetings . . .

—That's all true, and up the Hill Road, Master. There was that day when I was going for a creel of turf and your car was planked there at the side of the road at Ardeen More, and the two of you over beyond in the glen . . .

—OK, forget about that now, Guzzeye Martin, until some other time . . .

—But for all that, Master, I also remember that day when I got the news about the pension. Not one of us in the whole house had the least clue, by the mebs of the Devil himself, what it was about. "The Old Master is the boy for us." I says. I went on over to Peter the Publican's place and stayed there until all the students had gone. I went back then. When I got back to the schoolhouse all I could hear was moaning and groaning and sighing. "I left it too late," I says to myself, "pretending to be proper, according to myself. He's gone off home." I gawked in through the window. Saving your presence, Master, there you were with her, bonking and beasting away . . .

—I wasn't. I wasn't, Poxy Martin, no I wasn't.

—Ah, but you were, Master, there's nothing better than telling the truth . . .

—Good for you, Master! . . .

—You have no reason to be ashamed, Master.

—Who would ever have thought it, Breed? . . .

—We were sending our children to him, Kitty . . .

—If the priest had caught him, Joan . . .

—It was Whit Sunday, Poxy. I had the day off. "We should go

down to Ross Harbour," I said to her, after dinner. "Getting out and about will do you no end of good." She did. We went. I really thought, Martin, that I knew what she was all about, that night on Ross Harbour . . . The long summer day was fading in the west after its long labours. Both of us were lovingly stretched on a rock observing the stars glittering on the shiny surface of the sea . . .

—Yes, I get that too, Master . . .

—Gazing at the candles being lit one by one in the houses shining on the far side of the bay. Gazing at the whisk of the will o' the wisp wending on the seaweed on the well of the tide. Gazing at the sparkly dust of the weather coming in from beyond the mouth of the harbour. I can tell you, Martin, on that wonderful night I felt myself part of all those stars and lights and flashing phosphorescence and the wonder of the weather and the sweet soughing of the surf and the elevation of the air . . .

—Ah, yea, sure, I get it all, Master. That's the way it is . . .

—She swore to me, Martin, that her love for me was deeper than the deep blue sea; that she was more faithful than the rising and the setting of the sun; more permanent than the ebb and flow of the tide, than the stars and the mountains, that her love for me predated tides, and stars, and mountains. She swore to me that her love was of a piece with eternity itself . . .

—She said that, Master! . . .

—She said that, Poxy Martin. She said that, by the hammers of hell! . . . But hang on a minute. I was on my deathbed. She came in and she had just made the Pilgrimage of the Cross, and she sat down on the edge of the bed. She took my hand. She said that if anything happened to me her life would not be worth living, and her death would not be a death unless we should both die together. She promised and pledged no matter how long she lived after me that she would spend the rest of her days done down and depressed. She promised and pledged that she would never marry again . . .

—She promised all that, Master! . . .

—She swore and asseverated, Poxy Martin! . . . And despite all that she had the poisoned serpent in her heart all that time. I was only buried a year—one short miserable year compared with the eternity she had promised me—and there she was swearing fealty to someone else who wasn't me, someone else whose kisses, not mine, were on her lips, and someone else's love that wasn't mine in her heart. Me, I was her first love and her husband, me laid under the cold sods of the grave and she hot in the arms of Billy the Postman . . .

—True, hot in the arms of Billy the Postman, Master! I saw it myself . . . We have to forget about a lot of things, Master . . .

—And now, there he is on my bed, and she giving him gung-ho and giddy-up and go-for-it, looking after him from morning to night, going on retreats for him, sending for doctors, three of them, from Dublin, to look after him . . .

. . . If she had sent for even one doctor from Dublin to look after me, I would have been all right . . .

—You'd never believe what she told me about you, Master? I went into her with a bag of spuds just a week after you were buried. We were talking about you. "That was terrible news about the Old Master," I said, "and there was really no need for it. If he had stayed in bed with that flu, and looked after himself, and drank a few quaffs of whiskey, and sent for the doctor at the beginning . . ." "Do you know the real truth, Poxy?" she says to me. I will always remember exactly what she said, Master. "Do you know the real truth, Poxy Martin, all the doctors in the world couldn't save the Old Master. He was too good for this life . . ." That was it, bejasus, Master, and she said something else that I had never heard before. I think it's an old saying, but I can't be sure. "He whom the gods love, dies young . . ."

—The bitch! The witch! The cuntinental cow! . . .

—De grâce, Master. Speak nicely if you please. Don't be like Caitriona Paudeen. The chaplain came to visit her one day. He was new in the parish. He didn't know where Nell's house was. "Nell, that whore," Caitriona said. Honest! . . .

—You tramp of the Toejam trollops! You so-and-so! . . . Hey, Margaret! . . .

5.

—. . . He was there ready and waiting for Blotchy Brian collecting his pension every Friday. "You'd be well advised to grab a fist of insurance for yourself from now on, Briany," the wretch says. "Who knows, any one of these days you might go the way of all flesh . . ."

— "There's no guarantee that that useless old crockery wouldn't take out insurance himself," Blotchy Brian said to me one Friday in the Post Office, "or on anything apart from Nell Paudeen's little pup who used to come in regularly and sniffle around on Caitriona's floor."

—I was over with Brian myself getting the pension the day he was buried.

"The insurance lad didn't last too long after, either," I said.

"There he is heading away there now, the sewer sucker," Brian says, "and if he goes up, he'll piss The Man Above off with his never-ending guff about the accident that happened ages ago, and trying to get him to insure his holy and angelic property against the pyromania of yer Man Below. And if The Man Below gets it, he'll piss him off getting him to insure his few embers against the wiles of yer Man Above. They both of them couldn't do any better to that louse lackey than what Fireside Tom did to him: every time he didn't want Nell's cattle on his patch of land, he drove them into Caitriona's, and then Caitriona's cattle into Nell's . . ."

—Did you hear what he said when that headbanger Tim Top of the Road died?

— "Sweet Jumping Jesus, boys, St. Peter had better be looking after his keys from now on, or this new blow-in will have filched them from him in no time . . ."

—And I'll tell you one thing for nothing, do you know what he said to Fireside Tom when Caitriona died:

"Thomas, my beautiful angel," he said, "Yourself, and Nell, and Baba, and Nora Johnny's young one will have to be constantly calling into the Celestial Smithy to get their wings mended, that is, if God grants that you be allowed around the same place as herself. I'd say I only have a very slim chance of getting wings, though. Caitriona never thought me good enough. But do you know what Thomas, my gentle dove, you'd have no problem at all with anything broken if I could get myself a little cubbyhole of my own near her . . ."

—Ababoona! Brian next to me to torture me! God forbid! What would I do at all? . . .

—The Postmistress told me that she couldn't open any letters when I died she was so busy with the telegrams . . .

—My death was in the newspaper . . .

—My death was in two newspapers . . .

—Listen to the account of my death in the *Daily News*:

"He was of an old and highly renowned family in the area. He played a significant part in the national movement. He was a personal acquaintance of Eamon de Valera . . ."

—This is the description of my death in *The Irish Observer*:

"He belonged to a family that was very well liked in the area. He joined the Fenian Scouts when he was a boy, and after that he joined the Irish Volunteers. He was an intimate friend of Arthur Griffith . . ."

—. . . Coley told the story of "The pullet who was born on the dung heap" at your wake, also.

—You're lying! That's a disgusting story to tell at any respectable wake! . . .

—But, wasn't I listening to him! . . .

—You're lying, you were not! . . .

—. . . A row at your wake! A row at a wake where there were only two old pensioners!

—And one of them as deaf as Fireside Tom when Caitriona was trying to persuade him to come to visit Mannix the Counsellor about the bit of land.

—All true, and every vessel in the house was overflowing with holy water.

—There was a row at my wake . . .

—There sure was. Fireside Tom took it upon himself to say to Blotchy:

"You've drunk enough of Ned of the Hill's buttermilk since you came in, Tom, that you must have enough already for churning."

—There were two barrels at my wake . . .

—Three at mine . . .

—That's true, Caitriona, there were three of them at your wake. That's the bare honest truth for you, Caitriona. There were three of them there—three fine big ones—and a few shots from Ned of the Hill's magic waterworks also . . . And even if I was the oldfella, I still drank twelve mugs of it. To tell you God's honest truth, Caitriona, there's no way I would have swilled that much if I knew that my heart was a bit dicey. What I said to myself was, as my eyes were staring at the pints of porter: "Wouldn't it be a lot better for this guy to buy a colt rather than to be getting pissed with shit artists . . ."

—You pompous piss artist! . . .

—That's what they were. Some of them were laid out smashed drunk on the ground in the way of everyone else. It even happened that Peter Nell fell on top of the bed you were laid out on, Caitriona. His leg was gone, the one that was injured.

—The sneaky swill slurper!

—The best of it all was when Breed Terry's youngfella and Kitty's son started beating the crap out of one another, and then smashed the round table before they could be separated . . .

—Holy fuckaroni! Ababoona! . . .

—I split them up. If I knew then that my heart was a bit dicey . . .

—. . . It appeared to me, anyway, that you were laid out in the proper traditional way, unless my eyes were deceiving me . . .

—Then your eyes didn't see the two crosses on my breast . . .

—I had two crosses and the scapulars . . .

—Whatever they had on me, or they didn't have on me, Kitty, it wasn't a dirty sheet like there was on Caitriona . . .

—Ababoona! Don't believe a word from that mangy maggot's mouth . . .

—. . . You had a coffin that was made by the little scutty carpenter from Gort Ribbuck. He made another one for Nora Johnny and 'twas as small as a bird's cage . . .

—Your coffin was made by a carpenter as well . . .

—That may be so, but it wasn't the jobber from Gort Ribbuck, but a proper carpenter who had served his time. He had qualifications from the Tec . . .

—My coffin cost ten pounds . . .

—I thought yours only cost eight pounds: just like Caitriona's one . . .

—You're a liar, you microphallic muppet! I had the best coffin from Tim's shop . . .

—Little Kitty laid me out.

—Me too, and Biddy Sarah keened me . . .

—Then she didn't make a very good job of it. There's a kind of a lump in Biddy's throat and it doesn't melt until about the seventh glass. Then she starts up with "Let Erin Remember" . . .

—Anyway, I don't think anyone keened Caitriona at all, unless her son's wife or Nell sang a few bars . . .

—. . . Your altar was only six pounds ten . . .

—Mine was ten pounds.

—Hang on a minute now, 'til I see what mine was . . . 20 by 10 plus 19, that makes 190 . . . plus 20, that's 210 shillings . . . that comes to 10 pounds, 10 shillings. Isn't that right, Master? . . .

—Peter the Publican had a huge altar . . .

—And Nora Johnny . . .

—That's true, Nora Johnny had a big altar. I would have had a big altar too, only nobody knew about it, I went too quickly. The heart, God help me! Just the same as if I had been laid up and had bedsores . . .

—I would have had fourteen pounds exactly, except that there was a bad shilling with it. It was only a halfpenny that somebody had covered with fag paper. Blotchy Brian noticed it, and he copped on to the trick. He said that it was Caitriona Paudeen put it there. She had put many bad shillings like that on the altar. She tried to be at every altar like that but she couldn't afford it, the poor wretch . . .

—You lying son of a poor rat bastard! . . .

—Oh, I forgive you, Caitriona. I wouldn't give a tinker's curse or an itinerant's malediction about, if it wasn't for the priest. "They'll be plonking their old rotten teeth on the plate for me soon," he said . . .

—I only ever heard "Paul this," and "Paul that" from yourself and your daughter that time when she jizzed up the Great Scholar in the parlour. But there was no mention of Paul when you had to put a shilling on my altar . . .

—After I had drunk forty-two pints I tied Tomaseen up, but not one of his kip and kin or anybody from his house bothered their arse to come to my funeral, even though we're in the same town land. They hardly put as much as a shilling on my altar the lot of them together. They all had a cold, or so they said. That was all the thanks I got, even though he was stuck like shit to a blanket. Imagine, like, if he had to be tied up again? . . .

—I didn't have a very big funeral. Most of Bally Donough had gone to England, and Gort Ribbuck also, and Clogher Savvy . . .

—. . . And what do you think of Caitriona Paudeen, Kitty, who didn't as much as darken the door of our house since my father passed away, despite all the cups of tea she polished off . . .

—That was the time she was going to Mannix the Counsellor about Fireside Tom's land . . .

—Do you hear that old strap Breed Terry, and manky Kitty of the piddly potatoes? . . .

—I had to clamp my hand three times over the mouth of that old windbag over there, where he was singing: "Martin John More had a beautiful daughter" at your funeral, Curran . . .

—The whole country was at your funeral, journalists and photographers, the lot . . .

—And for a good reason! You were blown up by the mine, all of you. If you had died on the old bed just like me, there wouldn't have been a journalist or a photographer next or near the place . . .

—*Bien de monde* was at funeral *à moi. Le Ministre de France* from *Dublin* came to mine and he laid a *couronne mortuaire* on my grave . . .

—There was a representative of Eamon de Valera at my funeral, and the Tricolour was on my coffin . . .

A telegram from Arthur Griffith came to my funeral and shots were fired over the grave . . .

—That's a lie!

—No, you're the liar. I was First Lieutenant of the First Company of the First Battalion of the First Brigade . . .

—That's a lie!

—God save us, for ever and ever! Wasn't it a disaster that they never brought my bag of bones east of the Fancy City!

—The Big Butcher came to my funeral from the Fancy City. He respected me, and his father respected my father. He often said to me that he respected me because of the respect that his father had for my father . . .

—The doctor came to my funeral. That was hardly a surprise, of course. My daughter Kate has two sons doctors in the States . . .

—Now you tell us! That was hardly a surprise, indeed. So that he wouldn't be entirely shamed—after all the money you had given him—he came to your funeral. And you twisting your ankle every second month . . .

—The Old Master and the Mistress were at my funeral . . .

—The Old Master and the Mistress and the Foxy Cop were at my funeral . . .

—The Old Master and the Mistress and the Foxy Cop and the priest's sister were at my funeral . . .

—The priest's sister! Tell me, was she wearing the pants? . . .

—It was a disgrace that Mannix the Counsellor didn't come to Caitriona Paudeen's funeral . . .

—It was, disgraceful. Nor the priest's sister . . .

—Nor the Foxy Cop . . .

—He was checking out the dogs in Bally Donough that day . . .

—No dog would survive on the flea-ridden baldy bumps of your place . . .

—. . . "Fireside Tom's grin was as wide as a gate,

He'd have Nell now, as buried was Cate . . ."

—I'm telling you, Caitriona Paudeen, if I could have helped it at all, I would have been at your funeral. It wouldn't be right for me not to be at Caitriona Paudeen's funeral, even if I had to crawl there on my hands and knees. But I never heard a whisper about it 'til the night of the burial . . .

—You're an old codger, Chalky Steven. How long are you here? I didn't know you were here at all. The bad pains . . .

—There were gangs of people at my funeral. The Parish Priest, The Chaplain, The Chaplain from Lough Shore, A Franciscan and Two Brothers from the Fancy City, The Schoolmaster and Mistress from Derry Lough, The Master and Mistress from Kin Teer, The Master from Clogher Savvy, The Master from Glen Beg, and the Junior Mistress, The Assistant Teacher from Kill . . .

—No doubt about it, every single one of them, Master, and Billy the Postman too. To tell you the truth he was very helpful that day. He fastened and screwed down the bolts on the coffin, he carried it out of the house, and he slid it down into the grave. In all fairness, he wasn't either slow or sluggish. He threw off his jacket with gusto and grabbed the shovel . . .

—The robber! The homuncular homo! . . .

—There were five cars at my funeral . . .

—Yea, that gimp from Derry Lough, his car got stuck right in the middle of things, and your funeral was an hour late . . .

—There were as many as thirty at Peter the Publican's. He had two hearses . . .

—Just as you mentioned it, I had a hearse as well. The old woman wouldn't rest easy until she had got one: "His guts would be all shook up if he was up on their shoulders, or being hauled in an old cart," she said . . .

—Oh, it was easy for her to talk, Tim Top of the Road, with my turf . . .

—And my wrack from the sea . . .

—. . . There weren't enough there to even haul Caitriona to the church they were so mouldy from the booze. Even they started to act the maggot. They had to let her corpse down twice, the way they were. I swear they did: smack bang in the middle of the road . . .

—God help us! Ababoona!

—I'm telling you God's honest truth, Caitriona, love. There were only six of us from beyond Walsh's pub. The rest of them went into Walsh's, or else they fell by the wayside. We thought we'd have to get the women to carry the corpse . . .

—Ababoona! Don't believe him, the bollocks . . .

—That's the whole bare unadorned truth, Caitriona. You were heavy as hell. You weren't sick that long, and you had no bedsores.

"The two old buckos will have to lift her," Peter Nell says just near the lane at Clogher Savvy. The old men were great, Caitriona. Peter Nell was on crutches and Kitty's youngfella and Breed Terry's youngfella were beating the shit out of one another, metaphorically, like: each one blaming the other about smashing up the round table the night before. The truth is always the best, Caitriona. There is no way I would carry the coffin, or even go a step of the way with you, if I knew then that I had a dicey heart . . .

—Too busy piddling around with periwinkles, you piss artist . . .

—"There she is, still acting the mule. You wouldn't know from hell if she wanted to go to the church or even to the cemetery," Blotchy Brian said, while himself and myself and Kitty's youngfella were lifting you up to take you in along the church path . . .

"Not a word of a lie, my good friend," Peter Nell says, as he dumps his crutches, and goes in up and under the coffin . . .

—That's really the pits! The slut's son carrying my coffin. Blotchy Brian carrying me. The beardy bastard. If that twisted hunch humped whore was carrying me, then the coffin was baw ways. Abooboona boona! . . . Blotchy Brian the bum! . . . Nell's son! Margaret! Margaret! . . . If I had known all about it I would have burst. I would have burst on the spot . . .

6.

—. . . Are you telling me now, that they don't take any insurance on colts? . . .

—Well, my kind of insurance broker wouldn't take it anyway, Johnny.

—You'd think you weren't taking any chance with a fine healthy young horse. It would be well worth it, before anything happened, to get a big pot of money . . .

—I nearly got a big pot myself, Johnny, in the crossword in *The Sunday Scandal*. Five hundred pounds . . .

—Five hundred pounds! . . .

—That was it, by Jaysus, Johnny. I only had one letter wrong . . .

—I get it . . .

—What they wanted was a word in eight letters ending in "e." The clue said that it meant something that flew through the air by means of mechanical propulsion.

—Yea, I still get it.

—I immediately thought of the word "aeroplane," as I had seen them flying in the sky. But that was nine letters . . .

—Yea, still with you.

—"That can't be it," I said to myself. I spent ages and aeons wracking my brains and torturing myself. Anyway, in the end I put down "aerplane," as I couldn't think of anything else . . .

—I get it.

—But what do you know, when the answer came out on the paper it was "airplane"! Fuck that new spelling anyway Johnny! If I had a handgun I'd blow my brains out. That was one of the reasons why my life was cut short . . .

—Now, I really get it.

—. . . By the oak of this coffin, Chalky Steven, I swear I gave her, I gave Caitriona Paudeen the pound . . .

—. . . He had a broad grin on his mug . . .

—That stupid grin that the Junior Master makes is a good sign, anyway! He might go the way of the Old Master, who knows. There's some kind of curse on our school that the women don't get on with the masters there . . .

—. . . I'll tell you now the advice I gave to Cannon after he won the semifinal for Galway:

"Cannon, my hero," I says to him, "even if you don't manage to kick the ball in the final against Kerry, kick something. There must be some kind of equality in clocking people. The ref will be up for Kerry anyway. Why else would they have won so many All-Irelands? You can do it. You have the guts and the balls for it. Every time you clobber something, I will raise the roof . . ."

—Hitler is my darling! I can't wait for him to get to England! . . . I'm sure he'll damn them all to hell and the devils will be dancing on the dunes of England: that he'll give the bum's rush to their snotty snoots: that he'll plant a million tons of mines in their belly buttons . . .

—God help us all! . . .

—Ah, come on, you can't say anything bad about England. There's lashings of work there. What would the youth of Bally Donough, or for that matter, the crowd from Gort Ribbuck, and Cloghar Savvy do without her . . .

—Or the old gom over here who has a slice of land up above the town land that is the very best, beyond measure, for fattening cattle up . . .

—*Après la fuite de Dunkerque et la bouleversement de Juin 1940, Monsieur Churchill a dit qu'il retournerait pour libérer la France, la terre sacrée* . . .

—You shouldn't let any black heretic like that insult your religion, Peter. It was fucking lucky I wasn't there! I'd have asked him straight up, no bullshit: "Do you believe in God at all? Maybe you're just like a cow or a calf, or like a . . . cunty little pup." A dog doesn't give a fuck about anything only to fill his gut. A dog would eat meat on a Friday, I'm telling you that. It would be just great, just great for him. But, of course, not every dog would eat it, either . . . I had a smidgen of meat left over when I was in the town, one time. "I'll drag it out 'til Saturday," I says, "Tomorrow's a fast day, no meat" . . .

Coming in from eating out on Friday when I was returning from the fields with a fist of spuds, I saw the Minister passing by, heading off hunting. "Maybe you'll get away with it, you damned heretic," says I. "Of course I'm fully aware that you won't get past Friday without fresh meat . . . or even a young pleasant pup. Of course, without speaking crudely, you are very like a cow or a calf . . . or even a little plump pup." When I went in clutching my fist full of small potatoes, the loop was missing from the dresser. Every single fillet of flesh gone! "It's a cat or a dog for certain," I said. "When I get you, you're done for." Eating meat on a Friday. Amn't I the stupid eejit that didn't put them out, and close the door after me! I caught them on the way up. The Minister's dog gobbling the meat, and my dog growling at him trying to stop him. I got a hold of the pike. "You'd easily know who you belong to," I roared at him, "guzzling meat on a Friday." I thought I'd gut him with the pike. The filthy wretch got away by the skin of his teeth. I offered the meat to our own dog. May God forgive me! I shouldn't have been tempting him. He wouldn't refuse anything. Not a bit. Now do you feel any better? He knew it wasn't right . . . It's a pity you didn't tell him that, Peter, and not give him the chance to insult your religion. Lord God, if it had been me . . .

—How could I? The Minister's dog never took a bit from me . . .

—But the Spanish eat meat every Friday, and they're fine Catholics . . .

—You're a liar, you piece of mush! . . .

—The Pope gave them permission . . .

—That's a lie! You black heretic . . .

—. . . O, is that so, Master, my old pal? If I rubbed—what's that you call it again, Master . . . Oh, yes, if I rubbed methylated spirits on me in time, I'd never have got bedsores. Ara, but Master, there was nobody any good looking after me. They were all thick. You can't beat the bit of education, after all. Methylated spirits. Who'd have thought of it! You say it comes in a bottle. Do you know what, Master, they must be the same bottles that the Mistress buys from Peter the Publican's daughter. I'm told she buys loads of them. For Billy . . .

—Not them, Poxy Martin. You wouldn't get them in a pub at all. She's drinking the stuff, the dipso. Certainly downing it. Or else Billy is sloshing it back. Or the two of them together. That's one way with money, Poxy . . .

—Really and truly honest to God, Poxy Martin, I would have burst my gut to be at your funeral. It wouldn't have been right for me not to be at Poxy Martin's funeral, even if I had to crawl on my hands and knees . . .

—Margaret! Margaret! . . . Do you hear Chalky Steven bull-shitting again? He's a terrible pain . . . Hey there, Margaret! Did you hear? Hello, Margaret! . . . You're very quiet recently. Do you hear me, Margaret? . . . It's about time for you to say something . . . I'm talking about that blubby blabber, Chalky Steven. I didn't know he was here at all until a while ago. There's a very dour lot here, Margaret. They'd tell you nothing. Look at the way they stayed dumb about Chalky Steven . . .

O, I know full well, Margaret, that Chalky Steven is here. I was talking to him. They thought they'd dump him in on top of me . . .

That's true, Margaret: anybody is easy to recognise when there's a cross over his grave. It won't be too long now before my own cross is ready, although they say that the Connemara marble is getting used up, that's it's hard to get enough stone for a proper cross. Poxy Martin says you'd only get one now if you knew somebody. But he told me they were hurrying up with it, all the same . . .

He didn't say that, is that what you're saying, Margaret . . . There's enough marble left in Connemara to last for ever! Ah come off it, Margaret, stop talking through your hole! Why would I bother laying lies on a decent man? Neither himself nor myself are trying to compete in telling lies just because we have been dumped in this dive together . . .

You say that my daughter-in-law said that, Margaret: "We'll be well off in this life when we can afford to start buying a cross." Oh, I get it alright. You were eavesdropping behind closed doors again, Margaret, just as you used to do Up Above . . . Now, now, Margaret, there's no point in denying it. You were eavesdropping behind closed doors. That tale you told Dotie and Nora Johnny here about my life, where else did you hear that except from behind the door? . . .

What! You used to listen to me talking while I was walking the road! . . . And behind the ditch when I was working in the field! Well then, Margaret, isn't it just the same to be listening behind the door, and listening on the road, or skulking behind a ditch . . .

But, hang on a minute now, Margaret? Tell me this much, why are the people in the graveyard so set against me? Why can't they find someone else to chew the cud about apart from me? Because like . . .

Because like, I don't have any cross yet, is that it? What else? What else? . . .

They don't like me since I was stroppy about cooperating? How did I get stroppy, Margaret? . . .

Now I get it alright. I voted against Nora Johnny! Don't you know in your heart of hearts, Margaret, that I couldn't have done otherwise. The hairy molly of the Toejam trollops! The Fine Time that was had by all the sailors, the so-and-so . . . She was a candidate for the Fifteen Shilling Party after that, is that what you're saying, Margaret? And your shower didn't give a toss about Toejam Nora, nor about quacky ducks, nor about salacious sailors, nor about her toper tippling on the sly, nor about her being a so-and-so . . .

What's that you said the Master called me, you said? . . . A scab. He called me a scab because I voted against the Fifteen Shilling Party. But I didn't vote against the Fifteen Shilling Party, Margaret. I voted against Nora horse arse Johnny. You know full well that our family always voted the same way aboveground. Nell was the one who was different. Nell, the fucking fussock, did the dirty. She voted for this new crowd because they got a road built up to her house . . .

The Master called me that too, did he. Say it again, Margaret . . . A bowsie! A bowsie, Margaret! . . . Because I cursed Huckster Joan after she had insulted me! O my God Almighty! I never called her names, Margaret. It was she had a go at me, Margaret. I'll tell that much to the Master. I'll tell him straight up, without fear or hesitation. "Caitriona," she said, "Caitriona Paudeen, do you hear me?" she said. "I want to thank you for voting for us. You are a courageous woman . . ."

I never pretended, Margaret, I never pretended that I heard the sour tone in her voice. If I answered her at all, I would have said: "You fat floozie, I wasn't voting for you, or for Peter the Publican, or for the Pound Party, no way, I was voting against that so-and-so, Nora Johnny . . ."

She said that I was a turncoat because I called Nora Johnny . . . pretending to be friendly . . . after all the badmouthing I had given her since I came to the graveyard . . . Jesus, Mary, and Joseph, Margaret! Me calling Nora Johnny! . . . What's that Margaret? . . . He called me that! The Master! No, that's what he called Nora Johnny, Margaret. What else would he call her! . . .

He called me a so-and-so, Margaret. A so-and-so! I'm going to burst! I'm going to burst! Burst . . .

Interlude 7
THE MOULDING EARTH

1.

I am the Trumpet of the Graveyard. Hearken to what I have to say! Hearken unto my voice . . .

Here in the graveyard is the parchment whose weave of dreams is a feculent and enigmatic epigraphy; where the gauntlet of life's gallantry is no more than a smear of faded ink; where the majesty of our best moments melds into mouldy pages . . .

Aboveground all of earth, sea, and sky is a virgin golden parchment. Every hedgerow is a flourish. Every pathway is a streamline of colour. A field of corn is a golden letter. Every sun-kissed mountaintop and every curved cove under spangle-suffused sails is a compound sentence. Every cloud lenites the purple capital letters of the pirouetting peaks of the mountains. The rainbow is a semicolon between the half-quatrain of the sky and the other half-quatrain of the earth. Because it is thus that what is writ by this scribe can unfold its gospel of glory on the parchment of earth, sea, and sky . . .

But yet, even now, the deciduous trees are an uncompleted sentence on the crest of the hill. The cliff at the edge of the surging sea is a final full stop. And then, over there, on the hem of the horizon the unfinished letter ends in an inguttering of ink . . .

The quick of the quill is quenching, and weariness wends its way into the wrist of the writer . . .

The graveyard demands its dues . . . I am the Trumpet of the Graveyard. Hearken unto my voice! Hearken to what I have to say! Hearken you must . . .

2.

—. . . Who's that now? . . . Who are you? . . . Are you deaf or what? Or dumb? . . . Who have we here now? For fuck's sake, come on like, who are you?

—I haven't a clue . . .

—By all that's sacred and holy! It's Redser Tom! What's bugging you, Tom? This is Caitriona Paudeen talking . . .

—Caitriona Paudeen. You are Caitriona Paudeen. How's that for you? Caitriona Paudeen. Caitriona Paudeen, indeed . . .

—Yes, that's me, Caitriona Paudeen. You don't have to go on and on and on about it. How are they all up above anyway? . . .

—How are they up there? Up above. Up above there, is that it? . . .

—Why wouldn't you answer the person who speaks to you, Tom? How are they doing up there?

—Some of them are grand. Some of them are not so good . . .

—Yea, that's a great help! Who is grand and who is not so good? . . .

—It'd be a wise person who would know that, Caitriona? It would be a wise person, indeed, Caitriona. It would be a wise person who'd know who was grand and who wasn't. Wise indeed, no doubt about it . . .

—Don't you yourself know, and you living right next to them, wouldn't you damn well know if my Patrick is grand or not good, and his wife, and Jack the Lad? . . .

—Too true, they were just there near me, Caitriona. Right smack bang next to me, that's true. There's no lie in that much, sure that they were living right smack bang next to me . . .

—Come on, I said, show some balls. There's no point in funking it here, any more than there was when you were aboveground. Who's fine and who's crap, spill the beans . . .

—Well, Little Kate and Biddy Sarah are often sick. Maybe, even, it could be said that they might be a little bit poorly . . .

—Great stuff! I never remember anytime when they weren't sick, except when a corpse had to be laid out, or keened. It's about

time that they'd be sick from now on. Are they going to die soon? . . .
Do you hear me? Are Little Kate and Biddy Sarah going to snuff it
soon? . . .

—Some people say they'll be all right. Others say that they
won't. It would be a wise man who would do otherwise . . .

—And Jack the Lad? . . . Jack the Lad, what about him? How is
he doing? . . . Is your tongue tied to your teeth, or what? . . .

—Jack the Lad. Jack the Lad now. That's him, bejaysus, Jack
the Lad. Some people say he's poorly. Some people say he is poorly,
certainly. It could be the case. It could be so, no doubt about it . . .
But they say many things that are neither here nor there. So they do.
Maybe there's nothing wrong with him at all . . .

—Maybe you would stop pissing around and tell me directly is
Jack the Lad confined to bed . . .

—I don't know, Caitriona. I don't know, I swear. I wouldn't tell
you a word of a lie . . .

—"I wouldn't tell you a word of a lie." You'd think it was the very
first time you told a lie! What's up with Nell? . . . What's the story
about that bitch Nell? . . .

—Nell. Yes, right, like. Nell. Nell bejaysus. Nell and Jack the
Lad. Nell Paudeen . . .

—Yes, yes, yes. Nell Paudeen. I asked you what's the story about
her, how's she doing? . . .

—Some people say she's not doing well. Some other people she
is middling, others again poorly, no doubt about it . . .

—But is she? Or is it just part of her usual carry-on? . . .

—Some say she is, certainly. Some say she is, absolutely. It could
be true, that's the way it is. No doubt whatsoever that that's the way it
might turn out could be. But they say lots of things . . .

—Ah, fuck your gammy gums! You certainly heard if Nell was
coming and going, if she was confined to the bed . . .

—Confined to the bed. It could be, you know. It could be, of
course . . .

—Jesus, Mary, and Joseph! . . . Listen to me, Redser Tom. How
is our Baba doing in America?

—Your Baba that's in America. Baba Paudeen. She's in America all right. Baba Paudeen's in America, that's true . . .

—But how is she?

—I don't know. I honestly don't know, Caitriona . . .

—Ah, come on now, that's ridiculous, you must have heard some talk about her going around. Maybe that she wasn't that well . . .

—Some people say she isn't well. They say that certainly. It could be . . .

—Who says that?

—I swear I wouldn't tell you a word of a lie, Caitriona, but I just don't know. I don't really know. There's a chance there mightn't be anything wrong with her at all . . .

—Who'll get all her money? . . . Who is going to get Baba's money?

—Baba Paudeen's money? . . .

—That's it. What else? Baba's money . . . Who is going to get Baba's money? . . .

—I wouldn't have a clue about that myself, Caitriona . . .

—Did she make a will? . . . Did our Baba make a will yet? You really haven't a clue what's going on . . .

—I wouldn't have a clue about that, Caitriona. You'd want to be a very wise man to know that . . .

—But what are the neighbours saying about it, or your own neighbours for that matter? . . . Did they say that Patrick would get it? Or would it be Nell?

—Some people say Nell will get it. Some people say Paddy will get it. Lots of things are said that are neither here nor there. An awful lot. I wouldn't have a clue myself who'll get it. It would be a wise man who'd know that . . .

—You cheapskate chancer! Everyone else had something to say before you came along. What's with Fireside Tom? . . . Fireside Tom. Do you get me? . . .

—I hear you, Caitriona. I hear you no problem. Fireside Tom. By all that's holy, there's someone of that name there alright, I'm sure about that. There's not a word of a lie in that much, there's someone called Fireside Tom alright . . .

—Where is he now? . . .

—He's in your town land, Caitriona. Where else would he be? He's there in your town land. I thought you knew full well where he was, Caitriona. He was there in your town land all the time, every day, or so it seems to me, isn't that so? . . .

—Gum boils on your grin! What I asked was, where is he now? . . . Where is Fireside Tom right now? . . .

—I don't really know, unless I was to tell you a lie about where he is now, Caitriona. If I knew what time of the day it is now, but I don't. No I don't. He could be . . .

—But before you died, where was he? . . .

—In your town land, Caitriona. He was in your town land all the time, certainly. In your town land, I swear . . .

—But in what house? . . .

—I haven't a breeze really, Caitriona . . .

—But you'd know if he'd left his own house because of rain or a leak or anything . . .

—Some people say he's in Nell's house. Some people say he's in Paddy's house. They say lots of things . . .

—But he's not in his own house? . . . Do you hear me? Fireside Tom is not in his own house? . . .

—Fireside Tom in his own house? In his own house . . . Fireside Tom in his own house. It could be that he is. It could be the case when all is said and done, for all that. You'd need to be very smart . . .

—You're a piss artist, that's what you are, Redser Tom! Who has Fireside Tom's land? . . .

—Fireside Tom? Holy God, he has land alright. Fireside Tom has land, no doubt about that. Fireside Tom has a bit of land, not a word of a lie. He has some . . .

—But who has his land now? Does Tom still have it himself, or does our Patrick have it, or Nell? . . .

—Paddy? Nell? Fireside Tom? That's it now, Paddy. Nell . . .

—Cut out the pig acting and just tell me who has Fireside Tom's land! . . .

—Some people say that Paddy has it. Some people say that Nell has it. They say many things that are neither here nor there . . .

—But you're absolutely sure that Fireside Tom himself doesn't have the land? . . . You are certain, Redser Tom, certain that Fireside Tom himself doesn't have the land? . . .

—Fireside Tom's land, is it? Holy God, it could be, maybe so. You'd need to be a wise man to know who has Fireside Tom's land now . . .

—You're a shyster scumbucket piece of shit! That's a great present for me altogether: Redser Tom. A heap of crap! That serious illness brought you here. If it hadn't you wouldn't have come here until you melted. Your tongue wouldn't have killed you anyway! You're just more excrement in the graveyard, you ginger piece of poop! You snivelling smudge of snot! Fuck off! Get stuffed! Get the . . .

3.

—. . . Fell from a stack of corn . . .

—. . . A white-headed mare . . .

—. . . I hope the devil rides you all with your wasted waffle! Don't you see there's something bugging me, I don't know if your one at home would give the holding to the eldest son? . . .

—. . . I had a slice of land up on the top of the town . . .

—"The daughter of Martin John More,
She was as good as any man . . ."

—. . . *Monsieur Churchill a dit qu'il retournerait pour libérer la France, la terre sacrée. Mon ami*, the French *Gaullistes* and *les Américains* and *les Anglais* will occupy *la France*. That is *promis* by *Messieurs Churchill et Roosevelt* . . . That is a *prophétie* . . . *Prophétie* . . . A prophecy, *je crois, en Irlandais* . . .

—The Property, that's what we always called the bright meadows of the Pleasant Plain. That is the correct Old Irish for it . . .

—Ah, come on, listen to her again! . . .

—It was always and ever in the prophecy that the valley would be as high as the hill. I remember the time when people were scared shitless not to doff their hats to the bailiff and to the Earl's steward, never mind himself. More likely now people expect them to doff their hats to them. No word of a lie, I saw him the other day kowtowing to Nell Paudeen.

—The dirty yoke! The uppity sly slag! She gave him socks and chickens all for free so that he'd get her the road. There were no flies on her. She knew full well that it would be to his benefit to go hunting . . .

—There was another day, and I saw him kowtowing to Nell Paudeen.

—The Earl is a cultured man. Honest . . .

—Honest, my arse, Toejam Noreen of the smelly soles! . . .

—. . . There was an "evil omen" in the prophecy. That was the mine that killed us . . .

—. . . That Antichrist would come before the end of the world and take away a third of the people. My hunch is that we're close to that now. And just look at the state of the world today: those on the dole gorging themselves on meat on a Friday as gluttonous as any other black heretics . . .

—. . . And before the end of the world there'd be a miller with two heels on one foot. Peter Dickey, his name. That's what I always heard said. I was talking to the Junior Master, just after he was appointed to our school. I raised it with him. "Do you know what," he says, "that's just exactly the way it is with us we have it." He told me the precise place too, if I could only remember it. Somewhere out about there, anyway. "That's it, I'll tell you no lie," he says. "I know him well, and there's not a word of a lie in it: he has two heels on the one foot. He's a miller, and his name is Peter Dickey . . ."

—. . . And everyone would have to dip their bread in the sweat of their own brow. And, isn't that what they do? . . .

—O yes, they do! Look, there's Billy the Postman dipping himself in the Old Master's sweat, and do you actually think that Nell

Paudeen's youngfella, who got hundreds of pounds, is dipping himself in his own sweat? And Fireside Tom dipping himself in the sweat of Caitriona and Nell Paudeen. It won't be too long now before Nell dips into Baba's . . .

—Ababoona! May she never live that long! . . .

—And somebody called the Airy Fairy would be flying over Ireland. And isn't he? . . .

—That's not Colm Cille's prophecy at all, what you're spouting . . .

—You liar, of course it is! That's Colm Cille's prophecy every bit of it . . .

—Forget about Colm Cille's prophecy unless you have the right book. Only one book is the right book . . .

—That's the one I have: *The True Prophecies of Saint Columkille.*

—Hang on a minute now. Let me get a word in. I'm a writer. *The True Prophecies of Saint Columkille,* that was written to make fools of us all . . .

—That's a lie, you powder puff!

—Oh, it's a lie, and a big bad black bastard of a lie! . . .

—I'm a writer . . .

—Even if you had written more than would blot out the sky, you're still telling lies. A holy man like Colm Cille writing a book to make fools of us all! . . .

—Now you have it! A saintly man. You are insulting the faith. You're a heretic. No wonder that Antichrist is ensconced smack bang in the middle of the place. Do you think that God exists at all? . . .

—The old man of the graveyard. Let me speak . . .

—Only one person now had the true prophecy of Colm Cille: John Kitty from Bally Donough . . .

—How handy is that! And your own cousin and all . . .

—Rowty in Bally Donough knows it also . . .

—It seems that all the prophets hightailed it off to the nettly wastes of Bally Donough, and that it's a sacred ground now . . .

—At least the one and only true prophecy of Colm Cille is there, something you can't say about the flea-infested bumpy breasts of your own place . . .

—Our own Willy, the guy in our town land, he's a great prophet. I'd spend my whole life, and another one, listening to him. He talks a good deal of sense, and much of what he said has come true already . . .

—That's the false prophecy of Willy Clogher Savvy.

—It's not a false prophecy. It's the true and unadulterated prophecy of Colm Cille, the last one he ever made. But Willy often said that only one-third of it would come true, because Colm Cille left the other two-thirds to be unfulfilled . . .

—You're a liar! Colm Cille was a holy man . . .

—Oh, don't be in any way surprised if you see the Antichrist coming any day now!

—God save you all and your Colm Cille! We have the prophecy of the Dog Hound Gurrier in our place . . .

—And we have Conan's prophecy in our place . . .

—And we have the prophecy of the Son of the Sea Pirate's Stuffed Hole in our place . . .

—I heard Jaundiced Charlie's prophecy from a guy from Kin Teer . . .

—We knew all about Bung Knot's prophesy from a lad around our joint. He's in America now . . .

—Moaning Malachy's prophecy was very common around our way. The guy who knew it married in Lough Side. He used to say that Malachy was a holy man. He was living in the Joyce Country.

—My mother's brother knew Duggan's prophecy. "Duggan's Rule" he called it . . .

—There's an oldfella in our place still who remembers Dean Swift's prophecy . . .

—. . . That there'd be "a road on every track and English in every shack." And that's the way it is. Nora Johnny from Gort Ribbuck has tons of English and every road into Nell Paudeen's place has a few bridges on it . . .

—. . . And that the "Romans" would marry heretics. And didn't your one over there, didn't some of her family marry an Italian, a Jew, and a black! . . .

—Let everyone talk for himself, now! It won't be long before the Antichrist comes. Imagine, marrying a heretic . . . Do they believe in God at all? . . .

—My son, no more than your own, believes in God, even though he might have married an Italian . . .

—. . . And to turn the old man three times on the bed . . .

—Sorry to say, love, but sometimes they didn't turn me at all. If they had, my poor buttocks wouldn't be as infected as they are . . .

—. . . That Galway would win the All-Ireland in 1941 . . .

—In 1941, is it? Maybe you mean some other year? . . .

—No, I don't. No, that's not it. Why so? 1941. What else? Are you really set against the prophecy?

—This is "The War of the Two Foreigners." It was prophesied: "On the sixteenth year, Ireland will be red with blood . . ." And didn't that come true this year? There was fighting in Dublin and on the Pleasant Plain at Easter . . .

—Cop on to yourself, you eejit. That was thirty years ago, or about that . . .

—What do you mean, thirty years ago? The fighting was at Easter, and I died around Lady Day . . .

—Cop on, you eejit. You'd think you came here this year . . .

—But he's right about the sixteenth year . . .

—Ah, come on, you're the son of Paddy Larry, have some of sense. Colm Cille never said anything like that . . .

—Well, if he didn't, Ginger Brian said it: He has Ginger Brian's prophecy. And I'll tell you what else my uncle said:

"On the sixteenth year after thirty, Ireland will be bloody with guns,

And on the seventeenth the women will ask 'where have all the fine men gone?'"

The women of Bally Donough, Gort Ribbuck, Clogher Savvy, Glen Booley, Derry Lough, and Shanakill are all asking that already.

How will it be in another few years when there won't be even one man left?

I remember my uncle telling me that according to Ginger Brian's prophecy, a woman and her daughter would be standing on the bridge at Derry Lough and they'd spot a man coming towards them. He'd be a black, but that didn't really bother them at all. Then they'd go for him like a dog and give him a job. The man himself would be scared shitless. But then they'd start hassling one another, saying that he belonged to them. The man would get away by the skin of his teeth because of all the messing. I'm telling you, that's when the men will be scarce!

—That's hardly a surprise while they're marrying Italians, and Jews, and blacks.

—Since they heard about that, nearly every man was taking off to England. I'd say now that it won't be long before we get "the Autumn of watery women," as my uncle calls it. The women of Gort Ribbuck won't be able to get anyone to look after them, nor the women of Bally Donough, or Clogher Savvy. Wasn't that the reason I vanished myself to England: the women would have torn me limb from limb . . .

I'd be like Billy the Postman . . .

—Hey, son of Paddy Larry, yourself and your uncle have slandered the women of Ireland . . .

—Doesn't the Old Master make exactly the same point! . . .

—Hey, son of Paddy Larry, yourself and your uncle have insulted the faith. Dirty heretics . . .

—Everyone says that the best and the brightest of men are leaving the country. That's because I think that the Antichrist is about to appear and the end of the world is drawing nigh, and if the way down to Hell is near here there'd be no end of blackguards from the Fancy City, and Dublin, and England, of course, crawling around here. I'd be very afraid for our sisters . . .

—Shut your mouth, you grabber of Paddy Larry's!

—Shut your mouth, you grabber! . . .

—I think it won't be too long now before we see England being cast into the pits of Hell, all the way. Hitler . . .

—Caitriona Paudeen's prophecy says that her daughter-in-law will be here at the birth of her next child . . .

—God save us all! Ababoona! . . .

—I would lend credence to prophecies myself. I wouldn't desire that there would be any ambiguity about this. I do not necessarily believe in any one particular prophecy, but it seems at least in the realm of possibility that some people do indeed possess that gift. There are certain gifts which the material sciences know nothing thereof, gifts which cannot be demonstrated by experiment. The poet is not unlike unto the prophet, if all be told. The Romans had the appellation *vates* for the poet; somebody who saw visions and experienced epiphanies. I referenced this in my monograph "The Guide to Knowledge" and also in my collection of poetry *The Yellow Stars* . . .

—May the devil bugger you! You never did any good, never made a penny of money aboveground, only farting windy waffle . . .

—Shut your mouth, you little prick. How could you come to anything aboveground when your parents never put a bit of spunk in you. They'd leave you inside watching the sparks and talking crap, while they were outside working like slaves . . .

—It was foretold in the prophecy that the foreigners would come ashore at Kin Teer and they'd make their way to the east . . .

—'Twould be raining men then for the women of Gort Ribbuck, and Bally Donough, and Clogher Savvy . . .

—You're insulting the faith . . .

—Their great General will make his way down to the bridge at Derry Lough to give his horse a drink. An Irishman will fire a shot at him, and the horse will be killed . . .

—And there isn't a rib of that great General that won't be out searching for another horse. Come here to me, if he saw a big fine colt, do you think he'd steal it? . . .

—This is "The War of the Two Foreigners." I was down at the shallow hole footing turf when Patsy Johnny comes my way. "Hey, did you hear the latest news?" he said.

"Not a bit of it," I said.

"The Kaiser attacked the poor Belgies yesterday," he said.

"You'd really have pity on them," I said. "Do you think that this is 'The War of the Two Foreigners'?" I said.

—Cop yourself on, you nitwit. That war is over ages ago . . .

—. . . The Old Master said only the other day that this must be the War of the End of the World, as the women have got so fickle . . .

—Fireside Tom said exactly the same thing. "Do you know how it is," he said, "it's the end of the world, as the people have lost all decency. Look at my little shack and the roof dripping with leaks . . ."

—When that insurance man started off, every house he went into, he said it was the War that was prophesied to come:

"If you never did it before," he said, "this is the time to take out a little bit of insurance on yourself. They'll never kill the people who have insurance as they'd have to pay out far too much at the end of the War. All you have to do is to carry your insurance papers around with you at all times, and to show them if . . ."

—I know! The chancer robbed me! . . .

—Just the tricks of the trade . . .

—Caitriona herself said the other day that it must be the War of the Continents. "The Connemara marble is all used up," she said, "and it was prophesied that when all the Connemara marble was gone, it would be the end of the world."

—Ababoona! Connemara marble! Connemara marble! Connemara marble! I'm going to burst! . . .

4.

—. . . Take it easy now, Coley! A bit of patience . . .

—Let me finish my story, please, my good sir:

"I laid an egg! I laid an egg! Hot and fresh on the dung heap."

—That's fine, Coley. Despite the fact that it is devoid of art, I surmise that there is a deep interior meaning lurking within. It is always thus, in stories of that *genre*. You will be aware of what Fraser said in *The Golden Bough* . . . O, my deepest apologies, Coley. I misremembered that you were unable to read . . . Now, Coley, give me a chance to speak . . . Ah, come on, Coley, allow me to speak! I am a writer . . .

—. . . *Honest*, Dotie. Maureen failed. If she had been like me or my daughter she wouldn't have failed. But she took after the Paudeens and the Lydons. The nuns in the convent weren't able to put the tiniest jot of learning into her head. You'd hardly believe it, Dotie, but she started calling her teachers bitches and whores! . . . Honest Injun, Dotie, they couldn't clean the filthy talk out of her mouth. How could it be otherwise, she's listening to that kind of talk since she was born, in the same house as Caitriona Paudeen . . .

—Ababoona! Noreen . . .

—Pretend you don't hear her at all, Dotie darling. Isn't it obvious now that "a heavy hand was laid upon her at birth," as Blinks put it in *The Hot Kiss*? . . . You're right on the button there, Dotie. He's a cousin of Maureen's. It's no surprise at all that he is going to be a priest. He was surrounded by a great deal of culture since he was a boy. The priest would call around to the house every half chance he had. There were also fowlers and hunters from the Fancy City, from Dublin and from England around. Nell is, of course, his grandmother, and he was always with her. Nell is a cultured woman . . .

—Oh! . . . Oh . . .

—His mother, Blotchy Brian's daughter, was in America, and she bumped into a lot of cultured people there. America is a great place for culture, Dotie. The grandfather, Blotchy Brian, would hop over there from time to time, and even though you'd never think it, Brian is actually quite a cultured man in his own way . . . He's like that too, Dotie, but he had enough culture anyway not to marry Caitriona Paudeen. Honest . . .

—Oh! . . . Oh! . . . You infested foul mouth of fleas! . . .

—Pretend you don't hear her at all, Nora . . .

—Yep, Dotie . . . Isn't it amazing the differences between two families nonetheless! . . . My son's son in Gort Ribbuck is another cousin of Maureen's: the youngfella that the Old Master is always talking about. He managed to become a petty officer on a ship, Dotie.

Isn't that fantastic for him! Marseilles, Port Said, Singapore, Batavia, Honolulu, San Francisco . . . Sun. Oranges. Blue seas . . .

—But it's getting very dangerous at sea, now since the war began . . .

—"The hero never evades the daring of danger," as Frix said in *Two Men and the Powder Puff*. The sailor's life is a happy, happy one, Dotie. Wearing beautiful romantic clothes, every woman's dream come true . . .

—I told you already, Nora, that I'm a bit of a landlubber . . .

—Romance, Dotie. Romance . . . I gave him the key to my heart, Dotie. Honest! But don't whisper a word about that. You understand, Dotie dearest, you are my friend. Caitriona would only love to savour a bit of gossip. As she has no culture at all herself, she'd not quite get that kind of thing . . .

—Pretend you don't hear her at all, Nora . . .

—Yep, Dotie. I gave him the key to my heart. He was like a price-less urn into which the breath of life was blown. She was the sparkling star reflected in the wild pools of his eyes. His hair was black silk . . . But his lips, Dotie. His lips . . . They were on fire . . . On fire, Dotie. They had been warmed by the kiss of the vine . . .

And the stories he told me about foreign countries, and about harbour towns in strange places. About stormy seas and the white foam blowing in blond blasts to the tips of our topsails. About inlets of virgin sand in the embrace of bosky elfin woods. About scary scrubby mountains snuffed with snow. About meadows of solar warmth on the borders of deep dark woods . . . About strange birds, weird fish, and untamed beasts. About tribes whose money consists of stones, and other tribes who go to war in order to capture their brides . . .

—That's very cultured, alright, Nora . . .

—About tribes who worship the devil, and about gods who lust after milking maids . . .

—That's very cultured too, Nora . . .

—And about his own adventures in Marseilles, in Port Said, in Singapore . . .

—Cultural adventures, undoubtedly . . .

—Oh, I would have given him the last drop of my blood, Dotie. I'd have gone with him as his sex slave to Marseilles, Port Said, Singapore . . .

—But you broke up nevertheless . . .

—We didn't know one another that long then. Just an ordinary true lovers' tiff. That's all. He was sitting next to me on the couch. "You are beautiful, Norita," he said. "Your hair gleams more brightly than each rosy dawn of sunrise on the snow-topped peaks of Iceland." Honest, he said that, Dotie. "The sparkle in your eyes, Norita," he said, "shines more brightly than the North Star peeping out from the horizon to the lonesome sailor as he crosses the equator." Honest, Dotie, he said that. "Your features are more beautiful, Norita," he said, "than the white waves on the smooth beaches of Hawaii." Honest, Dotie, that's what he said. "Your posture is more stately, Norita," he said "than the palm trees that grace the *seraglio* walls in Java." That's what he said, Dotie, honest, no word of a lie. "Your unsullied body is more gentle, Norita," he said, "than the lighthouse which smoothly guides the sailor to the shores of the Fancy City and that calls me to give a warm and loving hug to my precious Norita." Honest, Dotie, he said all that. He kissed me, Dotie. His lips were on fire . . . On fire . . .

"Your legs are more shapely, Norita," he said, "than the moon which appears as a bridge of silver over San Francisco Bay." Then he dropped his hand down on my leg, on the calf of my leg . . .

—He grabbed the calf of your leg, Nora. You're away now! . . .

—Honest, he did, Dotie. "De grâce," I said, "Don't touch my leg." "The curve of your legs is more beautiful, Norita," he said, "than the graceful swoop of seagulls in the wake of a ship." He grabbed my leg again. "De grâce," I said, "hands off my leg." "Your legs, Norita," he said, "are more splendid than the rainbow cast on its back away beyond the oozy ocean." "De grâce," I said, "but you better take your hand off my leg." I grabbed a book I was reading off the window shelf and I clobbered him with the back of it on his arm . . .

—But you told me, Nora, that you hit him with the handle of a pot, just as I did . . .

—Dotie! Dotie! . . .

—But that's what you told me, Nora . . .

—De grâce, Dotie . . .

—But then, he pulled a knife on you, Nora, and tried to stab you; and then he apologised and said that was how they did it in his country, if somebody fancied somebody else, they put their hands on her leg . . .

—De grâce, Dotie, de grâce . . .

—But that you hooked up together again after that, and he wouldn't as much as sniff his snot rag anytime his ship came in to the Fancy City, before he'd be hot foot after you . . .

—De grâce, Dotie. "Sniff his snot rag." That's very crude and uncultured.

—But that's exactly the way you described it, Nora. You also said that he'd write to you from San Francisco, Honolulu, Batavia, Singapore, Port Said, and Marseilles. And that you were pining and whining when no letter came, until another sailor told you that he had snuffed it, some guy had stuck a knife in him in a bistro in Marseilles . . .

—Ah no, no! Dotie. You know I am a very sensitive soul. It would really upset me if someone heard that story. Honest, it would. You are my friend, Dotie. What you said just now would ruin my reputation. That he'd pull a knife on me! That I would do anything as uncultured as to hit somebody with the handle of a pot! Ah, come on! . . .

—That's what you told me a good while ago, Nora, but you didn't have as much culture then as you have now . . .

—Hum, and ha, Dotie. It's only an ignorant crude person like Caitriona Paudeen would do something like that. You heard Maggie Frances saying that she threw boiling water at Blotchy Brian. She must be a right terror. Honest! . . .

—It's a shame to God Almighty that he didn't stick the knife right into your guts, you sailors' bicycle! Where was that place you said he sat down next to you? Lord God, his luck had run completely out. You'd easily tell he was going to be stabbed in the end, anyone who'd sit down next to the One of the Toejam tribe. He got a lovely present leaving you, though: a nest of nits . . .

—Don't let on you've heard her at all, Nora . . .

—Redser Tom, now, for God's sake listen to me. I'm screaming at you for the last hour and you take no notice of me no more than if I was a slobber of frog spawn. What's up that you won't take any notice of me? Wasn't I one of your palsy-walsies up above? . . .

—One of your palsy-walsies, Master. One of your palsy-walsies, like . . .

—Redser Tom, just one question. Is Billy the Postman in a bad way? . . .

—Billy the Postman? Billy the Postman, is that it? Billy the Postman. Billy the Postman, bejaysus. There's a Billy the Postman there, I'd swear, Master. Billy the Postman is there, no doubt about it . . .

—Ara, fuck Billy the Postman, and I hope he'll wallow on the deathbed of Alexander Borgia, and roast in the hot house of the devils and the demons! I know full well that he's there! Do you for a moment think, you Redser Tom, that I don't know about Billy the Postman? Is he in a bad way, the foam-lipped little prick? . . .

—Some say he is, Master, and some say he isn't. They say a lot of stuff that's neither here nor there nor anywhere at all. But he could be bad all the same, he certainly could. No doubt about it, certainly? It would be a wise . . .

—I'm humbly asking you, Redser Tom, is Billy the Postman in a bad way . . .

—Oh, he might be Master. He might be, certainly. It could be, Master. Definitely, certainly. Ah, sure, I wouldn't know myself . . .

—I am asking you in the ancient name of neighbourly gossip to please tell me is Billy the Postman in a bad way . . . That's it, Redser Tom! . . . Fair play to you, Redser Tom! You're my golden boy, Redser Tom, but please tell me is Billy the Postman in a bad way, or is he going to die soon?

—Only a wise man would know that . . .

—I'm begging you, Redser Tom, as someone who always said the right thing about women—just like myself—to please tell me, is Billy the Postman in a bad way . . .

—He could be . . .

—I love you, Redser Tom, you are the apple of my eye, my rippling rill, my saviour of life . . . Do you not believe in private property at all, at all? . . . In the holy name of everybody to preserve the natural state of marriage, I am begging you to tell me, please Redser Tom, is Billy the Postman in a bad way . . .

—If I was to say anything, Master, I'd tell you before anybody, but I won't say nothing, Master. You'd be well advised to keep your trap shut in a place like this, Master. It's not the kind of place for someone to be blabbing and blathering. Even the graves have ears . . .

—May you be seven thousand times cursed tonight and tomorrow and a year from tomorrow, you Communist you, you Fascist, Nazi, atheist, spawn of the red Antichrists, you perfect pustule of the plebeian pricks, you dirty dregs of the dingy damned, you fester of fever, you fly's fart, you maggot's mickey, you earthworm's slime, you belching bollocks that even frightened death himself so he had to send you a disease in the end, you muck muppet, you clap of crap, you rusty wreck of a useless git! . . .

—De grâce, dear Master! Keep a grip on yourself. Remember that you are an upright noble living Christian. If you hang on, you'll soon be able to have all the hassle in the world with that wretch, Caitriona Paudeen herself . . .

—Answer her, Master, come on, Master, answer her. You are educated, Master. Answer her. Answer Noreen . . .

—Pretend nothing, Master, pretend you don't hear that so-and-so at all . . .

—So-and-so! So-and-so! Noreen Johnny is calling me a so-and-so! I'm going to burst! I'm about to burst . . .

5.

—. . . It was a bad bottle, I'm telling you. A bad bottle. A bad bottle . . .

—. . . There was another time and I saw the two of them at the house, Paddy Caitriona and Peter Nell . . .

—Do you think I don't know about that? . . .

—Well, certainly, Breed Terry, if I could have helped it I'd have been at your funeral. It would not have been right for me not to go to Breed's funeral . . .

—Chalky Steven bullshitting away again, or is it? God knows it's hard to get ahold of any story here. I spit on all that useless lying gossip! The best place for it is to go through one ear and out the other! This latest wafted over from Maggie Frances's grave. That place is rife with gossip. Even so, Maggie took it up, no problem. She had a filthy place aboveground anyway. Her floor covered in dirt as tall as a ship's mast, and grime stuck to every piece of furniture in her house. It's no wonder she's perfectly at home in the muck here. You wouldn't mind, but she's worse herself! You could grow potatoes in her ears, and she never gave her shoes a lick going to Mass. You'd recognise the streaks of soil she got in the gutter that she left on the floor of the church. And then, she'd never rest easy until she had slid in beside Huckster Joan and Nell next to the altar—the sneaky sow! If Maggie had married Blotchy, they'd have been well matched. He never washed himself either, unless the midwife did it when he was born. They say that cleanliness is a virtue, but I'm not too sure of that. The dirty shower seems to prosper nonetheless. I kept a clean house all the time. Every single Saturday night without exception I cleaned and washed and scrubbed myself underneath the roof of my own house. If I hadn't enough strength left in me to swat a fly, I still did it. And what did I get for it in the end, nothing, only it shortened my life . . .

What's this? What kind of a racket is this? Even though my ears are stuffed up, it still goes through them . . . Another corpse. The rotten dose . . . The coffin is only like an old hen box. Just about, like. They'd chuck a tinker down on top of me if they could . . .

Who are you anyway? . . . Damn and blast you, will you speak up! My ears are stuffed up . . . They said they'd put you in this grave beside your mother. I don't recognise your voice, though. But you're a woman. A young one . . . You were only twenty-two. I think you have it all arse ways. If you could turn your shroud inside out, you might make some sense. All my daughters are dead a long time . . . Why the fuck don't you speak out and tell me who you are! . . . Do I need any spiritual assistance! . . . What are you on about, spiritual assistance? . . . What the hell is spiritual assistance? . . .

Big Colm's daughter, bejaysus! Blotchy Brian is your uncle! You have little enough sense to try and scrounge your way into the same grave as me. There are far too many of your lot rubbing up against me here. You're not related to me in any way, and I don't want to have anything to do with you. Toddle off down to your mother over there. I heard her sniffling and snuffling just a while ago. I caught my death coming from her funeral. It was pissing rain from high heaven all day . . .

Shit! Stay away from me! The bad dose of Letter Eeckur. Stay away from me, if you have any sense. It was a bad idea to try and sneak in beside your uncle, Blotchy Brian . . .

What's that you said now? . . . You knew full well it was a bad idea! . . . You were against it all the time . . . You never darkened his door for the last year. That did you no harm at all, I can tell you, my dear . . . You can say that again, my dear! Isn't that exactly what I said a minute ago. Not a drop of water touched any part of his body since he was born . . . Do you know what, you're right there: your father was a very clean man. You'd never think he was related to that other bastard. Your father took after your mother. He was a very mild and kind man . . . You visited Blotchy Brian about a year ago . . . You asked him if you could give him any spiritual assistance. How was it any of your business to be offering the old ugly bastard any kind of assistance at all? . . . Oh, I see, you went there on behalf of the Legion of Mary . . . Too true again, he never said a rosary since the day he slimed into the world . . . That's what he told you . . . He told you to stuff your spiritual assistance . . . He said that the Legion were a shower of jennets! And he's a guy who doesn't give a snail's shite for God or for his Holy Mother . . .

The old bastard is coughing and spluttering at last. Bad luck to him, it's about time . . . That's what he said:

"I think I'll take a trip over thereabouts any day now . . . And be

sure and be certain that it'll be the right time to dip into those holes
. . . If Paudeen's mules are . . ." Are you sure now he didn't finish what
he was saying? . . .

Didn't I tell you already that I don't need . . . what's that you
call it? . . . spiritual assistance . . . Nell is talking about building a new
house with a slate roof . . . They're breaking up stones for it already.
I don't believe it! . . . That's what the little hunchback runt says: it
would be just right now, and the road all the way up to the door.
The little twat! . . . "Won't be long now before we have a priest in the
family, God help us all!" The mouldy bitch! . . . Her legs are giving
up. It would serve her right if she could never walk on the new road
. . . All that stuff you know nothing about now, you'll know plenty
about it in another week's time . . . But everyone was too afraid to go
near you in your house . . .

What's that you're on about now? . . . Jack the Lad is very sick.
That's it now, the death sickness. St. John's Gospel. Nell and Blotchy
Brian's young one will get another pile of money . . . You never heard
about St. John's Gospel . . . You didn't know that Jack needed any
spiritual assistance. He needs all the help he can get now, the poor
creature . . .

Black Bandy Bartley was anointed . . . Little Kitty and Biddy
Sarah are also very poorly you say . . . They never stir out of the house
one way or the other now. They'll neither sleep nor weep that much
anymore now, so . . .

Guzzeye Martin's cross went up the other day . . . and Redser
Tom's too. That foxy bollocks is no time here . . . You heard that: Nell
advised my Patrick not to erect a cross of the best Connemara marble
over me . . . You'd have known for certain in another week. That's fucking great! . . . Oh be damn sure, my lovely, that it's the whole truth.
She'd say that all right—the whore—and Blotchy Brian's young one
and Nora Johnny's young thing urging her on . . . Blotchy Brian said:

"If I was Paddy, I'd give that demented hag enough of Connemara marble to last her a lifetime . . . Dig her up from her hole . . .
Shunt her over to the Island . . . Straddle her up on the highest spike
there . . . Like your man on top of the big column in Dublin . . ." That

is really appalling, even though he is on the verge of death, God's breath does not decorate his mouth . . . Look, I'm telling you, I don't need and I don't want any spiritual assistance . . .

So Nora Johnny and Blotchy Brian's young ones, and Nell are all talking again. You'd easily know it. Hardly likely there'd be any fighting one way or the other if it wasn't for that little grabber of Paddy Larry's . . . That's it too, my lovely. A load of hot air, all their squabbling. They're a bunch of tinkers . . . You'd have known it all in about a week, yea, right . . .

So, a letter came, did it? . . . She didn't say who'd she leave the money to . . . Oh, OK, she wrote to Patrick also . . . Wasn't she the cheeky cunt writing to Blotchy Brian's house, and she has no relation or connection with him! . . . You're sure now, she said that he was bad . . . And she had made her will. By dad! . . . And she has a tomb ready and waiting and all written up in the Boston cemetery. Think about it, a tomb! Just like the Earl has. Our Baba has a tomb! May she rot in Hell if she's gone and got herself a tomb . . . She put money in the bank so that the tomb would be looked after for ever and ever! By the holy hokey! . . . And money for Masses . . . Two and a half thousand pounds for Masses! The will is only diddly squat now. Blotchy Brian's family in America will suck the rest of it up. In fact, I don't give a toss any more. Nell won't get that much one way or the other. She won't be crooning "Eleanor Aroon" as she is strutting up and down outside our house . . .

You think that Patrick never wrote back to Baba. He's a proper thicko if he didn't! . . . Will you shut your gob about the definite knowledge you'd have in a week! What use is it to me what you might know next week? . . . The Young Master doesn't write letters for anybody anymore . . . Far too busy . . . What was he doing, did you say? . . . Studying the form . . . That is, studying the form. That's a weird thing to say . . . Betting on racehorses. Oh, tell me more! . . . He doesn't do a stroke in school, only read about them and study the form . . . The priest is very against it. I thought the two of them used to be off going for walks together. Or is that a lie? You can't believe anything at all here . . . He gave a sermon about it . . . As true as a bull has balls, everyone knew who he was talking about, no need for any names or to spell it out . . . "Dissipating their money on gambling and cavorting with drunken loose women in the Fancy City," he said . . . "I heard about a certain man in this parish who drank forty-two pints, and about girlish guzzlers who could down a cask of brandy without losing as much as a puff of the powder on their cheeks . . ." My God, if he only knew about Nora Johnny! . . . They say there's a chance that he'll fire the Junior Master . . . Oh, here we go again! You'd have known in another week . . . You'll know a lot more in a week's time, I'm telling you, my little darling! . . .

Up the yard! Ababoona! The letters for America that the Junior Master wrote for Patrick, he forgot completely to post them in the letter box . . . And when he changed his digs, Mrs. Keady found them stuck in some old clothes he had left after him . . . I don't believe it! She told Nell everything that was in them . . .

There's something wrong with Patrick: why could he not have taken them himself and stuck them in the post? Do you think that I ever left my letters behind to be posted by the Old or the Junior Master? Schoolteachers are a weird lot. I always copped on that there was something else going on in their heads apart from my few letters. Didn't I see the Old Master over and back from the table to the window as restless as fleas in an armpit just to see if could he get a gawk at the Schoolmistress strolling on the road! . . .

The Schoolmistress wasn't writing letters for anyone either, is that it . . . Too much to do, looking after Billy the Postman. The sleazy slouch! Oh, if Patrick had listened to me he wouldn't be beholden to anyone now, if he had just gone into Mannix the Counsellor. He was the guy who could pen a perfect letter for seven shillings and sixpence. But Nora Johnny couldn't bear to spend even a halfpenny . . . You heard that Patrick didn't give a sugar about the will . . . That's more of Nell's sneaky stuff, the slippery tit . . . You didn't think for a minute that she was getting a bad conscience about my son when she was doing the same thing with her husband . . . "Paddy was perfectly all right until Besheen passed away." Blotchy Brian would say that . . . Leave me alone with your gabble about spiritual assistance . . .

Maureen's going back to college again. She'll do the business this time. Sure, she wasn't thrown out the last time at all, just that she came home herself. A bit of homesickness, the poor thing. You don't know what she's doing this time, do you? . . . To be a schoolteacher, I suppose . . . That's what you heard . . .

Patrick has lots of cattle on his land. Good on him! . . .

Fireside Tom has left his house . . . The rain coming in got rid of him . . . It should have happened a long time ago. That's what he said: "I swear to God the dirty drop was smacking me, sometimes in my mouth, then in my eye. It didn't matter where I shifted the bed. I think I'll go and arselick the quality for whatever time I have left . . ." He stayed two nights with Patrick and then he slung off to Nell's house completely. Nell will get the land so . . . Do you know did he sign it over to her or not? Only someone like Mannix the Counsellor would be able to answer that . . . It doesn't matter a tinker's fart what you would have known in a week's time! It's what you know now . . . Fireside Tom said that: "Nell had a much bigger heart than Caitriona. I'd far prefer to stay in Nell's house where I could rub shoulders with high society. Nobody with any decency visits Caitriona's house." Fireside Tom's midget head would be a wonderful sight to behold! . . . "The best people always have the best smokes and they also have fine-looking women." That hard-hearted harridan will soon have him craving women all right. If she senses anything happening to herself, she'll get St. John's Gospel from the priest, and Fireside Tom will be the first out the door. Isn't it a great pity that there's nobody alive up there to warn the poor fucker! What's the world coming to at all when Fireside grotty Tom can think he's going to rub shoulders with the high and mighty and the rich and famous? . . .

Lord Cockton came fishing every day to Nell's place. He could leave his car right up to the door . . . The priest drives his right up to her door, too . . . Ababoona! Lord Cockton took the slag bag out in his car . . . He took her out for a stroll to Rosses Cove. He must have had very little respect for his car to take piss flaps like her out in it! . . .

The priest's sister was up there on the hunt also. Was she wearing the pants or a dress? . . . The pants . . . Herself and Lord Cockton were out on the hunt together. How could a priest have anything to do with them! I suppose that Lord Cockton is a black heretic. They were all saying that she was going to marry the Master in Derry Lough . . . Oh, for God's sake almighty, you'd have known all about it in a week's time! We'll have to get permission to hoist you up again next week . . .

You think the marriage is all off? I thought that that Master in Derry Lough was a decent kind of a guy, never touched a drop . . . What's that you're saying? My ears are all stuffed up . . . She has a thing going with Tim Top of the Road's son. It's a queer world all right, no doubt about it! . . .

Tim Top of the Road's son said that to Lord Cockton: not to go hunting with her anymore, unless he was there . . . John Willy's son heard him say that . . .

What's this? Where have you gone? . . . They're shunting you away . . . They know this is not your grave . . . Good luck to you, wherever you're going! Even if you're related to Blotchy Brian, it was good of you to talk. You're not like that other worthless wanker, Redser Tom . . .

6.

—. . . I was swapping a word for every pint with the Great Scholar . . .

—. . . The Big Butcher often said that he had great respect for me because of the respect that his father had for my father . . .

—. . . And I was down to my last shilling . . .

—If the Junior Master isn't down to his last shilling now . . .

—. . . "'I laid an egg! I laid an egg' . . ."

—*C'est l'histoire des poules, n'est-ce pas?*

—. . . Honest, Dotie. My mind is totally gunked up for the last while. I need culture as desperately as the stalk of wheat needs the heat of the sun. And there is not a twitter of culture here anymore. The Old Master should be ashamed of himself. You'd think that when someone descended down into the grave that he'd leave the petty pissy grievances of the other life above behind and that he'd use his time to perfect his mind. I often said that to the Master, but what's the point? He can't help it now, but think about the Schoolmistress and Billy the Postman. Something has to be done to help him. Honest, I swear, Dotie. We don't have that many educated people with some kind of culture that we can do without even one of them. We'll have to stop him aping Caitriona Paudeen's slabbering and slattering. Every second word he bawls out now is "bitch" and "witch" and "wagon." Caitriona is a pernicious influence on him. She should have been kicked down to the Half Guinea Plot . . .

—Mange-pocked Nora . . .

—Don't let on you hear her at all, Norita . . .

—Yep, Dotie. I have every intention to proceed and to establish a cultural communion in this place. I think that a lot can be done to improve the depth and breadth of our cultural consciousness. When I establish this communion of souls we will dispute about politics and relationships, economics and science, learning and education and so on. And they shall be discussed with due academic objectivity, notwithstanding gender, race, or religion. Nobody shall be prevented from expressing his opinion, and there shall be no other qualification for membership apart from his or her being a companion of culture . . .

—Do you think for some reason that I was thinking of culture when I grabbed the handle of the pot and chucked it at . . .

—De grâce, Dotie. "God forgives the big sinners, but we ourselves, can we not find it in our hearts to forgive our small sins," as Eustasia said to Mrs. Cruikshank when they were fighting over Harry. We'll try to broadcast information about other aspects of life—strange and foreign aspects certainly—and by that to enhance peoples' understanding of one another. We will have regular debates, lectures, *soirées*, Pub Quizzes, Symposiums, Colloquiums, Plentiful Periodicals, Chapters, Summer Schools, and Weekend Schools and Information on Demand for those in the Half Guinea Place. This communion and get-together will be a wonderful device and stratagem in the pursuit of peace and in the communication of culture.

This kind of thing is called a Rotary. Only cultured people like the Earl have anything really to do with the Rotary . . .

—And sailors!

—And just don't pretend, Norita, that you hear her at all . . .

—Yep, Dotie. I won't. But that's exactly one of those nutcase ideas that should be properly crushed with the grace of the Rotary. Caitriona is not the only one who thinks thoughts like that. If she wasn't it wouldn't matter that much, but she's very common. Sailors are very interesting, as you know. Only a narrow bigoted uncultured mind would even think to condemn them . . .

—All apart from those knives they have, Norita?

—De grâce, Dotie. That's another one of those weird ideas that needs to be squashed . . .

—So, who else will be in the Rotary, Norita?

—I can't absolutely say, with complete certainty yet. You yourself, of course, Dotie. The Old Master. Peter the Publican. Huckster Joan . . .

—The poet . . .

—He can go and fuck himself, the little scut! . . .

—. . . But you never read *The Yellow Stars,* Nora.

—No infernal odds, old man! You're not acceptable. *Honest!* You're *decadent!* . . .

—Breed Terry should be accepted. She went to a film in the Fancy City once . . .

—By gaineys! I was with the little messer, that time we bought the colt . . .

—Hold on there now! Take it easy. I am a writer . . .

—We couldn't take you. If we did the whole graveyard would be ripped from limb to limb. You insulted Colm Cille.

—. . . There's no point in you reading it. I am not going to listen to your "Sundown." Honest, I'm not. I'm not going to listen to it . . . There's no point in bugging me about it: I won't do it. I am very broadminded really, but at the same time and at the end of the day one must hold on to a certain amount of propriety . . . I am a woman . . . I will not listen. No way, honest! . . . We could not accept you.

The stuff you write is Joycean gunge . . . There's no point in being at me about it. I don't want to hear "Sundown." You really have a disgusting lowdown mind to write something like that . . . You're writing "The Dinosaur's Dream" . . . No, I won't listen to it. "The Dinosaur's Dream"! A right Joycean galoot. You are really a lowlife form . . . There's no way you are going to be accepted until you learn *The Seventy Sermons* off by heart . . .

—I propose that we accept the Frenchie. He's a real Irishman. He's bursting his guts learning the language . . .

—He's already writing a thesis on the dental consonants in the Half Guinea's dialect. He says that their gums are sufficiently worn out by now that they can make a learned study of its sounds . . .

—The Institute has delivered the judgement that he has learned too much Irish of a kind which has not been dead long enough according to the appropriate approved schedule, and that there is a suspicion that some of it is "Revival Irish," they are of the opinion that he must needs unlearn every single syllable of it before he shall be qualified to pursue that study.

—He also wants to collect every piss and piddle of folklore that he can, and save it so that every new generation of Gaelic corpses will know in what kind of republic former generations of Gaelic corpses lived. He says that there is no other storyteller who could hold a cat's candle to Coley this side of Russia, and that the likes of him we will never meet again. He says it would be easy to make a Folklore Museum of the Cemetery, and that there'd be no problem getting a grant . . .

—Come off it, wasn't the little flyboy fighting against Hitler! . . .

—Let us accept him. Bring it on . . .

—I am so grateful to you, *mes amis! Merci beaucoup* . . .

—Hitler is against the Rotary . . .

—Ara, so what, shut up your old trap and your asshole Rotary! . . .

—A man who drank forty-two pints! They wouldn't even take him in Alcoholics Anonymous or in Mount Mellery. Nowhere at all, apart from "Drunken Pissartists Limited" . . .

—I drank those forty-two pints, too true . . .

—But Nora Johnny drank twice as much on the sly . . .

—Shut your gob, you grabber!

—But you couldn't think that you would accept any of the Dog Eared lot, could you? If you do, you'll know all about it . . .

—. . . How could they let the likes of you into the Rotary, and you don't even know your tables? . . .

—But I do. Listen now, like. Twelve ones, twelve; two twelves . . .

—. . . Why would they take him: a guy who murdered himself going to look at Cannon? It was a very uncultured way to die . . .

—The bookseller will be acceptable. He handled thousands of books . . .

—And the Insurance Inspector. He used to do the crossword . . .

—And Chalky Steven. He was a great one for going to funerals, death kept him alive . . .

—. . . So, why is it they won't accept you? Isn't your son married to a black! The blacks are a cultured race, kinda.

—They're more cultured anyway than the Italians, and one of them old bags is married to your son . . .

—Caitriona Paudeen should be accepted. She has a round table at home . . .

—And Nora Johnny's wardrobe . . .

—She was a good friend to Mannix the Counsellor . . .

—And her son's daughter is training to be a teacher . . .

—Big Colm's daughter should get in also. She was a member of the Legion of Mary. She gives people spiritual assistance . . .

—Easily known and all she knows. She hasn't kept her gob shut since she got back home . . .

—This is very offensive . . .

—If that's the way it is they should accept the Postmistress also. She was the Legion's Information and Investigation Officer, and there's no way she wasn't stuffed full of culture when you think of everything she had ever read . . .

—And Kitty too. Her son was deputy head bottle-washer in the Legion, and she belonged to a Credit Corporation . . .

—And Tim Top of the Road. His old one stuck a hearse under

his arse in case his bowels would be bollixed, or his guts would be gandered . . .

—So it goes, as you might say yourself . . .

—Everyone in Tim Top of the Road's House was in the Legion . . .

—And his son is all up for the priest's sister . . .

—Everyone in his house stole my turf . . .

—And my hammer . . .

—You are all insulting the faith. You are all bad black heretics . . .

—You're all right, you'll be accepted. The Big Butcher attended your funeral, didn't he? . . .

—Fireside Tom would have made a good Rotary person, wouldn't he? He was always a friend to culture.

—And Blotchy Brian. He was in Dublin . . .

—And Nell Paudeen. She meets up with a lot of the Rotary crowd. Lord Cockton . . .

—Let me speak. Give me a chance . . .

—John Willy will give the first lecture to the Rotary Club. "My Heart" . . .

—Then Kitty: "A Loan" . . .

—Dotie: "The Mild Meadows of the Pleasant Plain" . . .

—Guzzeye Martin: "Bedsores" . . .

—The Old Master: "Billy the Postman" . . .

—Yer man over here: "The Direct Method for Twisting Ankles" . . .

—Caitriona Paudeen: "Handsome Blotchy Brian" . . .

—Bugger off! Brian the bastard, bummer Brian . . .

—Then Redser Tom . . .

—I'll say nothing at all. Not even nothing. Zilch . . .

—You'll give a talk about the prophets from Bally Donough, won't you? . . .

—And you on about the flea-ridden knoblets of your own little townlet . . .

—To be honest, Dotie, I was always hot into culture. Whoever said to you that I started here is displaying an ignorant prejudice. When I was only a young girl in the Fancy City, as soon as I came home from the convent and had eaten my dinner I was hightailing it out in search of culture. That's exactly the time when I met the sailor . . .

— But you never said anything to me, Norita, about you attending the convent . . .

— De grâce, Dotie. I told you all the time, but it's gone clean out of your head. You must realise that I was putting the finishing touches to my education in the Fancy City, and I was staying with a relation of mine, a widow, as it happens, Mrs. Corish . . .

You're all gab and guts and a filthy liar, you Toejam Nora you. You're not related to her in the slightest. You were only her skivvy. I have no idea why she let you or your bag of fleas ever into her house. But as soon as she found out you were having it off with sailors she stuck a nettle up your arse and sent you off home to Gort Ribbuck, Gort Ribbuck of the ducks, the puddles, the nits, and the gummy glue between the toes. And, for all that, you went to school in the Fancy City! . . .

— Just don't pretend you hear a word she says . . .

— My goodness me, Dotie, that old wagon isn't allowed to speak. There she is, without a cross or a crucifix just like a letter that was sent without any address . . .

— You can thank your eejit of a brother, Noreen . . .

— Your son is at home, and he can't pay Fireside Tom's insurance. As soon as Tom heard that he upped and offed the fuck out of there, and awayed to Nell's place . . .

— Oh! Oh! . . .

— It doesn't matter if it's Oh or Pee, that's the way it is. Your son, Paddy, has let his land to Nell, and Nell's cattle are there renting their ruminating on his fields all the time . . .

— Oh! Oh! Oh! . . .

— If he lives a bit longer, he'll have to sell the land, the whole lot. Pity the woman that her man can't look after her. I gave him my daughter, as no way did I want to obstruct the ways of true and romantic love. That was the only reason he got her. I was always romantic. But whether I was romantic or not, if I really knew what I was on about, and if I really knew what she was up to . . .

—... What's that? ... Another corpse ... A new one ... I'll have no time for you in this place. A corpse's corner is its castle. Everyone here believes in the sanctity of private property ...

—Fuck off! By the oak of this coffin, they're not going to dump you on top of me. I'm going to join the Rotary ...

—... Peace is all I want. Not company. I'm joining the Rotary ...

—... That will injure me. I've already got bedsores ...

—... I have a dicey heart ...

—Go away and get stuffed out of this grave. I'm going to tell you nothing. The graves are full of ears. You'd think that we should be easily recognisable. We have crosses to tell who we are. But even so, they've left that grave far too close to mine. Oh! Head off over there to Caitriona Paudeen's. Over as far as Caitriona's! ...

—She loves to welcome a new corpse. It gives her a plentiful supply of jabber and clatter ...

—They dump everyone else down on her, people for whom they can't find any other hole in the graveyard. She'll keep them clattering and clappering about the neighbours ...

—You're wrong about that, that they were sent to her. After all, she has no cross ...

—And the Rotary won't accept her ...

—Redser Tom! Redser Tom! Maggie! Kitty! Breed Terry! Guzz-eye Martin! John Willy! Redser Tom! Redser Tom, he has something to say! I'm going to burst!

Interlude 8

THE HEATING EARTH

1.

I am the Trumpet of the Graveyard. Hearken to what I have to say! Hearken unto my voice . . .

The unturned sod is unwelcoming and sour with its lining of ice. The heart of the earth is acid sharp. As this is the meadow of tears . . .

Aboveground life is putting on the raiment of Spring. The pert peek of serendipitous stalks and the fresh smile which breaks on the bare earth are the basting thread of this suit of clothes. The radiant rays of the sun agleam on the shoulders of the clouds are its hem. Its buttons are the clumps of primroses waving from the banks of every hedgerow and whispering behind every rock. Its lining is the love song of the lark chirping above in the high empyrean and pouring down through the diaphanous air on the ploughman, while the brushwood is the mellifluous melody which accompanies the birds in their bundling. The spring in the step of the youth who has just found his lost lamb in the rough rocks and the lively lilting of the boatman while he skims his skiff along the frieze of the tide are the seams of hope with which the transient beauty of the eye and of the heart stitch the tunic which is the sempiternal spark of glory of land, sea, and sky.

But already, the thread which the tailor teases through the eye of his needle is an emaciated rainbow on the horizon. The scissors of a gale is tearing the buttons out. The clothes are being unravelled by the ripping of the elegant twill. The aurora of gold in the field is being unburnished as the corn dips its head. The tempest fairy wind is roaring through the barn and sweeping away every ear, wisp, and grain left over from last year's harvest . . .

The refrain the milkmaid sings as she returns from the summer pasture is flagging and fading. She knows well that soon the farm implements will be stored in the yard beside the house . . .

For spring and summer have retired. They have been gathered up by the squirrel in his haunt beneath the tree. They have flown away on the wings of the swallow and with the slipping sun . . .

I am The Trumpet of the Graveyard. Hearken to my voice! Hearken unto me . . .

2.

—. . . "Ho-oh-row, then Maureen, with your belts and buckles My love in the stook of barley . . ."

—What the heck is this? . . . Black Bandy Bartley, by the hokey, singing to himself. You're very welcome, Bartley! . . .

—"Ho-row, oh Maureen, with your belts and buckles . . ."

—Well, isn't it great for you, you son of a Black Bandy gun . . .

—Bloody tear and 'ounds, who's that? . . .

—Caitriona. Caitriona Paudeen . . .

—Bloody tear and 'ounds and that, Caitriona. We'll be neighbours again . . .

—They're not putting you in the correct grave, Bartley.

—Bloody tear and 'ounds, Caitriona, but it doesn't matter a damn where they stick your heap of bones? "Ho-row, oh Maureen . . ."

—Jaysus, Bartley, you'd hardly think that death had taken anything out of you. What caused it, anyway?

—Bloody tear and 'ounds, Caitriona, don't you know that even the best can't go on for ever, as Blotchy Brian said about . . .

—Oh, the loud-mouthed scuzzy bastard! . . .

—No reason at all really, just lay back until the last drop drained away. Bloody tear and 'ounds, isn't that reason enough! "Ho-row . . ."

—How's she cutting up there anyway, Bartley? . . .

—Bloody tear and 'ounds, Caitriona, same as always. Some

coming, some going, some neither here nor there. Isn't that the way it is, and it has to be. Just like loading a gun and giving it a blast, as Blotchy Brian said . . .

—I'm telling you, he was some smart guy with a gun . . .

—He never stirred out, Caitriona, never since that time when he was looking at Redser Tom after he was anointed. He was very cut up after Tom . . .

—They were well suited to one another, the dour-faced copper-knobbed scum and the snivelling snotty shit head . . .

—I was listening to him that very night up in the room telling Tom what he should do. "Bloody tear and 'ounds," he says, "if it ever happens, Redser Tom, if it ever happens that you make the trip across, and if you happen to meet her on the way, make sure she learns nothing from you. She'll be whoring after gossip, or else she has changed completely . . ."

—But, who's that Bartley?

—Bloody tear and 'ounds, Caitriona, but it wouldn't be right or proper of me to disclose that . . .

—Ah, for God's sake, Bartley, no need for you to be like Redser Tom. That's exactly his carry-on since he landed in the cemetery clay . . .

—Bloody tear and 'ounds, if there's going to be a row, well then, let there be a row. It's you. Yourself. Who else, Caitriona? . . .

—Me, Bartley? Me, whoring after gossip! That's a filthy lie. That nutjob will always have the bitter word until death clogs up his tongue . . .

—I wouldn't say it will be that long now, Caitriona.

—He'll be more than welcome . . .

—Bloody tear and 'ounds, don't you know he's easy come, easy go, and he didn't have enough spunk to go to Jack the Lad's funeral! . . .

—Aba bloody boona una! Jack the Lad's funeral! Jack the Lad's funeral! Jack! Jack jaysus Jack! You're spitting out lies now, you seed of the son of Satan . . .

—Bloody tear and 'ounds, he's here three weeks already!

—Jesus, God almighty, St. Joseph, Mary, and her Blessed

Mother! Jack the Lad is here this long, and neither Maggie nor any of them would tell me a bit about it! Toejam Noreen has this place totally fucked up, Bartley. Have a guess, what do you think she's up to now? . . . A Rotary!

—Bloody tear and 'ounds, who'd imagine that, a Rotary. "Horow, then Maura, with your belts and your buckles . . ."

—Jack the Lad! Jack the Lad! Jack the jaysus Lad here. You'd easily know he wouldn't have too long to live. St. John's Gospel and all . . .

—Bloody tear and 'ounds, St. John's Gospel, Caitriona . . .

—That's John's Gospel that that fugly wheedled out of the priest, what else? Jack the Lad, Jack the joke Lad! Jack the Lad done down and buried for the last three weeks unbeknownst to me. The ghouls down here would tell you fuck nothing, especially since the stupid Election. They'd stuff that mong John Willy, and Breed Terry the blow rag, and that clod churl Redser Tom into the same grave as me. Jack! Jack the langer . . .

—Bloody tear and 'ounds, Caitriona, it doesn't matter a snivelling snot—unless you are totally out of your tree—who gets dumped in the same grave. "How-ro, oh Maura . . ."

—One way or the other, Nell was hopping around like a heron on the griddle the day of the funeral! All flash and fashion and not a thought about the poor hoor that was laid out. They put him in the Pound Place, of course? . . .

—The grave just next to Huckster gombeen Joan . . .

—Huckster Joan, the scrubber! Too bad that she's next to poor Jack. That old bag will buy and sell him. But Nell wouldn't give a toss, the sly slut, she'd be happy to dump him into any old hole . . .

—Bloody tear and 'ounds, Caitriona, she got a nice dry grave right next to Huckster Joan and Peter the Publican; and hired a hearse; more than everything for people to stuff themselves at the wake and at the funeral, but she didn't let anyone get drunk; and then a High Mass just like the ones that Peter the Publican had, and Huckster Joan; four or five priests singing and ceremonising, the Earl up in the gallery with that other fancy fowler who used to be there . . .

Bloody tear and 'ounds, what else would you expect? . . .

— She really has a soft spot for the priests and the lords and ladies all the time. But I'd swear she never shed as much as a tear for the poor fecker. Neither herself nor Blotchy Brian's daughter ever gave as much as a fiddler's fart for him, all they wanted was that the poor old skin would be swept out of their way . . .

— Bloody tear and 'ounds, Caitriona, Blotchy Brian and herself cried their eyes out. And everyone said they never heard wailing as beautiful as that of Biddy Sarah's . . .

— Biddy Sarah! I thought that that freeloading dipshit had completely taken to the bed by now . . .

— And bloody tear and 'ounds, she has so! Isn't this exactly what Blotchy says about her, and about Catty Kitty and Billy the Postman too: "The priest has smeared enough oil on the three of them," he said, "that there won't be a drop left for any of us, whenever we want it . . ."

— No doubt about it, that bollocks Brian would need a lot of greasing! And didn't Biddy Sarah go to Nell's . . .

— Bloody tear and 'ounds, didn't Nell send a car for herself and Catty Kitty. But Kitty walked there nonetheless . . .

— She got the whiff of a corpse, what else?

— "Bloody tear and 'ounds," she says, just as she's laying Jack out, "it's like, even if I was going to peg out myself the next day, I couldn't not turn up, considering who asked me especially."

— Biddy Sarah, the sponger! Catty Kitty, the gossip! They went off to Nell, but didn't bother their arse about decent people at all. I wouldn't blame Jack the Lad one bit, the poor creature, if it wasn't for that other smarty pants. Jack the Lad! Jack . . .

— It won't be too long now before someone else will be weeping for Biddy Sarah, anyway. Bloody tear and 'ounds, she collapsed and fell on the way back from Jack's funeral, and they had to bring the car up to the house again . . .

— A drunkard! She was often off her tits plastered . . .

— She got a bit of a turn. Didn't get up out of the bed since. "But ho-row oh Maureen, with your belts and your buckles . . ."

—Nell has no recollection of coming here? . . .

—She said she wasn't well enough. But bloody tear and 'ounds anyway, she came to have a gawk at me, and I'd say she was as much of a fine fresh filly as ever she was . . .

—That's why she was thrilled and delighted to dump Jack the Lad out. Jack! Jack! . . .

—Bloody tear and 'ounds, Caitriona, hasn't she got it nice and easy with a car under her arse to bring her wherever her fancy takes her! . . .

—Lord Cockton's car. Has she no shame or decency to be gallivanting around the country like a young thing! Jack the Lad . . .

—Bloody tear and 'ounds anyway, Caitriona, but why wouldn't she do what she liked with her own! . . .

—What do you mean her own? . . .

—The only thing that was bugging me was that I didn't get a lift there at all. Herself and Peadar had promised they'd take me any place I wanted in the County, but bloody tear and 'ounds, I laid back and croaked without a groan! . . .

—Ababoona, boona! You can't be serious, you son of the Black Bandy Bugger, that she actually owns the car! . . .

—Herself, and her son Peter. Bloody tear and 'ounds, Caitriona, how is it you never heard she bought a car for Peter? . . .

—Never! No, she didn't. She never did, you son of the Black Bandy Bugger! . . .

—Bloody tear and 'ounds, Caitriona, and so he did. He can't really do the hard work anymore with his bad leg. He won't bother her that much anymore with his bandy leg, although you wouldn't know there was much wrong with him. He's doing all right shuffling people in a panic here and there and left and right and over and out and up and down in his car . . .

—I suppose you don't know what kind of a racket it makes going up and down by our house. Aren't I lucky, Bartley, that I'm not alive! . . .

—Bloody tear and 'ounds, but sure, she also wears a hat any time she leaves the house and goes out and about! . . .

—Ah, come on, Bartley! Bartley the son of the Black Bandy Bugger! A hat . . .

—A hat, just as fashionable as the one that the Earl's wife wore . . .

—I just don't believe, Bartley, that she hasn't already sucked off some of the money from Baba . . .

—Bloody tear and 'ounds, Caitriona, she's done all that, and four months ago! Two thousand pounds! . . .

—Two thousand pounds! Two thousand pounds you Black Bandy Bugger's bastard!

—Two thousand pounds, Caitriona! Bloody tear and 'ounds, she bought the car with it, and now she's going to put a real plushy posh window in the church! . . .

—She has good reason to suck up to the priest. I'd swear by the Holy Bible itself, Bartley, Baba wouldn't loosen her claws on that money until she died! . . .

—Bloody tear and 'ounds, sure didn't she die ages ago! Nell got a thousand before she died, and another thousand since. She has to get the odd hundred here and there yet, and she'll hump them into the bank to spend on that guy who's going to be a priest . . .

—Ah, forfucksake! My own Patrick won't even get enough to tickle his palm . . .

—They say he'll get more than enough, but he won't get as much as Nell. Bloody tear and 'ounds, the old dog always returns to his vomit! . . .

—Nell herself has her knickers in a twist about it . . .

—"Ho-row, there Maureen, your belts and your buckles . . ."

—Oh, Jesus Christ Almighty! Baba's will. Poor Jack, like a piece of useless crap thrown to one side, and her son kept alive with St. John's Gospel. A new road up to the house. Her grandson going for the priesthood. A new house with a slated roof being made for the puss-face. A car. Fireside Tom's land. Jack . . .

—Bloody tear and 'ounds, Caitriona, nobody has Fireside Tom's land.

—But isn't he living with Nell? . . .

—Bloody tear and 'ounds, not for a long time now. He's in your

Paddy's place, and Paddy's cows graze in his field. He never liked the nobs who came to Nell's house. "I mean, like," he said to Pat, "they're not half as generous as they are cracked up to be. I couldn't get a wink of sleep up there. Cars roaring and revving up all around from morning 'til night: hacking and hammering and blasting away from the crack of dawn to the drawing down of the light. They're bursting their guts to build the new slate-roofed house. I mean, like, for Jaysus's sake, think about me in my own shack and it didn't matter diddly shit where I shifted my bed around, there was always a drop of water piddling down on my eye or into my mouth . . ."

—No word of a lie there about the slate-roofed houses, anyway . . .

—Baba left him two hundred pounds in her will, and bloody tear and 'ounds, he never lifted his lips from a pint since then. Nell's house is too far away from the pub for him . . .

—He's the sly skunk alright, Fireside Tom . . . !

—Sly skunk is right. That's God's honest truth, Caitriona. A sly skunk. Bloody tear and 'ounds, I often said myself that he was a sly skunk. What else would you call someone who snuck out of Nell's house out of sheer stubbornness because they wouldn't let him get into the car . . .

—But wasn't he just the same, Bartley, just the same as the rest of the riff raff that snivelled around there? . . .

—Bloody tear and 'ounds, Caitriona, when Nell got her arse under the car first, she hardly let it out at all, apart from herself. Off she went, showing her snout to the rest of the country every other day—off to the Fancy City, to Lough Shore, to Ross Cala—herself and Blotchy Brian . . .

—The slitty slut . . .

—Bloody tear and 'ounds, Nell's Peter would hardly be there, but then the kids would be there too. He wanted to make a few bob and it didn't suit him that those little knackers were hogging the car at the same time. It's mouthed about that that's what finally did for Blotchy Brian, he was forbidden from getting into the car. Anyway, it was around that time, that he started shacking up in the house . . .

—God's curse on him anyway, wasn't it time for him! He'd look a holy show in a car, Blotchy buffer Brian!

—Bloody tear and 'ounds, Caitriona, didn't he look just as good as Fireside Tom! Tim Top of the Road's youngfella brought himself and Peter Nell and the priest's sister to a dance in the Fancy City. Fireside Tom had just come back from Peter's Pub, and bloody tear and 'ounds, do you know what, he plonked his arse straight up and into the car! "I'm going to the dance too," he announced, "I swear to God there'll be fine things and hot lashers there."

—The senile slapper . . .

—He was puffing and smoking like crazy, and bloody tear and 'ounds, what do you know, but the next thing is he chucks up a big green glob of scummy spit and fires it off! Nobody said nothing much, Caitriona, but I heard that Blotchy Brian muttered later that the priest's sister had to change her clothes before she went to the dance . . .

—Good enough for her, the little shit, getting into a car that belonged to a blow rag butch bitch . . .

—Peter Nell told Tom to shag off in home. "I will yea," he said . . . "No fucking way . . ."

—God bless him, and give him long life! . . .

—Blotchy Brian's daughter asked him to go in . . . "I'm telling you all, I swear, I'm going to the dance," he says with vehemence.

—He was right, of course, not to take a bitch of a bit's notice of what Blotchy Brian the Bummer's frump of a daughter said . . .

—Bloody tear and 'ounds, Tim Top of the Road's youngfella should grab him by the balls, fuck him out head over heels onto the street, and give him two big whopping boots up the bum! Bloody tear and 'ounds, he should take off down to Paddy's house right now no messing, he's skulking there this long while . . .

—That's a real smack in the face, a real beauty for Nell! He'll leave all the land now to Patrick . . .

—Bloody tear and 'ounds, Caitriona, so it goes, nobody has the least clue who Fireside Tom will leave his streaky rasher bit of land to. When they'd be off gallivanting in the car, Blotchy Brian was always nagging him to sign the papers to leave it to his daughter, but small chance! . . .

—Serves them both right, Brian the snotty smart-arsed jerk and mincy meddlesome Nell! I suppose you heard nothing about a cross, did you, Bartley? . . .

—Crosses. Bloody tear and 'ounds, they hardly talk about anything else. John Willy's cross, Breed Terry's cross, Redser Tom's cross, Jack the Lad's cross that they've done nothing about since . . . Bloody tear and 'ounds, Caitriona, but it doesn't matter by the hangers of the halls of Hell whether you have a cross or not when you are dead! "Oh-row, Maureen . . ."

—You won't be piping that tune much more when you're here a bit longer, Bartley, listening to Nora Johnny. You'd think she was the mother of the Earl. But, come here to me, did you hear that Patrick was going to stick up a cross over me anytime soon?

—Himself and Nell are often away off and yonder in the car ever since Jack the Lad was buried. Stuff about crosses, stuff about wills . . .

—But it wouldn't do him any good to be going off with that scum scuzzy slag . . .

—Bloody tear and 'ounds, Caitriona, but he's doing all right, God bless him! He never had as many cattle on his land. He raised two litters of pigs recently: you never saw the likes of them, lovely luscious lusty pigs with loaded backsides as hot and heavy as bullocks on the boil. Bloody tear and 'ounds, isn't he sending two of them to college! . . .

—Two of them? . . .

—Yeah, two, that's it. The older one and the young one after her . . .

—God help them, like! . . .

—And the one after that will be going in the autumn, they say. Bloody tear and 'ounds, isn't that exactly what Blotchy Brian said! . . . "Ho-row, then Mary, your belts and your buckles . . ."

—But what exactly did he say, Bartley?

—Bloody tear and 'ounds, it was just a slip of the tongue, Caitriona! "Ho-row . . ."

—No harm, Bartley, no harm. I can't exactly contradict him, can I? God bless you anyway, Bartley, but hey, listen, just tell me. It'll do me good . . .

—Bloody tear and 'ounds, Caitriona, it'll do you no good, no good at all. "Ho-row, then Maureen . . ."

—I'm telling you it'll do me a power of good, Bartley. You'd never credit the lift we get from a bit of news here. The crowd down here would tell you nothing at all at all, even if they could get back up again for a while as a reward. See! Jack the Lad buried in his grave for the last three weeks! Jack the Lad! Jack . . .

—"Ho-row, then Maureen . . ."

—Ah go on! Let it out. Good man, Black Bandy Bartley! . . . Straight up now. They'll know soon enough up above that this is the wrong grave . . .

—Bloody tear and 'ounds, Caitriona, it doesn't matter diddly squat where they chuck your old bag of bones! . . .

—But tell me anyway, Bartley, what did Blotchy Brian say . . .

—Well, if it's going to cause shit, Caitriona, it's going to cause shit. "Paddy is away on a hack," he said, "ever since he left that meddling muppet of a mother in the hole of the graveyard. He should have boiled a blazing pot years ago, lit it up with burning flames, and dumped her into it like you'd do with a kitten . . ."

—They've blotted you out, you bastard Black Bandy Bartley! Jack the Lad! Jack the Lad! . . . Jack the Lad! . . .

3.

—. . . I was crushed when I heard that the *Graf Spee* was sunk. I came here a fortnight since then . . .

—The mine nearly got us. Apart from that, Mrukeen was going to take the five . . .

—. . . Stabbed me through the twists of my kidneys. The Dog Eared Shower always had that sneaky stab . . .

—I caught the death of me from sweating in my sleep, that time I cycled to Dublin to see Cannon . . .

—... Fell off the rick of oats and broke my hip ...

—Pity you didn't break your tongue, as well! ...

—Your legs took you a long way up, up on a rick of oats ...

—I swear that you'll never fall from a rick of oats again. I swear you won't ...

—If you hadn't fallen from a rick of oats, you'd have died some other way. You'd have got a kick from a horse; or your legs would have given out ...

—Or he'd have given you a bad bottle ...

—Or your daughter-in-law wouldn't have given you enough to eat, seeing as you lost your pension because you had money stashed in the bank.

—You can be sure you would have died anyway ...

—To fall is a terrible thing ...

—If you fell in the fire like I did ...

—It was the heart ...

—Bedsores. If only they had rubbed a bit of hot stuff into me ...

—Joan, ya jizzer ya! You caused the death of me. Lack of fags ...

—And your coffee, ya ugly Joan ya ...

—One way or the other, that's the reason I died ...

—Bloody tear and 'ounds, there was no reason for me to die. I just laid back and drifted away ...

—The reason the Old Master died was ...

—An excess of love. He thought that if he died the Mistress thought her life wouldn't have been worth living without him ...

—That's not it, but it dawned on him that he'd be doing the dirty on Billy the Postman if he hung on any longer ...

—No way, but Caitriona cursed him after he wrote a letter to Baba. "May not another corpse come to the graveyard before her!" she'd say. "Going from the table to the window ..."

—The reason for Jack the Lad's death was that Nell sent him off with St. John's Gospel ...

—Shut your hole, you grabber! ...

—It's true! It's too true. The little whore's git got St. John's Gospel from the priest ...

—. . . You died from shame. Your son marrying a black in England . . .

—It would have been a lot worse if he had married an Italian, like your son did. From that day on you had no luck. I saw you going home one day. "He's done for," I said to myself, "he's like a dead man walking. Since he got the news that his son married an Italian he's been wasting away. Pure shame. Nothing would surprise you . . ."

—. . . The guy from the east of the town died because we let the English market go . . .

—. . . He was so pissed off mulling over whether or not to stick his foot out the door.

—Blotchy Brian said that Curran died because he was totally pissed off 'cos he couldn't do a hatchet job straight down through the middle of the Guzzler's donkey that he found gobbling the oats in his field . . .

—I thought it was Tim Top of the Road's donkey . . .

—Up his arse anyway, it was Top of the Road's donkey, but I'd have much preferred it if it was his daughter rather than his donkey . . .

—Colm More's daughter died because . . .

—The sad sickness of Letter Eektur . . .

—No way, no way, at all. But since she got a belt nobody visited the house apart from the doctor, and there wasn't a stir out of her . . .

—You are insulting the faith. You're a black heretic . . .

—The insurance man was only one letter short in the crossword. He had abbreviated . . .

—The reason for Redser Tom's death was that his tongue was too loose . . .

—What happened to me? What was wrong with me? What saw me off? You'd want to be very smart to know that . . .

—Chalky Steven died with sheer disappointment that he heard nothing about Caitriona Paudeen's funeral . . .

—. . . One way or the other, as you say, the reason I popped my clogs was the old guts . . .

—. . . Hoora! Did you hear that? The guts! His guts, like! It was

God's great revenge that he killed you, Tim Top of the Road. You stole my turf . . .

—It bugged him that he wasn't made the Grand Inquisitor . . .

—The wrath of God, Peter the Publican. You were watering the whiskey down . . .

—I was robbed blind in your house, Peter the Publican . . .

—Me too . . .

—God's justice, Guzzler. Drinking forty-two pints . . .

—"Nobody could ever say that I was just one of God's windbags," I says. "To go between hell and a hot place. Even if I had said a full and proper act of contrition, but I had hardly gone beyond the second bit of the credo, when the young one from the house beyond came looking for me. You're all lucky, you Tom types, that I have drunk forty-two pints . . ."

—Didn't God himself hassle you, you being an insurance man, that you were pulling a fast one on Caitriona Paudeen about Fireside Tom? . . .

—Ah come on now! I never did that, I never did . . .

—Too true, Caitriona, you never did, and you never didn't. The tricks of the trade . . .

—And when the Goom rejected my collection of stories, *The Yellow Stars* . . .

—You were better dead than alive, you poor shagger. Inside next to the fire praying by the ashes. "O Holy Ashes!" . . . Dear frozen blood that was spilled so that the balls of my bowels could be warmed! . . .

—He's a dirty black heretic . . .

—The *Irish Paddy* wasn't happy to publish "The Setting of the Sun." Nobody in the six parishes wanted to hear me read it . . .

—God's justice, no doubt about it! You said that Colm Cille made a prophecy just to fool the people . . .

—. . . No wonder that you died. I heard the doctor saying that nobody could keep their health on the nettle-infested fields of Bally Donough . . .

—The priest himself told me that twenty years ago, nineteen

households paid for it on the flea-infested hillocks of your own pissy little town, but now . . .

—Jack the Lad's funeral did me in. I crawled up out of my bed just to keen him. I collapsed on the way home. I burst out in a sweat. I was still sweating my guts out when I pegged out . . .

—Jack the Lad's funeral did me in also. I started swelling up after that . . .

—Ababoona! No harm in that when you think how you stuffed your greedy gut there! How long are you here, slippery Sarah, and you, clippity clappity Kitty? . . .

—Bloody tear and 'ounds, Caitriona, we nearly all popped off together. I went six days before Biddy Sarah, and ten before Little Kitty . . .

—That'll teach them to stay in their beds! They were wetting themselves trying to get a hold of that grubby clatterer, Nell. Pure nosiness. They wouldn't bother their barney searching out half-decent people . . .

—There'll be nobody left now to lay out or to keen Fireside Tom or Nell Paudeen . . .

—Serves her right, the fart face! . . .

—It was God's judgement that killed Caitriona Paudeen, no doubt about it. Honest! . . .

—That's a filthy lie, Noreen! . . .

—He persuaded her to ruin Fireside Tom, to rob Breed Terry's old man's tea, Kitty's spuds, and to pinch John Willy's periwinkles . . .

—That wasn't it at all, Nora Johnny, but St. John's Gospel that Nell got from the priest for your daughter. If it wasn't for the daughter wouldn't your daughter have been here at her next birth. She was always a bit sickly until Caitriona died. She was flying after that . . .

—Ababoona boona boona! Not a word of a lie! I swear I'd never have thought of that deep down! . . .

—That's it, I'd like to know how Huckster Joan would die. Force her to drink her own coffee . . .

—. . . Wear her own clogs.

—I know the death that I'd have liked for you, ya Greedy Guts, pour pints of porter down your throat until it came out every hole in your body, your nostrils, eyes, ears, under your nails, squelching out of your armpit, your eyebrows, fingers, knees, elbows, through the pores in your scalp, until you sweated seven different kinds of stout . . .

—. . . The death you'd deserve would be to keep you alive until you'd witness Kerry beating the crap out of Galway in the All-Ireland in 1941, and to have to listen to "The Rose of Tralee" being played on Cannon's arse . . .

—. . . The way I'd have you and every other descendent of the Treacherous Dog Eared Crowd, that you'd . . .

—Be forced to shout, "Up de Valera" . . .

—Not good enough, the way I'd do for Tim Top of the Road . . .

—To leave him to me so that I'd stick one of his thatching yokes down his throat, through his windpipe until it'd burst out through his guts . . .

—Leave him to me so that I'd clock him with the mallet he stole . . .

—I'd have no problem lopping his head off with my scythe . . .

—Wouldn't it be a lot easier to hang him with my rope . . .

—Peter the Publican? Drown him in his watered-down whiskey . . .

—Paul? Keep his throat parched while he had to listen to The Great Scholar reading the lesson . . .

—He can go and stuff himself with his windy waffle! Don't give the little prick anything to eat, the cheapskate dickhead, only his "Holy Ashes" . . .

—I know the death Caitriona Paudeen would give Nora Johnny. She'd get her to disinfect herself, especially her feet . . .

—Shut your hole, you grabber!

—. . . The writer guy, is it? He insulted Colm Cille, the lousy lickspittle. Make him do every second turn over and back, just as the Mistress does to Billy the Postman . . .

—Force him to stitch *The Thirty-One Sermons* onto his gut . . .

—Force him to renounce his heresy and his insults to Colm Cille before the congregation; to grovel and seek forgiveness for all the stuff he ever wrote; for all the innocent young maidens whom he sent astray with his writings; for all the couples who broke up because of him; for all the happy homes that he destroyed; for being the precursor for the Antichrist. And after that to excommunicate him, and to burn his bones. Nothing else would be good enough for a heretic . . .

—. . . I know the death the Old Master would give to Billy . . .

—The robber! The death I'd give to that knob gobbler . . .

—The Postmistress! I know. Make her go a week without reading any letters only her own . . .

—Too true. A full week without gossip killed Colm More's daughter . . .

—They say the Mistress said that what caused the Old Master's death was . . .

—That he was too good for this life . . .

—That's exactly what she said. I'll never forget the words she spoke. "He whom the gods love . . ."

—Oh, the bitch! The scrag! The dipshit! . . .

—De grâce, Master! Don't be copying Caitriona again! . . .

—. . . Don't you remember that I am the old man of the graveyard! Let me speak . . .

—. . . Little Kitty! To keep her away from corpses . . .

—God help your fruitcake head! The Afrika Korps couldn't keep her away, if she got the whiff of one . . .

—Blotchy Brian, I know the death he'd like Caitriona Paudeen to have . . .

—Squashing a sneaky cat under the lid of a pot! . . .

—Force her to stand out on her own road; then Nell to go by with her fancy hat in her lovely car; give a sharp sweet smirk in at Caitriona while she blew the horn with vigour . . .

—Oh, listen to me! Listen! I'd burst . . .

—Isn't that just what I said!

—I'd burst! I'd burst! . . .

4.

—. . . "'Would you not come home with me, I have room beneath my shawl

Ah, why not Ja-ack . . .'"

—*Écoutez-moi, mes amis. Les études celtiques.* We'll have a Colloquium now.

—A Colloquium, bejaysus boys. Hóla, the lot of you, Breed Terry, Chalky Steven, Guzzeye Martin! A Colloquium . . .

—A *Colloquium*, Redser Tom! . . .

—I'm saying nothing. Nothing at all . . .

—Isn't it a pity to God that Fireside Tom isn't here! He'd be a great man for a *colloquium* . . .

—There's the results of my study of the dialect of the Half Guinea Place. I'm afraid this won't be a proper *colloquium* at all. I'm not fluent enough, nor are any of you, in the only language in which a *colloquium* could be properly delivered . . .

—Fluent? . . .

—Fluent, *mes amis*. The first requirement for a *colloquium* is to be able to talk. I have to say, my friends and colleagues, that my research has left me sorely depressed . . .

—Oh, God help us, the poor man! . . .

—*Mes amis*, you can't really do any learned research on a language which many people speak, like English or Russian . . .

—I have my doubts, I think he's a filthy heretic . . .

—You can only research a dialect—or it wouldn't be worth it anyway—that is spoken by two or three people, at the most. There has to be three slobbers of senile snot for every one word . . .

—There was a day like that, Peter the Publican, don't deny it . . .

—There's no point in researching somebody's speech unless every word of his is stand-alone like a crow on the sand . . .

—Eight into eight, that's once; eight into sixteen, that's twice . . .

—. . . This *colloquium* is a God-sent opportunity for me to read "The Sunset" . . .

—*Pas du tout!* This is a *Colloquium convenable* . . .

—I'm not going to listen to "The Sunset." No way. Honest! . . .

—Just a minute now, you fancy Frenchie! I'll tell you a story . . .

—*Écoutez, Monsieur* Coley. This here is a colloquium and not a university lecture on Irish literature . . .

—I'll tell you a story. I swear to God I will! "The Little Pussy who Smudged and Smattered the White Sheets of the North of Ireland . . ."

—. . . "Big Johnny Martin's young daughter

Was as huge as you could imagine . . ."

—. . . "At dear Doughty Dublin he met Mogcat of the Massive Thighs. 'Don't budge even another inch,' says Mogcat, 'I've just come back from seaman Dublin having done the dirty on all the clean sheets there. "Dublin of the Ford of the Stickies," they'll call it from now on. I left as my heritage this fine piece of nasty nonsense splattered on the country—Reidy's Rump—and before that I had smudged and smattered the nice virgin sheets of the South of Ireland. The South of Ireland, do you get it, derived from Smog Cat, that is a huge cat in Old Irish . . .'"

—*Ce n'est pas vrai!* The word is Magnacat. Matou. Magnatude. Magnacalves.

—The real authentic word for "cat" in Old Irish was "gast."

—*Mais non!* Like a gate, a trap, a trick, a snare, a snatch, a device, a thingy, a yokemebob. "My gate of gates, I have gotten you in the get up of go," in the words of Stitched Arse as he was discarding his robes . . .

Modern Breton: *gast:* a woman who has a whole wheelbarrow full of blessed stuff which she will sell as a cheapo *pardon* in the Lyons fair. In the dialect of Gwynedd . . . sorry I'll have to look up my notes, Coley, just to check that out. But the *thèse* is spot on: Old Irish: Gast; "S" giving way to "T"; Gat: Cat: Pangar Bawn; Panting: Panther. The Huge Humungous Fluent Flying Mogcat of Learning and Knowledge . . .

—Hang on a minute now, like, my good man, and I'll relate to you how the robes were whipped from off the back of Arse Stitch . . .

—Ah, come on Coley, John Kitty over in our place says just that he only lost them . . .

—John Kitty from your place! Of course, everybody from your place was always decent and proper, as we know . . .

—By the oak of this coffin, Little Kitty, I gave her the pound, I gave Caitriona Paudeen the pound . . .

—. . . She had a lovely fur coat on her, Redser Tom, just like the one that Baba Paudeen had, but she had to dump it because of all the streaks of soot that had soiled it in Caitriona's house . . .

—That's another lie, Breed Terry! . . .

—I just want a bit of peace. Why don't you just shut the fuck up and give me some peace, Caitriona . . .

—. . . Might I, if you please, Chalky Steven, be permitted to give you some spiritual assistance? . . .

—. . . Billy the Postman, is it, Master? Bloody tear and 'ounds, if somebody dies, they dies. If Billy is on his way out, bloody tear and 'ounds, come on, like, Master, he'll just lie back and there won't be a puff left in him . . .

—. . . That's what you say about the young colt that died! . . .

—About the young mare that died! . . .

—It's a long time since we heard that story, but Black Bandy Bartley told me that the young colt hadn't long died . . .

—It was a long time for me, anyway. A queer thing. I bought her at St. Bartholomew's Fair. It was no bother to her to haul a ton and a half up a hill. I had her, just about two years . . .

—As soon as Black Bandy Bartley said that the young colt had died, "The weather whacked her," I said, "The youngfella hadn't put a roof on the pen, and he left her too long exposed." "Bloody tear and 'ounds, that's not what happened at all, no way, never," he said . . .

—It was around the time of Bartholomew's feast day, of all days. I was bringing the young mare up to the New Field beside the house. She had chomped and chewed all the way down to the chalk. I met Nell and Peter Nell at the top of the meadow, and they were heading off back home. "Any chance you'd have a match?" Peter asks me. "Bejaysus, I might," I said. "Where are you off to with the young mare?" he asks. "Bringing her up to the New Field," I says . . .

— "So it goes," I says to myself. "Bloody tear and 'ounds, that wasn't it all, at all," Black Bandy Bartley says . . .

— "She's a lovely little mare, God bless her, and God bless you," Nell says. "She'd be fine," says Peter, "if you could control her at all." "Control her!" I says. "She doesn't even break sweat pulling a ton and a half up a hill . . ."

— "Glanders," I says. "Bloody tear and 'ounds, no it wasn't the cough," Bartley says. "No, that wasn't it at all . . ."

— "You're not thinking of putting her in for the competition this Bartholomew's Day, are you?" Peter said. "Ah, sure, I wouldn't have much of a clue about that," I says. "You win some and you lose some. I hate to ditch her. A great little hoor of a young mare. But I haven't much apart from her this winter."

— "Worms," I says. "Bloody tear and 'ounds," says yer man of the Black Bandy . . .

— "How much are you looking for her now, God be good to her?" Nell says. "Ah, like, if I brought her to the market, I'd look for twenty-three pounds," I says. "What do you mean, twenty-three pounds!" Peter says, as he wends his way up the bit of road. "Would you be happy with sixteen pounds?" Nell asks. "Do you know the way it is, Nell, I wouldn't," says I. "Seventeen pounds," she says. "For crying out loud, what do you mean by seventeen miserly pounds!" Peter exclaims. "Get the fuck out of here!" The mother went off out behind away after them, while she cast every second glance back on the white-headed mare . . .

— "What do you mean, worms!" he screams. "Bloody tear and 'ounds, she hadn't as much as a worm wriggling inside him as I did! Wasn't she opened up! . . ."

— Caitriona Paudeen appeared from behind the little Hedge Fields, her own lot. "What was that pus bitch saying?" she demanded. "I'd let her go for twenty, or maybe even nineteen. I'd sell her for a pound cheaper than I would to any blow-in. 'Twould raise my spirits to see her trotting past every day. I'd say because she liked her so much herself or her son would be knocking on my door before the morning was past. They won't let me bring her to the fair." "Arrah, was it that small snouty smelly bitch?" Caitriona says. "She'd destroy that lovely fair-headed mare of yours, going up the cliff path with her. But if she buys her, bad luck to her . . ."

—"God knows so," I says, "what use would that little colt be. Any chance she'd have a dicey heart? . . ."

—Do you know what, she said something like that, John Willy? "Hop off to the fair," he says, "with your white-headed mare, and get what you can for her, and don't believe a word from that saccharine sly slinky slut . . ."

—"Bloody tear and 'ounds," the Black Bandy fucker said, "why would she up and lie down and die on us? . . ."

—"Go away off to the fair with your white-headed mare," Caitriona says again. I wouldn't have taken a blind bit of notice, if it wasn't for the terrified look I saw in the eyes of the young mare . . ."

—It's tough luck now on the poor youngfella that the young colt is gone. He'll be hard put now to get any kind of a woman . . .

—That very evening the colt was coughing and spluttering. The very next morning at the crack of dawn Peter Nell turned up at my door. The two of us headed off to the New Field. 'Twas a total disgrace, John Willy. She was laid out from ear to arse, dead to the world . . .

—Just like the young colt . . .

—"How it goes," I says. "The evil eye."

—They always said that Caitriona had the evil eye. I refused to buy any young colt as long as she was around . . .

—Come off it! Ababoona! Nell, the bitch, gave the evil eye.

—She went by me without as much as a "hallo," and I hadn't even put two more stumps up on the stook when I collapsed . . .

—I swear to God she never even gave me a nod, and I twisted my ankle that very day . . .

—And of course, the Old Master never had one more day of decent health since he wrote that letter for her. A curse . . .

—She obviously never gave Mannix the Counsellor the evil eye, as he's still alive . . .

—Don't believe them Jack! Jack the Lad! . . .

—. . . How is it you never heard, Kitty, how is it you never heard that Fireside Tom has moved again? . . . He did . . . I swear, a fortnight ago . . .

—Ababoona! . . .

—There was no way he could get a wink of sleep in Paddy Caitriona's house, what with the pigs snuffling and sniffing from morning till night. The sow had some young ones, and they were brought into the house. "You'd really think they'd need a snorting of sows," he says. "Look at the likes of me who never had a smell of a sow. I'm off up to the house where there's no grunting or growling of pigs, and what's more, a house that has a slate roof." On his way up to Nell's house, he drove Patrick's cattle clean out of his own bit of land . . .

—The little slime skin, that's Fireside Tom . . .

—You'd be far more disgraced, as you said yourself, if he upped and offed and married an Italian. Those blacks are a fairly slick lot. Remember the black guy who was a butler to the Earl, a long time ago now?

—But that black guy was a rough enough diamond . . .

—Yea, true, sometimes he could be a bit rough. Well, God knows, what will happen to the guy left at home? The priest's sister asked him to marry her, as it happens. They're still talking and hanging out together, one way or the other.

—That's exactly what happened to my youngfella in England too. He was knocking around or knocking up this black yoke for a while, and then she asked him to marry her. And do you know what, the fucking eejit upped and married her . . .

—By the holies, as you say yourself, that's how it goes. Stupid senseless lads. I heard that there was great crack in that one Nancy, back home—I think she's called Nancy too—but if I was alive I know what I'd tell him: "Take it nice and easy now, boy. What could that young one do in a country house? Do you think she'd lift a load of turf, or carry a creel of seaweed? . . ."

—Isn't that exactly what I wrote to my son in England! "You've hitched up with a right floozie there," I says to him. "If you ever dare to come home, you'll have a right queer gang hanging out of you: a little black picanniny, and a whole flock of small blackies skiting around the town. You'll be the talk of the whole country. They'll come from north and south and east and west to get a gawk at them. Of course, there's no way she'll be able to raise a sweat on field or on shore. There wasn't a smell of either turf or seaweed where she came from . . ."

—You could hardly get more stupid than that, as you'd say yourself! Our guy, you couldn't talk any sense into him. He was always a bit of a . . . What's that Nora Johnny called him? . . .

—A dolthead? . . . A bowsie? . . . A dosser?

—Ah no, not at all. He was never a dosser. I brought him up good and proper, and not just because I'm saying it. How is it that I can't remember how Nora Johnny described him? . . .

—Adonis! . . .

—That's it exactly, now that you say it. Nancy took him into the Fancy City, and got him to stick a ring on her finger. The old one was beside herself with excitement . . .

—You can say that again, and my old one too! She thought that the negress was some big important upper-class lady until I pointed out to her that the colour of her skin was exactly the same as the Earl's butler's. They had to call for the priest after that . . .

—That's how it goes, as you say yourself. The priest was trying to get Nancy to marry the Derry Lough schoolmaster, but I swear didn't she tell him straight out without sparing her tongue, that she wouldn't, no way. "That poncy microphallus is already married to the school," she says, "so why would he bother marrying me? I don't like him, I don't like the Derry Lough master," she said. "There's no jizz in him! He's only a wimp and a wanker . . ."

—My son was a bit of a wimp anyway. You'd think for a minute that there was a shortage of opportunities in London, a city in which there are as many people as in all of Ireland, or so they say . . . Her hair, I hear, is as curly as an otter's . . .

—Sheer stupidity, as you say yourself. "I won't marry the Derry

Lough wimp," Nancy says. "Tim Top of the Road's son has a motor-bike. He's a hunter, a fisherman, a fiddler, and he dances like a dream. He scrubs up brilliantly. He threatened to shoot Lord Cockton, if he ever saw him around me again. His house is like a *vile*"—that's the word, *vile*, that she used, I swear!—"his house is so spacious and sheer class. It cleans the cockles of my heart every time I go near it . . ."

—It's easy for you to be blathering and boasting about your classy house, Tim Top of the Road. Classy . . .

—Because of my stolen seaweed . . .

—Honest, Dotie. Every word I said is the complete truth. Caitriona Paudeen never paid for anything: the round table, Kitty's pound . . .

—You're a liar!

—And her son is like that too, Dotie. He wasn't paid for her coffin yet, in Tim's shop, or for the booze at her wake, or her funeral at Huckster Joan's . . .

—You're a liar, Noreen!

—A bill lands on her son's lap every second day concerning them, doesn't it! Honest. Why else do you think that Peter the Publican and Huckster Joan are so pissed off with her here . . .

—Ababoona, Noreen, Noreen . . .

—Not one miserable cent was paid for her burial, Dotie, apart from the fact that my son paid for Gort Ribbuck, and for the tobacco, and the snuff . . .

—Oh, Noreen, the margarine legs of every maritime man! Don't believe her, Jack the Lad . . .

—God would avenge us . . .

—And it was Nell, too, who paid for her grave here, simply out of shame . . .

—Oh, the whore, the wretch, the wench, I did not, I did not! Don't believe a word from that rancid rump from Gort Ribbuck! Don't believe her, Jack! I'm going to burst! I'm going to burst! I'll burst! . . .

5.

—... It was I who laid you all out, good friends and neighbours ...

—You were all right, Little Kitty, if the truth were told ...

—I never took neither a pound, a shilling, nor a penny from any man or beast. When the Earl's mother died, the Earl called me up. When I had laid her out, "How much will that be?" he asked. "It's up to yourself ..."

—They'd lock you up for ever, Little Kitty, if you even tried to lay a finger on her, or get to within a smell of the room she was laid out in ...

—'Twas I laid out Peter the Publican ...

—No, Little Kitty, it wasn't you. It was two nurses from the Fancy City decked up in dresses and white hats. Some people say they were nuns ...

—It was I prepared the Frenchman ...

—If you as much as laid a hand on him, Kitty, you'd have been locked up for violating Irish neutrality during wartime ...

—I laid out Huckster Joan ...

—You did in your arse. My daughters wouldn't give you a whiff of a puff of a half-nostril of the air that was in the same room as my body. Why would they? There you would be pawing and poking at me! ...

—There was only a whiff of a glance of Joan's body anyway, Kitty ...

—The Old Master ...

—Not you at all, Little Kitty. I was up working in our own field, beside the road, just next to the house. Billy the Postman called me over:

"He's on his way to the lost property office," he says. You and me, Kitty, were in the door as quick as a rat out of a hole. We shot up the stairs and rattled off a raft of prayers with the Mistress and Billy.

"The poor Master has passed away," the Mistress said, whimpering so. "You'd easily know it. He was too good for this life ..."

—Oh, the thundering bitch! ...

—Then, Kitty, you went over and stretched out your hand to

close his eyes, but the Schoolmistress stopped you. "I'll do whatever has to be done to the poor Old Master," she said . . .

—The twerpish tart twat! . . .

—Now, remember, Master, that Guzzeye Martin saw you at school . . .

—Nothing beats the truth, Master . . .

—"You go off on down to the kitchen, and take it easy, Little Kitty," she says. She said that Billy should go and get some food, and drink and smokes. "Spend whatever money you need," she said to Billy. "I couldn't begrudge the Old Master anything . . ."

—With my money! Aaah! . . .

—When we came back, Kitty, you were still in the kitchen. Billy went up to the Mistress, who was still bawling her eyes out . . .

—Oh, the skunk! The poxy shitmonkey! . . .

—When he eventually came down, you spoke to him, Kitty. "That poor thing has every reason to be distraught," you said. "I'll go up and try to help her." "It's alright, take it easy there, Little Kitty," Billy says. "The Mistress is so heartbroken over the death of the Old Master that she needs some time to herself," he said. He took a razor out from a cabinet and I held the belt for him, until he sharpened it . . .

—My own razor and belt! I kept them on top of the cabinet. He found them, the fecking filcher! . . .

—You were hopping around the kitchen, Kitty, just like a dog with fleas.

—Like Nora Johnny moseying around Caitriona's house . . .

—Shut your mouth, you grabber! . . .

—"I'll have to go up and keep him on his side while you are shaving one side of his face," you said. "Don't worry, the Mistress will do that," Billy says. "You just relax there, Little Kitty . . ."

—Oh, the poxy prick!

—Don't take a blind bit of notice of that, Master. I laid you out. You were a gorgeous-looking corpse, too, God love you! That's exactly what I said to the Mistress when I had you dickied up. "You have nothing to be ashamed of, Mistress," I says. "He's a gorgeous-looking corpse, God help him, and so he should: a man as fine as the Old Master! . . ."

—One way or the other, Kitty, it wouldn't matter how you dressed any one of us, but I'd say you'd be very much at home doing your thing with a schoolmaster . . .

—. . . I was five days looking after you, Mister Eastman; up and down to your house; up and down the hillock to look back at your place, to see if there was any sign of you. You were rambling and raving and rabbitting on about that slice of land at the top of the town, the very best for fattening up cattle. You'd think you didn't want to go at all unless you could take it with you . . .

—And the chancer blah blahing all the time about the market in England . . .

—. . . It was I laid you out, Curran, and even so, you were very reluctant to depart. There's no way you were going to go with the first death rattle. I was always just about ready to close your eyes, when you'd jump up again. Your wife took your pulse. "He's passed away, may God have mercy on his soul!" she said.

"May his soul have a calm crossing and a good day!" Blotchy Brian said, he just happened to be there. "He's got his passage at last. But by jaypurs, I never thought he'd sail away without Tim Top of the Road's daughter along with him."

"May he have a bed in paradise tonight!" I said myself, and I got them to prepare a basin of water. Of course, just at that very second you decided to wake up! "Make sure that Tom doesn't get the large holding," you said. "I'd rather see it blown away in the wind, than that it would be left to the eldest son, unless he marries some other woman except Tim Top of the Road's daughter." You sat up a little bit more: "If you let the eldest son get his claws on that land," you said to your wife, "I swear by all the devils in hell that my ghost will have you by the balls all day and all night! Wasn't it terrible that I didn't get a lawyer to make an unambiguous will! . . ."

Then you rose up the third time: "That spade that Tommy's daughter borrowed for the new potatoes, somebody better go and get it, seeing as they don't have the common decency to return it. The devil fuck them! Make sure too that you get a summons served on Greedy Guts up there about his donkeys wandering about and destroying our oats. And if you don't get any satisfaction in the court, the next time you catch any of them inside your fence, take a few horseshoe nails and drive them through their hoofs. The devil fuck them all! Don't be either lazy or listless and remember to get up well before dawn to keep an eye on your turf, and if you ever catch that Tim Top of the Road . . ."

—I thought it was the old one who did the stealing . . .

—Neither himself nor his old one nor his four children ever failed to do the wrong thing . . .

—. . . You were near enough to your last breath when I came in. I went down on my knees for the prayers. All the time you were saying, "Jack, Jack, Jack." "Isn't it great that the poor man is thinking all the time about Jack the Lad," I says to Nell Paudeen, who was on her knees beside me. "They were always great pals." "God give you some small bit of sense, Little Kitty!" Nell spluttered. "'Black, black, black' that's what he's really saying! The son . . ."

—I heard it said, Kitty, the last warning that Caitriona gave her son was . . .

—To bury her in the Pound Place . . .

—Erect a cross of Connemara marble over her . . .

—Ababoona! . . .

—Go to Mannix the Counsellor to write a stiff letter about Baba's will . . .

—Let Fireside Tom's house fall down . . .

—Poison Nell . . .

—Ababoona! Don't believe any of that, Jack . . .

—If Nora Johnny's daughter doesn't die at the next birth, to divorce her . . .

—You are insulting the faith, you grabber. The Antichrist won't be long coming now . . .

—. . . Ara, it quickly turned into a riot up and down the town land:

"Fell from a stack of oats."

"Fell from a stack of oats."

"Fell from a stack of oats, it's what the man did."

I took off up to your house straightaway. I was dead certain I would find a nice clean corpse waiting for me. But instead of that you were there like the useless article you are gobbing away telling all and sundry how your left leg slipped . . .

—But 'twas true, Kitty, I made junk and jibbets of my hip . . .

—What good was that to me? I thought I'd have a nice clean corpse all ready . . .

—But I did die, Kitty . . .

—I never saw a twit as uncomfortable as you were in the bed. One leg hanging out . . .

—I knew, Kitty, that I was on the way out, so I thought I'd go all the way and butcher the murderer. "Take two spoons of this bottle . . ."

—Bloody tear and 'ounds anyway . . .

—I poked away down your windpipe. "Where's the bone that choked her?" I asks. "The doctor plucked it out," your sister said. "May God's mercy know no end!" I said. "Nobody should be a glutton. If that woman wasn't gulping it down like a pig when she should have been eating, we wouldn't be laying her out now . . ."

"She hadn't eaten a pick of meat since St. Martin's Day," your sister said . . .

—Bloody tear and 'ounds anyway, isn't that exactly what Blotchy Brian said, that she'd be alive and bitching today, if it wasn't that she drove Caitriona Paudeen's dog out of the house before dinner. "He was so raving and ravenous," he said, "that he could have jumped down her thick throat and brought the bone back . . ."

—Oh, Brian, the bastard!

—. . . It was during the summer and the sweat was as thick as jam on your skin. "He must stink of sweat," my mother said. "My lovely boy, he had always a bit missing, and all signs on it now. That journey he brought on himself all the way to Dublin on his old crock of a bike, and he slept out in the open all night! I hope God won't punish him for it . . ."

—If I had been alive a month later, I'd have seen Cannon beating seven kinds of crap out of Kerry . . .

—In 1941, was it? If so . . .

—. . . You made my head go grey, and Maggie Frances's too. We scrubbed and scoured, and scoured and scrubbed you, but it didn't make a toss of a difference. "They're not dirt marks at all," I said to Maggie at the end. "There's five or six of them there," Maggie said. "Some kind of symbols to do with Hitler," your daughter said. My head is gone now, I can't think of what he called them . . .

—Tattoos.

—Swastikas . . .

—By all that's holy, that's it! We had used up three pots of boiling water on you already, four pounds of soap, two boxes of Rinso, a mountain of Monkey Brand, two buckets of sand, but there was no trace of them coming off. You wouldn't mind, but you weren't the least bit grateful after all our sweating and scrubbing! . . .

—You'd have got more only for the *Graf Spee*, otherwise I'd have branded every single screed of my skin. It's only what Hitler deserved . . .

—"Ara, let him go to blazes! Leave them be," said Maggie. "You couldn't let him off like that, the state of him," I says. "He's all over the place like a stray letter! Put another pot on the fire, for God's sake."

Blotchy Brian was there at the same time. "It looks to me that you intend to scrub the poor man like you'd scrub a swine," he says . . .

—He was the scrubber all right, and an ugly scrubber at that! . . .

—. . . Just like the other one, I was worn to bits trying to clean you. There wasn't a pinch of your flesh that wasn't covered in ink. "Just like somebody that was dipped in an ink trough," I said. "It's exactly the same as if he was," your sister said. "The ink shortened his life. Sucking it into his lungs from morning 'til evening, and from night until morning . . ."

—Writer's cramp from scribbling away, according to himself . . .

—It doesn't matter anyway what got him. He was a dirty heretic. He should never have been buried in consecrated ground. It's a wonder God didn't make an example of him . . .

—. . . I copped it as soon as I came into your room. "Did anyone spill any booze or something here?" I asked Curran's wife who was there. "I couldn't really tell if they did or didn't," she said . . .

—It wouldn't do him much harm: a man who could down forty-two pints no problem . . .

—There wasn't as much as a drop of booze in my stomach the day I died. Not as much as a drop! . . .

—It's true for you. Not a drop. All because of Little Kitty, the dirty gossip. She was gagging for a drink when she said that to Curran's wife . . .

—. . . But that's what it was, Little Kitty. It rotted my guts, Huckster Joan's coffee.

—. . . Your feet were as brittle as wood that was going to break into sawdust, big black lumps on them, and they were clattering away like a cow on spindly sticks . . .

—Huckster Joan's clogs, of course . . .

—I don't suppose you ever made it as far as Gort Ribbuck, Little Kitty. If you only caught a glimpse of Nora Johnny's feet who never wore clogs! That is, if what Caitriona says is true . . .

—Shut up your mouth, you grabber! . . .

—. . . As soon as I came to the door, I got the whiff of the small potatoes in the dregs of the fire, Kitty. "Serve up these few spuds," I says, "until the corpse is all ready." "There are no potatoes ready," Mickey says. "And unfortunately, there wasn't since morning either. She guzzled too many of those small potatoes. They were too hard on the heart. They crushed her stomach . . ."

—Bloody tear and 'ounds I've never heard the like, Kitty floored, flahed out, as if there wasn't a drop left in her . . .

—. . . They did nothing to you until you had gone cold. You were bundled up there, four of us around you, and not a clue between us. "Why doesn't one of you go and get your man's mallet," Blotchy Brian says, "and then you'll see how I'll straighten out the knees . . ." "Bloody tear and 'ounds, anyway," the Son of the Bandy Bollux said, "didn't Tim Top of the Road steal it from him! . . ."

—He certainly did, no doubt about it. A lovely mallet . . .

—. . . The mark of the creel of potatoes, John Willy, that you hauled from the Partick Field was etched on your back . . .

—When I was easing it off in the house the strap unravelled and it came down arseways. I got a little dart in my side. The dresser started to dance. The clock on the wall went up the chimney, the chimney came through the door, the colt out there in front of me in Garry Tee took off into the air, and deep down the path and away up the road. "The colt!" I screamed and headed for the door out after him. My heart, though . . .

—I got the stink of the bed from you straightaway, Guzzeye Martin . . .

—Too true, the bedsores done for me in the end . . .

—I don't really want to spread it around, but you, as a poet, you were covered with a crispy crust of crud from the knob of your noggin down to the thick of your toes . . .

—. . . His "holy ashes." The devil fuck him, the little latchiko! He never washed himself once . . .

—Myself and one of your aunts pointed it out, when it was only like a pimple on your butt. It nearly had us beaten. "There's a hard lump of dirt stuck in here," I says to your aunt. "Buckets of boiling water and sand." Your mother was out and about trying to get the shroud. She came back just then. "That's a birthmark," she announced. "Whenever my lovely boy felt the urge to write poetry, he'd scratch himself right there, and the words would pour out of him . . ."

—He was always easy to manage, a big softie, a lump of lard. We had a job to do and business to finish one way or the other . . .

—I never met a corpse whose eyes were as difficult to close as Tim Top of the Road's. I had my thumb pressed down on one of his eyes, while his old one had hers jammed on the other, but as soon as I closed mine the other one would just pop up open . . .

—Just to see could he spot a mallet which had gone astray . . .

—Or summer seaweed . . .

—I never ever smelled a smell as sweet as that from the Postmistress . . .

—That was the smell of the stuff she used to open and close the letters. The back room of her place was like a chemist's shop . . .

—Not at all! The kettle did the business. The perfumes in the bath. I had a bath myself just before I died . . .

—True for you, Postmistress. There was never any need to bathe your body one way or the other . . .

—I have no idea, Little Kitty, whether that's necessary or not. Gosh, like! If you came next or near my corpse the Minister for Posts and Telegraphs would have sued you . . .

— . . . Whoever laid you out, anyway, I'd say he got the smell of nettles from Bally Donough from you . . .

—A bit better than the smell from you . . .

—I never encountered a cleaner corpse than Jack the Lad's. The throes of death didn't leave a mark on him. He was like unto a posy of flowers. His skin was as smooth as silk, you might say. You'd think he was just lying back and relaxing . . . What matter, but every stitch he had on him was like the white "flour" that they threw on the earl at the door of the chapel when he was getting married! Of course, they'd never have been in Nell Paudeen's house if it wasn't otherwise . . .

—The sly slut! The cock piss artist! . . .

—They say, Kitty, that Caitriona's corpse . . .

—Caitriona's corpse! That thing! They called me, but I wouldn't go next nor near it . . .

—Ababoona! . . .

—It would have disgusted me . . .

—Ababoona! Little Kitty, the gabbler! Little Kitty, the gabbler! I'll burst! I'm about to burst! . . .

6.

There's no God up there but he'll avenge the two of them! You'd easily know. I had no particular pain. The doctors said that the kidneys wouldn't kill me for a while yet. But that whore from Hell Nell cajoled St. John's Gospel from the priest for Nora Johnny's daughter, and they bought a single ticket for me to this place, just like Jack the Lad, the poor old codger. Wasn't it clear to a wedge of wood, if there wasn't some kind of jiggery pokery involved, that Nora Johnny's young one would be here at her next birth! Instead of that she hadn't a sign of a pain or an ache . . .

Too bad, there were no flies on that bitch! She knew right well as long as I had a flea's fart of breath left in me that I'd keep at her about Baba's will and Fireside Tom's bit of land. But she can pull the wool over Patrick's eyes, anytime she likes . . .

Two thousand pounds. A slate roof on the house. A car. A hat . . . The Son of the Black Bandy Bartley said that Patrick would get a fistful of the readies, but that's not much of a consolation when he won't get the whole lot! It was an injustice to God that your one over there didn't leave every greasy grimy halfpenny that she had to some priest! . . .

Jack the Lad had an altar worth twenty-three pounds! And he never allowed a shilling leave his own house to be sent to any funeral! . . . A High Mass. Priests. The Earl. Lord Cockton. Four half-barrels of stout. Whiskey. Cold meats . . . And, of course, it was no bother to that bush pig to light twelve candles for him in the church. Just to have one over on me. What else? I wouldn't begrudge poor Jack anything, but for that bitch making his corpse look so garish, the old cow. Easy for her—the tricks of a tart . . .

Jack the Lad wouldn't sing a song that last day. All the heart had gone out of him. It doesn't matter to him now having spent his life with that slag. And the only respect she had for him in the end was to fetch St. John's Gospel so he could die! . . .

When I told him that the other day he said neither yea nor nay, nothing except "God might punish us . . ." I'd say he's like a red raging bull now because of the way she messed him around . . . And the muppet didn't know a thing about it. There was never any harm in him. If there was he'd have known that that blowrag Nell was making a fool of him when she asked him to marry her. "I have Jack," she said triumphantly. "We'll leave Blotchy Brian to you now, Caitriona" . . . But I'm cosying up to Jack more closely now than she is. I can speak to him anytime I like . . .

If Patrick hadn't listened to Nora Johnny's waffle I'd be right up next to him now in the Pound Place. That other wench, Huckster Joan, is right beside him. She has only a bad word for me too. She's told him a bellyful of lies about me already. That's why he's so cagey . . .

I wouldn't mind only that Toejam thing trying to entice him into her Rotary! And Biddy Sarah and Little Kitty endlessly groaning and moaning about the funeral. You'd easily know it wasn't the poor guy that killed them off. Go away with yourselves now, sure, but they never stop boasting and prattling on about the way they put that bitch sitting up on her bed . . .

All their tongues are worn out praising Nell too, Maggie Frances, Kitty Small Potatoes, Breed Terry, John Willy, the Foxy Cunt and Guzzeye Martin. But they won't say anything up to my face, as I would have nothing good to say about her . . .

Say anything or nothing. You'd think they were trying to avoid me. I love somebody who comes straight out and tells you brazenly to your face . . . This graveyard is worse now than those places the Frenchie was yacking on about the other day: Belsen, Buchenwald, and Dachau . . .

—. . . If I was alive, I'm telling you, Jack the Lad, I'd have been at your funeral. I wouldn't be found wanting . . .

—. . . Come here to me now, my good man. Did you ever hear the nickname that Conan had for Oscar? . . .

—I swear by the oak of this coffin, Biddy Sarah, I gave her the pound, I gave Caitriona the pound, and I never saw a penny of it ever again . . .

—You're spouting lies, you itchy arse bum! Margaret! Margaret! Do you hear what the Slut of the Small Spuds is saying again? . . . Hey, Margaret, I'm talking to you! Hello, Margaret! Why are you taking no notice of me? . . . Margaret, for Jayz sake! . . . Why won't you say something? Because I'm a loudmouth, is that it! . . . All I'm good at is causing trouble . . . There was peace in the graveyard until I came along, is that what you're saying? You should be thoroughly ashamed of yourself, Margaret, trying to ruin somebody's reputation like that! . . . The place is like Bricriu's Feast with all my lies! Ah, come off it,

Margaret! You don't have to go that far from your own hovel to find a pack of liars. I never told lies or spread rumours around, thanks be to God for that! . . .

Hello, Margaret! Do you hear me? It was your Pack who were the Pack of Liars . . . You're going to pay no heed to my piping from now on, is that it? Piping, forfucksake! And it was always the whole truth and nothing but the truth! . . . Hey, Margaret! Margaret! . . . Mother of God, not a word. Hi Hi Hi, Margaret! . . . Why don't you give your tongue a wakeup call? . . .

Hello, Little Kitty! . . . Little Kitty! . . . It's not about neighbourliness, Kitty . . . John Willy! . . . Do you hear me John Willy? . . . Not a peep! . . .

Hey Breed Terry? . . . Are you out there, Breed Terry? . . . Tell me Breed Terry, what did I ever do on you? . . .

Guzzeye Martin! . . . Guzzeye Martin! . . . Kitty! . . . Kitty! . . . It's Caitriona. Caitriona Paudeen . . . Ah come on Kitty, for God's sake . . .

Jack! Jack! . . . Jack the Lad! . . . Hello, Jack the Lad, it's me Caitriona Paudeen . . . Hey, you in the Pound Place, call Jack the Lad! Tell him that Caitriona Paudeen wants him! . . . Jesus, Mary and Holy St. Joseph, Jack! . . . Huckster gombeen Joan, Joan! May God give you every blessing, Joan, but please call up Jack the Lad He's right there beside you . . . Joan! . . . Jack! . . . Jack! Jack! I'll burst, I'm going to burst, I'm about to burst, burst, I swear I'll burst . . .

Interlude 9

THE WASTING EARTH

1.

—The sky is mine, the sea, the land . . .

—The hinterland is mine, what is upside down, the insides, the lower depths. You only have the edges and the contingent . . .

—The light of the sun is mine, the shining moon, the sparkling star . . .

—The mysterious recesses of every cave are mine, the jagged pits of every abyss, the dark heart of every stone, the unknown guts of every earth, the hidden stem of every flower . . .

—Mine is the sunny south, brightness, love, the ruddy rose and the maiden's smile . . .

—Mine is the dour north, darkness, misery, the shoot that gives life to the rose petal, the web of veins that drives the diseased blood of melancholy routing laughter from the cheeks to lighten the brightness of the face . . .

—Mine is the egg, the sprout, the seed, the source . . .

—Mine is . . .

2.

—. . . *Monsieur Churchill a dit qu'il retournerait pour libérer la France. Vous comprenez, mon ami?* . . .

—His Irish is slipping away again, no problem, now, since he's taken up the higher learning . . .

—. . . Fell from a stack of oats, Chalky Steven . . .

—. . . I heard "Haw Haw" with my own two ears promising revenge for the *Graf Spee* . . .

—. . . The Big Butcher came to my funeral, Chalky Steven . . .

—. . . Hitler himself will cross over to England and stuff a small bomb, about the size of a loaf of bread, down inside those big baggy trousers that Churchill wears . . .

—. . . I spend my time giving people spiritual assistance. If you ever feel the need for some spiritual assistance, I'm the . . .

—I won't, I'm telling you. And I'm warning you now, even if you are Colm More's daughter, to leave those black dirty heretics to me, and don't stick your nose into it one way or the other, or else I'll . . .

—. . . Christ save us all, if England is decimated like that, where will the people sell anything? You have no land at all up at the top of the town . . .

—*Mon ami*, the United Nations, England, *les États Unis, la Russe, et les Français Libres* are all defending human rights together . . . *Quel est le mot?* . . . Against the barbarism of *des Boches nazifiés*. I told you already about the concentration camps. Belsen . . .

—Nell Paudeen is up for Churchill. All those fowlers and fishermen from England, of course . . .

—She was always treacherous, the witch! *Up Hitler! Up Hitler! Up Hitler!* Do you think there's a chance, if he comes on over, that he'll flatten her new house down to the ground?

—The Postmistress is all up for Hitler. She says that postmistress is a highly valued position in Germany, and if she suspects anyone, she had a bounden duty to open that person's letters . . .

—Billy the Postman is on Hitler's side too. He says . . .

—Oh, the scabby skunk! Whatever other side would he be on? Of course, he doesn't believe at all in private property or in the traditional values of western Europe. He's a communist, an antitraditional revolutionary, an Antichrist, an old fogey fart of a blackguard, a demon from hell just like Hitler himself. Up Churchill! . . . Shut your gabbling gob, Nora Johnny! You're a disgrace to womankind! Even to say that that filthy shit sucker had a romantic streak in him! . . .

—Good for you there, Master! Don't cool off now when it comes to the White Beauty of the Toejam trotters! . . .

—Redser Tom says that Fireside Tom . . .

—Fireside Tom! Which side is he on? It would take a wise man to say which side Fireside Tom was on . . .

—. . . Are you saying that I don't know already? . . .

—Nobody would really know, only those in the same town land . . . Fireside Tom fancied his own little hole of a hovel as much as a king hugged his crown . . .

—Son of a gun, anyway, I'm telling you, they let the whole hovel fall down on me in the end! . . .

—Ababoona! Fireside Tom is here! . . .

—There was a constant drip drop, drip drop into my mouth and eyes, no word of a lie, no matter where I planted the bed. They were bad. They were really bad, I'm telling you. Caitriona Paudeen has one mong of a youngfella, and Nell had another one, and they were a fairly miserable lot that they couldn't even put a strip of straw on my shack! . . .

—Fireside Tom is in the Fifteen Shilling Place, Kitty!

—That's it Breed, Fireside Tom is in the Fifteen Shilling Place! . . .

—That's the least you could expect, that they'd bury him in the Fifteen Shilling Place. He has his own bit of land, and they'll get a dollop of money from the insurance . . .

—But Nora Johnny swears that Paddy Caitriona welched on his insurance payments after his mother died.

—She's a liar! That swamp Toejam Hag! . . .

—Even if he didn't, what difference will that make to the insurance, after all that Tom had paid? Caitriona's praying for his death was no help at all. We'll ask the insurance man . . .

—Fireside Tom, how long are you here? . . .

—Do you know what now, like, I'm only just about here, Caitriona, my lovely. I never even had a pain nor nothing, and I died just the same as all! I went off exactly the same as all the others. I'll tell you what the doctor told me . . .

—It doesn't matter a damn now what the doctor told you. Nell buried you first . . .

—She's not great, Caitriona. Not great. She spent three weeks in bed, but she's hopping about again . . .

—The bitch, she would . . .

—And look at me, Caitriona, never had a pain nor nothing, and I died just the same as the rest of them! . . .

—Did you think you were going to live for ever? . . .

—Well, to tell the truth, I thought I would Caitriona, and the priest wasn't one bit pleased, he sure wasn't. The day he was up visiting Nell, he passed me by on the road, just as I was on my way to get a plug of tobacco from Peter the Publican . . .

—Peter the Publican's tobacco was better than anybody else's . . .

—True, Caitriona, my lovely. And you'd get a halfpenny's worth for next to nothing. "The way it is, Father," I says, "that poor woman up there is totally knackered" . . .

—You cunt you! . . .

—"It certainly doesn't look as if she is a hundred percent," he says. "I feel she is far too long in bed. Where are you off to now, Fireside Tom?" he says. "Off to get a plug of tobacco, Father," I says. "They say, Fireside Tom," he says, "that you really fancy that place over there; and that you never take your snout out of the booze . . ."

—That whore's git told him that! She'd always twist the knife in you . . .

—"Ah, sure, what harm, I take a drop the same as any man, Father," I says. "A drop would be no problem, Fireside Tom," he says, "but they also say that you'll never know when they'll find you stretched out on the side of the road dead as a doornail and you on your way home." "There's not a bit of bother on me, Father," I said, "I never had a pain nor nothing, thanks be to God, and of course, I have the new road under my feet all the way to Nell's door now."

—Hitler will rip up that road yet, with the help of God!

—"My advice to you now, and I'm telling you for your own good, Fireside Tom," I says, "my advice is to stay away from that place beyond there, and give up on the old booze. That won't really suit you from now on. And this lot over here have enough on their plate without having to scrape you off the ground and drag you home every night . . ."

—Holy God Almighty, hasn't the whore's melt got him by the balls! She wouldn't fuck with Hitler so easily . . .

—"For crying out loud, like, Father!" I says, "don't they have a car?" "If so, Fireside Tom," he says, "nonetheless, they have no petrol in the tank. There I am, and look at me I have to go on my bike! They say too, Fireside Tom," he says, "that you're like a shopping trolley over and back between the two houses. You'd think now, Fireside Tom," he says, "that you'd have a small smidgen of sense and settle on one of the two houses. Good luck to you, Fireside Tom," he says, "and not a word to anyone." "If that's the way it is," I says to myself, "I won't give them the satisfaction of bringing me home every night. There are far too many priests hanging around the house up there. It's not as if they need more priests . . ."

—That's not a word of a lie, Fireside Tom, not a word of a lie . . .

—"I'll toddle on down to Paddy Caitriona's house where I'll get a bit of a break," I says. I turned off down the path towards the Alla in case there'd be a few of Caitriona's beasts chomping away on my land. But there wasn't. A few of the useless fences were down. "I'll tell Paddy Caitriona to come up in the morning and to mend those fences and to put his own animals on my land," I says to myself . . .

—You got it bang on there, Fireside Tom . . .

—I came back around to the top of the path again, and I turned down to head towards Paddy's house. But I swear to Jesus, I'm telling you now, all of a sudden I couldn't budge a foot or mutter a word! Half of me was dead, and the other half alive. I never had a pain nor nothing, Caitriona, and yet I died the same as the rest of them! . . .

—Burst smack bang on the side of the road just like a puncture in a bicycle tube! That's Nell's evil eye for you, you poor fucker! . . .

—But I didn't actually die on the side of the road, dearie. Peter Nell came along as luck would have it and shunted me up to their house in the car. If it wasn't for that, I'd have died in your place, Caitriona. But there I was stretched out on the bed in Nell's house before I could get my breath back, and when I did I thought it wouldn't be right to take me down to Paddy's house . . .

—You always made a balls of everything, Fireside Tom, any chance you got . . .

—I only lasted the best part of ten days. My speech was coming and going. To tell you the truth, I haven't a clue if the priest helped me or not. I was never sick nor nothing . . .

—You never gave yourself any reason, me boyo! . . .

—Sacred Heart of Jesus, Caitriona my lovely, I did huge dollops of work. I slaved all my life . . .

—Even so, Fireside Tom, it wasn't for your own good. You spent most of your time slaving away at booze and boorishness . . .

—To tell the truth, Caitriona, I did get a bit pissed the odd Saturday, after Friday . . .

—Oh, you did alright, Fireside Tom, and every Saturday, and every Sunday, and every Monday, and a gaggle of Tuesdays and Wednesdays too . . .

—Your tongue is as ready as always, Caitriona. I always said that Nell was much more pleasant than you . . .

—You're an old fart! . . .

—I'll tell you what I'd say, Caitriona. "Caitriona wouldn't have been arsed looking after me if it wasn't just to spite Nell," I'd say. If you saw the way she looked after me after I was clocked, Caitriona. Two doctors and all . . .

—She called them entirely for herself, Fireside Tom, if the truth be known. That little hussy, nothing bothered her at all!

—As it happened she called them for me, Caitriona. No sooner was I brought into the house than she leaped out of the bed to look after me . . .

—She leaped out of the bed! . . .

—Leaped isn't the word, Caitriona, and then she stayed there sitting up and just looking at us . . .

—Oh, you eejit! You total fucking eejit! She had you on. She

244 *Máirtín Ó Cadhain*

made a total asshole of you. You never had a pain nor nothing, sure you didn't, Fireside Tom . . .

—Hardly ever, Caitriona, and see how I died just the same as everybody else who was racked with pain. Son of a gun, like. I'm beginning to think that the priest didn't help me one way or the other . . .

—You can swear to that, Fireside Tom! The prick-teaser managed to get St. John's Gospel from him that night, and she dumped you instead of him, just as she did with Jack the Lad . . .

—Is that what you think, Caitriona? . . .

—You can't see it yourself, Fireside Tom! A woman who had her arse in the air one minute, and the next was flitting away like a butterfly! That's what you deserved for yourself if you went next or near that bitch. If you stuck with my Patrick you'd be alive and kicking today. But anyway, what did you do with your patch of land? . . .

—A, sure, Caitriona, love, I left it to them: to Paddy and to Nell . . .

—You left them half and half, you little bollix!

—Ah, no, I didn't go that far, not half and half. I used to say it like this to myself, Caitriona, when the words came to me: "If it was any more than that, I wouldn't go one way or the other. There's no point in chopping it up half and half. Blotchy Brian always said it wasn't worth dividing up . . ."

—Of course, he said that, in the hope it would all be left to his own daughter . . .

—"I'll have to leave it to Paddy Caitriona so," I said to myself. "I'd have left it all to him if I had been that close to the house when I got the puck. But Nell was always very good to me too. I couldn't not leave her something seeing as I was about to die in her house . . ."

—Oh, you cunt! You bad baldy ball-less bollocks of a cunt!

—The priest was there and all to write down what I had to say, that's when it came to me: "Divide it in two, Fireside Tom," he said. "Either that, or leave it all to one of them."

—You'd think after all that crap, Fireside Tom, that you'd make a better fist of it than that. Why didn't you just saunter in nice and easy to Mannix the Counsellor in the Fancy City? . . .

—By the hokey, now Caitriona, I could only get the words out sometimes, and you'd have to have nails of ice on your tongue to start spitting words like Mannix the Counsellor. No matter anyway, Caitriona, I never really fancied having much to do with that same Mannix ever . . . Your Paddy was there: "I don't really want it," he said, "I have more than enough myself already."

—Oh, the eejit! I knew that Nell would make a complete asshole of him. He misses me . . .

—Isn't that exactly what Blotchy Brian said! . . .

—Blubbering Blotchy Brian!

—Maybe so, Caitriona, but he sent for the car to have him visit me . . .

—To help Nell about your patch of land. And if not, it wasn't for your good, Fireside Tom. Sending for the car! He'd look a sight in the car. A big bush of a beard. Teeth like a rabbit. Bent over. Stuffed nose. Clubfoot. Filthy flaky skin. Never washed himself . . .

—"If the mediator over at that gable-end was here," he said, "I'd say now, Father, that it would be Mannix the Counsellor rather than yourself who'd be accompanying Milord in by the fireside past the gander . . ." Nell slapped him in the mouth. The priest shoved him on out the door . . . "We don't want your patch of land either, Fireside Tom," Nell spluttered . . .

—That's another downright lie, the cocksucker! Why wouldn't she want it? . . .

—"I will leave my portion of land to Paddy Caitriona and to Nell Johnny," I said, when words came back to me. "You can have it, good luck to you." "What you say is a total crock, Fireside Tom," the priest said. "It'd only cause confusion and the law would be dragged in, if it wasn't for the good sense of these decent people . . ."

—Decent people! Oh! . . .

—I never spoke another single word after that, Caitriona. I never had a pain nor nothing, and see, I died all the same! . . .

—You're not much good to anyone dead or alive, you gimp! . . .

—Listen up now, Thomas. That's the dote. That tiff with Caitriona won't . . .

—What do you mean, a "tiff"?

—All that vile vituperation will only vulgarize your mind. I will have to establish a relationship with you. I am the cultural relations officer for the cemetery. I will give you some lectures on "The Art of Living."

—You, son of a bloody gun, . . . "The Art of Living"? . . . What next?

—A progressive section of us thought we had a duty to our fellow corpses, and so we set up a Rotary . . .

—Some bloody good, a Rotary! Look at me! . . .

—Exactly, Tom. Just look at you! You're a red-blooded romantic, Tom. You always were. But romance always requires the regulated support of culture beneath it to raise it above mere anarchy, and for its superior point to penetrate the meadows of Cupid in this twentieth century, just like Mrs. Crookshank said to Harry in . . .

—Hold it right there now, Nora dear! I'll tell you what Eeval Enema said to Tight Arse in "The Rape of the Cloak" . . .

—Culture, please, Tom.

—Up outa that! I don't believe that this is Nora Johnny from Gort Ribbuck at all, can't be? . . . Do you ever think that I'd ever learn to speak like that in the dirty dust? Come here 'til I tell you now, Nora, you used to have great Irish talk in the old days! . . .

—Don't pretend for one minute, Norita, don't bother your barney with him at all, at all.

—Goo Goog, Dotie! Goo Goog! We'll have a bit of a natter between ourselves in a minute. Just between the two of us, like. A bit of pleasant banter between us, you know what I mean. Goo Goog!

—I was always very cultured, Tom, but you were never able to tell. It was very plain to me the very first *affaire de coeur* that I had with you. If it wasn't for that I might have been able to do something with you. Agh! Such an uncultured person! A partner should really be a companion. Look, I'll give you a talk, with the help of the writer and the poet, of course, on Platonic love . . .

—I'll have nothing to do with you, Nora Johnny. Sweet fanny all! . . .

—Good on you there! Fireside Tom!

—I used to be hobnobbing with the nobs up in Nell Johnny's house . . .

—The bad brasser! . . .

—Oh, I'm telling you, those foreign ones are great fun, Caitriona. There was a big ugly Orange floozy fishing up there with Lord Cockton this year, and I'd say she smoked every fag that was ever made. She would have, and the priest's sister along with her. She keeps them in big fat boxes down in her trousers pocket. Tim Top of the Road's youngfella is shagged trying to keep up with her. Too bad for him, the gobshite! But I swear to you anyway, that she's gorgeous. I sat in the car right next to her. "Goo Goog, Nancy," I says to her . . .

—Your mind is a plenitude of raw and rough substance, Tom, you dote you, but I promise you I will reorganise it, and shape it, and mould it, and polish it until it is a beautiful bright vessel of culture . . .

—I'll have nothing at all to do with you, Nora Johnny. I swear I won't. I've had enough of you. No sooner would I be in through the door of Peter the Publican's than you'd be in on my heels, scrounging a drink, and on the bum, and tippling away. I bought you many fine frothy pints, not that I begrudge you any of them . . .

—Don't pretend anything, Norita . . .

—Go for it there, Fireside Tom! God give you long life and good health! Give it to her now hot and heavy, Toejam Noreen of the stinky feet. Always on the scrounge! Were you in Peter the Publican's when she got the goat drunk? . . . God bless you, but tell that to the rest of the graveyard! . . .

3.

—. . . I keened every one of you, my family and friends! Ochone and ochone again! I keened every single one of you, my family and friends! . . .

—You certainly had a fine wild whinging wail, Biddy Sarah, to tell the honest truth . . .

—. . . Ochone, and ochone again! You fell from the cursed stack, didn't you my darling!

—For all you know he could have fallen from a flying boat! Like falling from a stack of oats, like! That wouldn't kill anyone, but somebody who was dead already, dead to God, or dead to this world. If he drank the bottle that I drank! . . .

—Woe and alas and ochone! You drank the bad bottle, my lovely!

—You're always going on about your bottle. If you drank forty-two pints like I did . . .

—Ochone and Ochone again! You'll never drink a pint, ever again! And to think of all the pints that were slugged down in the gullet of that gut of yours . . .

—Ara, he's bored a hole through the wax of my ears, with his forty-two pints and all! If you had sucked that many barrels of ink into your lungs as the writer had . . .

—Ochone, and alas and alack! My wonderful writer laid low now and for ever . . .

—God help us for ever and ever . . .

—Sloppy sentimentality again! . . .

—I keened you Dotie, my Dotie! Oh, my love, my darling! Didn't you die far away from your native plains, sad to say! I feel it for you, I feel wrecked to the core of my being that they wrenched you over this way and you knew nothing about it! You are far from your friends and relations! You died beside the wandering wave! Your bones will be thrown . . .

—In the mean barren clay and the sandy seaweed . . .

—I keened every single one of you, my good people! . . . My precious, my love! . . . Whatever the future brings, he won't write a thing! . . .

—Just as well. The fucking heretic! . . .

—I keened you certainly! No doubt about it! Ochone oh! I'm totally destroyed! A fine chunk of land up at the top of the town! He won't set a foot on it now, not in autumn nor in spring! . . .

—Was it you said, Breed, that you couldn't beat it as regards fattening up cattle?

—I sure did, Biddy Sarah: I was listening to you. And then you started up on "The Lament for the Ejected Irish Peasant." . . .

—. . . I keened you! I'm telling you I keened you! Ochone and alas and alack! He will never again get into the saddle of the white-headed mare, never again . . .

—Aha, Caitriona Paudeen gave him the evil eye . . . !

—That's a filthy lie, Nell! . . .

—. . . I cried my eyes out because of you, Old Master. Ochone and woe is us! The Old Master going to his grave still a young man! . . .

—Ah, come off it, Biddy Sarah, you didn't keen the Old Master one way or the other. I know it full well, as I was there closing up the coffin along with Billy the Postman . . .

—The maggot!

—The Mistress was sobbing and simpering. You took her by the hand, Biddy Sarah, and you began clearing your throat. "I haven't the least clue," Billy the Postman said, "which of you—you Biddy Sarah, or you Schoolmistress—has the least sense . . ."

—Oh, the robber! . . .

—Feck off out of here and shag off down the stairs, every single one of you who doesn't live in the Other World, and stay there until we close up the coffin," Billy shouted. They all slid off, apart from you, Biddy Sarah. "But we have to keen the Old Master," you whined to the Mistress. "God knows, it's the least he deserves," the Mistress said . . .

—Oh, the fat arsed diddy! . . .

—"Whether there's keening or no keening today," Billy says, "unless you fuck off right now out of here and out of my way Biddy Sarah, he won't be on time for today's delivery." Then you came down the stairs, Biddy Sarah, snotting and snorting and foaming at the mouth. Billy was making an unholy racket up above twisting and turning screws. "Your one, he won't leave her after Billy," said Blotchy Brian. "If you drove the same number of screws into Mannix the Counsellor's tongue, Caitriona might go to another lawyer altogether about Baba's will . . ."

—Ababoona! The nasty louser!

—Just then, Billy appeared at the top of the stairs. "Get ready now lads, the four of you," he ordered.

—I remember it well. I twisted my ankle . . .

—"It wouldn't be right or proper to allow the Old Master out of the house without shedding a few tears for him," you said, Biddy Sarah, and you took off up the stairs again. Billy stopped you. "He has to go to the graveyard," Billy insisted. "There's no point in keeping him here any longer . . ."

—Oh, the uppity brute!

—"By gaineys, no point at all in keeping him here any longer," Blotchy Brian said, "unless you're thinking of putting him in aspic! . . ."

—You keened me, Biddy Sarah, and I certainly wasn't grateful, or even half-grateful or a tiny bit grateful to you. Oh, yes, you certainly made enough noise all around me, but you were barking up the wrong tree all the time. You didn't open your mouth about the Republic, or about the treacherous Dog Eared Lot who stabbed me because I was fighting for it . . .

—But I told you the people were grateful . . .

—That's a lie. You never said any such thing! . . .

—Biddy Sarah had nothing to do with politics, any more than myself . . .

—You coward, you were hiding under the bed when Eamon de Valera was risking his life . . .

—You never had any luck, Biddy Sarah, you never said that it was Huckster Joan's coffee done for me, you never said that while you were keening me . . .

—And Peter the Publican's daughter knobbled me . . .

—And me too . . .

—And you never said nothing, when you were keening me, about Tim Top of the Road swiping my turf . . .

—And my seaweed on the shore . . .

—Nor that your man down here died because his son married a black . . .

—I think what that fellow says is true, Biddy Sarah has nothing to do with politics . . .

—I'd have keened you a lot better, only I had a frog in my throat that day. I had keened three others the same week . . .

—It wasn't a frog or hoarseness, but drink. You were scuttered mouldy with the stuff. When you tried to start up with "Let Erin Remember" as you always did, out came "Will Ye No' Come Back Again?" . . .

—No it wasn't, it was "Some Day I'll Go Back Across the Sea to Ireland" . . .

—I'd have keened you, Black Bandy Bartley, but I couldn't get up out of the bed that time . . .

—Bloody tear and 'ounds, Biddy Sarah, it doesn't matter a pig's mickey if he is keened or not! "Ho row, Oh Mary . . ."

—And how come, Biddy Sarah, that you never came to keen Caitriona Paudeen, seeing as they sent for you?

—Yes, tell us why you didn't come to keen Caitriona? . . .

—You had no problem going to Nell's house, even though you had to get up out of bed . . .

—I hadn't it in me to refuse Nell, and she sent the car as far as my front door for me . . .

—Hitler will take the car from her . . .

—I'd have keened you alright, Caitriona, no doubt about it, but I'd hate to be in competition with the other three: Nell, Nora Johnny's daughter, and Blotchy Brian's young one. They were whining and whimpering and huffing . . .

Nell! Nora Johnny's daughter! Blotchy Brian's young one! . . . The three you got St. John's Gospel from the priest to kill me. I'll burst! I'll burst! I'm going to burst! . . .

4.

—. . . Hey Jack, Jack, Jack the Lad! . . .

—. . . Goo Goog, Dotie. Goo Goog! We'll have a bit of a natter now alright . . .

—. . . What would you say, Redser Tom, about a man whose son married a black? I'd say he's as much of a heretic as his son . . .

—Could be, you know, could be that . . .

—The sins of the children are visited upon the fathers . . .

—Some say they are, some say they aren't . . .

—Wouldn't you say now, Redser Tom, that any man who drank forty-two pints was a heretic?...

—Forty-two pints. Forty-two pints bejaysus. Forty-two pints...

—I did that, I drank the lot of them...

—Fireside Tom was knocking around with heretics...

—Fireside Tom. Fireside Tom bejaysus. You'd have to be a very wise person to know who Fireside Tom was...

—To tell you the truth, I wouldn't be that sure either about the Old Master, Redser Tom. I'm very wary of him for the last while. I'll say nothing until I find out more...

—A body would be well advised to keep its clap shut in this place. All the graves have huge ears...

—I have my doubts about Caitriona Paudeen too. She swore black and blue to me that she was a better Catholic than Nell, but if it turns out that she had the evil eye...

—Some people said she had, some people said...

—That's a pack of lies, you foxy fool...

—...Ah come off it, Master, you know full well he's going to die. Look at me who never had nothing wrong with him, and I died same as the rest of them! I went off just the same as somebody who had...

—But seriously, though, Tom, do you think he is going to die?...

—Don't you know full well, Master, that the weeds will be up through his ears shortly!...

—Are you sure, Tom?

—Don't worry one bit about it, Master. He'll die, no doubt about it. Look at me!...

—With the help of God, the shithouse slug!

—Ah, come off it, Master, isn't she gorgeous...

—Oh, the strapper!

—Do you require any spiritual assistance, Master?...

—No, I don't. No, I don't, I'm telling you. Leave me alone!... Leave me alone, or I'll chew your ear off!...

—Son of a gun, come here 'til I tell you, Master, I heard it said that she used to have jobbers knocking around in the kitchen, while you were stretched out on your dying bed...

—*Qu'est-ce c'est que* jobbers? What the fuck are jobbers? . . .

—Fireside Tom is not a jobber because he has his own plot of land. Nor the Bally Ser man either. He had some land on the top of the town that was the best you'll ever get for fattening cattle. But Billy the Postman was a kind of jobber. All he ever had was the Master's garden . . .

—Billy used to be hanging around all right, Master. I often heard him stirring things up when he came in asking for you . . .

—Oh, the tramp! The slinky sneaky skank! . . .

—Be that as it may, Master, the truth must out when all is said and done. The Mistress is gorgeous. Myself and herself would be down in Peter the Publican's. His nose was stuck in everything and everywhere his legs could carry him! I met her up at the Sharp Ridge on the mountain road, just a few months after they buried you. "Goo-Goog, Mistress," I says. "Goo-Goog to you to, Fireside Tom," she says. I didn't get any chance to have any kind of a chin wag, as Billy the Postman comes down on his bike having delivered his letters . . .

—. . . They say if you don't fill in the first papers correctly that it's a doddle to disqualify you from the dole after that. The Derry Lough Master filled it in for me that first time the dole came along. He scribbled something across the page in red ink. Long life to him, they never took the dole from me since! . . .

—But they took it from me. The Old Master filled my form in. He did nothing apart from drawing a stroke across the paper with his pen. I've no doubt, but he didn't do it with red ink either . . .

—The Old Master was always very touchy when he was thinking of the Mistress. I'm not sure if you ever heard what he'd get up to just staring out the window madly penning letters to Caitriona!

—But she never got anything from it, the Mistress, couldn't he just fill up a dole form properly! . . .

—I always got eight shillings. The Foxy Cop did it for me . . .

—Just as well. He was riding your daughter on the nettle-infested fields of Bally Donough . . .

—I was completely deprived of the dole. Somebody wrote in to say I had money in the bank . . .

—God bless you, anyway! People are happy when their neighbours do well. Do you see there, Nell Paudeen's daughter who was getting the dole for yonks, even though his scrubland was valued more than two pounds, and Caitriona dumped him out . . .

—He never earned it! He didn't deserve a penny of it! He had money stashed away in the bank and he was still getting fifteen shillings dole every time. She must love it, the bitch! . . .

—I hear what you say, as you put it, that you had a dollop of dole . . .

—You got a good slice of dole too, Tim Top of the Road . . .

—No wind ever blew, Tim Top of the Road, that didn't make things better for you. The stray sheep, it always wandered into your fold . . .

—The wodge of wood that wandered into the shore on the West Pier, you can be sure you grabbed it . . .

—And the seaweed on the strand . . .

—And the turf . . .

—And the bits and pieces . . .

—Everything that was left round and about the Earl's house, you snatched it up . . .

—Didn't you hang on to the darkie's leg that the Earl had? I saw one of your chicks being born on the sly, and you made a balls of the cover on Caitriona's chimney . . .

—Even if it was the priest's sister who was up and away and whistling and showing off her arse in her jeans, she still hung out with your son . . .

—Hey, do you hear the tailor bullshitting and boasting? You made a jacket for me, and a bus would get lost in it . . .

—You made a pants for Jack the Lad and nobody's legs would go into it, apart from Fireside Tom's . . .

—God knows . . .

—Not a word of a lie, love, but my feet slid into it, no problem, just right . . .

—Easily known that's how it would be, and then you bring your clothes to the Half Eared Tailor who stabbed me! . . .

—But what's the point of talking, you carpenter from Gort Ribbuck? Didn't everyone see Nora Johnny in the coffin you made for her . . .

—. . . She was the very first of the Toejam gooey gams that ever was laid in any kind of coffin . . .

—She'd have been better off without that coffin, Caitriona. She was as full of holes as any chimney that Tim Top of the Road made . . .

—I couldn't do anything about your chimneys, as you didn't pay me . . .

—I paid you . . .

—Well, grand, fine, if you paid me, there were four others for everyone who didn't . . .

—I paid you too, you chancer, and you fucked up my chimney a lot more than you ever fucked it down . . .

—You paid me, fine, as you say, but there's another family whose chimney I repaired just before that, and but do you think I ever got as much as a sniff of the money they owed me . . .

—Is that why you screwed up my chimney, you chancer? . . .

—But I told you to get a small chimney brush . . .

—And I did. Top to bottom, but you left a mess . . .

—I hadn't a clue, as you say, who would pay me or who would not. A local woman comes up to me and says. "We'll have the priest," she said. "The chimney smokes away when there is an east wind. If there was an east wind when the priest came, I'd be ashamed. Nell's chimney smokes with every wind." "I'll stop it smoking with the east wind, just as you say," I says. I just redid the top of it. "You'll see now," I says, "that there'll be no smoke with the east wind, just as you say. I'll say nothing about that, as you're neighbours and all that, just as you say. A pound and five shillings"' "You'll get it on market day, with the help of God," she says. Market day came, and I didn't get my pound and five shillings. What a hope! I never got as much as a whiff of a sniff of my money . . .

—Isn't that exactly what I told you, Dotie, that Caitriona never paid nothing. Honest! . . .

—Why in God's name would I pay the chancer—Tim Top of

the Road—to put a few planks on the top to call them with smoke signals! Even though it was a west wind, it was nothing like the blast that blew the day the priest came. It would have whipped the child from the fireside, that west wind. When Tim Top of the Road was finished with it, it wouldn't even draw a puff of smoke except with the east wind. I offered to pay him, if he did the same job on the winds as he did with Nell's chimney. But he wouldn't lay a hand on them, ever again. It was Nell, the bitch, who pulled a fast one on him and sold him a pup . . .

—That's true, Caitriona, Tim Top of the Road could be easily fooled.

—Anyone who bought my seaweed.

—To tell you the truth, Caitriona, it wasn't Tim Top of the Road who was at fault with your chimney, however bad he is, but it was Nell who got St. John's Gospel to look after her own chimney . . .

—And to blow the smoke over to Caitriona's, just because she thought she could get at Blotchy Brian . . .

—Hoora! Hoora! I'll burst! I'm about to burst! . . .

5.

—. . . I could sue him because he poisoned me. "Drink two spoonfuls of this bottle before you go to bed, and then fast again," the murderer said. Fast my arse! I was just lying down on the bed . . .

—Bloody tear and 'ounds, didn't you just lie back and die! . . .

—"Ha!" he exclaimed to me, as soon as he saw my tongue. "Huckster Joan's coffee . . ."

—"I never had either pain or sickness, dear," I says to him one day when he was inside in Peter the Publican's place. "That may be so, Fireside Tom," he says, "but you're still swilling too much porter. Porter isn't good for someone your age. You'd be far better off with the odd half-one of whiskey." "That's brilliant, that's what I used to drink all the time!" I said. "But it's getting scarcer and dearer all the time." "Peter the Publican's daughter will give you the occasional half-one anytime," he said. She sure did, no doubt about it, and anything else

I wanted, but from the second one onwards she charged four pence, and from the sixth eighteen. The doctor that Nell brought in from the Fancy City insisted it was the whiskey that done for me, but myself and Caitríona Paudeen thought it was the priest . . .

—God doesn't want us to say anything bad about our neighbours . . .

—He said to the Old Master: "You are too good for this life . . ."

—Shut your mouth, you grabber! . . .

—The doctor in the hospital, he stuck the bottle under my nose as I was stretched out on the table. "What's that, doctor!" I asks. "It's only a gadget," he says . . .

—Bloody tear and 'ounds one way or the other, wouldn't it be grand just to lay down on a bed and die, as Blotchy Brian says, instead of being stretched out on a trolley in the hospital and never get up again, and he as chopped up as the free beef that Clogher Savvy's butcher had.

—. . . "Up there's the problem," I said. "Up there in my chest." "No it's not up," he said, "it's down, down there in your legs. Take off your shoes and socks." "No need for that, doctor," I said. "The problem's up here. It's up here in the top of my chest." He took no notice then or now of my chest.

"Throw off your shoes and your socks," he said. "There'll hardly be any need for that, doctor," I said. "There's nothing wrong with me down there . . ."

"If you don't whip your socks and shoes off pronto," he says, "I'll see to it you're in a place where they'll get them off fast . . . It would be hard for you not to be infected," he said. "Did you ever wash your feet since you were born?" "Down by the shore, doctor, last summer twelve months . . ."

—I was all bunged up in myself. Completely bunged up. People are very reluctant to say anything about it. "I'm very reluctant to admit that to you, doctor," I said. "It's not very appropriate."

—So it goes, as you said. I sat up again. Manning from Minlough was in the next bed, as he always was. "I didn't think they were going to carve you up for the next couple of days," I said . . . "Here, wake up," says I, "and don't be like a sack of potatoes any longer." "Leave him alone," the nurse said. "When you were taken down to the operating room, he got all sentimental, like. We didn't put as much sugar on the knife for him as we did for you. That's why he hasn't come round yet." Those nurses never put a tooth in it, as you say yourself.

— "Decorum!" he howled. "What's that!" he shrieked. "Decorum, treat me with decorum! Did you kill somebody or what?" "By the Cross of Christ, doctor," I said, "I swear I didn't!" "What's pissing you off so?" he says. "Let it rip." "Ah, well, like, it's not a very seemly story to tell, doctor," I said. "I'm all bunged up . . ."

—Bunged up, as you say. I never got a taste for food for the next four or five days. "Toast," I said to the nurse. "Ara, go and stuff yourself!" she says. "You think I have nothing else to be doing only to be supplying you with toast." That's the way they are, as you put it. I asked the doctor for the toast the next morning. "This gentleman has to have toast from now on," he said to the nurse. I swear he did. There wasn't a word out of her . . .

—. . . "Twisted my ankle," I said . . .

— "I'm bunged up," "Bunged up," he said. "With all due respects now, doctor," I said. "My body is bunged up." "If that's all it is," he says. "I'll fix that for you. I'll make up a good bottle for you." He mixed up some white and some red stuff. "This will sort you out, no problem," he says . . .

—. . . "You'd feel sorry for the poor old Belgies," I said to Patchy Johnny. "Do you think this is 'The War of the Two Foreigners'?" . . .

—Cop yourself on, man. That war is over for thirty years . . .

—That's what he said, just as you put it. "You better get her to get ordinary plain bread for me," Manning from Minlough muttered. "What's this?" the doctor said. "Isn't this bread just as ordinary and as plain as you'll get?" "But I usually get toast," the Minlough guy mumbled. "Oh, now I remember you," the doctor said. "You created an unholy fuss when you were admitted, demanding toast. The ordinary bread here wasn't good enough for you." He was gnashing his teeth with anger. That's the way it is with the likes of snobs like him, just as you say. "I'll never even get a smell of a sliver of a slice of toast," your man from Minlough says. "I'm paying up here and I have to get what suits me." He said that, no doubt about it. He was very stroppy with them. "And you thought that the ordinary plain bread wasn't good enough for you here when you were admitted," said the doctor. "Then maybe you should be the doctor here!" "I don't think it's that unusual for the old guts do a great lot of grumbling, after they're carved up on the operating slab," your man from Minlough said . . .

—. . . "Too true. My twisted ankle," I said.

— "This won't cost you anything at all," he said. "God bless you and keep you, doctor!" says I. "This bottle is magic," he said. "Certainly the ingredients are expensive. You'd never credit what that beautiful bottle cost me in the Fancy City?" "A pretty penny, I'd say, doctor," I said myself. "Eight shillings and four pence." "Forty-two," he said . . .

— That's the way it goes, as you might say yourself. From then until now I couldn't even stomach to look at ordinary bread, and Manning from Minlough wouldn't offer anything better. If I got every penny that was owed to me from the mess about the chimney, I couldn't even suck a smack from the pipe, even though I was mad about it before that. What about the Minlough guy who'd smoke a whole bog, and think about it, here's a guy who never stuck a pipe in his gob until he landed in hospital! . . .

— "Everything's absolutely fantastic and hunky dory here since this stupid war started," he says, "and it wouldn't matter much, even if things were as they are." "Listen to me, doctor," I said, "Aren't there enough people around! If things go on as they are, we'll have nothing to depend on, only the grace of God . . ."

—Oh, there's tons of people around, just as you say. "My guts are totally bollixed," the Minlough guy says to me just as we are strolling down outside, a few days before we were sent home. "I feel as if my guts are like a pants that are too small for me, or somesuchfucking thing. I take two bites and I feel swollen up to the gills. Look at me now, forfucksake! . . . My stomach is as delicate as a live wire," he says. He was a humungous lump. He was head and shoulders above me, and up for it. "The way it is," I says, "as you might say yourself, but my bag of guts isn't too good either. I don't think all the food in the hospital would fill it up. They're a bit baggy, like they were a few sizes too big. If I move at all, they're like cow's udders wobbling and yanking this way and that . . ."

—. . . The Big Butcher often said he had plenty of time for me because he had plenty of time for my father . . .

—"This bottle will set you back seven and sixpence," he said. "But it's the best." "God bless you and save you, doctor!" I says myself. "If it wasn't for you, I don't know what anybody would do. I swear I don't. You're a good man even with all the bad news. You tell it like it is . . ."

—A man for the bad news, as you say. After that, myself and Manning from Minlough wrote to each other every week. All he'd say in every letter was that his appetite had changed. He was always moaning that he couldn't taste either potatoes, or meat, or cabbage anymore. He'd give the whole world below and the blue sky above just for some tea and some fish, two things I took a complete turn against. But as you say yourself, you never saw anything like it. I never really liked either meat or cabbage, but since I was in the hospital, I'd claw them half-raw out of the pot. Them and potatoes. I'd guzzle potatoes three times a day if I got the chance . . .

—. . . "The old ankle is twisted again," he said. "By the hairy balls of Galen and the belly button of the Fenian doctor, if you even as much as approach me again with your bloody scuttered ankle . . ."

—"Seven and six," he says. "I don't owe you seven and six," I says myself. "I'll give it to you, fine, if you give me a decent bottle . . ."

—To do you good, as you'd say yourself. But nothing would do me any good. I was a greedy guts. Potato, meat and cabbage for my breakfast, my dinner and my supper. "It's the old sooty chimney that's sharpening your stomach," the old one said. "The soot is lining your guts." "That's not it, at all," I says, "it's just that my belly is ravenous . . ."

—I'm telling you then, boy, he gave a leap and he smashed the bottle on the floor . . .

—So be it, but if I gave a leap, as you put it, my guts would start wobbling and yanking around, and they wouldn't stop for half an hour. I told this to an Irish scholar who was staying with us the summer I died. He was a medical student. He was to qualify the following year. He really interrogated me about the way they had done the operation. "Yourself and the guy from Minlough were together on the same operating table," he said . . .

—. . . *Qu'il retournerait pour libérer la France* . . .

—Then he crushed the bits of the bottle under the table. He gave the shelf a kick and scattered everything that was on it. "If it wasn't that they'd disqualify me, I'd force you to eat all those bits of bottle," he said. Then he fecked off to Peter the Publican's . . .

—Bloody tear and 'ounds anyway, weren't you haunted lucky. If you had drunk that bottle of poison, you'd have been stretched out dead, like your man we were talking about a while back . . .

—He'd have been stretched out, certainly, as you put it yourself. "Your guts are gluttonous since then," the young doctor said. "But I'm afraid that you have Minlough Manning's stomach. The doctors and the nurses had a few too many at the dance the previous night!" he said. "That's the way they are, as you put it yourself," I says. "You'd never believe it," he said, "but when they were stuffing the guts back into you the next time around, they put yours in the Minlough guy, and his in yours. That's why you gave up smoking . . ."

—But you never gave up your robbery, Tim Top of the Road. After they opened you up you still nobbled my seaweed from the shore . . .

—And my mallet . . .

—Careful now, maybe he swiped the stomach of your man from Minlough! . . .

—Certainly if his guts were hanging around loose and nobody claiming them . . .

—He never said nothing to me except that I was stabbed through the walls of my liver. "You've been stabbed through the wall of your liver," he said, "and that's that." "Those treacherous Dog Eared thickos! I said. "Swear by your lily liver, doctor! You'll swear as much as any man in Ireland. They'll hang them yet . . ."

—Caitriona made her way over to him. "What's up with you now?" he asks. "Nell was here the other day," she said. "Do you think, now, doctor, that her present ailments will do for her? Be honest now, doctor, God bless you!" she says. "Some people say that you've got access to poison. I'll divide Baba's will with you! Nobody will ever know anything about it if you let a little drop into the next one and swear that it's a fantastic bottle: just two spoons before bedtime and fasting after that . . ."

—But Nell could sue her and the doctor then . . .

—Ababoona! The doctor never let me out that day . . .

—And I never got a smell of my pound from that day until I died . . .

—. . . And the little clack-box asked him to poison me. He never said it straight out, but . . .

—. . . But tell me anyway, Joan, did she ever return the silver teapot?

—. . . I easily knew the way the doctor spoke to me that day . . . Kitty small potatoes! Don't believe her Jack! Jack the Lad, don't believe poxy Kitty! . . .

—God forbid, Caitriona, say nothing . . .

—I'll burst! I'm going to burst! I'm about to burst! . . .

6.

—. . . I know like, as you say, but I fixed up her chimney at the same time . . .

—. . . That's the way she was, my dear, not saying anything bad about her, but she scrounged some money from me that time when she wanted the round table. She had her heart set on a round table. Look at me! . . .

—You little cunt! Money from you! . . .

—. . . Too bad, Curran, we lost the English market! I had a patch of land . . .

—Feck that too, nobody under the stairs of heaven had better land than me. No way, dear. But I was totally flahed out at the end running all over the place trying to keep Nell and Caitriona's cattle out. Between them they had me totally shagged, not that I'm saying anything, like!

—But look at the state of my own big holding, gone to rack and ruin! Curran's donkey and Tim Top of the Road's beasts making total crap of it every day and night! The eldest youngfella always having it off with Top of the Road's daughter, even though she was expressly forbidden from the day she was born to even as much as step beyond my rick of turf . . .

—Bloody tear and 'ounds, isn't that what she said to Blotchy Brian, that there was a nest of weasels in his own rick!

—The devil fuck her! She made a complete eejit out of the eldest guy. She had this little box of pictures and she pretended she was the one in the little skimpy clothes. Black Bandy Bartley used to say that most people expected that the second boy would be sent packing and the whole lot would fall to the older guy. Over my dead body, she does! . . .

—. . . Exercise: a donkey would devour the grass of four square perches of land overnight. My question now, Curran, is this, how many times would four square perches of land go into seventeen acres of yours: seventeen by four, multiplied by forty . . .

—. . . Honest, Dotie, Caitriona didn't have a romantic bone in her body. All she wanted was the place. Thought she could rob some of the nobs who came there. It certainly wasn't out of concern for Jack the Lad . . .

—Don't believe her Jack. Don't believe Clammy Calf Johnny! . . .

—God would punish us if we said anything . . .

—. . . She just completely failed to get herself a man, Dotie. Blotchy Brian used to say that she had a recurring cold. No sooner was she spat out of your mouth than she snotted her way back up through your nose . . .

—Oh, Jack, don't believe a word! Jesus Christ Almighty and his Blessed Mother! Blotchy Brian! . . .

—. . . Honest, Dotie. Every single night she'd crawl her way over the old path from her own place just to be there as he came back the other way, while he'd be out visiting . . .

—Oh, Mother of God! The blubbershite!

—. . . She asked him to marry her, twice or three times at least . . .

—Blotchy Brian! Marry Blotchy Brian! . . .

—. . . Honest, Dotie . . .

—Goo Goog, Dotie! . . .

—Goo Goog, Fireside Tom! . . .

—Honest to Heavens, Dotie! It's just not appropriate to be bleating "Goo Goog" like that all around the graveyard. What would those in the Pound Place say? It's just a bad example to those in the Half Guinea Plot. Say "Okeedoh" if you like. But why would you say either hump or lump to the old Pain in the Bunk? . . .

—Unrequited love, Norita . . .

—. . . Blotchy Brian, Jack! Blotchy bung-nosed bent-hipped, buck-toothed, bum-bearded Brian. Blotchy Brian who never washed himself from . . .

—God would punish us, Caitriona . . .

—. . . I'm telling you life wouldn't be half as bad if it wasn't for women . . .

—Did you hear the one that Coley told the other day! This skivvy gave the Pope the hots, and Rory McHugh O'Flaherty—a holy man in this country way back—was called immediately just to get him to watch himself. He rode the Devil all the way to Rome . . .

—Take that stinko strapper from the Fancy City that's threatening to sue the Junior Master, if he does anything else . . .

—Tim Top of the Road always said that the women were worse than the men. The priest's sister nagged the master's son to marry her . . .

—The Old Master himself says . . .

—Oh, that's the way it is, it's always the woman's fault! . . .

—It's always the woman's fault, Breed Terry? . . .

—Didn't I see what those scuzzies looked like in those photos! . . .

—I swear to God you did, and me too, Breed. Didn't I say to the young tosser with me while Mae West was leering at us: "My advice to you now, is to have nothing to do with anybody like that," I said. "She'd be alright after being ridden by a bucking bronco, I'd say, but nonetheless . . ."

—Listen, John Willy, as the man said, women are just like a rainbow on its arse . . .

—Well, that's something, an old crotchety crock like you giving out about women, and you never had anything ever to do with them, only see them pass by on the road! How the fuck would you know? . . .

—I know full well. A man told me ages ago. He was an old man who was very old . . .

—The women are a hundred times worse than the men. Much worse, indeed, I'm telling you. No doubt about it . . .

—Ara, will you all just shut up and listen to me! Look at my eldest boy who wouldn't even dream of dumping Tim Top of the Road's daughter even after he inherited the huge chunk of land! The Devil f . . .

—And this guy over here, whose son married a black . . .

—I am a woman, and undoubtedly I would be up for women if it came to that. But is that all you have to do, just listen to Caitriona Paudeen badmouthing Jack the Lad morning, noon and night . . .

—I swear now, but Caitriona isn't the only one buried here who has her tongue slobbering on about that yoke of a young jerk . . .

—I never ever saw anyone as bad as her. Do you know what she said to him the other day, that Nell tried to pull a fast one on him when she asked him to marry her. How's that for a brass neck? . . .

—I swear by the oak of this coffin, this is what I heard her say: "The women around here, Jack," she said, "they really appreciate you talking to me. But be as wary as hell of them, I'm telling you! . . ." Whatever shame she had she left it six feet above . . .

—"Maggie Frances," she shouted at me, "the barb is gone from my heart, and I don't notice the time passing, no more than if I was at a concert, since Jack came." "Have you actually banished every bit of shame by now, Caitriona?" I asked.

—Did you hear, Margaret, did you hear the words she spat back at me? "Breed Terry," she gloated, "doesn't it just serve the old bitch right! 'I have Jack. I have Jack.' She doesn't have Jack wrapped in under her little rag of a shawl anymore, Breed Terry . . ."

—I'll speak to Jack the Lad. I would and you would too, you scabby scum, if he'd speak back to you. It's not for want of trying he won't talk back to you, you tight-arsed twat . . .

—Leave off your insults, Caitriona! Peace is all that I want . . .

—May God not weaken you, Caitriona. They really deserve that tongue-lashing! You'd never think to listen to them that the coven of cunts here in the graveyard thought about anyone else except Jack the Lad! You wouldn't mind, but they're all married! . . .

—But the Old Master himself admitted the other day that death dissolves the bonds of marriage . . .

—So why is he so pissed off about Billy the Postman? . . .

—He said that: death dissolves the bonds of marriage! I should have kept my eye on him. Definitely a heretic . . .

—Say nothing now, until you hear the whole thing! If that's all Caitriona said it would be alright . . .

"Breed Terry," she says to me, "there's a . . ." Decency doesn't allow me to repeat exactly what she said, there are some men listening . . .

—Just whisper it, Breed . . .

—Whisper to me, Breed! . . .

—To me, Breed! . . .

—I'll tell it to Nora . . . Are you ready for it now, Nora? . . .

—Upon my word! I'm shocked! Who'd ever think that about Jack! . . .

—I think we should give Jack some advice, as Nell is not here . . .

—I'll advise him . . .

—You haven't a clue how to talk, not the same way as a woman . . .

—Do you require any spiritual assistance, Jack the Lad?

—Listen, Colm More's daughter, you have a damned cheek sticking your nose into this one way or the other, there are women here three times older than you . . .

—. . . Hey, Jack the Lad! Jack the Lad! . . . Maggie Frances here

. . . I have a bit of advice for you . . . In a little while. You'll sing a song first, Jack . . .

—Go for it, Jack . . .

—God bless you Jack, off you go! . . .

—Jack, you can't begrudge me, Breed Terry . . .

—Honest Jack. That new ditty: "Bunga, bunga bunga" . . .

—"Bunga, bunga, bunga"! Holy God Almighty, "Bunga, bunga, bunga," ya son of a gun, ya lovely lad ya! . . .

—You won't let me down, Jack. Huckster Joan . . .

—May God forgive you! . . . Why don't you all just leave me alone! . . . I told you already I wasn't going to sing you any song.

—Ah, come on Jack, Jack of my heart, that bunch of crazy women are as mad as a posse of porpoises panting after a school of sturgeon. Tell them, Jack, as you used to tell us when we were young ones on the bog jibbing and jibing at you: "I never dreamed the hunting started this early in the year . . ."

—God wouldn't forgive us if we were to say anything wrong, Caitriona. But I'm imploring you dear God Almighty and His Blessed Mother that the women in this graveyard will give me some peace . . .

—Toejam Nora, Low-lying Kitty, Twisted Joan, Breed Terry. Hoora, Jack bejaysus, I think I know them better than you do. You were always away at the arse end of the bog from them. And I'm here longer than you too. I'm telling you not to take a bit of notice of them! All very well, but songs too! . . .

—Every single minute, Caitriona. But God would punish us if we said anything bad about our neighbour . . .

—They'd say that for certain, Jack, and swear black and blue that he came looking for the loan of a pound and never paid it back. I'm telling you I suffered endlessly because of them and their lies! Are you there, Jack? . . . You've been promising me for a long time, but you better sing your song now . . .

—Don't ask me Caitriona . . .

—Just one verse, Jack. Just one small measly fucking verse! . . .

—Some other time, Caitriona. Some other time . . .

—Come on Jack. Now . . .

—How do I know that I wouldn't be just like any old hag who died in the parish? . . .

—Oh, if that's all that's bothering you, Jack! It's only the rheumatism that's at her now, and they won't be bringing her corpse to the graveyard for another twenty years! . . .

—She's never that well, really, though, Caitriona . . .

—She hasn't as much as an ache or a pain, Jack. I hope her corpse stays miles away from this graveyard! Sing the song. Go for it, Jack! . . .

—She was always a very good woman, I'm telling you Caitriona, and not just because she is your sister . . .

—It doesn't matter a ghoul's ghost whatever sisters say in this life, Jack, just sing the shagging song . . .

—I'm not trying to be awkward, Caitriona, but there's no point in badgering me. It's strange the way things happen, Caitriona, my dear. The night before I got married, there I was in your parlour and the whole gang were at me to sing a song. Breed Terry was there, and Kitty, and Maggie Frances. I don't want to speak ill about anyone, but the three of them were hassling me no end! I was whining and wheezing like an old bit of clattered clapped-out coffin all through the night. "Jack won't sing any more songs," Nell said, half-mocking, whole in earnest, while I was sitting in her lap . . . "except when I ask him . . ." You won't believe me, Caitriona, but they were the very words that were swimming through my head the following morning when I was there down on my two knees before the altar rails in front of the priest? May God forgive me! It was a grievous sin! But the ways of the world are weird, Caitriona. Every time I was asked to sing a song afterwards, that's exactly what I remembered!

—Ababoona, boona, boona! Oh, Jack. Jack the Lad! I'll burst! I'm going to burst!

Interlude 10

THE GOOD EARTH

1.

— He doesn't want to go . . .
— It's a blessed release. . . .
— He finds it distressing . . .
— It's a blessed release . . .
— He's afraid of the unknown . . .
— It's a blessed release . . .
— He finds it scary . . .
— It's a blessed release . . .
— But . . .
— It's a blessed release . . .

2.

— Son of a gun, I swear to God, you couldn't even hear Oscar threshing because of all the hammering and blasting. And that's the truth . . .

— Was there any letter from Brian Junior? . . .

— God bless your brains! A young man going for the priesthood has better things to be doing than sending letters off to that hole. Making the postman sweat . . .

— Nell was laid up for a while too, wasn't she, Tom?

— Just rheumatism, dear. The old rheumatism. She got up the day I went down . . .

— She was always a decent woman, Tom . . .

—I always said, Jack, that she had a much kinder nature than Caitriona . . .

—God doesn't want us to speak ill of our neighbours, Tom . . .

—Be that as it may, there was always the bitter word amongst neighbours, dear! If she didn't have a kinder nature she'd hardly offer to pay for Caitriona's cross, or to send three of Paddy's children to college. And one thing's for sure, they need some education. Look at me! . . .

—Every penny she ever had, Tom, she did some good with it . . .

—You never spoke a truer word, dear. I always say to myself, if Nora Johnny had got the money from that will she wouldn't be sober even one day in the year . . .

—God doesn't want us to say anything bad about our neighbours, Tom. There was never as much as a bitter word between myself and Nell . . .

—Son of a gun, sure, you don't know what happened, dear, she cried a cupboard full of big bright hankies when you died. She bawled her eyes out, dear. And on top of that, she got tons of Masses said for you! I heard it said that she stuffed two hundred pounds into our priest's paw, not to mention what she gave to other holy priests in other places . . .

—Bloody tear and 'ounds, isn't that what Blotchy Brian says: "If the priests can't get the Lad up on that ladder and give him a kick in the arse up to the loft, then nobody can . . ."

—Holy shite, like, Black Bandy, you don't know nothing, nor half of it. You couldn't hear a bang on the ear with all the talk they had about Masses. Masses for Jack's soul, for Baba's soul, for Caitriona's soul . . .

—Charity isn't lessened when you spread it around, Tom . . .

—That's exactly the same as Nell used to say. "You're getting piles of Masses said for Caitriona," I said to her one day, when we were talking about this. "Give good for evil, Fireside Tom," she'd say to me . . .

—God forbids us to say anything bad about our neighbours, Tom. Poor Caitriona can't help it. The poor creature is tormented because she has no cross . . .

—So it goes, dear. You couldn't hear a bang on the ear with all the carry-on about crosses. Caitriona's cross was ready to go, paid for and all, but when you died Nell and Paddy agreed to leave it until her own and yours could be erected together . . .

—Bloody tear and 'ounds, isn't that what Blotchy Brian said that it was no wonder the world was in a mess when you think of all the hard-earned money being squandered on a heap of old stones . . .

—Game ball, Black Bandy, you never heard nothing, nor even half of it. I don't know if all that yackety yack about crosses helped me one way or the other. Crosses from morning to night, and from night until morning. A fellow couldn't have a quiet pint to himself without some goofball going on about crosses. You couldn't walk your bit of land without imagining there were crosses sprouting up all over. I escaped down to Paddy Caitriona's house, where they don't talk much about crosses at all. I could do with . . .

—. . . *Qu'il retournerait pour libérer la France* . . .

—. . . Off again. Then back. Every day I'd drink at least twenty pints . . .

—God help you and your twenty pints! I drank forty-two . . .

—Even so, my dear, the doctor who brought Nell back from the Fancy City said it was Peter the Publican's whiskey did for me. That's what he said. "I swear, dear," I says, "the doctor insisted I drink it." "Which doctor?" he asks. "Our own doctor, bless him," I says. They were his very words, my dear. Peter the Publican's daughter was listening to him. If you don't believe me, toddle into her on your way back. I don't blame the doctor one little bit. I was well used to drink, and it never bothered me. But I can tell you now, I blame the priest. Son of a gun, I swear to God, I don't think he helped me in the slightest . . .

—May I offer you any spiritual assistance, Fireside Tom? . . .

—Goo Goog to you, Colm More's daughter. Goo Goog! Just a bit of a natter . . .

—I mean, even the priest didn't succeed.

—The priest didn't succeed! The priest succeeds at everything. You're a heretic . . .

—. . . By the oak of this coffin, Jack the Lad, I gave her the pound . . .

—God will punish us, Kitty . . .

—Wills! If it wasn't for Baba Paudeen's will, Fireside Tom wouldn't have been sent packing quite so soon . . .

—His own fault! The booze would have stayed in the same place only Tom decided to bring his gut to where it was already. The will didn't bring Nell any bad luck. She bought a car and a hat with peacock feathers . . .

—Oh! Oh!

—We've seen all of this before, anyway! Wills kept Bally Donough alive for years. Or, if not, it was nettles. Women who hardly had gloves one day, we saw them flaunting themselves in their hats and their frills the next. Too bad for them: soon hens were laying eggs in their hats . . .

—The people of Bally Donough had enough guts and gumption to go to the side of the sun, even to the ditch of the devil himself, to get what they could from people's wills. If the spas from your place left their pissy little hills, they'd be pining over the fleas they left behind . . .

—Did you hear of the guy from our place who was buried and all he had was a shilling! . . .

—That man from our place wasn't buried with just a shilling, but it was the best thing that ever happened to him, if true. He had his feet on the ground until he got the big moola. Neither God nor ghost saw him after that except he was flashing around with his grin gawking out at you from every corner. Did you see him? I bet you couldn't see him without his gob glowering at you . . .

—It might make some sense if your gob was smashed, but remember that young scut from Clogher Savvy—he's related to me—he got a fortune, and nothing would do him except to go and break his neck. That's exactly the way to say it: nothing in this whole wide world would satisfy him except to go and break his neck . . .

—Don't you see that smarmy lout from Derry Lough! Some old witch in America left him a few thousand. The dregs of Huckster Joan's tea were hardly drained from his belly, but there he was in Dublin with a monster motor under his bum. He also took up with a little strip of a woman who was up for it, and he upped and offed with her. She didn't stay that long with him. The gurgle of the engine was grating on her guts. She took off on her own again into the night. They called the car Tight Arse. May I never leave here, but it never budged an inch until he got a gang of local langers and yobbos from the top of the road to push it with him!

—Didn't I twist my ankle! . . .

—They'd push it to the nearest pub. It was left there until morning, and then they'd push it back again. Its wheels and body were left at the top of the road in the end. But it had a great horn! . . .

—Just like on Nell Paudeen's car . . .

—Especially passing Caitriona's house . . .

—Ababoona! . . .

—All very well, for a car that was got from a will, it rattled along no problem . . .

—Maybe, with the help of God, Hitler will be here soon . . .

—Not as much as a drip of a drop ever leaked out from Mannix the Counsellor about Old Wood's will. He told me that much the day I was with him trying to sue Tim Top of the Road about my mallet . . .

—. . . "The arse will fall out of Wall Street, as it did before," he says, while his eye is wandering over towards the axe. "It'll all fall apart, and I'll lose another will, just like it happened before . . ."

"I wouldn't give a toss," Caitriona said, who was there at the time, "if it fell out in one big plop, as long as it fell with the same noise out of Nell's . . ."

—Tim Top of the Road's old one got a slice of a will also . . .

—That's what gave her the flashy house . . .

—No it wasn't. It was my turf . . .

—I got a great *coup* from the insurance at the same time. Top of the Road and his eldest daughter . . .

—I sold a whole set of *The Complete Carpenter and Mechanic* to his son . . .

—Credit that, as you'd say yourself . . .

—He came into a will that time when Peter the Publican's daughter was teasing him in the parlour . . .

—The Old Master got a will . . .

—Billy won't be short of doctors so . . .

—Oh, the thief. The little pimply prick face! . . .

—. . . That's another lie! It wasn't because of a will that that Dog Eared butcher stabbed me . . .

—. . . He could pay for forty-two pints, couldn't he! Somebody with not enough land that the donkey could only plonk his two hind legs down on it! He had to stick his front two on Curran's land next to him . . . That's him all the way! Pushing the car for those knackers from Derry Lough was the best he did . . .

—And Curran too, he got the lump of land he wanted his son and Tim Top of the Road's daughter to move into . . .

—The devil fuck her! I'll be bollixed if she lets that one in on her land! . . .

—Top of the Road's young one has insurance . . .

—. . . If that's the way it is, then Caitriona is delighted she didn't get the will. If she had . . .

—She'd have made two slate-roofed houses . . .

—She'd have bought two cars . . .

—She'd have erected two crosses . . .

—And two hats . . .

—You'd never know, and maybe even a pair of pants . . .

—Bloody tear and 'ounds, isn't that what Blotchy Brian said when his daughter's son went off to college to be a priest: "If that cud-chewing cunt were still alive," he said, "she'd never have rested easy until she had forced Paddy to dump his wife, and packed him off for the priesthood."

—If you tell me Caitriona how many pounds were to be got in the will, I'll make out the interest on it for you:

$$\text{Interest} = \frac{\text{B.A.} \times \text{A} \times \text{R.}}{100}$$

Isn't that right, Master?

—They'd be enough there anyway to repay Kitty her pound.

—And Tim Top of the Road for the chimney . . .

—And Nora Johnny for the spoons and the silver knives . . .

—Oh Holy Mary, Mother of God! Silver knives in Gort Ribbuck! Silver knives! Oh, Jack! Jack the Lad! Silver knives in Gort Ribbuck! I'll burst! I'm going to burst! . . .

3.

—. . . She said that, Master? . . .

—She said exactly that, Guzzeye Martin. She said . . .

—. . . "Up there the problem is," I said . . .

—. . . "'Diddley die de dum,' Caitriona sings, 'a fine big pig for roasting . . .'"

—. . . "Martin John More had a buxom young daughter . . ."

—How long do you think before she marries again, what do you think? . . .

—Ah, go on, Kitty, my neighbour, how would I know, I haven't a clue . . .

—Of course, she'd have no problem getting a man, that's if she has any notion to marry again. She's a fine sprightly flighty young woman, God bless her pins and what else! . . .

—That's very true, Margaret, you were my neighbour! . . .

—That's if she never said anything about it when she saw that you were gone . . .

—That wasn't it, Breed . . .

—Maybe the Junior Master might marry her . . .

—Or the Master from Derry Lough, since the priest's sister dumped him . . .

—You are really a dote, Billy. Honest, cross my heart and hope to die. Tell us if the Schoolmistress said anything about getting married again . . .

—Ah, come on like, was that the way it was so, the sponger, the wanker, the twisted thicko, the runt, the sweaty scumbag warm-arsed bollix! Where is he, let me at him, the crooked cunt? . . .

—This is a very nice way to welcome people to the graveyard . . .

—Son of a gun, cop on now, Master, don't you remember what I said to you? Didn't he die though? . . .

—Where is he so? . . .

—Come on now, Master, my good friend, easy now, easy! We were always good neighbours up above. Did I ever open one of your letters? Ah, come on now, Master, stop telling lies! . . . If that was the case, Master, it wasn't me who did it . . . The Postmistress could do anything in the world she wanted, but don't call me a liar, please, Master . . . That's a dirty lie, certainly, Master! I never gave your letters to anyone, but straight up to your house, and stuck it straight from the bag into your hand. I'm telling you now, not every postman would do that! . . .

Oh, Master, Master, God forgive you Master, God forgive you! I didn't deliver your post so promptly every day just to see your wife. Oh, come on, I hope that that idea never even entered your head! . . . Oh, come on, Master, you were my neighbour, stop that now. Don't tell lies about her. She is still there above treading on the bright daisies of mendacity while you are here below in the dark pushing up the daisies of truth . . .

Believe every word I say, Master, that I was very sorry that you died. You really looked after people who visited your house. And it was always worthwhile listening to you too. You'd blast away there about life . . . Ah, come on, Master, don't say things like that! . . . Ah, come off it, Master! . . .

There wasn't a day passed, but I gave my condolences to herself . . . Ah come on, my good neighbour, for God's sake, stop going on about that! "That's a great one about the poor Old Master," I'd say to myself. "It's not the same place since he left. I'm telling you, Mistress, that I'm really sorry for your trouble . . ."

. . . Take it easy now, Master! Easy there! Can't you just keep it to yourself! "Billy the Postman," the old codger would call over to me, "but, sure, I know that. He really liked you . . ." Ah come on now, Master. We can talk about this, Master! "I did my best for him, Billy, but it was beyond the doctors . . ." Oh, Master my darling! Oh, Master of my heart!

. . . "The way it was, Billy, one way or the other, the Master was far too good . . ."

"Ah, come on now Master, don't disgrace yourself and all the neighbours listening! Remember always that you are a Lord of Learning, and you must always give a good example . . . Just be patient now! Come on now, Master, you are really doing my fucking head in. This is a great welcome, no doubt about it, to the dirty dust . . .

— Do you think it possible, Billy the Postman, that you might require some degree of spiritual assistance? . . .

— Oh the snot-snuffling sot shit, he does . . .

— De grâce, Master! Keep a grip on yourself. Billy is really a very romantic guy. Honest, he is . . .

— You were like that too, Master . . .

— I swear I saw you, Master . . . in the school . . .

— It's no wonder our kids marry heretics and blacks . . .

— . . . To make a long story short, Master, it was Whit Monday. It was a holiday. I went for a stroll up along the road just, as we say, to take the air . . .

. . . Now, I'm asking you, my neighbours, what harm is there in going for a stroll? Only once in a blue moon did I ever get a chance to stretch my legs . . . It wouldn't have done my health any good to go the other direction down the road . . . Just shut up a minute! . . . As I was just going past the gate of your house, I noticed she had the car out on the road. I had put air in its tyres for her . . . So what, Master, so what if I did? It was just an effort to be a bit neighbourly . . . "God be good to the poor old Master," I said to myself. "He really took a shine to that car." "Billy," the one says to me, "the Old Master was never destined to be happy. The Old Master was far too good . . ." Oh, Master, I can't help it? . . . But hang on a minute, Master! The rest of the story . . .

"Sit in there, Billy," she says. "You'll drive the car for me fine. I have to get out and about one way or another after all this time in mourning and widow's weeds. Nobody will think anything about it. You're an old friend of the family, Billy . . ." Keep ahold of yourself there, Master. Can't you see that everyone is listening. I never thought you were that kind of a man! . . .

To cut a long story short, Master, the place was deserted apart from the two of us. If you were ever down around Cala Ross that time of the day, Master, you'd know that there are very few places as beautiful. The lights were glimmering on the headlands and on the darkling pastures on the other side of the bay. I really felt it, Master . . . Ah, for God's sake, Master, have some sense of decency! . . .

. . . To cut a long story short, Master, she swore to me that her love was deeper than the ocean . . . Just hold your horses, Master! Calm down! Come on, Master, I was convinced you weren't like that . . .

"God be with four years ago!" she said. "The Master and I were here in this same spot looking out at the lights, up at the stars and down at the will o' the wisp shimmering on the seaweed . . ." Looks like, Master, that you're going to get a bad name! But hang on now! Easy! . . . "The poor Old Master," I said. "The poor Old Master," she says, "it was a great pity. But he was too good for . . ." . . . Master, Master my good friend, why won't you just listen to the story! . . .

"He whom the gods love, Billy," she says, "dies young. Do you know what, Billy, he was really very fond of you . . ." What could I do, Master? . . .

—Come on now, Master! Guzzeye Martin spotted you . . .

—No doubt about it, Master, you were having it off with her . . .

—. . . But what would you do yourself, tell me Master, if you were as I was down there at Cala Ross looking out at the lights, mooning at the stars and wondering at the will o' the wisps shimmering on the seaweed? . . . Come on, cool down a bit, Master! . . . To cut a long story short, Master . . . Ah, come on Master, you're a neighbour . . . Don't lose the bop entirely, Master . . . Why are you taking your bad mood out on me? I don't deserve this . . .

But to cut a long story short, Master, she got three doctors from Dublin to examine me . . . What do you mean, you never met the likes of me since you were born! Why are you taking it out on me, Master? Anybody who knew you when you were six feet above would never believe you were anything like this . . .

"What happened to the Old Master won't happen to you," she

said, "or it's too bad for me" . . . God be good to you, and take it easy Master. You'll disgrace yourself. You're a schoolmaster after all . . .

. . . To cut a long story short, Master, I had a vicious pain in my side and in my kidneys. I got a little bit better in the afternoon. The lift before dying. She sat on the side of the bed and took my hand . . . God help us, she said! Do you see the state he's in? . . . I couldn't do anything about her, could I?

—To cut a long story short, Master: "If it happens that you don't come out of this, Billy," she said, "my life wouldn't be worth living without you . . ." Ah, come on, Master, don't be so nasty . . . If she marries yet again, can I do anything about it? . . . Have a bit of cop on, Master! . . .

. . . To cut a long story short, Master, I was just on the edge of eternity, when she screamed into my ear: "I'll bury you properly, Billy," she shouted, "no matter how long I live after you . . ." Back off, Master, take it easy! Give me a break for God's sake, Master! . . . But I think my peace is gone, actually . . . If she had only thought to bury me in any other place in the graveyard except right next to this nutjob. But I suppose she couldn't help it, the poor thing. She didn't really know what she was doing . . . Come on, patience Master, get ahold of yourself! . . .

—Bloody tear and 'ounds anyway, isn't that what Blotchy Brian said when Billy was struck down: "That little wanker isn't too far from the graveyard," he said. "By dad, he'll be lucky if he's buried at all. If he died in Dublin he'd be dumped in a bin. But she'll slash him in one big scoop on top of the Old Master in the same hole. Then the two of them will gouge one another like two dogs whose tails are tied together . . . '

—. . . God help us all, and fuck you too! . . . Blotchy Brian was right this time . . . Two dogs whose tails are tied together . . . Do you know, this time he was right! . . . Our tails were tied together, Billy . . .

—You got it right this time, Master . . .

—We were bucklepping around, wagging our tails you might say and just lounging there when we were seduced by the magic of the lights, the sparkle of the stars, the wonder of the will o' the wisp and the pleasure of promises. Do you know what, Billy, we thought that will o' the wisp was like unto the candle that is never extinguished . . .

—That's so true there, Master . . .

—We believed at that moment that the heavenly stars would be our wedding present; that we would sup of the harvest home wine wherein no dregs lie . . .

—Oh my, how romantic! . . .

—Ah come on, Billy my pal, it was only all the kind of mushy mush that our egos inflict us with. We were caught in a trap. Our flighty tails were nailed and tied down. She was only, my good pal Billy, but a bushwhacking brasser of a woman who knew how to play the game. "One day I'm in Rathlin, and the next in the Isle of Man . . ."

—It's "One day in Islay, and the next beyond in Kintyre," my good Master, my good neighbour . . .

—You've got it in one, Billy my boy. That woman isn't worth the steam of your piss or even a hard word or a moment's worry. Billy boy, she got two stupid dogs who let her trap them and tie up their tails . . .

—Never spoke a truer word, ya Master ya . . .

—Listen Billy, my good man, we are obliged from now on not to put any strain on our tails, but just to be pleasant and neighbourly to one another . . .

—Well said, Master! Now you're talking, chalk it down. Peace and quiet, Master. That's the best possible thing here six feet under, Master: Peace and quiet. If I thought even for a minute that I'd be lying here next to you, I'd have never married her . . .

—It doesn't matter a dog's dinner what anybody does! She is the way she is, but you made a right proper hames of it anyway, you tramp, you thief, you tinker! You should have been pitched into the gas chamber, you fart face, you pig's puke, you . . .

—Ah come on, Master, zip your lip for a minute, easy up now, easy! . . .

4.

—If I'd lived a bit longer . . .

—It was a blessed relief . . .

—If I'd lived a bit longer . . .

—It was a blessed relief . . .

—I'd be getting the pension by St. Patrick's Day . . .

—Another few months and I'd have been in the new house . . .

—God save all here! If I had lived just a little bit more, maybe they would have brought my heap of bones beyond the Fancy City . . .

—. . . I was to be married in a fortnight. But you stabbed me right through the walls of my liver, you nasty murdering bastard. If I had survived for just another bit, I wouldn't have left a Dog Ear within a sight of us . . .

—I'd have got the Old Wood's land from my brother. Mannix the Counsellor told me as much . . .

—I never thought I'd die until I got the satisfaction from the seaweed that Tim Top of the Road stole . . .

—Oro, I hope the devil fucks him! If I had lived even another short while, I'd have hightailed it into Mannix the Counsellor, and made a proper will. And then I'd have dumped out on his arse the eldest boy, and would have got a woman for the other youngfella, Tom. Then I'd have served a summons on the boozer Crossan and his drove of donkeys, and if the court didn't fix it up for me, I'd have driven nails through their hooves. Then I'd have gone into hiding during the night just to catch the Top of the Road shower trying to steal my turf, and then I'd hammer them with the bitch of a summons . . . And if the court didn't solve it to my satisfaction, I'd get a few sticks of dynamite from the boss himself. And then . . .

—Then I'd sue Peter the Publican's daughter . . .

—Bloody tear and 'ounds, I'd get a lift the likes of which I never got before in Nell Paudeen's car . . .

—I'd see "The Sun Set" published . . .

—If I had lived just another bit, I'd have rubbed—what's that you called it, Master? . . . that's it, right, I'd have rubbed methylated spirits on myself . . .

—By the oak of this coffin, I'd have pursued Caitriona Paudeen about that pound she owed me . . .

—God wouldn't forgive us, Kitty . . .

—I'd have made a love letter of my body covered with tattoos of Hitler . . .

—The Postmistress said the other day that the Irish Folklore Commission and the Director of Official Statistics asked her to give them the complete lists of the number of xxs that were on every letter. The Master averaged about fifteen, and Caitriona always appended about seven normally to Blotchy Brian: one for his beard, another for his hips, another . . .

—. . . Easy! Easy! Come on my good Master!

—. . . Don't believe him Jack . . .

—I'd have gone to England just to earn money and to hang out with the lads from Kin Teer . . . My spies tell me there are hundreds of them in London . . . some of them wearing fancy jackets . . . and poncy monocles . . .

—I'd have travelled the world: Marseilles, Port Said, Singapore, Batavia. Honest, I would . . .

—*Qu'il retournerait pour libérer la France* . . .

—If I'd have lived another while, you wouldn't have killed me, ya ugly witch ya, Joan. I'd have switched the ration cards . . .

—. . . I'd have gone to your funeral, Billy the Postman. It wouldn't have been right for me not to go to a funeral . . .

—I'd have keened you, Billy, I'd have keened you softly and sweetly . . .

—I'd have laid you out, Billy, I'd have tended you as gently as a young girl would tend her first love letter . . .

—If I had lived any longer, I'd have insisted they put me in a different grave . . . Master, Master, come on, fix it up, forget about it! . . . I know, but listen to me, Master! Two dogs whose tails are tied . . .

—Of course, and certainly I'd drink whole tons of porter . . .

—. . . We would have won the game. I had the nine, and it was my partner's chance. Fuck the mine anyway, it exploded just at the wrong time! . . .

—I'd sue the murdering bastard because he poisoned me. "Here, drink two spoons of this stuff . . ."

—I would have too, even though I have no time for trying to argue with Mannix the Counsellor. Son of a gun, that's not to say, like, that I wouldn't sue him. He told me to start downing some whiskey. That's what he said, no doubt about it. If I had stayed on the pints I'd have been alright. I never had a pain or a sickness, nor nothing . . .

—If I had lived, I'm sure I would have cracked the crossword. And, of course, I'd have got a huge scoop of insurance money from Jack the Lad's place. I'd have put "God be with the days of the sim-plified spelling" as a *nom de plume* on the first ticket in the sweep-stake . . .

—. . . "Say 'cheese' now, nurses," I'd have called it! . . .

—"Cala Rossa," Billy would have called it . . .

—I'd have gone to the pictures again. I swear to God I'd have given anything even to see that woman in the fur coat once more. It was just exactly like the coat that Baba Paudeen had until the soot came tumbling down in Caitriona's place . . .

—That's a lie, ya scrubber!

—Back off from me, Caitriona. I just want peace and quiet. I don't deserve you bitchiness . . .

—. . . If I had lived another while! If I had lived another while, for jay's sake! What would I have done? What would I have done, that is the question. A wise man might be able to deal with that . . .

—If I got as far as the election, I'd have given the lie to Corsgrave and his crowd. I'd have said to him that they were only sent over as plenipotentiaries, or messenger boys, and that they went way beyond their remit . . .

—I lived though, thanks be to God, I lived long enough to say to de Valera that they were sent over with full powers. I told him that to his face. To his face. I told him straight up to his . . .

—You're a liar. You never said nothing like that! . . .

—I remember it well. I twisted my ankle . . .

—If you lived for another bit, you'd have seen the young ones from Bally Donough sucking and smoking pipes. They started that since the fags got scarce. Some people say that dock leaves and nettles are just brilliant in a clay pipe . . .

—If you lived as long as Methuselah and the Hag of Beare, you'd never have seen the end of the fleas being fucked off the hillocks of your own place . . .

—If the Postmistress had lived another while . . .

—She had no need to. Her daughter picked up where she left off . . .

—If I'd lived for another while . . .

—Why would you live anyway? . . .

—I'd have seen you buried, that much . . .

—If Fireside Tom had lived? . . .

—He'd have moved on . . .

—He'd have gone on the sauce again . . .

—He'd have kicked Patrick Caitriona's cattle off his own patch of land . . .

—Nell's cows, careful now!

—If Caitriona had lived . . .

—And buried that bitch before her . . .

—If I had lived, I would have dispensed spiritual assistance. Even if I had lived just another week I would have been able to tell Caitriona precisely what she needed to know . . .

—Hey, Colm More's daughter, didn't you used to be in at the Rosary just to eavesdrop and find out were all the neighbours saying their own Rosaries . . .

—I'd have gone to Croke Park to see Cannon . . .

—Billy the Postman saw your ghost after the final and there you were sobbing and sniffling and whining and whimpering . . .

—I'd have finished the pen and the colt would not have died . . .

—Didn't everyone in the place see your ghost! . . .

—. . . I don't believe, Redser Tom, that there's any such thing as a ghost . . .

—Some people say there is. Other people say there isn't. You'd want to be very wise . . .

—But, of course, there are ghosts. God forbid that I'd tell a lie about anyone, but I saw Curran driving the Guzzler's donkey and Tim Top of the Road's cows out of his corn, and he was dead a whole year! . . .

—Wasn't the first thing that happened to Billy the Postman, wasn't it that he saw the Old Master the day after he was buried rummaging around in the cupboard of his own kitchen? . . .

—. . . Easy up now, Master! . . . Oh, come on, take it easy, take it easy! . . . I never shaved myself with your razor. Go away with yourself now, Master, and just listen up a minute. Two dogs . . .

—Tim Top of the Road was seen . . .

—By the hokey, as you'd say yourself . . .

—But it could have happened! I have no doubt he was stealing my turf . . .

—Or mallets . . .

—They say, God help us, that a ghostly airplane is heard over Cala Lawr every night since the Frenchie was downed there . . .

—Not at all, that's the regular airplane on its way to America from somewhere in the North, or from Shannon! . . .

—Are you saying I wouldn't recognise a normal airplane! I heard it clear as a bell, when I was saving seaweed late at night . . .

—Maybe the night was dark . . .

—Come off it, what's the point of dribbling shite talk! For Moses' sake, what's this about it not being a regular airplane. Any gobdaw would know a regular airplane . . .

—*Mes amis* . . .

—Let me speak! Let me get a word in, please! . . .

—When all is said and done, though, it looks like it. I never gave a petrified puke about ghosts until I heard about John Matthew who's buried here, in the Half Guinea place. His own son told me about it. I've only fallen under the hatch since then myself. He was himself up in the land of the living at the time, but he'd never say his father was a liar. The last thing his father begged them to do, just when he was dying, to bury him here along with the rest of his people. "I'll die happy," he said, "if you can promise me that much." They're a shower of drippy dossers over there in Kin Teer. They threw some dust there just in front of the door. For the next month the son was pitching dried seaweed over by the shore. He told me straight out of his very own mouth. He saw the funeral coming out of the graveyard. He told me it was a clear and present to his own eyes—the box, the people, the whole lot—as clear as the clutch of seaweed he was pitching on the heap. He moved over closer to them. He recognised some of the people, but he'd never even dream of calling them by their names, he said. He was a bit scared at first, but as he got nearer to them, he plucked up a bit of courage. "Whatever God has in store for me," he said, "I'll follow them." He did. They moved along the shore, and he kept after them step by step, until they came to this graveyard, and they put the coffin down here, and buried it in the Half Guinea place. He recognised the coffin. He wouldn't tell a lie about his own father . . .

—Where's John Matthew? If he's here, nobody heard a peep out of him . . .

—I wouldn't know anything about that any more than I would about the Pope's tooth, but just as his son said, and he wouldn't tell a lie . . .

—The dead didn't budge a bit. Call up the Half Guinea gang and they'll tell you whether he's there or not . . .

—Look it! Listen to those clack boxes!

—I won't listen, no way will I listen. Hey, you over there, you in the Half Guinea place! . . .

—. . . Bridey Matthew is here . . .

—And Colie Matthew . . .

—And Paddy Matthew . . .

—And Billy Matthew . . .

—And Matthew himself . . .

—Johnny Matthew is buried over in the cemetery at Kin Teer. He was married over there . . .

—He never told a lie about his own father! . . .

—It's not as easy to switch around like that like it is to go from one political party to another. If that were the case, Dotie would have shifted a long time ago to the bright shiny meadows of the Smooth Fields . . .

—And the Frenchie . . . But maybe it's only his ghost is here . . .

—It's not any weirder a yarn than what Billy the Postman spun me: that Fireside Tom is often seen shooing the cows off of his own patch. Paddy Caitriona and Nell chopped it in two between them, but neither of them is happy about it. Every second week either Paddy or one of Nell's sees him. If one house sees him one week, the other doesn't. Nell hauled the priest in and got him to walk the land and say a whole protective wall of prayers, not to mention St. John's Gospel, or so he said.

—She'd do that alright, the old biddy. God grant she'll never make a single rotten fucking penny out of it! My Patrick has lashings of land without that . . .

—It's mouthed about, Caitriona, that you haven't given Jack the Lad a second's peace since you died . . .

—God would punish us . . .

—Nell told Fireside Tom that you made a right sucker out of him . . .

—Wasn't she mooning after Blotchy Brian? . . .

—Oh, Jesus Christ Almighty and his blessed mother! After Blotchy Brian! . . .

—Bloody tear and 'ounds, isn't that exactly what he said . . .

—"O row there Mary, with your bags and your belts . . ."

—What did he say? . . .

—What did he say, Black Bandy Bartley, boy? . . .

—What did he say, Bartley?

—The same Blotchy Brian says the most ridiculous things . . .

—"O row there Mary . . ."

—What did he say, Bartley?

—Bloody tear and 'ounds, Caitriona, it won't do you the least bit of good . . .

—It would do me good, Bartley. Spit it out . . .

—That's the dote, Bartley! Let us have it . . .

—Hey, do you hear scrunty Johnny. Don't put a tooth in it, Bartley . . .

—You're a dote, Bartley. Spill the beans . . .

—Don't say it, Bartley! Don't breathe a word! . . .

—Honest to God, Bartley, you'll be a right meanie if you don't tell us now. Did he say that every time he opens his eyes her ghost is hovering above him? . . .

—If you dare tell it to Johnny Sparrow's sow, Bartley! . . .

—Honest to God, Bartley, you are awfully mean! I should cut off all cultural relations with you. Let me see now. Did he say that because he wouldn't marry her when she was alive that her ghost is his phantom lover now? . . .

—Ababoona! A phantom lover to that ugly maggot! Watch it, Bartley!

—On the level, Bartley. Did Caitriona's ghost tell him to go and shave his jowls, have a shower, shite, shampoo, and a scratch, or to wash himself, or to pay a visit to some shoulder and shank specialist? . . .

—Bloody tear and 'ounds, Nora! . . . Bloody tear and 'ounds, Caitriona! . . .

—The skin off your nose if you breathe a word, Bartley! . . .

—Honest to God, Bartley!

5.

—. . . That's true for you, Fireside Tom. God would be fierce angry at anyone who'd suggest that that ugly string of misery would be my lover . . .

—. . . You fell from a stack of oats . . . Did you ever hear of the Battle of the Sheaves? . . . I'll tell you that one. "Cormac MacAirt Mac Conn Mac Bulging Muscles Baskin was one day making a stack of oats in Tara of the Assemblies. Gabby Clump was chucking them up to him. Then came the Seven Battles of Learning, and the Seven Battles of Everyday Knowledge and the Battle of the Small Fry . . ."

—. . . There's a lot of talk about moving him. A lot of talk . . .

—But what's the point of moving him, unless he was going to be smashed up, or killed, or drowned or hanged, or squashed like a cat after that. This cemetery is in a mess because of that sponging squatter, Billy. "Take two teaspoons of this bottle," the murderer said . . .

—Maybe, yet, neighbours, he might be smashed up. It could

happen yet after he beat seven kinds of crap out of a man from Bally Donough who offered him a red ticket. But I don't think he'll be executed . . .

— Ah, sure, that's no good then! I'll tell you what should be done with him: he should be suffocated under a pisspot. Look at me, he gave me poison! . . .

— By the holy souls, didn't he tell me to drink whiskey? That's what he said, exactly. The bastard! What harm, but I never had a pain, not a day sick in my life! . . .

— Galway have a good football team this year, Billy? . . .

— They have a fantastic team. Everybody says that even if they were hobbling around on crutches, they'd win the All-Ireland. *Green Flag* said as much the other day . . .

— Cannon will bite their arses that day . . .

— Cannon is only a sub!

— A sub! A sub! If that's the case what are you on about? They'll never win. They won't win. They . . .

— They have a brilliant bunch of young players. The best. They'll win, I'm telling you. Wait and see yourself . . .

— Come on, put a cork in it! What's the point in blabbing on about it? I'm telling you that those young players aren't worth frog spawn without Cannon! What's the point of screaming "They'll win! They'll win!" . . .

— Listen now, neighbour, in all fairness, you'd think that you'd prefer that they'd be beaten with Cannon than to win without him! Being right is a great thing. Cannon was to blame for most of it in 1941. I was never as pissed off leaving Croke Park as I was that day . . .

— That's the truth, Billy . . .

— Billy was always obliging . . .

— He'd always be thrilled to bring you some good news . . .

— And even if it was bad news, I swear that all his gabble and chatter was a kind of a safety belt . . .

— Who laid Fireside Tom out, Billy? . . .

— Nell and Blotchy Brian's daughter, and Tommy's wife, Kate . . .

— And who keened him, Billy? . . .

—Nell and all the local women, Biddy. But yourself and Little Kitty were sorely missed. Everyone was saying: "May God have mercy on Little Kitty and Biddy Sarah, the poor creature. Didn't they just love to lay a man out and to keen him! We'll never see the likes of them again . . ."

—Your good health, Billy! . . .

—Bloody tear and 'ounds, who gives a toss who lays you out or keens you! . . .

—. . . Hitler is still hammering them to bits, good on him!

—Easy now, neighbour, easy . . .

—What do you mean, easy! Shouldn't he be landed in England by now! . . .

—Not so, neighbour, but the English and the Yanks are both back in France . . .

—They are, yea! You're just spouting lies, Billy the Postman! This is not just bullshitting about sport, you know . . .

—It's months now, neighbour, since I had a chance to read a newspaper, so I can't tell you exactly how things are. Everyone said that time that the English and the Yanks would never get a toehold in France on D-Day . . .

—Why Billy, dear, why do you think that they would? They were driven back leaving heaps of skulls on the beach, driven into the balls of the devil, into the sea . . .

—I suppose that was it, neighbour . . .

—And Hitler pursued them this time—something he should have done that time at Dunkerque—and he's in England now! *Der Tag!* I think there's isn't a single Englishman left there now . . .

—*Non! Non, mon ami! C'est la liberation qu'on a promise. La liberation! Les Gaullistes et Monsieur Churchill avaient raison* . . .

—Hoora, you gutty, you plonker, you blind bollix!

—*C'est la liberation! Vive la France! Vive la République Française! Vive la patrie! La patrie sacrée! Vive de Gaulle!* . . .

—I suppose you heard, Frenchie, my neighbour, about the stuff that was in the papers about your heroics: you were presented with the Cross . . .

—*Ça n'est rien, mon ami. C'est sans importance. Ce qui compte, c'est la liberation. Vive la France! La France! La patrie sacrée!* . . .

—Hoora, do you see how the little shit is all over the place! He's even better than the Old Master . . .

—Come here, I want you, Billy, was there any talk at all that we'd get the English market back?

—Do you hear again the midget mewling?

—The English market will be fine, neighbour . . .

—Do you think so, Billy?

—No doubt about it, my neighbour. No hassle. I'm telling you that the English market will be hunky dory again . . .

—God be good to you, Billy! You have taken the bitter dart out of my heart with your beautiful talk. You're certain it will be alright? I have a bit of land up on the top of the town . . .

—. . . It's published, you know, your book of poetry . . .

—*The Yellow Stars!* Oh, Billy, my dear Billy, it can't be true . . .

—I didn't see it myself, but the Postmistress's daughter told me as much . . . Don't worry about it, neighbour. Your book will be published soon too, before too long . . .

—But do you think it might, Billy? . . .

—I'm certain it will, neighbour.

—You know something the rest of us don't, so, Billy?

—Ah, sure, I'd hear bits and pieces, you know the way it is, neighbour. I got to know a lot of people round aboutish. The Postmistresses's daughter . . . Ah, come off it Master, cool it now! Take it easy! . . . Master, please! . . .

—Have a bit more manners than that, Master! . . .

—There's lots and loads of money to be made in England still, Billy, isn't there? . . .

—Not as much as before, good neighbour. Scraping through can be hard enough. The crowd from Shana Kill, Clogher Savvy, and Bally Donough are all back home . . .

—Taking their ease in the superior nettles of Bally Donough will do them the power of good . . .

—. . . Your own son, his wife, and two children, they're back at home also . . .

—Now you're telling it, Billy!

—Well done and good for you, neighbour! By the holy finger itself! . . .

—And did he bring a black wife home with him?

—Yes, of course, and two children too . . .

—But, come on now, Billy! Tell me the pure unadulterated truth. Are they as black as they say? Are they as black as the Earl's own little house black?

—Don't worry about that, neighbour. Not a bit like that . . .

—Are they as black as Top of the Road after he's been stuck up a sooty chimney? . . .

—Ah no, really, nothing as bad as that.

—As black as Big Nob Knobbly Knacker? . . .

—Don't worry about it, neighbour, nothing like that . . .

—As black as Baba Paudeen's fur coat after she visited Caitriona? . . .

—Shut your hole, you grabber!

—As black as Blotchy Brian sweating stew after a night's piss-up? . . .

—Blotchy Brian was as happy as a pig in shit coming up before the judge after he went to see the geyser in Dublin, as happy as one of those saints you see in the window of the church . . .

—Blotchy Brian sweating after a night's piss-up. About as black as that, yes . . .

—Well, in that case, they're hardly niggers at all . . .

—The kids aren't as black as the mother, then . . .

—Did they have to call on the priest for the grandmother? . . .

—Too true, neighbour, she was in a bad way. She didn't want to let them into the house at all, at all. All the neighbours gathered around, and many of them wanted to stone them and to drive them away. But anyway, to make a long story short, they were brought over to the priest who splattered them with holy water and dipped them into the font, and the granny was happy after that . . . She has great fun with them now. She even brings them to Mass every Sunday . . .

—If that's the way it is, Billy, then I'm not really dead at all. I thought her heart would break into little bits . . .

—Come here, like, have you any news at all about that young-fella of mine, Billy? . . .

—John Willy, that youngfella of yours is a real cute hoor and knows which side his bread is buttered on. He bought a colt the other day . . .

—That's great news, Billy! If he only had a bit of a thing of a woman now . . .

—Don't worry about that, Johnny. From what I hear, it won't be long now. Someone from over by Kin Teer who was in England. A woman of substance, or so they say. The Postmistress's daughter says that the Junior Master will get married any day now . . . That's her. The one in Barry's Bookies in the Fancy City . . . The priest says nothing about it now, neighbour. She took the pledge a little while ago . . . Don't worry about it. You're always going on about what you did. Some people saying you did it, and others saying that you'd have to burst . . .

—Explode or burst or whatever, Billy! That's the truth as clear as the dew. I drank forty-two pints . . .

—Do you think that Antichrist will come soon, Billy? . . .

—Don't worry about it, neighbour. I don't think he will. I reckon that he won't. To make a long story short, my considered opinion is that it is unlikely that he will . . .

—I think myself, Billy, that it won't be long now . . .

—It'll be great anyway, neighbour. Believe me, wait and see, you'll know yourself . . .

—Do many people require spiritual assistance, Billy, or do they even say the Rosary?

—Didn't I tell you often enough, Colm More's daughter, didn't I tell you often enough to leave heretical matters to me . . .

—Do you really think, Billy, that the prophecy is going to come true? . . .

—I think so, neighbour. That story will be . . .

—Do you think that John Kitty in Bally Donough believes it is going to come true? . . .

—The last time I was in Bally Donough they all gathered round—those of them that weren't in England—they were all gathered around John Kitty under a bunch of nettles between the houses, and there he was prophesying away.

—Did he say that England would go up in a ball of flames and in a bunch of ashes right up to the sky?

—In a ball of flames and ashes! Ball of flame and ashes! He said that the priests would be just as hungry as the people. Hang on a minute, now . . . He said that you wouldn't know a man from a woman. Wait now . . . He said more . . . He said that the pint would be only two pence again.

—Your women know fuck all about fuck nothing! Did he say that England would go up in a ball of flames? . . .

—He didn't go that much into it actually, neighbour. He had only got to the bit where Tight Arse was woken up in the cellar, and that he'd flourish his sword to free Ireland. And then I pulled out income tax returns on their wills . . .

—John Kitty is right. Every single word of it is about to come true . . .

—. . . Did I hear you right, Billy, Eamon de Valera is winning . . .

—That's all wrong! Billy said that Richard Mulcahy is the one who's winning . . .

—Eamon de Valera and Richard Mulcahy were outside the church after Mass, just a month ago. It was a joint meeting . . .

—A joint meeting?

—A joint meeting?

—Had dad! A joint meeting? . . .

—Crikies! A joint meeting? . . .

—A joint meeting about the emergency services . . .

—Eamon de Valera spoke about the Republic?

—Richard Mulcahy spoke about the Treaty? . . .

—No, they didn't say a word about the Republic, or about the

Treaty . . . To make a long story short, they both said much the same thing: they were thanking the people . . .

—Ah, now I get it, Billy! That was a neat trick of Dev's to fool the other crowd . . .

—That's a lie! Every old stopped clock in the cemetery knows that it was a plan of Mulcahy's to make de Valera go the other way. Would you agree with me, Billy?

—Watch it now, Billy! You have reached the age of reason and understanding, and remember we got you a pay rise and promotion. Remember now, that you were only "An Assistant Rural Postman" . . .

—My friends and companions! I am here today! . . .

—If you were here during the election . . .

—Just like me, Billy has no interest in politics . . .

—Ya knobber ya. Get back in under the bed . . .

—You witch! . . .

—Where are you, Paul? Your friend was out and around the country again this year . . .

—The Great Scholar! I don't believe it! . . .

—He didn't go near Peter the Publican one way or the other . . . You won't make a total langer out of him there anymore. You just watch, but Peter the Publican's daughter won't be pulling the wool over anyone's eyes any longer, neighbour! . . . Oh, every why for ever! The foxy fuzz catching her one Sunday here at the second Mass. There was nobody here from Shana Kill, Clogher Savvy, or Bally Donough who were home from England who weren't inside in the boozer. They said that the Great Scholar tipped off the police to raid the place. He has a big job in the government . . .

—She won't try her tricks in the parlour any more . . .

—She ripped me off . . .

—And me . . .

—I had nothing to be grateful to her about. Certainly not. After the second half-one it was four pence, and after the sixth it was eighteen. I tell you what now, the doctor from the Fancy City was right: it was only any good for the small gut, stout was what suited the bigger gut. Too much whiskey destroyed the small gut, and the big one shrivelled up with fever. There was no pain . . .

—. . . She needn't have worried, good neighbour, if the only thing against her was that she opened on Sunday, but more people said that she watered down the whiskey . . .

—Will she lose the license? . . .

—Could happen, neighbour. Maybe so. But somehow I doubt it . . .

—Then what was it all about, what good was it? . . .

—Huckster Joan will certainly lose her license to do what she is doing. She's being tried at the Military Tribunal . . . Tea on the black market. The sergeant nabbed her . . .

—The sergeant, imagine that, and she used to give him tea and fags on the side! . . .

—You killed me, lousy ugly Joan! . . .

—The Dog Eared crowd was it, neighbour? The youngest one of them has fecked off with a tailor in England . . .

—Good man, Billy! Good man! . . .

—He sliced Rootey's youngfella from Bally Donough . . .

—Oh, yes, the same sneaky kidney stabbing that the Dog Eared crowd did on me! They'll hang him yet . . .

—They say he'll be locked up . . .

—He'll be hanged . . .

—They say, neighbour, that it's easy enough to hang somebody in England, alright. But I don't think he'll be hanged all the same. He'll get a couple of years in prison, maybe . . .

—A couple of years in prison! Fuck that for a brass monkey of a prison! If they don't hang him . . .

—They say that the Postmistress's daughter will get eighteen months, or even a couple of years . . . Letters that had money in them, neighbour, but the bloodhounds from the Head Office smelled a rat when it was about letters from the Great Scholar . . .

—My goodness me! After I spent twenty years teaching her . . .

—I swear now, Postmistress, believe me now, neighbour, I

wouldn't like anything to happen to your daughter . . . Easy now, dear Master, easy! . . . I swear by the blessed finger that I never once opened one of your letters! . . . Oh, maybe she did, Master, but I never helped her . . .

—My eldest lad, Billy, is he hanging out all the time with Top of the Road's daughter? . . .

—I think so, neighbour. Himself and Top of the Road's two daughters will be at the next court. They say that that other son of yours . . .

—Tom . . .

—They say that himself and Tommy's son caught them rolling in the hay in the morning early . . .

—The second son, and Tommy's son caught the eldest boy swiping turf from Top of the Road's snotty sooty shower! . . .

—I haven't actually a clue, neighbour, I only know he has a summons . . .

—The gammy teeth of the devil ride him! He's just a little brush in the huge sweep of Tim Top of the Road's filching fingers! . . .

—Your wife has given them another summons, this time about their cows trespassing on your land . . .

—Yes, of course! Overnight! Good for her! She'll do the job now, I'm telling you! Isn't it a pity that the eldest guy hasn't been thrown out on his head to the four winds, and some class of a young thing hauled in by the second boy to look after all the land! Do you think, Billy, that Tommy gave back the spade that he borrowed to lift the feed of new spuds? . . .

—I couldn't tell you that now, neighbour . . . To make a long story short now, neighbour, the Top of the Roads are whacked with the law these days. To tell the truth, I thought that the priest was like somebody whose lapdog had taken a bite out of him last Sunday. He was up early in the morning, and he caught a gang snitching his own turf. They say it was the Top of the Road's gang what done it . . .

—Even though they were licking his eyebrows . . .

—I don't actually think, neighbour, that the priest would take the trouble to put an umbrella between the Top of the Road's gang and a drop of rain, especially now that the son got six months in prison . . .

—Tim Top of the Road's son? . . .

—Tim Top of the Road's son, seriously! You're spouting lies? . . .

—And they nearly gave another six months to Tim Top of the Road's old one for receiving stolen goods . . .

—My seaweed on the shore, certainly! . . .

—No, it wasn't that this time, neighbour, but he cleaned out Lord Cockton's car, the whole lot, fishing gear, his gun and stuff. He broke into the Earl's house in the middle of the night and made off with his dinner jacket, tennis shorts, gold watches, and ornamental cigarette cases. And then a couple of thousand fags from Huckster Joan's, and he sold them for three pence each to the young straps from Bally Donough. They were pissed off with the clay pipes . . .

—More bad luck to Huckster Joan's daughter! . . .

—And the Earl! . . .

—And the young ones from Bally Donough! . . .

—And Tim Top of the Road's son, the clot. Son of a gun, I'll tell you the truth, I've always been saying he deserves it! He has had it nice and easy with his . . .

—He stole the priest's sister's pants too, but nobody said anything about that. John Willy's son and some of the young scuts from Shana Kill saw Top of the Road's daughter wearing them on the bog, but she had some kind of a skirt over it . . .

—That sack slapper that my son is knocking around with . . . That's her! She'll be sewn into those pants now so as to get a rise out of the older guy . . .

—The priest's sister, Billy, it upset her that Tim Top of the Road's son was sent to prison, didn't it?

—Ara, you know full well that it did, Breed! . . .

—Listen, Breed, my good neighbour, it never even darkened the slightest furrow on her brow. "What good is a man in prison to me?" she asks. "Top of the Road's son is an old impotent worrywart . . ."

—She'll marry the Master from Derry Lough now, so? . . .

—The Master from Derry Lough is just another one of her exes for a long while. She's hooked up with some Scottish dude in Shana Kill now, and she spends her time drawing pictures. He wears a bit of a kilt . . .

—How's that for you! A bit of a kilt. And tell me now, Billy, confidentially like, does she wear the pants when she's out with him? . . .

—Not at all, Breed Terry, just a skirt. Top of the Road's son stole the best pants she had—the stripy one . . .

—The pants that Fireside Tom snotted the spit on? . . .

—While we're talking about Fireside Tom, the Postmistress's daughter told me that Paddy Caitriona . . . Easy now, Master! Cool down, Master! . . . Back off, Master! . . . I never ever opened one of your letters, Master . . . Listen to me, Master. Two dogs f . . .

—A bit of balance, now Master. What was that she said about my Patrick, Billy? . . .

—That he got the insurance money on Fireside Tom, and that Nell got a nice little nest egg from Jack . . .

—Good for you, Billy, my comrade in arms! If you'd believe Nora Johnny's viperous tongue you'd think that Patrick never paid that insurance after I died! Since I came here, I'm the receptacle for every single spit she squirts out of her slobby gob. Do you hear that, sponger Johnny? God be good to you Billy, tell her that—tell swamp slut Johnny—tell her that Patrick got . . .

6.

—God would punish us for saying something like that, Caitriona . . .

—But it's the truth, Jack . . .

—Not so, Caitriona. I was very poorly for years. She brought me to every single doctor who was any good in the Fancy City. An English doctor who used to come fishing down our way about eight years ago told me to the day exactly how long I would live. "You'll live until," he said . . .

—. . . "Yea," I says myself. "Locked up in my body . . ."

—. . . "My ankle is gone again," he says, "By the hairy balls of Galen . . ."

—. . . You'd never really believe, Caitriona, my good neighbour, how much I owe to your Paddy. Not a single Sunday would pass but himself and his wife would come to visit me . . .

—The Toejam trotter crowd . . .

—Howandever, Caitriona, neighbour, there isn't any bit of earth that doesn't have some kind of weed. Look at the change that came over the Old Master there! You wouldn't have met a nicer man on the pilgrimage to Knock than him . . .

—But did you see the way that she and that suet brain Nell got me, Billy? They got St. John's Gospel from the priest and I got dumped down into this casket thirty years too soon. They did the same dirty trick on poor Jack . . .

—God will not forgive us . . .

—That's only all old guff, Caitriona. If I was you I wouldn't believe a word of it . . .

—Believe it, Billy, even if it's all only old guff, as you say. The priest is able to . . .

—I believed a lot of that stuff too, Caitriona, neighbour. I did really, even though you mightn't think it. But I asked a priest once—he was a very learned priest—and do you know what he said to me? He told me something I should have known ages ago only that the old guff was still stuck in my mind. "All the St. John Gospels in the whole wide world wouldn't keep you alive, Billy the Postman," he said, "when it's God's will to call you home."

—I find it hard to believe that now, Billy . . .

—Another priest said the exact same thing to my wife—to the Schoolmistress—Caitriona. He's a very holy priest, Caitriona, the two eyes in his head are bursting out of him with holiness. The Mistress did every single pattern and pilgrimage in Ireland and Aran for me . . . Take it easy, now Master! Back off a minute! . . . Stop making that racket! What could I have done about it? . . . "You should make the pilgrimages," he said, "but you never know when God is ready to perform a miracle . . ."

—But a pilgrimage isn't the same as St. John's Gospel, Billy . . .

—I know that, Caitriona, but wouldn't St. John's Gospel be a miracle too? And if God wanted to keep someone alive, why would he have to take another in his place? You don't think for a minute that God in his heaven has as much red tape as the Post Office, do you? . . .

—Bloody tear and 'ounds, anyway, isn't that exactly what Blotchy Brian said . . .

—. . . "Do you think this is 'The War of the Two Foreigners'?" is what I ask myself . . .

—Get your act together now, man . . .

—. . . It was my wife who filled in the papers for Paddy Caitriona . . . Cool down for feck's sake, Master! Back off, will ya! . . . Grand so, Master, if you say so. I know she was your wife . . . Hang on there, Master! Patience now! Like two dogs . . .

—. . . There were days like that, Peter the Publican. Don't try to deny it . . .

—. . . Paper under the roof, Caitriona. But Paddy is putting a slate roof on the house! . . . That's it, a two-storey house, Caitriona, bay windows and all and a windmill up on the hill for electricity . . . If you saw the government bull that he bought, Caitriona! All of ninety pounds. The cattle dealers are very happy. All the bulls around the place were a posse of pansies . . .

—Bloody tear and 'ounds, isn't that exactly what Blotchy Brian said: "The bulls have gone awful quiet since England put a stop to de Valera's cattle and since the Massacre of the Innocents . . ."

—And he has plans to buy a lorry to deliver turf. We could do with it badly in our own hole of a backwater. We don't have sign or sight of a lorry since Paudeen's was taken from him . . . I'm telling you, neighbour, five or six hundred pounds . . .

—Five or six hundred pounds! Anybody's pocket would be very lonely if that much was removed from it, Billy. Nearly as much as Nell got that time in the court . . .

—His pocket wasn't lonely at all, Caitriona, especially since he got the will . . .

—But Nell got the big fat wad of notes all the same . . .

—Bloody tear and 'ounds, didn't Blotchy Brian say that Paddy

Caitriona wouldn't recognise paper money any more than Fireside Tom would recognise the sweat of his brow, or . . .

—Wouldn't you think, Billy, with a whirlwind of notes like that flying around the place that somebody would remember to pay back the pound that I loaned to Caitriona . . .

—You little drizzling shit! . . .

—. . . The Postmistress's daughter told me as much . . . Calm down, Master! . . . It's a dirty lie, Master . . . I never opened any letter . . .

—Don't take a blind bit of notice of his ranting, Nora. Remember always that he was a noncommissioned officer in the Murder Machine . . . I won't have the opportunity to read any more of "The Sunset" to you again, Nora. I am far too busy with my new draft, "The Piglet Moon." I got the idea from Coley. His grandfather could trace his family tree back as far as the moon. He spent three hours every night staring up at it, just like our ancestors. When the new moon rose his nostrils developed three different kinds of snot: one golden, one silver, and the good old dependable genuine solid Irish snot . . .

—. . . She told me, Caitriona, that Baba said that you were her favourite sister ever, and that you would have been grateful to her too, only that you died first . . .

—I did my best and I did my worst, Billy, but I failed to bury Nell . . .

—Be japers, Caitriona, neighbour, maybe it made no difference one way or the other. Paddy himself told me, and told the . . . the Mistress, that Nell left him a lot of bits and pieces that were never in the will. She'd only take half of Fireside Tom's land from him, and believe you me, Caitriona, not a Sunday passes without the priest saying a Mass for your soul and Jack the Lad's . . .

—For my soul, and Jack the Lad's . . .

—Bloody tear and 'ounds, didn't Blotchy Brian say that . . .

—For my soul, and Jack the Lad's . . .

—And Baba, and . . .

—. . . "The only comparison you could ever make with the gang of Paudeen's daughters," he said, "is that they're like the two scabby pups that I saw once with their eyes glued to a nag of a mule that was in the throes of death over in Bally Donough. One of them was yapping and yowling trying to keep the other away. It stressed him so much that he burst his whole guts out in a glob of gunk. No bother to the other dog, as soon as he saw that the mule was dead and had him all to himself, didn't he just up and away and left him there for the dead dog . . ."

—Looks like he missed that trick all right! He thought that his own family would get its paws on every crumb of the will! That I may be killed stone dead . . .

—I'll tell you no lie, Caitriona, neighbour, himself and his daughter aren't cosying up to Nell now as much as they used to . . .

—No harm in that . . . For my own soul and that of Jack the Lad . . .

—He can't make up his mind, Caitriona, whether to come or to go. He was anointed the other day . . .

—It won't make him any younger! He's twice my age . . .

—My own . . . Mistress took a jaunt up to see him. Do you know what message he sent back with her? . . .

—The hard and bitter word unless he has totally changed . . . I swear . . .

—My own uncle never received any spiritual assistance from the time I was looking after him, or do you think, Billy, that he says the Rosary? . . .

—Bloody tear and 'ounds, isn't that what he said . . .

—What he said to the Mistress was this: "You'll tell Billy the Postman," he said, "if he pops off before me to tell them all back there that that I'll be on my way flying in no time at all. He'll tell Redser Tom that I'll take the lump out of his throat, if he didn't bother to take my advice . . ."

—Neither herself nor anyone else ever managed to put one over on somebody else because of what I said, Billy. And I have to tell you too that that all the graves are riddled with holes . . .

—... "He'll tell Black Bandy Bartley to strike up a bar of a ballad as soon as he hears I'm on my way ..."

—"And ho row there Mary, with your bags and your belts ..."

—"Marty John More had a young one

And she was as strong as any man ..."

—... "He'll tell Greedy pint-guzzling Guts that I'll crack the willow whip on the hide of his old crock of a donkey for being ready and waiting in my field of corn, especially since she started Curran making his pilgrimages to the courts ..."

—Bloody tear and 'ounds, Billy, go on, keep going ...

—... For my soul and for ...

—That's what he said, neighbour. But if he did my ... the Mistress never told me about it ...

—Bloody tear and 'ounds, what's the point of making a Redser Tom of himself! If it's going to rip, let it rip. "And he'll say to my own little darling, Caitriona," he'll say, "that they were sending for the long tubes of the fire brigade to quench me after the scorching I got from the geyser in Dublin, but that I'm not in any way scared now of its boiling water ..."

—Ababoona! Ababoona! Black Bandy Bartley! Billy my friend! How do we know they won't dump the ugly waster ... the stuff-nosed ... stoopy slanty-shouldered ... yob, down on top of me ... Oh, go away Billy dear, I don't believe he ever washed himself in Dublin ... Bury him next to me! Like fuck they will! They have their glue! ... The room ... The grin ... "You can have Blotchy Brian, Caitriona ..." Oh, Billy, I'd burst, I swear I'd burst, I'd burst ...

—Don't worry your noggin about it, Caitriona, neighbour. Everything will be fine.

—But just look where they buried you, Billy ...

—The poor creature didn't really know what she was up to ... Back off, Master! Take it easy! ... Don't take a blind bit of notice of him, Caitriona. That leech is as fresh and as clingy as the ivy ...

—That kind of stuff doesn't matter in the end. Holy Mary, Mother of God, the Earl's little black boy wouldn't disgust me as much . . . What's this now, Billy? Another body coming in! Sacred Heart of Jesus, Billy my good friend, suppose it's him. Shut up a minute and listen! . . .

—How are you all cutting! Are you plugging away? John Kitty from Bally Donough has just arrived . . .

—See where he's buried . . .

—The Great Professor of Futurology of the Western World is dead and his prophetic skull is laid down at Bandy Bartley's feet . . .

—Bloody tear and 'ounds, his skull could do with an extra pillow alright.

—Tell us now, John Kitty, what do you think of the old life now, or do you think that the prophecies will come true? . . .

—I'll keen for you now, John Kitty, as is only right and proper for your calling and for your fame . . . Ochone and Ochone Oh!

—. . . Ara, get up the yard, John Kitty! All that bullshit talk about Red Ball O'Donnell! Will England get blasted to bits and be blown away in a storm of ashes in this war? Is that in your prophecy? Hey, Black Bandy, Give him a jab of your toe in his prophetic skull . . .

—Oh Billy my dearest! . . . I'm going to have no peace here six feet under in the dirty dust . . .

—Don't let it bother you, Caitriona. The priest has arranged to make a completely new map of the graveyard. Top of the Road's old one was bitching away recently. "Weren't things bad enough for the twattish twerps of Clogher Savvy," she says, "but now they have to go and put their rotting legs across the sensitive stomach of the old boy himself . . ."

—I'm telling you, no coffin or blanket will last too long on that corpse! See the way he stole my mallet! . . .

—. . . But Caitriona dear, you'll have the cross up over you anyway . . .

—I wish they'd hurry it up, Billy! I wish they'd hurry it up before the witch herself is dead . . .

—It will have been worth waiting for, Caitriona. Everyone who has seen it says it is absolutely beautiful. The priest himself came hot foot to look at it, and the Junior Master was there, and my . . . the

Mistress, they were all there the same Saturday having a good gawk at the inscription in Irish . . .

—Did you say that Billy, did you tell that to Nora Johnny and Kitty and Redser Tom? . . . Oh, Billy dear, if it's not on me . . .

—It will be, Caitriona. Don't let that bother you one bit, my good neighbour. It's been ready for ages, but they were just waiting to stick your own one and Jack the Lad's up together . . .

—My cross and Jack the Lad's cross going up together . . .

—Fireside Tom's cross is holding them up now . . .

—My cross and Jack the Lad's . . .

—Everyone says, Caitriona, that your one is much nicer than Kitty's, or Nora Johnny's, or even Huckster Joan's . . .

—My cross and Jack the Lad's . . .

—It's nicer than Jack the Lad's too, Caitriona. My . . . the Mistress says she'd prefer it to Peter the Publican's . . .

—It's of Connemara marble so, Billy?

—I couldn't say that for sure, neighbour. It was bought in McCormack's yard in the Fancy City anyway.

—Bloody tear and 'ounds, how could that gom know anything seeing as that he couldn't raise his head from his pillow for yonks past? . . .

—If it's not Connemara marble, Billy, it won't be worth a tinker's curse or a gypsy's grunt as far as I'm concerned . . .

—I thought that all the Connemara marble was all used up . . .

—Shut your hole, you grabber!

—It's of Connemara marble!

—It's not of Connemara marble!

—I'm telling you it is of Connemara marble!

—I'm telling you it's not of Connemara marble!

—McCormack's never have Connemara marble. Only Moran's have it now . . .

—Ara, away out of that, what's the point of going on about it? Didn't Nora Johnny's and Kitty's come from there, and weren't they all of Connemara marble! . . .

—And Breed Terry's . . .

—And Huckster Joan's . . .

—I certainly did hear, Caitriona, neighbour, that Nell had ordered a cross of Connemara marble for herself . . .

—The Big Butcher from the Fancy City came to my funeral. He often said he had plenty of time for me because his father had plenty of time for my father . . .

—. . . Nora Johnny's cross is of Connemara marble . . .

—. . . I was twenty and I played the ace of hearts . . .

—. . . Kitty's cross . . .

—. . . *La liberation* . . .

—. . . Breed Terry's cross . . . Huckster Joan's cross . . .

—I was the first corpse in the graveyard. Don't you think that the oldest resident in the place should have something to say? Let me speak! Let me speak! Let me sp— . . . !

—Let him speak!

—Go on ya good thing! Off you go! . . .

—. . . Nell's cross . . .

—Go on! . . .

—Go on, you headbanger! . . .

—. . . Is not Connemara marble . . .

—. . . After you nearly bursting your guts for thirty-one years getting permission to speak . . .

—. . . Too true for you, Master! Now you're talking! Two dogs . . .

—. . . Neither my cross nor your cross, Jack the Lad . . .

—. . . You're allowed to talk now, but it seems you're happier to keep your gob shut . . .

—. . . Neither my cross nor your cross is Connemara marble . . .

MÁIRTÍN Ó CADHAIN was born in an Cnocán Glas, Cois Fharraige, Connemara, in 1906. He was educated locally, and a scholarship allowed him to become a National School teacher. On graduating from St. Patrick's College, Drumcondra, Dublin, he returned to Connemara, where he taught in local schools, including Camas and, later, Carnmore. During the Second World War he was interned in the Curragh camp in Kildare for membership in the proscribed Irish Republican Army (IRA). He subsequently became a translator in Dáil Éireann, and Trinity College Dublin appointed him lecturer in Irish in 1956, naming him professor in 1969. He died in 1970. He is best known for his novel *Cré na Cille* (1949); his short story collections include *Idir Shúgradh agus Dáiríre* (1939), *An Braon Broghach* (1948), *Cois Caoláire* (1953), *An tSraith ar Lár* (1967), *An tSraith Dhá Tógáil* (1970), and *An tSraith Tógtha* (1977). Another novel, *Athnuachan* (1997), and a piece of continuous imaginative prose, *Barbed Wire* (2002), were published posthumously.

Born in Cork in 1947, ALAN TITLEY is a writer and scholar. He is a member of the Royal Irish Academy and Professor Emeritus of Modern Irish in UCC, and former head of the Irish Department at St. Patrick's College, DCU. Apart from his scholarly work, he is the author of seven novels, four collections of short stories, numerous plays, one collection of poetry, and several film scripts on literary and historical topics for television.